# NIGHTRUNNERS OF BENGAL

# THE STORY-TELLERS

## *Nightrunners of Bengal*

JOHN MASTERS

SOUVENIR PRESS

First published in Great Britain by
Michael Joseph Ltd.

This edition first published 2000 by
Souvenir Press Ltd.,
43 Great Russell Street, London WC1B 3PA

ISBN 0 285 63552 2

Printed in Great Britain by
The Guernsey Press Co. Ltd., Guernsey, Channel Islands

*To*

**THE SEPOY OF INDIA**

**1695–1947**

# Author's Note

ALTHOUGH most of the incidents in this story of the Indian Mutiny are drawn from local tradition, official reports and contemporary letters, this book is a work of fiction. My object has been to make the fictional whole present a true perspective of fact—the facts of environment, circumstance and emotion. In general, the people actually met with in the story, and the places they visit, are fictitious; the people and places that remain offstage are or were real, and notes on many of them are included in the glossary. Where I have had to use a Hindustani word I have tried to make its meaning clear in the context; the precise meaning of such words, and their pronunciation, are given in the glossary.

# Contents

★

# PART ONE

# The Upstairs Room

# 1

RODNEY reined back to a walk and sighed. A thin crowd, scattered round the holy man's tree, was blocking the Pike ahead. He saw a horse tethered by its reins to an outer branch of the tree and recognized it, and sighed again; a little of Caroline Langford went a long way. He brought Boomerang to a stop and peered over the heads of the crowd. The day's work was done, the year's work done, and he was in no hurry to get back to his bungalow. He might as well see what was going on.

Men yawned in the washed afternoon sunlight, and stretched their arms. Brown naked children splashed in the puddles. Women glided down to the river, carrying bundles of clothes on their heads. The holy man sat on a raised earth platform, revetted by loose stones, which had been built up round the bole of the peepul tree. Miss Langford stood at the edge of the platform, facing him. She was young, and of medium height, and the severity of her grey jacket emphasized her slightness of body. A hard black hat perched on the front of her head, which was small, and she carried a riding crop in her hand; her wrists were thin and brittle-seeming. She stared steadily at the Guru, and Rodney noticed that habitual concentration had cut a frown deep into her forehead. She was so cold, so English, against the warm colours. He saw that there were a couple of sepoys of his regiment, the 13th Rifles, Bengal Native Infantry, in the crowd. He waited patiently.

The holy man faced north, sitting erect, his legs crossed under him and his hands limp at his sides. He was naked except for a dirty loincloth well below his navel. A fresh wind blew down the river, and raindrops glistened on him. He breathed slowly, the bony face immobile but not at peace. His cavernous eyes were fully open, and Rodney, musing, imagined them as focused on something far away. They did not absorb these living greens and browns of Central India; surely they sought something beyond the curve of the plains and the cities hidden in the north—and did not find it. Perhaps their pale fires were the glitter reflected from the ice walls and fluted snow battlements of the Himalaya, the silvered trumpet-horns of a forgotten monastery?

Caroline Langford's voice, startling in the depth of its pitch and timbre, interrupted Rodney's reverie. She spoke slowly at the holy man, in Hindustani.

"The people say that animals understand you. Is it true? How do you do it? I wish to know the truth."

Rodney's eyebrows rose, and he looked at her with new respect. She was the cousin of the wife of an officer in his regiment, and a mere visitor to India. She'd been away from Bhowani for six months, as a guest of the Rajah of Kishanpur. She must have studied hard there, because that Hindustani was surprisingly good. After six years in India, Rodney's wife Joanna knew twenty words, and could use her verbs only in the imperative mood.

Miss Langford looked up and caught his expression. Her frown deepened, and she said curtly, "Good afternoon, Captain Savage." The sepoys glanced round then and saluted hurriedly; they were both in his company and he knew them well. He smiled back and winked slightly, in token that he disavowed the miss-sahib's blunt inquisition.

The holy man's body glowed in the diffused light under the tree. The rain had cut runnels in the ashes and dirt, and there the brown skin was wrinkled gold, the leprous patches smooth silver. His forearms and hands were like parts of a bright statue. The crowd waited in silence. The holy man would answer in his own good time, if he wished; and when he did, the white woman might wish he hadn't.

The waiting and the silence became embarrassing. Rodney glowered down at the unyielding determination of her profile. She had chosen an unpredictable man to pester with her questions. There was a yogi who lived in meditation at the other end of the city; he would never break his silence to answer her, or anyone. There were charlatan fakirs who trooped up and down the Pike in naked insolence; they would beg a rupee and give her a sarcastic blessing. But this old leper was the Silver Guru of Bhowani; and he was in his way a true guru—a teacher—and might explain to her what he knew—or he might flay her with ironic praise and threats of damnation. His temper was growing noticeably worse as the years passed. The townspeople and sepoys feared him, but pointed him out to visitors with proprietary pride. His influence over Indians of every religion was enormous and widespread; as far east as Patna, as far north as Meerut, they had heard of the Silver Guru of Bhowani.

Rodney looked away over the heads of the crowd, at the steam drawn by the sun out of the decaying brick and mud walls of the city, at the terraces by the river, dotted now with brightly clothed women and scavenging pariah dogs, at the swirl of a fish under the bank, and up through the branches at the sky. Thousands of feet above the city and the river two kites planed in slow circles; a troop of minivets twinkled and stirred the leaves, and cheeped *swisweet sweet sweet*; he saw no other bird anywhere.

The Silver Guru raised one hand and turned his eyes down on Miss Langford. The minivets left the tree in a cascade of scarlet and gold sparks, and flew away. Boomerang stamped and tossed his head, and the snaffle clinked; the mare began to sweat and shiver and back up, tugging at her looped reins.

A crow landed on the earth platform, with one harsh caw and a creak of wings. It cocked its head, its eyes sharp and brown, and hopped forward. Two more joined it, then three, then another one. Rodney's scalp tingled and he looked quickly around. To west and south black dots pockmarked

the sky, swelling out and taking shape as they came closer—
crows, flying fast to the peepul tree. They landed beside the
Silver Guru in fours and squadrons until they overflowed the
plinth. Then they crawled on top of one another at the feet
of the crowd, and in silence flapped their wings and opened
their beaks. Their eyes glinted with an awful obedience.
Rodney knew suddenly that at a signal the slithery wings
would smother him, the dirty beaks peck his eyes out. The
air under the tree stank of putrid meat.

The Guru laughed harshly and held out both silvered
hands over the crows. "Many have come. Are you all, then,
the ghosts of dead tyrants? . . . You? . . . And you? . . . And
which one ruled this morning in the east, eh?"

As if his voice had hammered off invisible shackles, the
crowd, so still and taut, burst into struggle. They breathed
hard and fought to get away while Boomerang squealed and
Rodney leaned over to hold the snorting mare. Even then the
girl hesitated, looking at the Guru.

Rodney's nerve snapped, and he shouted, "Don't be a
fool! Mount!"

She rode pale and silent beside him, and did not speak till,
at the cantonment limit, she said, "I don't understand."

"There are many things you do not understand."

An English girl had no business to involve herself with
gurus and fakirs and the edges of magic. Besides, he had
lost his nerve and she must have noticed it. He spoke curtly,
and meant to be rude, but she showed no anger. Frowning
intently, she did not speak again until they reached the foot
of the Hatton-Dunns' driveway. There she raised her head
and said, "I will find out."

Rodney saluted coldly and trotted on alone towards his
own bungalow. His chin sank forward on his breast, and the
black vision of the crows shone in the puddled road. He
shivered. He did not understand either. Hadn't old Bulstrode
talked of something similar, done by a fakir up country in
'42—and the fellow saying the crows only gathered when
catastrophe was in the air?

As he turned in under the bare branches of the gold-mohur tree at the entrance to the drive of his bungalow, a pot-bellied brown infant ran out of the bushes and stumbled howling in his path. He reined in, dismounted, and picked him up. It was the gardener's youngest son; tears coursed through the kohl round his screwed-up eyes.

Rodney cried softly, "Ho, mighty one! Are you tired of life already? There, there, you're all right."

The gardener's wife hurried down the drive and took the child away. She threw Rodney a quick shy smile before adjusting the end of the sari to cover her face. He dropped the reins on Boomerang's withers, whispered, "Go to the stable, boy," and walked slowly forward.

The bungalow, low and square and dull white, sprawled in the long tree shadows; a colonnaded verandah, ten feet wide and paved with red flagstones, encircled it. Short flights of stone steps, without balustrades, ran down at the front under the carriage porch and at the back under a covered passageway leading to the separate kitchen block. Rodney's son, Robin, in a blue dress and a big straw hat, lurched across the grass on the right of the drive, yelling at the black-and-white kitten, Harlequin; the kitten skittered about like a mad thing under the spreading banyan tree, its bottle tail streaming. Moti, the ayah, waddled splay-footed along the side of the bungalow, picking at her teeth with a thorn twig, her dress sharp white against the purple bougainvillaea twined on the colonnades.

Everything was all right; he forgot the crows. He saw no carriages waiting in the compound behind the house, and whistled gently with relief. Joanna's gossip-and-lace factory must have dispersed.

Sher Dil, the butler, tottered rheumatically out on to the front verandah and stood there in bent, dignified immobility, the general of the servant army. Lachman, the bearer, hurried down to take Rodney's cloak. The assistant cook, the dish-washer, the water-carrier, the washerman, and the dogboy, who were smoking rolled-leaf cigarettes by the stable wall, scrambled to their feet, bowed, and put both hands to their foreheads in salaam. From inside the kitchen the cook shouted, "The sahib has come." The gardener, crouched two hundred feet away among a mixed bed of larkspur and pink Clarkia, straightened his back and stood in meditation. The untouchable sweeper, squatting with basket and broom on the verandah outside a bathroom door, rose and made salaam. Jewel, the bull terrier bitch, pulled her head out of an unkempt oleander, barked twice, and returned to the interesting smell.

Robin threw down his big hat and galloped erratically across the drive, shouting, "Daddy! Daddy!" Two female voices called him back, one the ayah's shrill "*Baba! topi pher lagao! ek dum!*" the other an English voice, nearly as high-pitched, with the same message. "Robin! Put your hat on again! At once!"

Rodney caught his son, swung him shrieking to his shoulders, and looked up. His wife, Joanna, stood at the head of the front steps, the pink and white oval of her face set in a petulant frown. The sunlight touched a golden throat locket hung against the dark blue of her dress; one hand was pushing at the masses of her golden hair.

"Rodney, put his hat on, please. He'll get sunburnt and brown, like a subordinate's child."

He put the boy down, jammed the hat on his head, and went up on to the verandah. Joanna said, as she presented her cheek to be kissed, "I don't care if the sun is nearly down. He must always wear his hat out of doors."

She walked down the hall and into the drawing-room. Rodney shrugged, turned into the bedroom opposite, Lachman at his heels, and sat, yawning, on the edge of the bed. Lachman eased the bottle-green tunic from his back, then knelt, pulled off his spurred boots and strapped green trousers, and pushed slippers on to his feet. A smoking jacket of maroon velvet hung on the back of a chair, the tasselled cap on top, the trousers underneath. Rodney looked at his watch; an hour to dinner, three or four hours before

he'd have to change for the ball—time enough to relax.
Lachman held out the smoking kit for him, piece by
piece. Sher Dil stood in the open doorway, supervising the
operation.

In the drawing-room Rodney dropped into a high-backed
armchair. The lamplighter, who was also the night watchman, sidled apologetically through the jungle of furniture to
light the oil lamps. A fire burned in the grate; Rodney
stretched his toes, looked into the flames, and gathered comfort from their assurance that the hot weather was not due
for a few weeks yet. He felt tired and realized he had not
said a word to Joanna yet, not even to ask about her salon.
He couldn't be bothered. Sher Dil had brought the brandy;
the bottle stood on the table beside him. He hesitated,
glanced at her, poured out a glass as silently as possible,
filled it with water, and drank.

Joanna spoke, without looking up from her petit-point
frame. "Did you have an interesting day in the lines, dear?"

"Not particularly—drill parade, company accounts—
but . . ." He did not want to remind himself of the crows.

She said, "But what?"

"A rather weird thing happened on my way back . . ."

He told her and went on, his own mind ensnared again now
that he had to try to make someone else see the reality of it.
"Of course I've heard my father and Curry Bulstrode talk
about even stranger things—but that doesn't explain them.
What do you think?"

"Did you say Miss Langford wasn't wearing gloves, or a
cloak, or a veil?"

"Eh? No—yes—I mean she wasn't. I asked what you
thought about the Silver Guru and the crows."

"Oh, it's a trick, of course. That young lady must be
spoken to. I'm surprised Lady Isobel hasn't done it already.
She must not be allowed to let us all down in front of the
blacks."

"Joanna, will you *please* remember to call Indians by their
race and caste, or, if you don't know, 'natives'?" He became

angry, as he always did when this familiar subject came up, and he gripped the brandy glass more tightly. "God damn it, you ought to know better. We of the Company's service *live* here all our working lives. We do our work and enjoy ourselves and lord it over the country entirely by the goodwill of the average native—especially the native soldier, the sepoy. If you even think of them insultingly, of course they know it and resent it——"

"Don't blaspheme, please. I'm sorry. But I think you're too sensitive about it. And haven't you had enough to drink?"

She eyed the brandy bottle and did not look at all sorry. He poured out a peg, with deliberation.

After a pause she continued in sudden vivacity, "Wait there. I'll show you what I'm going to wear at the ball."

She edged between the furniture, the curve of her breasts parodied in the enormous billow of crinoline below. In a minute she came back and held up a low-topped dress, the satin slip shimmering through white tulle, three deep flounces at the left side caught up with loops of pearls.

"And that will be over hoops, of course, and I'll wear my big pearl earrings and the triple necklace with the sapphire pendant, and one of the fillets in my hair."

Rodney did a quick sum in his head; five months' worth of his pay, transmuted into pearls, would be on show with the dress. Few other captains of Bengal Native Infantry adorned their wives in that style. Perhaps they did not love their wives; or perhaps they had too much damned sense to throw their savings into the great social competition. It was never a fair competition either; Lady Isobel Hatton-Dunn had a big allowance, a few others had private means of a sort. He stared moodily at his wife's face and thought the petulance was beginning to make permanent creases.

She turned the dress this way and that. He forced a smile and said, "Mrs. Savage, tonight you're going to look like a queen."

"It is pretty, isn't it? And Mr. Dellamain has booked three

waltzes—with your permission of course, dear, but I knew
you wouldn't mind. He has only asked Lady Isobel for
two."

Feet scampered down the hall, and the handle of the door
rattled. Robin rushed in, in an embroidered nightshirt, his
long near-white curls wet and plastered from the bath.
Joanna snatched the ball dress up out of his way and put
down her cheek. "Careful! Good night, my sweet child.
Run along now and say your prayers and get into bed."

Rodney kissed him; his breath smelled cool and baby-
sweet, and his wide eyes searched for something that could
keep him here. "Want dink bandy *pani*! Yes!"

Rodney pulled his ear. "No, you little toper. Off to bed
with you!"

Ayah led him out; Rodney poured another brandy. Great
Dellamain the Commissioner, the lord of a million souls, the
first prize of feminine intrigue—poor Dellamain, his dinner
plates the Sangreals of society. The idea gave him a certain
malicious pleasure because he did not like Dellamain; but
then neither did any other man in Bhowani, and none of
them could say why.

Back at her frame, Joanna chattered on. "I hear Victoria
de Forrest is going to wear a maroon dress—really most
unsuitable. . . . Mrs. Cumming swears she saw Captain
Hedges holding Victoria's hand, near the Sixtieth's manège
at three o'clock yesterday afternoon—she said actually
fondling it. He's such a wild man, and she *does* look voluptuous. It's a pity her father has not married again; that's
what she needs. . . ."

Rodney nodded drowsily. His mind wandered into familiar
channels—details of next Friday's parade . . . where on
earth had Sepoy Manglaram's bayonet got to? . . . When
would the regiment get the new-pattern rifles from Dum-
Dum . . . that would mean new cartridges, new loading
drills. . . .

He dozed off, a tall man of thirty with black whiskers
curling up on high cheekbones. His right hand, the sinews

standing out on it, gripped the arm of the chair; his left hand
hung at his side. The same duality, of calm and impulse, was
in his face; the jaws were hard, the mouth sensitive; the hair
classical-black and long, the nose high-bridged and un-
classical. The firelight painted his sunburnt skin with bronze,
and blurred the crosshatching of fine wrinkles at the corners
of his eye sockets. A log cracked and he opened his eyes
quickly; they were blue and frosted, and eager. But there was
nothing. The room was quiet and the fire silent. His eyes
dulled; the corners of his mouth settled a little downward.
Only peasants and beggars travelled the Pike these days;
there were no kings, no hunters, and no horsemen on desperate ventures. On this last day of 1856 deep peace lay over
India. The Moguls were gone and Clive long dead. Rodney
dozed again.

# 2

IN THE victoria she was a wrapped splendour of pearl
and gold, and the immensity of her skirts covered the
whole of the seat opposite him. The coachman's head
nodded against the night sky; the carriage mare blew through
her nostrils as the raw cold tickled them. The lamps outside
the quarter guard of the 88th Bengal Native Infantry were
haloed by the damp; the sepoy sentries paced slowly, their
red coats and brown faces vaguely seen, their white cross-
belts, cuffs, and collars standing out sharp. Opposite, the
court buildings and gaol loomed black against the stars. A
hundred yards farther on, lights glowed in the dim bulk of
the Commissioner's bungalow, and traced yellow paths across
the grass and shrubs of the garden. In the shadows of the
gates' stone pillars two watchmen leaned on iron-tipped
staves.

Colleen, the carriage mare, trotted incuriously past all these symbols of the colossal empire of the Honourable East India Company. Rodney had been born in and of that empire, but still it took his breath away when he considered the power created by those English merchants who had striven here and made themselves the masters of princes. Two hundred and forty-eight years ago their envoys had come to Agra and begged the Great Mogul to let them build a trading post beside the sea. A century ago they bowed and scraped for the favour of the King of Oudh. Today, by luck and aggressive skill, by courage and persevering deceit, their footholds had so expanded that their Presidency of Bengal alone extended seventeen hundred miles from Burma to Afghanistan, and seven hundred miles from the Himalaya to the Nerbudda.

Their other two Presidencies, Bombay and Madras, had swallowed the rest of India; the heir of the Moguls existed only as their pensioner; the King of Oudh had no kingdom. The map of India was a daub of British red, patched by yellow islands to mark the states of the remaining rajahs. On British sufferance, these states ruled themselves, but were forbidden to treat with each other or with any foreign power.

The Company had become a weird blend of trading corporation and administrative engine, and the English government in London controlled it. It traded as it wished, and dictated treaties. It minted money, made laws, collected taxes, and executed criminal and civil justice. It kept the peace—and made war from Persia to China. The man who was its chief representative in India, the Governor General, had direct and almost unlimited power over a hundred million people, and indirect power over other millions living in the states. When the Governor General spoke, the largest volunteer standing force in the world moved to compel obedience.

In fact the Governor General controlled three armies; each of the Presidencies maintained its own, and together they numbered 38,000 British and 348,000 native troops, with 524 field guns. The native soldiers, the sepoys, served under British officers in regiments raised by and belonging to the Honourable East India Company. The Company also maintained in each Presidency a few all-British regiments; but the majority of the white-skinned soldiers in India were in Queen's regiments, those raised by and belonging to the Queen. The English government hired out the Queen's regiments to the Company, for a spell of duty in India while they were on their rounds of the other British colonial possessions overseas.

Rodney smiled a little grimly. Colleen was a symbol herself—a country-bred carriage horse, trotting peacefully down a road made in some dim past by Indian slaves, rebuilt and maintained now by English engineers; trotting on, clip-clop, clip-clop, heedless alike of the Mogul ghosts, the brocaded hunters, the Mahratta horsemen, the centuries of pillage and destruction which had surged up and down this road. No more now though: the land lay quiet under a strong hand. The railways crept west from Calcutta, the telegraph posts strode across the millet fields, the dams rose in the rivers.

He found it a strange thing to hate his exile, and yet to love the country which was its place. His blood was pure English; could it be that the generations of Savages who worked and made love here had passed on to him this awareness of India? England was over the seas and in the north; he looked up at the blurred stars and sighed.

Joanna said, "What is it? Have you left something behind?"

"No. I was remembering the way the snow crackled under the wheels when Mother took me back to Charterhouse after my first Christmas holidays—the same at Addiscombe. The stars in England have a frosty glitter you don't see here. I wish—I wish I could make a lot of money and retire quickly —perhaps I don't. I don't know."

She put her hand on his. "Rodney, why don't you ask for employment under the civil? Mr. Dellamain would recommend you—though you're not very polite to him. Or go on the staff? They get much better pay."

"Perhaps." So that he would be considered a more important person in Anglo-India!

Nothing would induce her to give up this life and return to middle-class nonentity in England. For himself, he did not want to leave his regiment and the sepoys. Year by year he waited for some great thing to turn up for him to do. His father had found such a thing: not many people in England would have heard of the man who rooted out the system of religious murder and robbery called thuggee; yet every year ten thousand Indian travellers, who before William Savage's time would have vanished from the roads, now returned safely to their homes. Something like that might come to his hand, something as big.

The carriage turned into the Club drive, and he sat forward on the edge of the seat, clapping his white-gloved hands, for it was cold. Chinese lanterns hung along the front verandah, and string music pulsed out through the closed windows.

He repeated softly, "Perhaps, some day. But tonight let's dance in this New Year of eighteen fifty-seven. It will be the twentieth of the Queen's reign, the sixty-ninth of my regiment, the Company's two hundred and fifty-eighth."

They entered the centre hall. The earthy dark of the night was in his nostrils, so that the waft of flowers and scent struck cloying sweet, and the shaded lights seemed harsh. Plants stood in pots on tables in the hall and coloured loops of paper lent the pink-washed walls an air of provisional gaiety. Someone had sewn up the rent in the ceiling cloth where the rat fell through during the monsoon of '55. He hung up his greatcoat and shako, stretched his neck, and tugged at the back of his shell jacket. Relaxing, he paced slowly through the lounge towards the ballroom.

English people eddied about among scattered chairs and couches. Indian servants, white-clothed and red-sashed, slipped hither and thither with trays, the full skirts of their

robes swinging. Across the ballroom a Goanese band, hired
from Bombay, sat in chairs on a two-foot dais and fiddled
energetically at the alien music. The floor shuddered in the
rhythm of the dancers, and Rodney's feet began to tap
with the music. Lines of pleasure sprang to crease his face,
and his eyes lit up with clash and blend of moving colour.
Half mesmerized, he saw the officers of the 60th Bengal
Light Cavalry as grey and silver waves, swirling among the
scarlet and white ships of the 88th, breaking on the black
and silver rocks of his own 13th.

The women were drifts of foam—and Victoria de Forrest
a dull maroon anemone. The girl did look voluptuous. And
she was dancing with Eddie Hedges, who had curly fair hair
and a hard mouth, and didn't care a damn about anything
except his own pleasures. Rodney wondered if Joanna's hints
were true.

Joanna was coming towards him. As she reached his side,
a young man in the uniform of the 60th came up, tapped his
programme against the cords on Rodney's jacket, and cried
cheerfully, "Number five—mine, sir!"

Rodney grinned. Cornet Walter Percy Mervuglio, nicknamed Julio, whose family had been settled for three generations in England, thought English but still gesticulated
Sicilian.

Rodney said, "Wait a minute, Julio. Are you coming out
after snipe next Thursday—tomorrow week?"

The dark face smiled in sudden animation, while Joanna
moued prettily and swished her fan. "By Jove, yes. Three in
the morning at your bungalow, isn't it? And may I come
back to dinner, Mrs. Savage? Captain Savage is going to
help me plan my trip after tiger next cold weather." He
turned to Rodney. "You know that double-barrelled sixteen-
bore with twenty-six-inch barrels——"

Rodney interrupted laughingly. "For heaven's sake, Julio
—eleven months hence! That can wait; Joanna won't."

Smiling, he watched them go. Turning away, he found a
slim girl of fifteen at his elbow. She watched the dancing

with brown, deliberately slumbrous eyes, and pretended to be oblivious of his presence. Rodney caught one pigtail and pulled it gently.

"Hullo, Rachel."

She gave a realistic start and sighed heavily. "Goodness me, isn't this *boring*! Mother's in the lounge, talking nineteen to the dozen with that awful old stick Captain Gosse. Pa is in the men's bar, reading the Bible aloud to prove that dancing's wicked—you can hear him from the hall—and he has taken too much to drink."

Rodney gave the pigtail another tweak and said, "When's your big brother coming out?"

"William? In a few months—and he's going to get an ensignship in the Eighty-eighth, our regiment. It'll be wonderful. He's so handsome!"

Rodney listened, and wondered for the hundredth time what frolicsome god had attended the mating when Rachel was conceived. Kindly, stupid Two-Bottle Tom Myers, who wrestled drunkenly with the potentates of Hell, and prayed to God, God his punishing Father, to bend down and strike him with a thunderbolt that all these cynical fools might see how abominable was strong drink in His eyes; "Mother" Myers, twenty years an officer's wife and still in all her thoughts and ways a Sussex farmer's daughter—and from their union, this wildly imaginative dark sprite.

He wanted to laugh, but, looking into the girl's eyes, he controlled himself, smiled, and left her.

Joanna had arranged that they should join the Hatton-Dunns. He began to manoeuvre slowly through the crowd, stopping here and there for a word and a greeting, bowing to right and left. Geoffrey Hatton-Dunn was there, he saw, sprawled in an armchair, and Lady Isobel, and of course her cousin the Langford girl. As they sat side by side on a sofa the family resemblance was very noticeable—same grey eyes, same bone structure, same pallid skin; but Isobel was bigger, her face was squarer, and the other's tautness was in her transmuted to a relaxed assurance; Rodney liked Isobel very much. He saw that she had enticed poor Alan Torrance into the party as escort for Caroline, and that the boy did not look happy.

While he was still greeting them the music stopped, and Joanna joined them and sat down. The clatter and clink in the lounge grew louder, and Geoffrey poured champagne.

Alan Torrance ran a hand over his smooth hair. "Miss Langford's been lec—telling us about the Silver Guru's crows. Asking how it's done, what it means. Dashed if I know—do you, by any chance?"

Rodney shrugged. Why not forget the crows, on this of all nights? Tonight, if they all tried together, and all agreed to pretend that the servants were English footmen, their spirits would not actually be in India; they would be friends and neighbours meeting in an English country house.

To change the subject, Joanna said something light about the band, but Caroline Langford interrupted as though such small talk had no right to be heard at a moment like this. She leaned forward, tapping the table with her fan.

"I'll tell you why I must find out. After these six months at Kishanpur, living in a state, I have decided that we English only inhabit the surface of India. You know I was teaching the Rani our style of deportment, and improving her English? I saw the old Rajah too, and made him talk sense"— she lifted her head and her jaw line tightened—"after he'd tried to fob me off with the nonsense men think will satisfy a woman. Rajahs are so rich and autocratic that I'd expected them to be even more cut off from the common people than we are. It is not so. If something worried his people, the Rajah *felt* it. I think the crows, and what the Silver Guru said, worried all the Indians who were by the tree—so it ought to worry us, because we're supposed to be their friends, as well as their rulers."

Joanna was annoyed; she said, "Come, Miss Langford, we will begin to think you have quite gone native. It is no use bothering about the natives' superstitions, my husband says —don't you, dear?"

Rodney felt trapped and unhappy; that was not at all what he meant when he said, as he often did, that some things about India were inexplicable. He fumbled for words. "It's not quite that—it's a question of proportion . . ."

He hesitated, and Geoffrey stood up. "Proportion—exactly," he said. "If we worried about every queeah thing that happened, we'd nevah have time to school our chargers. . . . Theah's the music—mine, I think, Isobel?"

Lady Isobel gripped the arm of the sofa and pulled herself upright. She walked forward with a heavy limp, her left foot chunking on the floor and the cripple's boot on that side showing plainly under her skirt. Someone came to claim Joanna, and Torrance slipped away.

Rodney hardly noticed them go; he was watching Caroline Langford as she in turn watched her cousin. A sudden and unexpected grace softened her profile, and her lips were slightly parted. Rodney said quietly, "She is a wonderful person."

The girl moved her legs as if their true proportions angered her. She said, half aloud, "Her body's so awkward—her face is so calm." She turned her eyes on him. "I wish I was that way round." The words came in a rush, and she stopped short.

Embarrassed, Rodney struggled to get up, and asked her to dance. The stern lines jumped into place round her wide mouth.

"Sit down, sir. I will excuse you from your painful duty. And do not bother to explain away Geoffrey's levity—he ought to have been a poet, and he's shy. Tell me, where is the next English station?"

The abrupt change of subject notified him that she was back at her desk, again inquisitorial and impersonal. This game he would not play for long, not tonight, and he answered lightly.

"Agra to the north, a hundred and thirty miles; Gondwara to the south, a hundred and forty miles. East and west? No, nothing for impossible distances over impossible roads—just the states: Kishanpur to the east, where you've been staying; Lalkot to the west. The communications here run mainly north and south, like the rivers."

"So India is your palace, but you live shut up with yourselves in little rooms like this Bhowani Cantonment, and the next English room is always away at the other end of the palace somewhere?"

He looked at her curiously. It was a bizarre idea, and against his will it made him think. After a while he said, "In a way, I suppose we do. But, you know, we visit the other rooms too—the Indian ones. The civil—magistrates, revenue people, administrators, and so on—reach into every village. The Commissioner is the head of that here. You've met Mr. Dellamain?"

"Yes. But do *you* make these visits? Does your wife, or any woman? And even 'the civil,' as you call them, do they not merely visit, instead of live in, the Indian rooms?"

"Miss Langford, they do their best. We all do. But to feel India in the way you say your Kishanpur friends do, you must become Indian, gain one set of qualities and lose another. As a race we don't do it—we can't. Women, now— English ladies have to be careful. Indian customs are very different from ours, and we do not want any misunderstandings to spoil things." He avoided her eyes. "As for us officers, we know the sepoys, which means we know the classes and castes they are enlisted from. The Bengal sepoy is the salt of the earth, the most wonderful person anyone can have the privilege of knowing—though I suppose there are just as fine men in the other Presidencies——"

He caught himself up and looked sharply at her. He always did it, always gave these damned visitors and Queen's officers their opening to sneer at Anglo-Indian enthusiasm, to say something about "faithful blacks" and "doglike devotion."

But her face was interested, and though she said the usual thing she said it to get an answer, not as a barb of condescension. Besides, she accented the question as if it were his own particular faith which interested her. "*You* love them, don't you?"

He hesitated, analysing himself more carefully than he had ever done.

"Love? That's a strong word. One man here loves them—Colonel Bulstrode, oddly enough. He loves them—as a father loves a pack of half-witted sons. For most of us it's a sort of giving: we each give all we have, and we don't keep accounts. Of course there are things we don't know about each other—but aren't there things you don't know about your father, or your cousin Lady Isobel? Things you don't want or need to know? It's only trust that matters, and we do trust each other, we and the native officers and the sepoys—completely, unconditionally."

Her expression had softened again as he spoke. She said in a gentle deep voice, "I understand, I think. But don't you ever feel that you and the sepoys might be pulled in opposite directions—oh, by religion, or politics?"

He had to raise his voice to answer her, and lean forward in his chair, for the music of a polka crashed and swung, and around them men were laughing.

"It would have to be something so fundamental that we wouldn't have sufficient faith—loyalty, trust, whatever you like to call it—to bring it out into the open. Remember that every single native soldier is a volunteer. The people have for centuries been the toads under the harrows of a lot of vicious rajahs. Never again. They can look forward to peace for about the first time in the whole of India's history. Think what that means to a man who needs all his energy, all his life, to get a living out of this soil."

"Is that really all he thinks of?" the girl interrupted quickly. "Doesn't he want to be his own master?"

"Perhaps, if it were possible. But first he wants peace, and protection—which means power—and we're giving them to him." He filled his glass and went on. "That's why it's right—but sometimes I feel ashamed. Take this very Bhowani Territory. It used to be part of Kishanpur State, as I expect you heard when you were there. We took it on a forced lease—in perpetuity—but we really have no right here. Yet now the peasants and the lower castes generally would do anything rather than revert to Kishanpur rule and——"

The girl was looking up over his shoulder; he broke off and turned his head. The others had come back, and Joanna was standing by his chair, her full lips compressed. His face was very close to Caroline Langford's, and he stood up abruptly.

"Joanna, let's dance."

"Let me look. . . . I can't, Rodney. Major de Forrest booked it just now."

"Fine, he can wait. Come on."

She came then, with an obvious gladness, a display of happiness—and ownership. Caroline Langford was talking to Alan Torrance, and not looking at her. Rodney felt a fraction of the light spring leave his wife's step.

He swung her out on to the floor, pushed down his thoughts, and let the music take him. He must be a little drunk, but only partly on brandy and champagne. . . . The peasants had peace, and that was good and right—but oh, the dusty splendour, the silent trumpets!

The music stopped, and he demanded the next with Joanna too. In that dance he felt the increasing drag of her against him, saw the tiny curl of discontent on her lip; she was trying to make him behave more sedately. Oh, God, he couldn't live all his minutes in a staidly reasonable manner; he wasn't built like that.

But the sparkle died, and afterwards he led Joanna back to the table and began on the duty dances which filled his programme: Mrs. Caversham, Mrs. Bulstrode, Dotty van Steengaard, Victoria de Forrest—Caroline Langford. She waltzed surprisingly well and did not chatter, concentrating hard, as usual, but light and sure on her feet. In the lilting lift and swing of it he thought he'd like to talk more with her. She was plain, but interesting.

He saw her dress was very similar to Joanna's—white tulle, but with many fewer pearls. That couldn't have helped. Why did women take such instant likes and dislikes? And why did everyone stare at him so? He couldn't be that drunk —no, his partner was staring too, over his shoulder, across the ballroom and the lounge towards the centre hall.

A slight dark Indian stood in the outer doors, one of which had been opened. Mud splashes streaked his brilliant clothes, and the Club's head butler and two servants moved to restrain him from coming in. A raw draught blew through the lounge, and Curry Bulstrode's voice rose in a hoarse bellow above the music. "Shut that door, hey!"

The butler slammed the door to. Circling in the dance, Rodney could not see clearly, but Miss Langford said suddenly, "It's the Dewan of Kishanpur! Why is he here? And what are they doing to him?"

"The servants are making him take off his slippers."

"But he's the Prime Minister and Commander-in-Chief of the State. They can't treat him like that!"

"Can't they! He'd make *them* crawl on their stomachs. Anyway, they're acting for us. He is a bedraggled little peacock, isn't he? They're leading him through towards the billiard room. We'll hear all about it soon enough. Let's forget it—you really dance wonderfully well."

He saw she was perturbed, but she said no more. The hum of conversation rose; the band had never stopped playing; the incident hardly checked the momentum of the dance, because New Year's Eve at the Bhowani Club was something more than the occasion of a ball—it was a ceremony, and the exiles would play their roles to the end.

Fifteen minutes later, while dancing with Rachel Myers, he saw that a servant was bowing beside Curry Bulstrode's chair in the lounge. The Colonel heaved his twenty-stone bulk upright, drained a pony of brandy, licked round the glass with his tongue, and waddled away. Rodney watched the same servant wander round until he found Major de Forrest; watched him come to the doorway of the ballroom and slip closer through the dancers. When he reached Rodney, the man whispered, "Compliments of the Commissioner-Sahib, will you go to him in the billiard room, please."

By then Rodney felt no surprise; he had remembered that his company was on alarm duty this week. He excused himself, led Rachel back to her mother, and slipped off.

# 3

SIX MEN were grouped in the shadows round the far end of the billiard table. Mr. Dellamain, a big man in his mid-forties, stood facing the door. He was the Commissioner charged with the government of the Bhowani Leased Territory, and therefore indisputably the most important official in the room. As though he considered the precedence needed some further emphasis, he stood in a central position, in a pompously authoritarian pose. He was a portly man, dark-jowled, and had bulging flecked brown eyes.

Colonel Bulstrode had levered himself up on to the table so that his vast buttocks, tight in the blue trousers, bulged over its edge. Major Swithin de Forrest, the commanding officer of the 60th Bengal Light Cavalry, in silver and grey, sat on the higher of the two banks of leather-padded spectators' benches, and looked down like a malarial death's head. Gerald Peckham, the brigade major, sat on the lower bank; he was fair and pleasantly good-looking; a staff officer's notebook lay opened on his knees. Eustace Caversham, Rodney's own commanding officer, stood a little aside, his narrow head bowed, his fingers fiddling from nervous habit with the braid on his jacket.

The sixth man Miss Langford had recognised as the Dewan of Kishanpur. He turned quickly to face the door as it opened, and Rodney saw that smallpox had scarred the texture of the dark skin. The wide-set eyes examined him with the too alert interest he associated with a mind not firmly balanced. Red mud and rain had soiled the yellow coat and white jodhpurs. Rings twinkled on the Dewan's fingers as he played with the hilt of a sabre in a jewelled scabbard. In his right hand he held his slippers; on his head he wore a hard wide-brimmed black felt hat shaped like the flattened sail of a dhow, one side up, one side down, and decorated with pearls and diamonds.

Caversham peered at the doorway. "Savage? Your company is on garrison alarm duty, I think?"

"Yes, sir."

"Please sit down, and listen."

Mr. Dellamain grasped the lapels of his tail coat with plump hands. His voice claimed their attention—a full, ripe voice.

"Gentlemen, I will be brief. I have news that His Highness the Rajah of Kishanpur was assassinated today. He was thrown over the inner battlements of his fort into the court-yard, and died instantly." Rodney glanced round, but all the faces were expressionless. "There appears to have been a palace plot to remove both the Rajah and his only legitimate son, an infant, and place on the *gaddi* another, much older son by a concubine—though how the murderer expected to achieve recognition by the Governor General, I am at a loss to understand. This gentleman here is His Excellency Shiva-rao Bholkar, the Dewan of Kishanpur, and a devoted servant and trusted friend of the late Rajah. He has come here in person to bring me this sad intelligence."

The Dewan licked his lips and bowed uncertainly, as if not quite sure that he had followed the English sentences aright.

Bulstrode, sucking on an empty pipe, said, "When did it happen, Commissioner?"

"At about three o'clock this afternoon."

Rodney calculated quickly. Kishanpur lay forty-seven miles to the east, on the far bank of the Kishan River. The messengers would have had to cross the river and ride at least part of the way after dark, and it was unlikely they could have set out immediately after the assassination. He pulled out his watch; near twelve—not bad going.

Mr. Dellamain continued: "Her Highness the Rani was luckily able to take the assassins red-handed, and so save her infant son, the heir. Thereafter, she appears to have acted with considerable—er—energy. She at once ordered the ringleaders to be garroted—thirty-five of them, I think. It was thirty-five, you said, Excellence?"

"Thirty-five men, sahib—and three women."

Bulstrode in turn pulled a heavy full hunter from his waistcoat and opened it. He grunted. "Quick work, h'm! And no tales."

The Dewan's sloe eyes flashed momentarily. Rodney felt rather than heard a faint thumping; the lamps rattled in their chains, and the windows shivered. Midnight. They were singing "Auld Lang Syne" in chorus in the ballroom, arms linked and feet stamping. He glanced at Eustace Caversham and saw that he was pale. Every year, by Bhowani custom, Caversham allowed himself to be persuaded into singing the first verse, solo. Now the biggest moment of his year was lost and all his gargling gone for nothing; he'd have to wait till '58.

The Commissioner shot a quick, warning look at Bulstrode. "Three women, your Excellency? That is unfortunate —but we cannot judge these things by our own standards, can we, gentlemen?"

He began to pace the floor, head bent, one hand caressing his chin. Bulstrode watched him, his shrewd eyes sunk like tiny blue stones in the rolls of fat, a faint sneer hiding in the red-grey jungle of beard around his lips. The Dewan tugged at his moustache.

Mr. Dellamain turned at last and resumed his position.

"The treaty of 1809 makes my duty clear. We must keep the peace in Kishanpur until we have time to find the facts, recognize a new ruler, and see him firmly established. Is your army affected, Dewan?"

"Some—I am not trusting, except Bodyguard."

"I see. Colonel, what force do you consider necessary? I shall of course go to Kishanpur myself, so we must be strong enough to avoid any unfortunate—ah—contretemps."

Bulstrode took the pipe out of his mouth. "It's only a piddling little state. One company infantry, one troop cavalry will do. I'll send a galloper to Gondwara—ask the general to stand-by some artillery there, at six hours' notice. Kishanpur's not allowed guns heavier than six-pounders, hey? A company of our twelve-pounders will fix 'em if it comes to a fight."

Mr. Dellamain stroked his jowl. "I think Brigadier General Jones would have sent a larger force than that, Colonel."

Bulstrode frowned. "Jones was an old hen—Queen's service, too—didn't know the first damned thing about India! I've been out here thirty-nine years—two hundred John Company sepoys are more than a match for any damned pack of rajah's ragamuffins. Send your lads off at once, de Forrest—Mervuglio's troop? All right. And you'll send Savage, I suppose, Caversham? Good. He can march at sun-up, arrive the following day. Savage, arrange details direct with Julio. You command in Kishanpur as soon as you get there. Execute Commissioner's policy—use your own discretion how you do it. Clear? That all, Commissioner? Got to meet a curried duck in the supper room."

Without waiting for an answer, he heaved down from the table and waddled out of the room. Mr. Dellamain stared after him, his face mottled by some emotion halfway between shame and anger. The other soldiers hesitated and shuffled their feet, then followed the colonel and left the Commissioner once more alone with the Dewan.

Rodney slipped away and set about making the necessary arrangements. The orders were clear enough. Julio Mervuglio's troop of a hundred men of the 60th Light Cavalry would ride to Kishanpur as soon as they could and deal with any urgent trouble there. He himself would follow with his infantry company of the 13th, and on arrival in Kishanpur would be in command of the whole force.

He went in search of Julio, and found him in a corner of the bar, listening to de Forrest's dry orders and nodding energetically, obviously in a high state of excitement. When the major finished, Rodney settled with Julio details of the rendezvous, supplies, baggage and scales of reserve ammunition, and then returned to the lounge.

The supper interval was nearly over, and in the ballroom the bandsmen were taking their places on the dais. As soon as Rodney sat down, Torrance began to ply him with questions while men from other parties clustered round to hear the news. Before he finished outlining the story the band struck up, and in a few seconds his audience dissolved. Geoffrey, Isobel, Joanna, and Torrance began to talk about something else; Miss Langford stared at the ceiling.

In the billiard room there had been tension. He'd had a quick vision of an old man with grey hair and bright robes, dropping spreadeagled past the loopholes of a red wall, turning in the air as he fell; a dark and bloody excitement came from Kishanpur and filed the edges of his imagination. Not now, though; he and Julio would set off on a routine duty, and no one was at all excited. His exhilaration evaporated; he'd better get some sleep.

Caroline Langford lowered her eyes to his. "We haven't leased *all* of Kishanpur. Why do we interfere?"

Rodney answered wearily, "We—the Company—can't permit the endless succession-murders and civil wars that there used to be in the states. We don't allow any rajah to mount the *gaddi* until we have recognised him as the lawful heir to his state. Then we've forbidden many states—including Kishanpur—to have a big army; it might be dangerous. Well, when we prevent a rajah from defending himself, we have to undertake to do it for him—and we do."

Torrance stifled a yawn and raised one quizzical eyebrow at Joanna. Miss Langford was not satisfied; she bent her brows on Rodney.

"I do not believe one word of this story of the Dewan's. The elder son—the man they say did the murder—was as harmless as a mouse, and terrified of the Rani. Now she and the Dewan have had him executed—and all his fuddled hangers-on with him, I suppose. No one will ever hear anything but what the Rani says. The old Rajah was a good man—rather like the Duke of Wellington. He said his father signed a treaty of friendship with us and he was going to keep it in letter and spirit, though he hated us. He was hard, old-fashioned, and, to our ideas, cruel—but honourable and upright. I liked him. I didn't think there was a soul would want to murder him, or dare to, except——"

Her face was pale and serious, her jaw set; she must have looked like that when she faced the Rajah, cross-examined him, argued with him. Watching her, Rodney tried to imagine the feelings of a grim old man, uncompromisingly an Eastern prince, when confronted by this equally uncompromising freak of an English female. He pictured their first, formal meetings; she would ask him man's questions; he would try to fob her off with platitudes; she would correct him, goad him to astonishment and interest in her. He must have recognized her militant feminism and chuckled to see a woman angrily reject the extra weapons her sex gave her.

Joanna stared coldly at Miss Langford and then turned to Rodney. "Has the Kishanpur tiger hunt been cancelled?"

He'd forgotten that. It had been the old Rajah's custom to invite a small party from Bhowani to his annual tiger drive. This year invitations had come for the Hatton-Dunns and Caroline, among others, but not for the Savages.

Rodney said, "It wasn't mentioned—but I hardly think the Rani will go through with it so soon after this. It's in February, isn't it? Anyway, it doesn't concern us, dear."

"But if they do have it, and you're still there on duty, they'll have to invite me too, won't they?"

Caroline Langford tapped her knee with her fan. "I have something important to say. Please don't stop me, Isobel. Captain Savage, do you remember what the Silver Guru said to the crows this afternoon?"

Rodney started. He remembered. "Are you all, then, the ghosts of dead tyrants? And which one ruled this morning in the east, eh?" Kishanpur was in the east.

The others stared at him, for he had repeated the words aloud. He stammered confusedly. "But—but—he couldn't have known it! It was about five o'clock; the Rajah was killed at three—and Kishanpur's forty-seven miles away."

"Precisely. He could not have known. But he did."

His brain refused to focus on the worrying, misshapen idea. He shrugged impatiently.

Then he saw she was angry. Her eyes, and still more her expression, also showed surprise—and that stung him.

She exclaimed, "Do I understand that you—that no one is going to make inquiries? Or at least report to Mr. Dellamain?"

She was right, of course. Dellamain ought to be told, as a matter of routine. But the tone of her voice was infuriating.

"That is just what I do mean, Miss Langford. It is no business of mine, still less——"

"Rodney!" Joanna lined her reproof with a downy coo of approval.

"It is your business, sir"—the girl made an angry gesture towards the ballroom—"all of you! The natives almost worship this Guru. You know that. Even I have seen it. Now an honest old man has been murdered, and it appears that the Guru is in league either with the devil or with a clique of assassins—and you say it's none of your business!"

Torrance glanced at his nails and coughed. "Miss Caroline, it's just a coincidence—er, can't it wait until tomorrow?"

She took no notice but jumped to her feet and stared coldly round the circle. She had to raise her voice to make herself heard above the music and the yelling from the ballroom.

"Then it is clearly my duty to tell Mr. Dellamain myself —and ensure that he pursues the matter."

Rodney, trembling with anger, watched her sail through the empty lounge. Suddenly he regained his sense of humour and chuckled. "She'll be blushing in a minute!"

But the erect figure crossed the hall and disappeared under the lintel of the doorway leading to the men's bar; on it was written *Gentlemen Only*. Rodney swore under his breath. Nothing would stop the infernal woman, and her face would not be red. The idea of "ensuring" that the Commissioner pursued the matter!

Joanna purred, "She's a dear sweet girl, but so—intense. She really ought to get married, Isobel, don't you think?"

"I must apologize, Joanna—and to you too, Rodney. She's been like this—hard, almost harsh—since she came back from working with Miss Nightingale in the Crimea. You don't see the true Caroline until something very bad happens. Soldiers back from Scutari came to our house in London, where she was living then, just to thank her. And when I broke my thigh and everything went wrong, and they thought I was going to die, Caroline hardly left me for six months."

Joanna's face showed that praise of Caroline Langford could not hold her interest. She nodded her head as Lady Isobel finished speaking, and said, "How good and kind."

She lowered her voice. "I think we have a very suitable husband for her here in Bhowani." She gestured slightly with her fan.

From the corner of his eye Rodney saw Swithin de Forrest, Victoria's father, walk by, dabbing at his lips with a white handkerchief. God, Joanna was a cat sometimes. De Forrest had a thin nose and flat bloodless face, the skin shaped close on the bone structure; he was dead, inside and out, like a stick of cankered wood. Caroline Langford might be a nuisance, but she was too young and alive to associate with de Forrest's total disillusionment.

Joanna was pleased with herself and caressed him with warm eyes. There was something of champagne there, and something of triumph. What victory did she think she'd won, and in what war? Yet her full beauty, smiling and golden-crowned, hit him with physical force and made him catch his breath; she was his wife. Tonight she'd forget; tonight after all these months they could start again, find again a lost path. Tonight there would be no excuses.

He jumped up. "I must go and get some sleep. Are you coming, Joanna?"

He asked the question shyly, but surely he didn't have to; surely her eyes meant what they said?

She leaned back in her chair. "I think I'll stay on, Rodney, if Isobel does not mind an extra lady in her party. Geoffrey can escort me home. Is Mr. Dellamain going to Kishanpur?"

The others talked aimlessly among themselves, pretending not to overhear. The light shone on Geoffrey's sandy hair and long horse face. The blood mounted in Rodney's neck and he answered curtly, "Yes, but he won't leave the ball just yet. You may get your last dance. Good night. Good night, everybody."

He did not wake when Joanna came in, but she was there beside him when Lachman's repeated pulling at his foot aroused him. A lamp burned with a yellow light, the low voice droned on ,"*Huzoor, huzior,sarhe panchh baje sarhe panchh baje, huzoor . . .*"

He sat up slowly, rubbed his eyes, and looked at his half-hunter on the bedside table. Half-past five o'clock it was. He stirred the tea in a cup on the table and yawned. The company would be on parade in an hour. He dressed quickly while the feet of many servants padded about the house. He leaned over Joanna; she was warm and animal with the smell of sleep, and he could not be angry with her. He kissed her cheek and whispered in her ear, "Good-bye, darling. I hope I'll be back soon."

She stirred and spoke, her voice blurred in the pillow. "G'bye—don' be long—don' li' being lef' here 'lone."

She subsided back into sleep, and Rodney tiptoed along to the dining-room. Two beef chops were swimming in congealed gravy on a cold plate. That fool of a cook must have got up and prepared them at three a.m. He couldn't face them, forced down a thick slice of bread, drank some more tea, and went out into the open.

A sharp cold edged the morning, and the three servants, perched on top of the load in the bullock cart, had muffled themselves in blankets. He mounted Boomerang and rode down the drive, the groom at his stirrup, the cart lagging behind.

A mist carpet lay low over the river, and tendrils of mist entwined the trees and shops of the Little Bazaar. The Silver Guru sat under his peepul, his eyes open and fixed into the north. Rodney made to pull up and ask him what he meant by yesterday's words to the crows—but it wouldn't be any use; besides, he would feel such a fool. He wondered what the Commissioner had said to Miss Langford.

The company stood lined up at attention on the parade ground, awaiting his arrival. He gave the order to stand easy and called out the two Native Officers—Subadar Narain Pande, who was his second-in-command, and Jemadar Godse.

"*Ram ram, sidar log!* Is everything ready, Subadar-sahib?"

Narain was a big man, with sternly accentuated frontal bone and cheekbones, and drooping grey moustaches. Promotion did not come quickly in the Bengal Army; age had bowed his shoulders. He saluted.

"Yes, sahib. Two sepoys are sick, but otherwise we are full strength."

"And the baggage train? Rations for fourteen days? Ammunition? A hundred rounds a man in reserve in the train? Good! Fall in, please."

The Native Officers saluted, turned right, and marched to their places. Rodney raised his voice. "Stand to your front! Number Three—*Company!* Form—*fours! Left!* Right wheel, quick *march!* By the left—left wheel, forward."

He led them north again up the Pike, passed the Little
Bazaar and the motionless Guru, and turned right along the
main Bhowani-Kishanpur road. The wide unmetalled surface, deeply rutted, grass-verged, and lined like the Pike
with a double avenue of bulky dark trees, ran due east past
the northern outskirts of Bhowani City, and on out into
cultivated land. The column of men marched, silent and
sleepy, behind him. A skein of wild duck clattered overhead and swirled up river. Yesterday's rain had laid the dust,
and the road stretched brown and red ahead. The marching
sepoys began to wake up as the sun swung higher above the
Sindhya Hills; the blue smoke of morning fires rose from
the huts they passed among the fields.

An old man peeped out of a clean white house, shaded his
eyes, popped back inside, and scurried out to stand at last
on the side of the road, holding up a sword in his two hands.
Rodney leaned down to touch it as he passed, and smiled,
and said, *"Ram ram,* Father. Be of good health!"￼ Everyone
in Bhowani knew the rheumy old fellow. He was said to be
over ninety, and it was probably true, for as a sepoy in the
24th B.N.I. he had helped to capture a French colour at
Cuddalore in 1783. After reaching the highest of the three
ranks of Native Officer, subadar-major, he had retired from
the service—and that was long since. He shuffled out to greet
every body of troops that passed his land, and if given half
a chance would quaver on happily for hours about Wellesley,
Lake, Combermere—all the shot-silk fabric of the past. It
troubled Rodney, as he looked back along the column, to
see the old man bending in salaam to the Native Officers.
It should have been the other way round, for they were
younger, of lower rank; he was loaded with years and battles
—and he had been a subadar-major of Bengal Native
Infantry. Of course, they were high-caste. The old man
would be low, as most of them were in those old days. That
explained it. Just the same, Rodney did not like it.

The sun was well up now. Ahead, a thirty-mile-wide
tongue of the Sindhya Hills separated the valleys of the

Kishan and the Cheetah. Where the road entered the hills, the jungle began. There would be parrots, green pigeon, and troops of swinging monkeys; men working in tiny cultivated strips cut out among the trees; little villages with bright, shy women at the well; water wheels creaking as the oxen turned them; perhaps the garish music of a wedding procession. He'd take out his shotgun when they reached the day's stage at Adhirasta and try for jungle fowl. He swung up with an imaginary gun at another skein of duck and whistled with cheerful tunelessness in time to the plod of Boomerang's hoofs.

It was a lustrous and silver-gilt morning; he was riding away from Bhowani, and the tea parties, and the whist parties, and the bezique parties, and the interminable talk of sepoys' boots, officers' pay, and ladies' virtue. Caversham's tremulous tenor dropped back with the furlong stones, and Bulstrode's bass grunts, and McCardle's dour Calvinism, and Geoghegan's Catholic humour. He liked these things; they were Bhowani, Anglo-India. Yet—another India lay ahead and waited for him, a princely, Indian India. Caroline Langford's metaphor came to him; now, unless he deliberately shut his eyes, he would see into another room of the palace.

# 4

SHORTLY after noon on the next day, January the second, the jungle fell back on either hand, and he rode out into the open. Ragged fields sloped gently down to a curtain of trees. The trees grew along the bank of the Kishan River, and the grass under them was dotted with flat stones, black and grey piles of wood ash, and dustings of straw; here generations of travellers had rested and fed themselves and their animals before crossing the river. A clumsy barge floated at the edge of the water; in it the three ferrymen squatted round a hookah with a cheap pottery bowl and a hollow bamboo stem.

A troop horse, saddled and heel-picketed, cropped the grass; a trooper of the 60th stood by its head, scanning the oncoming infantry. He stepped forward as Rodney trotted up, and gave him an envelope. Rodney read, while the trooper shouted to the ferrymen to make ready.

*Capt. R. Savage, 13th Rif., B.N.I.*

*Sir:—The Commissioner has arranged accn. for your coy. in the fort. My troop arrived midday yesterday and is quartered in the Kishanpur Cavalry barracks outside the city. I am in fort. The Commissioner has intelligence from Dewan that there will be a riot tonight in the city, and urges that you make all speed. I do not consider situation serious.*

*I have the honour to be, Sir,*

*Yr m.o. servant*

*W. P. Mervuglio, Cornet, 60th B.L.C.*
*11 o'clock a.m. January 2nd, 1857, at Kishnapur Fort.*

Rodney folded the message away in his sabretache, dismounted, and ordered embarkation to begin at once. It would take three trips to get the company over; he'd better cross with the first party, ride straight to the fort, and find out how frightened the Commissioner really was.

Grunt by grunt the ferryman poled the barge out into the stream. Rodney stood in the bow, between the horses' heads, and in mid-channel passed from the direct power of the Honourable East India Company into the dominion of the Rajah of Kishanpur. Trees on the far bank hid the city, which the trooper had told him lay straight ahead. Half a mile upstream, to his right, the river curved. There the red stone blocks of the Rawan family's fortress-palace frowned down on the reach of smiling water. The high walls slid sheer from the battlements into the river, and the sky behind, a towering range of white cumulus cloud, emphasized the palace's angularity and dramatic bulk.

They were approaching the east bank ferryhead, and he saw that two roads led off from the crude ramp and landing platform—one straight on through the belt of trees, presumably to the city; the other right, and along the bank. He ran ashore with a light heart and a few minutes later, the trooper trotting a little behind him, he came to the fort. They skirted the shadowed north wall, seventy feet high, and rode round to the main gate in the east wall, the side away from the river. The double doors of iron stood open; two yellow-coated Kishanpur soldiers came clumsily to the Present, and they clattered past into the dim tunnel of the entry port. The port turned twice at sharp angles, then they rode out into a sunny courtyard.

Cloistered passageways surrounded it, and a fountain played in the middle. Julio sat on the balustrade of the fountain, pointing with his finger at a book open on his knee. The Indian beside him was bigger than the Dewan, and wore the same sort of primrose coat and black hat; he looked bored and puzzled, and Rodney knew that Julio, who was an amateur ornithologist, had been asking him whether he'd seen such-and-such a bird here. He wanted to smile, but this was business. He composed his face and walked Boomerang slowly up to them.

Julio dropped the book, jammed his cap hurriedly on his head, and saluted. "Good morning—I mean good afternoon, sir. I'm glad you have arrived—er, this is Prithvi Chand, the Captain of the Rajah's Bodyguard."

"Good afternoon. Good afternoon, Captain." Rodney looked down from the saddle. "Mr. Mervuglio, why have Kishanpur troops been left on main gatehouse guard if there is any doubt of their loyalty? Where is my company supposed to go?"

A woebegone expression settled on Julio's face. The captain made to interrupt. Rodney raised his hand. "I will speak to you later, Captain. Well?"

Julio explained, waving his hands. "I didn't like it, sir, but the Dewan told Mr. Dellamain that they're less likely to make trouble if no sign is given that they're distrusted. The Dewan has allotted your company several rooms over there." He pointed to the south cloister, where doors could be seen, and a dark passage.

"Who the devil is the Dewan to order Bengal troops about! Oh, it's not your fault, don't look so worried—and anyway we'll make short work of these people"—he glowered at the captain—"if they start trouble. But I wish the civil would keep their long noses out of military matters. Where is Mr. Dellamain? All right, I'll report to him when I've had a look round." He eased his chin chain, turned to Prithvi Chand, and said sternly, "Please show me the fort now, Captain."

He asked first to see the quarters allotted to his sepoys. They were dark cells, but clean and high-vaulted and certainly no worse than the ancient buildings of the Bhowani lines; they'd do. Then Prithvi Chand called for a torch, and ran himself to fetch it when one didn't immediately materialize. They traversed the fort from bottom to top.

The lower passages were an unlighted damp maze. At the end of one there had long ago been a water gate and a portcullis, but now the portcullis hung rusted in its slide and the passage ended against a stone wall where the gate had been removed and built over. Down there too, in the immense thickness of the west wall, were the cells and oubliettes. Tens of thousands of bats inhabited the darkness and crawled over one another on the ceilings; the dank air was acid with the taint of their droppings. And it was cold; even in the heat of May it would have been cold.

Higher up, the passages bent and turned, sometimes running along the courtyard side of the rooms, sometimes in the outer wall. At one place, on the highest of the four stories, a gold curtain hung across the passage. A sentry of the Bodyguard stood there, leaning on a rusty old Tower musket. The captain explained nervously that this was the entrance to the zenana and the Rani's rooms, where no adult male was permitted. Rodney hesitated—he'd want to know the geography there, in case of serious trouble; but Prithvi Chand had contracted a violent fit of the trembles and seemed about to burst into tears, so he turned away; it could wait. After a glance round the broad walk which circled the roof behind the crenellated stones of the breastwork, he asked to be shown to the Commissioner's quarters on the fourth floor. At the door he dismissed the captain with a word of thanks, knocked, and entered.

The Commissioner sat at an ormolu-encrusted table in the right-hand of the room's three wide windows, writing with a quill pen. Isfahan rugs covered the floor, and a large divan stood under the centre window. It was a light and luxurious apartment, obviously decorated and furnished for the use of British visitors. From the window the Commissioner could look out across the river into British territory. The door at the left must lead to a bathroom cell.

Mr. Dellamain greeted him with a friendly wave and, as Rodney began to make his report, swung round to listen. Rodney did not like him, and outside the door had summoned up reserves of aversion in order to fight the more forcefully for his views. But here in this cool sunny place, alone at his work, the Commissioner was not a man to be disliked. He was a middle-aged, cultured, intelligent gentleman; Rodney felt his resolve weakening. He tried to hold his ground—in vain: Dellamain discussed the problem of the gatehouse guard with such good humour and good sense that Rodney at last gave in cheerfully and told himself he'd been a fool.

After they had talked, almost like friends, about the march and the investigation of the fort, Rodney said, "Do you think there is going to be a riot, sir?"

The Commissioner leaned back and rubbed his chin. When he answered he spoke simply and without the usual fruity overtones in his voice. Rodney decided, with a small recurrence of malice, that one military officer was not a sufficient audience to warrant the Commissioner's *vox humana* stop.

"I fear so, Savage. The Rani is sure of it."

"I'll stand by, then. May I go out now in daylight to reconnoitre the streets?"

"Better not. It might precipitate trouble. The Rani tells me that the city's in a very uncertain mood. The Dewan or Prithvi Chand will accompany you if you have to go. We'll hope for the best. May I know your plan?"

Rodney had thought it over during the afternoon and replied at once. "If you send me out I'll leave my quarter guard in the fort, sir, and take the rest. I'll order Mervuglio's troop to stand by in their barracks, but won't call on them unless it becomes clear they'll be needed."

Dellamain nodded and looked out of the window. Sitting in a chair opposite, Rodney saw him three-quarter front; the light fell diagonally, and suddenly, as one sees a face in a fire, he was looking at a frightened young man with a weak mouth. He started involuntarily; the heavy jowl, the massive port were nature's shields shaped by the years to replace youth's vanishing resilience. Behind the barricades there lived a pleasant, pliable, clever, but perpetually fearful human being. He wondered, now, that he could ever have thought otherwise; the flecked soft eyes ought to have told him. He said gently, "You may rely on me, sir."

Outside the door he realized he had never used such a theatrical phrase in his life before. He shook his head and hurried down to the courtyard.

At midnight, sitting on the camp bed in his ground-floor room, he found that he could not concentrate on the adventures of Marco Polo. He shut the book with a snap and began to stride up and down the floor, his spurs jingling. The company had settled in by two o'clock that afternoon, and were sleeping under arms in their quarters across the courtyard. Through the evening the tension in the fort had

mounted, while yellow-coated officials scurried in and out
with messages and orders. Crowds were reported gathering
here, there, and everywhere, and the Dewan had worked
himself into a frenzy; but when Rodney climbed up to look
from the battlements the white city a few hundred yards to
the north-east seemed quiet. He wanted to go and see for
himself.

After dusk the oddly assorted trio of officers of the Bodyguard had stood about talking in strained undertones. Besides Prithvi Chand there was a surly Lieutenant Shivcharan,
and a slim golden-skinned youth of about sixteen, apparently the ensign. Rodney had heard little of their conversation, except that two or three times he'd caught the words
"rani" and "Her Highness." The Dewan, too, frequently
shouted that some order came "from Her Highness's own
lips," and Rodney noticed then with what alacrity men
obeyed. They did not argue or ask questions; they ran. The
woman stayed behind the golden curtain but she was everywhere, just the same. He felt a pang for what he'd said to
Prithvi Chand. The poor devil lived here and probably slept
with perpetual nightmares of rope and rack.

At nine o'clock he'd left the courtyard and its flares and
silences and sudden scurries, and come to his room. But the
Rani was here too, filling each corner with the same darkly
gilded premonition that had touched him in the billiard
room. He could not imagine what kind of human being it
was who could tear apart the chains of her sex and widow-
hood. According to the rules, she should have become a
person of no account, a woman by custom considered
dead.

Midnight. He could not read. The door swung open, and
the Dewan and Prithvi Chand, breathless and excited, stumbled into the room. The Dewan burst out in rapid Hindustani; Rodney buckled on his sword as he listened.

"The riot's begun, Captain-sahib! A terrible riot in the
city. I've told the Commissioner, and he says the sepoys will
put it down. He gave me a note for you."

Rodney glanced at the scribbled chit and said, "Which of you gentlemen is coming with me?" The Dewan answered, and they went out together. Two minutes later the company stood formed up in the silent courtyard, bayonets gleaming. The groom held Boomerang ready. As they began to move into the entry port the iron gates at the far end clanged open.

He halted them among a huddle of broken-down shops in the outskirts of the city and addressed the Dewan curtly in Hindustani. He did not want to be rude; he would have liked to feel sympathy, because the pockmarked little man was a Bholkar, and the Bholkars of Goghri had once been the greatest family in Central India—greater than the Rawans, so great that their head was called simply "The Bholkar." This Shivarao, as a young child, might have been present when British soldiers and Bombay Native Infantry stormed and sacked Goghri. Sympathy wouldn't rebuild the Bholkar glory; nothing could—but Rodney couldn't find even sympathy. The Dewan's air, alternately cringing and bullying—and both attitudes façades for something deeper—grated on him.

Against his will Rodney's voice rasped. "Which way is the riot?"

"Down there, sahib. They have set fire to the tax collector's office, and a tithe barn, and have already killed many officials."

Rodney called out; the sepoys moved, advancing deeper into the city. Crowds milled aimlessly about in the alleys; it was not easy to see details, except that some wore white cotton cloth and some dark coarse blankets. He thought that among the town-dwellers there must be peasants from the country—probably farmers just arrived with goats on the hoof and vegetables for the dawn market. One or two men were throwing stones at house doors, but they did not act in concert, and no one showed serious anger. The sepoys tramped forward, the thick wedge of them walling the street from house to house, the bayonets of the front rank levelled.

The mob surged, like fish in a crowded channel, and were pushed slowly forward. Ahead, where they were not directly in contact with the sepoys, they did not know why the pressure kept moving them on.

At his stirrup the Dewan looked up with eyes sparkling. "Open fire, sahib, open fire! Kill them!"

He did not reply. The lane at last debouched into a small square bounded on three sides by boarded and shuttered houses, and on the fourth by a sprawled temple. There the crowd was pressed too thickly together to move. A low building across the square was burning gently; the red flicker from it illuminated the upturned faces of the mob. They waved hand torches above their heads, and he saw more torches on the housetops. Drifting wisps of smoke dimmed the guttering lights, and a cloud of dust, heavy with the smell of sewage, hung over everything.

The grumbling mutter of the people in the square began to form words. He tried to make them out, while the Dewan screamed up at him, "They're destroying the Rani's property! They're killing officials! It's your duty to fire——"

Rodney snapped, "Shut up, you——"

—ugly, murderous little brute, he'd wanted to say. He heard distinct words in the crowd.

"Down with the murderess!"

That must mean the Rani. The news of the sepoys' arrival did not seem to have travelled through the mob; only those nearest had turned to face them. He patted Boomerang's neck and stared steadily down on them; they looked like honest men, puzzled and goaded. A big old fellow with a gauzy white beard shook his fist at the Dewan and yelled hoarsely, "Murderer! Adulterer!"

Round the speaker they surged forward, and a couple of bricks flew. Rodney saw that they were aimed at the Dewan, who was cursing beside him, but they crashed among the men. A sepoy staggered and spat blood and teeth into the road. Subadar Narain hissed, "Stand up, stand still!"

Rodney leaned down to the bugler at his other stirrup. "Bugler, blow three Gs."

The bugler held his rifle between his knees and took up the bugle dangling at his right hip. He wetted his lips, whispered "prrp prrrmp" into the mouthpiece, then flung back his head and blew.

At the brazen shriek the voices in the crowd fell silent, and Rodney heard the massed, heavy breathing. He stood in the stirrups and called out, "Ohé, people of Kishanpur! Disperse quietly to your homes! If you move this way, we fire!"

A sibilance of whispering soughed over the square. "*Sahib hai—Company ka sahib—Company ka sipahi!*"; then a ripple as they murmured, "*Dewan bhi!*"

He saw consternation in the faces turned to him, and disbelief. They hated the Rani and the Dewan, and they could not believe that he and the sepoys had come to uphold the rulers. Flushing, he raised his voice and shouted his order again. A farmer, conspicuous by a wall eye and a pinched toothless face, jumped out, joined his hands in salaam, and cried in a shrill thick dialect, "Sahib, rid us of the murderess —and rule us—or she will strangle us!"

Narain muttered under his breath, "Swine!" The Dewan fixed the speaker with a wide stare, a hungry almost loving look. More brickbats clattered on the house fronts, and a stick curved through the air.

"Make way!" Rodney edged Boomerang back till two ranks of soldiers were in front of him and he was no longer blocking their line of fire. "Front rank—*kneel!* Front rank, second rank—*cap!* Fire a volley at point blank—*ready!* Present when the sword drops."

He drew his sword and held it out level. From the corner of his eye the N.C.O. at the right of the front rank watched the point.

A long deep sigh shook the crowd. They began to move, peaceably, without panic or hurry. They edged away, pushed back, dispersed, dissolved. The dust drifted around the dark

soldiers, waiting, silent and still in perfect discipline. One
tried to choke a cough, and Narain snarled, "Quiet!" Rodney's sword arm ached.

At last he cried "Rest!" and slowly lowered the sword till
it lay across Boomerang's withers, and breathed out with a
long whistle. The square was empty of people. Several abandoned bullock carts stood in it, and a pair of goats, tethered
together, ran about bleating. He saw no bodies and no
wounded, and the fire in the shack opposite had burned itself
out. The housetops were deserted; a yellow light glowed on
the portico of the temple; his eyes moved nearer along the
second-storey windows.

He looked straight into the face of an unveiled woman,
statue-still, and ugly.

She was leaning out of an open window two feet above
him and not more than ten feet distant, her elbows on the
sill. She was in her late forties; her face was square and
powerful, and daubed with remnants of make-up. Red betel
juice stained her teeth and mottled her lips; thick black hair,
grey-streaked, fell in rats' tails round her face. He knew by
the contemptuous pride of her pose that she could be only
a princess or a whore.

The Dewan saw her and exclaimed in angry recognition.
Ignoring him, she said scornfully, "Of course they killed the
Rajah. I know it. You English—blind stupid fools!"

The Dewan pulled the pistol from his sash and sprang
forward. The woman inclined her head, pursed her lips,
and spurted a jet of red betel juice down into his eye;
she was gone, vanished into the dark behind her. The
pistol exploded, and a sudden orange flash glared on the
wall. The ball chipped the baked mud and sang up into
the sky.

The Dewan put up his pistol and turned back, breathing
hard. Rodney stared at him coldly, without moving. When
the sloe eyes dropped he snapped out a string of orders, and
the sepoys began to march. For an hour they explored the
silent jungle of the city.

At last he halted them and turned to the Dewan. "Where is the other damage? Where were your officials killed? What's happened to the corpses?"

The Dewan had recovered himself, and smiled crookedly. "It must have been exaggerated, sahib. But several men indeed died, so I was told. If not, we can remedy the matter tomorrow."

Rodney turned Boomerang's head without a word and led the sepoys back to the fort.

The riot should have settled something. Perhaps it had; but now he was on edge with suppressed anger and a certainty that No. 3 Company had somehow been tricked and misused.

In the courtyard of the fort, when he had praised and dismissed them, he detained the man who had been injured by the brick. The light was bad, and after a minute's vain peering he called impatiently for a torch. No one answered; the Native Officers had gone about their duties; the N.C.O.'s and sepoys were trailing off to their quarters; his orderly, Rambir, had disappeared, and the Kishanpur officers were nowhere to be seen. His frayed temper broke and he shouted at a shadow passing near him, "You there! Go and get a light, quick!"

The shadow stopped moving. After a short pause a woman's voice called softly, "Someone fetch a light to me, *quickly*!"

In five seconds Prithvi Chand panted up with a flaring torch. By its light Rodney saw that the shadow was a white burqa, the one-piece, top-to-toe garment worn by all Mohammedan and some high-caste Hindu women. Black eyes flickered behind the netting of the oblong eyepiece, and she was gone. He did not have to ask who she was. He frowned and turned to the sepoy.

When he had finished he set out to make his report to Mr. Dellamain. The Commissioner sat fully dressed at his desk. A pair of horse pistols lay beside the inkstand, the chewed stubs of cheroots filled the brass ashtray, and stale tobacco smoke permeated the room. He looked up quickly as Rodney entered.

"Well, was it serious?"

Rodney laughed shortly. "It was nothing at all. Someone had set fire to a shack in the square, and they were throwing a few bricks. Of course it might have got worse, but as it was the Kishanpur troops could have put it down easily."

"H'm. Was there much shooting? I did not hear any, but then the breeze might carry it away."

"We didn't fire a shot. The Dewan tried to murder a woman, but missed. Personally I doubt whether anyone was hurt, from beginning to end. I had a strong impression that it wasn't real, spontaneous."

The Commissioner rose, took a deep breath, and swelled to his full size. His voice was ripe again as he said judicially, "Now why do you imagine someone should have stirred up a riot—and whom do you suspect?"

"I have nothing to go on, sir, but . . ." He related how the crowd had behaved, particularly when he first saw them. "They may have been a bit boisterous. I think the Dewan made it out worse than it was, so that we'd be called in—which would prove that we're supporting the Rani."

He knew now the pattern of light and shadow which could reveal that other man behind the Commissioner's heavy features. He looked, and saw that Dellamain was twisting away from some fact, or fear, or suspicion, even while he spoke words of certainty and reasoned confidence.

"Ah, I suppose that is possible. The workings of the Indian mind are tortuous. But even so, it is a trifle far-fetched. The Dewan is essentially an honest man, unusually direct and—h'm—crude for an Indian. And I do not see that any harm has been done even if your suspicions are justified—a point, I may remind you, on which we have no evidence. Had he asked me outright, I would have been glad to dispatch you on a flag march, in order that the infant Rajah's subjects should be under no misapprehension. The Company's policy will certainly endorse him as the true heir, and the Rani as regent during his minority."

"But they hate her; we heard them tonight! They called her a murderess—that means they think she killed her husband the old Rajah. And they hate the Dewan. They're going to hate us too, and despise us, for supporting her. Some of them were shouting for us to take over the state."

The Commissioner, who had been pacing the floor and slowly shaking his head, stopped in mid-stride and said sharply, "Nonsense! A small section of rumour-mongers and sycophants in the mob, at most."

For a moment Rodney thought the man underneath, cornered, was going to lose his temper. Dellamain was struggling too draw around himself the Commissioner's detached firmness. At last he succeeded, and it was the great Commissioner of the Bhowani Leased Territory who laid an affable hand on Rodney's shoulder and gripped it, a gesture Rodney detested.

"There, my dear fellow, you have a sensitive nature, and I admire it in you. But in these matters of high policy we must subordinate the heart to the brain." Rodney stirred, and the Commissioner let his hand drop. "You have carried out your task tonight with efficiency and dispatch—and Christian mercy. Be assured I shall commend your conduct to Colonel Caversham, and I—ah—flatter myself I have some small influence with him. You have great responsibilities of your own; pray do not burden yourself with mine too. Now let me see, I think a word or two in the right quarter might effect your speedy return to Bhowani, eh? And to the charming and gracious Mrs. Savage. How would that suit you? Caversham could send another officer to relieve you. The sepoys may have to stay for some considerable period."

"Don't do that, sir. It's my company."

"No? Very well. Now go to bed like a good fellow. You must be exhausted. By the way, I would wish you to move your men out into camp somewhere nearby as soon as the immediate danger is over—say in a week? We must not give the impression that we have—ah—seized the reins of government."

"Very good, sir."

"Wait. Her Highness is very anxious that the officer who stays here should try to improve the efficiency of her army."

"What for, sir?"

Mr. Dellamain raised his eyebrows. "To assure her own protection and the young Rajah's, I presume. Perhaps a certain pride too—put on a better show for the Governor General than Lalkot does, you know—something like that. And of course the better her army becomes, the less chance there is that we'll have to come in and help."

"Very good, sir. Good night."

"Good night, my dear fellow."

Rodney saluted and walked quickly along the passage and down the spirals of booming stairs to his own room. The pompous Commissioner's parting clap tingled on his back; poor frightened Dellamain's contrived smile hovered before his eyes: two people in one, a composite man, committed by profession to the filth of politics, writing crooked démarches, saying something and meaning something else. He unbuckled his sword and for a moment let the cold steel of the scabbard touch his cheek. That was direct, honest; cruel—but clean.

# 5

HE WATCHED the dancing girls through half-closed eyes, for he was full of food and lazily content. He had been here seven weeks, each week settling more comfortably into the new way of living. Tomorrow, Saturday, February the twenty-first, it would all vanish under a resurrected formality. Tomorrow the British guests arrived for the installation of the young Rajah and the tiger hunt. He could gauge now the constraint their presence would put on him and the people here. After the tiger hunt he would return to Bhowani, his tasks completed.

There had been no more disturbances in the city, or, so far as he knew, anywhere else in the five thousand square miles remaining to the State of Kishanpur. Once a week letters came from Bhowani—the day he left, Robin had sat on a small scorpion; the dog, Jewel, recently had had a fight with a jackal; Joanna had bought the materials for a new bonnet from a pedlar, and the tailor had made it up for her—total cost, six rupees fourteen annas. She also "presumed" that she would soon receive an invitation to the tiger hunt; he knew she would not, but found it difficult to tell her in so many words. In his letters he "supposed that the Rani had never thought of the matter," and pointed out that he could hardly "stoop to outright cadging." It wasn't true; Sumitra *had* thought of it. Whenever he tried to manoeuvre conversation towards the subject, she as subtly guided it away again. After several attempts he knew she avoided it deliberately. She was a wonderful woman, but a princess, and an Indian, and his pride forbade him to ask favours of her.

The Commissioner had stayed only a week, and had taken Julio's troop with him when he returned to Bhowani. The six weeks since had passed quickly, and Rodney had been kept busy training the local army. He had not expected to achieve much in so short a time, and had set to work with mixed feelings. The work was interesting enough; on the other hand, half believing that the Rani was a murderess, he felt a strong distaste for the idea of setting her more firmly in power.

But after a few days the scruffiness and military ignorance of his pupils aroused his soldier instincts. In a week his only thought was that these people were a disgrace to his profession, and he worked on them as keenly as on his own company. He'd even fretted as his time ran out, but knew now that he would go back to Bhowani warmed by a little glow of accomplishment.

For Prithvi Chand he had begun to feel a genuine friendship. The fat captain seemed to be a court parasite, and if he owned a conscience of any kind he kept it concealed under a happy-go-lucky air and a flow of amusing stories. Rodney's military ferocity terrified him, and it took the Indian two or three weeks to realize that the same man who flayed him so rigorously on parade would joke and drink with him off duty. He reminded Rodney of a gross butterfly, but no one could help liking him, and at parties such as this he was a pleasant companion. Airily drunk with sweet wine, he reclined now on a bank of cushions at Rodney's elbow. The water bubbled in the silver bowl of his hookah; from time to time he belched explosively, for he too had eaten well and gave thanks therefor in the customary way.

Rodney turned to him. "Prithvi, do you and your friends treat all English visitors so—easily? I expected you to be reserved, correct; you have no reason to like us. But it's been more than that, especially in the last few weeks."

Prithvi Chand scratched his stomach and grinned slyly. "If you mean Her Highness, Captain, who am I to say? Now don' be annoyed, I'm only joking—but you know she likes you. She's very unusual lady." He glanced round automatically to make sure no one was in earshot. "The old-fashioned dragons wan-wanted her shut herself up rest of her life when the Rajah died—even become suttee. You know most of the princes are here already for the hunt? With their ranis and girls? I've got a li'l piece upstairs, she says she—she can't hear 'self think for the 'foreign' women d'nouncing our Rani's out-out*rage*ous behaviour! Bzz, bzz, clatter, clatter—at it all day!" He hiccoughed and waved a plump hand in the air. "Waste of breath. Rani says, ever since she's a li'l girl so high, she's going to be different. 'S not another woman of family in India dares do what she's done. She's wonderful—terrifies everyone. Woman like that's like tigress with wings—a freak? I say, you won' tell her this, will you? I'm drunk 's th' Archer-God."

Rodney shook his head and sucked on the amber mouth-piece of his own hookah. It was all true enough; she was like a fire, or a steel spring, and terrifying in the force and range of her passions. Her rages struck like lightning; she even stood still with a sort of passionate realization of her stillness. He had not sought a meeting with her, partly because he was ashamed of his outburst that night in the court-yard. Dellamain had presented him at an informal audience, and after that the Rani took the initiative. Rodney had tried to remain cold and official; it was impossible, because the emotions she aroused were powerful ones—whether of contempt, dislike, distrust, fear, or admiration. Within ten days after Dellamain's departure he had felt all those, in that order. She saw him two or three hours a day; never covered her face; cross-examined him on a thousand minutiae of his work and life; sometimes asked him to call her by her name, Sumitra, to help her "think English." She thought that way she would understand better what he was getting at. It was an impossibility, of course; there was no English-woman in the world quite like Sumitra, Rani-Regent of Kishanpur.

The music beat a louder tune; the dancers swung, their fingers gestured, their silver anklets clinked and crashed. Prithvi Chand raised his voice. "What a row! You know the miss sahib—Langford, wasn't it?—who was here six months last year? She an' the Rani hated each other, 'cos they're so much 'like." Rodney opened his mouth to protest. "Oh, *yes,* Captain. One's Indian, one's English—one has power do what she likes, other wants it. But why you find us easy—tha'ss because you fit in, yet you're still English as goddamn —'scuse me, Captain."

Rodney smiled. Perhaps it was true. Or perhaps they had some ulterior motive in view and wanted to make sure he would report favourably to the Commissioner. But it was a nice thing to hear. He said, "Thank you, Prithvi. You've all taken such a lot of trouble to see that I had a good time—all the shikar you've shown me . . ."

Prithvi Chand giggled; Rodney frowned, then relaxed in a sheepish grin. In the beginning, Prithvi, Shivcharan, and even the golden youth, had indeed taken him out hunting. One of them always went along to show him where the wild fowl flighted and the red jungle cock fed. They clung close and never left him to do his own explorations; once, wanting to take the morning flight and not thinking it necessary to disturb anyone at four a.m., he had slipped out alone. The surly Shivcharan came running after, and later blurted out the reason for his haste. The Dewan feared Rodney might lose his way or come to some harm in the jungle. The Rani would hold the Dewan responsible; so one of the officers was always to accompany him when he left the fort. The Dewan himself seemed to be away a lot.

All that was in the early weeks. For the last month it had been the Rani who came with him, talking without cease, demanding to be taught to shoot, asking his advice on the ordering of guns from England. She was a little over five feet in height, firmly built, and had big black moving eyes. It was she who sat over the kill with him when villagers brought in news of a leopard; she who shot the leopard and clapped her hands like a young girl.

He wanted to thank Prithvi for other benefits besides good hunting. He swept his hand in a gesture embracing the dancers, the bottle of imported brandy on a table, the liveried servants behind him, the strewn cushions. "And then there's all this . . ."

Prithvi smiled happily. "We want you to see our life, Captain, what we are. This is the best tr-troupe dancers in the state. You still look 's if you're on parade—jus' happen to be reclining. Can you *never* relax? Try, jus' thish once, feel like a prince—be Jonathan Savage."

"That was nearly eighty years ago, Prithvi."

"An' now you're not a'venturers any more? Jus' bits great pomp-pompous machine? C'mon, try, jus' please me." He subsided with a belch and closed his eyes.

Rodney thought perhaps he could afford to unbend a little;

Dellamain and Julio gone, no other Englishman here to stand in judgment on his behaviour. He forced a small musical burp and giggled.

In the Rani's court there were old men, Oriental Minnesingers; at night they told tales of Rawan history—of the magnificence, of hawking and hunting, of war, torture, and single combat. Rodney no longer read Marco Polo, for the old men's stories were as true and as thrilling. The Rani encouraged them to embroider the legendary splendour remembered of his great-grandfather, Jonathan Savage; of how he had lived like a prince, and gone away at last with presents and loot worth half a million rupees. Rodney wondered fretfully what in hades he'd done with it. *He* hadn't got it.

The room was warm; its luxury of gold and wine and music touched his jealousy. Four hundred rupees odd a month, Joanna's pearls not paid for, Robin's schooling to come—and there ought to be more children when she got over her fright or her pretended worry about her figure; or was it the fright that was pretence? Why did no one offer him a nice large bribe? What for? What reason on earth would anyone have to bribe a soldier these days? The civil, now! That was the place, and the middle of last century the time! India was a golden jungle then, and his own standards would have been different. Jonathan Savage took bribes and thought nothing of it. Even William, Rodney's father, who had never taken one so far as he knew, had not regarded venality as a form of social leprosy; neither that, nor sexual immorality, nor drunkenness, nor anything—except lack of physical courage. That had been the eighteenth century's code, the code of the Regency bucks. This damned Albert was the root of the trouble, imposing his stodgy German decorum on the Queen and through her on all her subjects. The English had been a riotous crew once; they were a damned dull lot now. It was too late; he'd been bred and raised in the new propriety. He couldn't take a bribe, even if he wanted to and if someone were fool enough to offer him one.

He brushed back the hair falling over his forehead and drank moodily. Prithvi Chand lolled on the scarlet silk covers, asleep now, his mouth open. Through drowsy eyes Rodney saw that only one lamp remained burning in a far corner. The few other guests, all men, had drifted away unnoticed, and the servants had gone. The weak glimmer of the lamp contracted the room so that its gold and scarlet hangings blurred close over him. The curtains were drawn on the musicians' balcony. An Indian violin etched arabesques on the night; a drummer beat with two hands on his drum; each hand beat a separate rhythm, each rhythm different from the violin's. The three rhythms followed their paths, came together at a point of sound, paused, separated, and in due time again met. Six girls danced; their hands writhed, slowing as the music slowed. Each girl wore two anklets on her right ankle; the anklets chimed, *chink-chink, chink-chink*. Shields and swords gleamed like silver ciphers on the walls. The light dimmed.

A brown girl trembled in the centre of the floor. She wore no anklets, or swinging skirt, or tight-drawn bodice. As her naked body moved, the glancing curves of light moved, and Prithvi Chand slept. The outer verges of darkness had swallowed the other dancers. Perhaps they lay beyond the light, locked with soldiers or courtiers, like the spread-eagled women of the temple carvings and the gods who grasped them with many hands—locked for ever, carved of one stone.

The girl was an arrow, straight and taut. She arched her back and was a bow, bent, straining to let go. The bow released; she was a woman and twisted in slow ecstasy. Her breasts pointed the way for her seeking, hesitant feet; her mouth drooped slack and wet and her eyes were blind. She twined around him, her restless body so slight it could not escape. His hands went out and took hold of her buttocks. He dug his fingers into her flesh; the flesh yielded.

He looked into her eyes, searching deep, his nostrils pinched and his breathing difficult. The keys lay there, not in him; a shameless splendour of desire would drive him on

until her desire was peace. She moved, and his fingers
tightened. She had brown eyes, and in their depths a flat wall
of—nothing.

He sighed softly and let his grip relax. Dear girl, dear
lovely arrow girl. She had done her best. He caressed her
bottom, smiled, and pushed her gently away. After a long
wondering hesitation she smiled and stepped back, pace by
slow pace, smiling, into the darkness. A moment longer she
remained as an image held on the retina—big eyes, tight hair,
a half-smile, and a whiteness of small teeth. Prithvi Chand
slept.

The violin crept down a stair of sound. At the foot the
rhythms met for the last time, and silence joined them. The
collar of his shirt constricted his breathing. He rose to his
feet, walked carefully out of the room and along the passage,
and climbed up through the fort towards the battlements.

It was cold in the open air; the day's clouds had passed
and the sky hung low, a roof of twinkling fire. Leaning
against the parapet, he lit a cheroot and saw the smoke drift
north against the stars; nearly always, at night, a breeze blew
down the river. He looked at the bulk of the fort, black and
enormously crouched below him.

A Rawan had built it on the site of a smaller house, in the
sixteenth-century morning of the Mogul glory. The plan of
the entry port showed the hand of a French engineer, and
Prithvi Chand had confirmed that another Rawan had commissioned a student of Vauban's to modernize the fort in
1710. Mahrattas, Rajputs, and Moguls had captured and re-
captured it, and at last the British. For five hundred years
the Rawans had ruled their lands from here. Their hold had
been now tenuous, now firm, but they had never altogether
relaxed their grip, whether as independent kings, as vice-
roys for the Mogul, as vassals of the Mahrattas, as caged
pets of the British. The fort lived on with them. The Rani
still held audience in the huge room on the ground floor;
soldiers and servants moved up and down the passages;
today no prisoners shared the dungeons with the bats, but

there were signs—a smell of ammonia, a pile of calcined
excrement in the corner of a cell—that there had been
prisoners yesterday, or last month, and might be again
tomorrow.

Yet the fort slept a last sleep; for all its mass it was a
ghost. Rodney paced slowly round the walk, and stopped
again on the south face, over the zenana. The fountains were
dry which had once played for waiting women. No one sat on
the marble benches under the grottoes which the builders
had imitated from Al Kadhimain. The kings were dead and
the disputes settled. The dispossessed crowded round him,
changeless, drowned in tides of history. What a wonder of
silk and steel this must have been!

He stirred, the unease of death in his bones, remembering
the tree roots that pushed apart the stones of the lower wall,
the lily pads and water weeds that grew along the river front
at the foot of the red masonry cliff. It must be fifty years
since canopied barges carried the prince and his court out on
the water. Now mangy dogs wandered in and out of the
wicket in the main gate and lifted their legs against the
cloisters, and a pile of ordure stank against the outside of
the north wall. The uniforms of the Bodyguard hung in
yellow tatters from their bodies; they had been rich and
splendid once.

The shape of the land showed only in a blacker blackness
against the horizon. He saw the quarter-guard lights in his
camp by the river, a mile upstream.

He had never talked with her here at night, and did not
know why he expected her. Leaning on the parapet, he turned
his head. She was a pale oval face, a vague spread of gold
and silver. The sari lay back in a sweep on her shoulders,
the stars gleamed on the central parting down her black
hair, and her eyes were on him—they had never been so
huge and moving-black. Her lips were painted dark. She had
a round red caste mark between her eyebrows; a ruby ring
on a finger of her right hand made a spark of fire. He knew
that she was not surprised to see him.

She leaned against the parapet beside him, and after a minute asked softly, "What are you looking at?"

"That light. It's in my camp." He pointed with his chin. She put her hand on his sleeve in a natural gesture.

"Why will you not let me come and see it? It is my land. I wish to know what a sepoy's camp is like. Show it to me tomorrow—please."

He smiled and drew smoke into his lungs. "No, ma'am. I will not."

He felt her stiffen, then at once relax. She left the hand resting on his arm and sighed. "I am sorry. I forget sometimes that I am not the queen of your English Company. But I wish to know. I have never been in any camp; *they* would not let me. When I go out to Kishan Falls on Monday, it will be the first time. Tell me about it."

The single light by the river filled the darkness, and he was there, standing beside it. The tents were ranged in a single row, facing the water; the sentries strode their posts; monkeys chattered suddenly by the Monkeys' Well behind; a leopard's sawing cough boomed across the river in front; the soldiers slept. She didn't want to know about all that. He answered her, pausing between his sentences. She spoke English well, if a little formally, and understood it without effort, but he had to speak slowly.

"You won't see the best part—choosing the place and pitching camp. With us the sepoys put up the tents on a bugle call, all together, and the men of each tent try to get it done first. Next, they dig drainage cuts round, and they're always very cheerful then—I don't know why. I have one tent to sleep in, and one as an office, and that's where I rest and read too. I eat outside unless it rains. The sepoys make a fireplace of mud for me in one wall of the tent. The orderly and the bearer spread my mats on the grass inside. The day we pitched camp down there, Rambir was imitating a Pathan carpet pedlar—you may not have seen one, but plenty of them come down from the north every cold weather. Rambir waved the mats about and made plocking noises, like boots being pulled out of wet mud. That's the way they imitate the Pathans' language, and it always amuses them; all the sepoys in earshot were chuckling as they worked. But Rambir's a great buffoon, and that wasn't enough for him. In the middle of all this gibberish he made one phrase come out clearly enough: 'Beautiful carpets—eight annas to you, eight rupees to a sahib!' Then everyone looked at me out of the corner of his eye to see if I had taken the point.

He laughed, warm with the memory.

"Then we clear the camp of stones, and settle down and make ourselves comfortable. Some officers have glass doors to their tents, you know. I like to clean my guns when there is nothing else to do. In the evening the Native Officers come to my tent and I sit there with my shirt unbuttoned and my legs stretched out, and we talk about the next day's work and so on. Sometimes I have to wear my greatcoat because it's chilly."

"What time do you start work?"

"Not very early yet. No one's heard the coppersmith bird or the brainfever bird, and we don't count the hot weather as really begun until we do. Reveille's still at six, first parade, seven—but I'll put them forward an hour soon. By eleven o'clock these days the sun is hot on your back. Those tunics are thick, and we perspire right through them. It's a good life; the best. The bats fly about under the trees. After dark I listen to the river—this fort stands up very big and square and black from there. I like that better than being in it, I'm afraid."

She put up the hand that had rested on his arm and adjusted her sari so that it hid the side of her face nearest him. "It is cold. You see my India as the men who paint pictures see it, yet you are a soldier. The greatest hero of our family was like that—Rudraparsad Rawan. You know, I too am a Rawan, of another branch? But you are a foreigner—oh, it is not true! None of you English are quite foreigners, or ever will be. I wish I did not think so."

Her low worried voice stopped. When she continued a minute later, she spoke lightly. "I should have been born a man. The outside smells better than those women in the zenana—phooh! Do you remember the hunting with the cheetah? Was it not beautiful, Rodney?"

He nodded. That had been at the end of January. The party had gathered in the courtyard at six in the morning; he remembered the cold tinkle of the fountain, the three monstrous, vague elephants soundlessly shifting their feet and waving their trunks. The fields on the way to the hunting ground were quiet, and the elephants pitched and rolled in a shallow sea of mist. The first light painted the fort behind them with a luminous pallor. The howdahs creaked, huts and trees drifted past, and no one spoke. Sumitra had gripped the basketwork rim and opened her nostrils to the sharpness of the morning.

A mile out they rode through the grove of seven tall trees and seven smaller ones which lay just behind his camp and was called Monkeys' Well. Slabs from the coping of a ruined well were scattered there on both sides of the trail. A band of long-tailed grey langur monkeys chattered and shrieked among the branches; their ancestors had given the place its name. She had pointed silently at the well; there a deep orange-black head rocked from side to side three feet above the ground. The hamadryad's throat shaded down to golden yellow, and its olive-green white-chevroned back curled out of sight between the stones. With hood fully expanded it watched them pass. Rodney looked back as the elephants strode on, and saw the snake uncoil and slither like a green hawser through the dust, while the monkeys chattered louder.

Did he remember all that? When she called him "Rodney" it was a code and meant she was trying to stand outside herself, to see as he, an Englishman, saw.

He nodded again. "I remember. Sumitra, do you know what that hunt reminds me of? Those tapestries in the audience chamber."

Through his telescope he had watched a tapestry hunt that day. The blackbuck ran, the cheetah ran—and the cheetah ran the fastest of all the animals. It was not sport, but it was beautiful. Its symmetry had surrendered the quality of motion; only the posed formality remained now in his memory. There had been not terror, but representation of terror in the morning sun; not movement, but a weft of running in a warp of earth. The figures would be embroidered on that valley still, and the buck would still be running, still alive.

He said, "It's nearly over now. I must go back. Bhowani will seem flat after this. You've made it for me, ma'am. I have no way to thank you."

She did not answer.

It was not "nearly over"; it was quite over. It had finished when the rajahs began to arrive for the hunt. For days past they had been coming, with their horses, elephants, and ornate carriages. Great Jamalpur from the far south had come; Gangoh, Tikri, Gohana, Kiloi, Mamakhera, and Ganeshghar from the east; the Sikhs, Phillora and Tarn Taran, from the Punjab, the land of the five northern rivers; the Mohammedan Nawabs of Jalalabad and Purkhas; Lalkot in force—they did not have far to travel, for only the leased territory of Bhowani lay between Kishanpur and Lalkot; once the two states had adjoined.

In his father's time such a gathering of princes would never have been permitted. It could have meant only intrigue or war. Now—the Company was strong, and the princes had to amuse themselves with mass tiger-hunting.

The Rani said abruptly, "The English party—they are all arriving tomorrow. The Lieutenant Governor from Agra I have met, and of course Mr. Dellamain. I think I have seen the fat colonel—Bull-estrode? The others I do not know. There will be a major general from Gondwara. What is he like?"

Rodney studied the long ash on his cheroot. He wished he knew what she was thinking about; it would be something unpredictable—perhaps it was better not to know. He supposed she was giving him a chance to hide his sadness, stifle his emotion, and be flippant. He answered her lightly and quickly.

"Sir Hector Pierce? He's only been in command at Gondwara since November last. Queen's service. Infantry, I believe. He stands as high as your knee, ma'am, and he has several nicknames—the Baronet, Napoleon the Noughth..."

"Is he a good general?"

He glanced up in surprise at the half-hidden intensity of her question. He had no idea what sort of general Pierce was. He didn't seem to have been in the Crimea and, in India at least, had no reputation of any kind. He said, "I don't know, but he's deceptive, I can tell you that. I've only seen him once. I was drilling some men on the square in Bhowani and didn't even know the general had come up from Gondwara. Then I saw this little square man, about five foot one, in a plain brown suit and a tall black hat. He was standing on a portable mounting block which I suppose his groom has to carry about everywhere. He held a rolled umbrella like a sword on one shoulder; his other hand was tucked into his breast and his head stuck forward a little—just like the pictures of Napoleon. The groom stood behind him, holding his horse— a grey stallion at least seventeen and a half hands high. A couple of my sepoys off duty were squatting in front of him, eyeing him nervously—and I don't blame them—but he took no notice. He has a pasty face, a hook nose, and a square beard. Of course I knew at once who it must be because all sorts of jokes were being made up about him even then. I wanted to laugh."

He turned, threw the stub of his cheroot over the parapet, and watched the falling point of light until it disappeared under the wall.

"I marched up to report myself. Then I didn't want to laugh. He has eyes like stones; he's very polite—never raises his voice above a whisper—smiles primly but with a sort of reserve you can't fathom. We talked a bit, then he scrambled

on to the colossal horse and rode away up the Pike with the
rolled umbrella on his shoulder. I watched him go. I still
don't know whether I want very much to see more of him,
or whether I never want to meet him again."

He couldn't manage any more; at this moment Sir Hector
did not really interest him. He'd have to break off, say good
night, ride back to camp. Sumitra's presence was warm and
familiar beside him, and all their hours together had led
naturally to this place and time. He knew her, and they were
friends within the agreed, unspoken limits.

He did not care now whether she had murdered her husband. Here in Kishanpur the idea of murder did not seem to
outrage him. Then, he thought, the old Rajah might have
tried to degrade her in some beastly way, and only she could
know it. Certainly she was resolute enough to kill—but
surely only in anger, or perhaps for love, or for this soil of
Kishanpur. She could not be a selfish killer.

There were barriers between them, defining their friendship. On her side, she would not discuss the real problems of
the state with him, and he would have liked to talk to her
about something so close to her heart; he had seen her
absently caressing the rough wall of the fort as though it
were her child's skin. But that was her barrier; she'd built it.
He put it down to fear of British interference and kept away
from the forbidden subjects.

On the other side there was a fence too, around the difference in their sexes. That one he had built himself, but he was
not sure now who was keeping it so carefully intact. In the
beginning she had flaunted her sex at him, loading her
slightest gesture with invitation, letting her body touch him
on-purpose-by-accident. It had amazed and alarmed him.
When he knew her better, he concluded that she was goading
herself to wipe out a sense of race superiority she presumed
him to have; that she wanted to force him to acknowledge
beauty in an Indian woman, and desire it. If he had been
another kind of Englishman, he would have felt degraded
by such desire, and she had intended to degrade him. There

had been a wall of nothing behind her eyes in those days—
like the nautch girl just now.

It was as well. His little fence was weak; he had a passionate love of women's bodies, and Joanna would not—
could not?—give it release, Oh, such embarrassment! He
frowned. Recently Sumitra had turned shy and hardly let
him see her eyes.

He braced himself to say goodbye and cut off this moment
of intimacy in the high air. The magic ended here, and he
could not find the right word. He searched in his mind for
something casual, but he said only, "Sumitra!"

She started up and interrupted him with sudden harshness.
"Captain Savage, I want to free my Dewan for his other
duties. I want you to command my army, instead of him. I
have decided that no one but a British officer can make it
efficient, and I want it to be."

"Why?" The startled question was jerked out of him by
an unthinking reflex.

"Because I do—oh, pride. Don't you understand?" He
nodded foolishly; that was what Dellamain had said. He
didn't believe it, and didn't know why. She was saying, "You
are good. I have seen you, seen the improvement in the
officers. It will be a contract for ten years. Perhaps you will
want to stay by then. Things change. You will have the local
rank of major general, with pay of four thousand rupees a
month. Let me know your answer by the end of the tiger
hunting."

Her voice cracked on the last words. She ran across the
roof walk, and he listened to the hurrying echo of her slippers
as it faded down the stairway.

# 6

"IT'S LIKE going out to sea in a little boat. Look, there's the city on the land, there are the fishing boats anchored in the harbour, there's the open ocean ahead, great dark waves with the sun shining on the crests."

Geoffrey Hatton-Dunn's wide sweep embraced the fort behind them, the huts in the misty fields, and the jungle-covered hills rolling away ahead. Rodney smiled, and Lady Isobel exclaimed, "What a lovely idea!"

The elephant swayed steadily on; the mahout dozed, squatting cross-legged on its neck. Geoffrey's imagination raced happily, and animation shone in his long face. His wife and friend listened, chuckling, and he forgot to drawl.

"Dash it, yes—but we're not in little boats. We're a battle fleet in line ahead. Now that the Lieutenant Governor's gone back to Agra, don't you agree that it's Dellamain's duty to make a signal: 'England expects . . .'? He could hoist it on that parasol they've put up in his howdah, or stream it from the elephant's tail—yards and yards of bunting."

Leaning forward, he gestured with his hands; the monocle, forgotten, swung and tapped the pearl buttons of his sleek tan coat.

"A fleet's too cramping. We have all *sorts* of nautical people. Look—ahead there on the next elephant: de Forrest —he's obviously poor Franklin frozen up somewhere in the Northwest Passage. Caroline—she's Bligh, browbeating the crew of the *Bounty*. I do hope Sir Hector doesn't make her walk the plank or anything. Sir Hector—h'm, he's just himself. Surely Napoleon couldn't have worn a great tall beaver hat like that on the *Bellerophon*? Let's say he's a low figure-head to overawe the poor Indian. Behind us we have Colonel Bulstrode, the gallant marine, spitting over the gun'l into the

sea and picking his teeth with a marline spike. What is it
really? Dash me, it's a hunting knife! Mrs. Bulstrode—she's
perfectly dressed for a voyage on an elephant, I mean a ship,
on a beautiful morning, and all the rajahs looking so romantic and princely. She's got eight hatpins to keep her hat on,
she can't see a thing through the veil, and she's *knitting*,
dash it; she's knitting the colonel a red wool cummerbund!
Let's pretend she's a bumboat woman."

"Geoffrey! that doesn't sound very polite."

"You're wrong, my dear, it is. Well, call her Lady Hamilton
if you prefer. Now there's Victoria with them. She's a spoil
of war and is about to be ravished—dashed if I don't think
it would do her a world of good."

"Geoffrey!"

They were passing through the grove at Monkeys' Well
and Rodney glanced over the side to look for the hamadryad,
but it was not visible. Trying to think, he listened with half
an ear to the others and did his best to join in. Isobel knew
him too well; she had eyed him questioningly once or twice
these past two days. He did not know why he shouldn't tell
her his problem, except that he guessed the Rani would
rather have it kept secret, at least until he had made up his
mind whether to accept.

It was a hell of a problem, because Joanna was at the root
of it. The pros were clear enough, and mainly benefited him;
the cons were not so clear, and affected Joanna. He'd have
to get away by himself and think. He might talk to Colonel
Bulstrode about it. Bulstrode knew a great deal about India;
at least he'd give a shrewd and unbiased opinion. Dellamain
would have to be asked too; it might have to go higher.
That depended: if the politicals really wanted Kishanpur to
have the assistance of a British officer, they would probably
have him seconded for indefinite duty but hold him on the
books of his regiment; if they didn't care much one way or
the other they might make him send in his papers before
allowing him to accept. That was a large con; he did not
want to resign his commission.

Lady Isobel was speaking to him. "Rodney, Joanna is a little—put out that they did not invite her to this, when you were here."

He shrugged and muttered that he'd done what he could, short of begging.

Lady Isobel pressed him. "Yes, but surely it's very extraordinary of the Rani. It isn't as if she were quite ignorant of what we call good manners——"

To his relief, Geoffrey turned and butted obliviously into the conversation. "You're looking peaked, old boy—been workin' too hard. Bhowani's been very gay, ha! while you've been rottin' heah. Twinkle won first prize for carriage horses at the show. Two-Bottle Tom finally got the D.T.'s; John McCardle took his Old Testament away and says he'll recover soon. Louisa Bell had a boy; Mrs. Caversham managed to look quite gracious at bein' a grandmother— better not remind her of it too often, though. Dotty van Steengaard's expectin' anothah in May. Eddie Hedges is mashin' Victoria, poor girl—but you'll have heard all this from Joanna. Haven't had a moment to talk to you since we got heah, except in that crowd on Saturday after dinnah, and then deah cousin Caroline was bombardin' you with questions about the riot——"

Rodney broke in hastily, anxious for Lady Isobel to forget the Rani and her unexplained rudeness. "By George, yes, she fairly cross-examined me, didn't she? Even de Forrest seemed interested—or pretended to. What's come over him? Did he go out yesterday to see the city with Miss Langford? She said they were going to."

Lady Isobel answered with an abstracted frown, "They did. They missed the Installation to do it. There was plenty of time before or after——"

"That Installation, or enthronement, or whatever you'd call it, was one of the most gorgeous sights I've ever seen," Geoffrey interrupted eagerly. "And do you know what I noticed most? The gold stripes down the Lieutenant Governor's and Dellamain's trousers! The rajahs and maharajahs

and nawabs and courtiers and all the rest of them were
lavish, brilliant—but formless. Then, in the front row, those
two in plain blue civil uniforms, and if you half-closed your
eyes the stripes down the outsides of their trousers—broad
gold stripes—absolutely dominated everything. They were so
—disciplined."

Lady Isobel said, "I noticed the little boy most. He looked
so pathetic, loaded with jewels and that toy sword—with
those huge eyes. You've seen the Rani, of course, Rodney.
Is he like her?"

"Yes."

At the Installation Sumitra had conformed to the Indian
custom and watched from a screened balcony. Rodney had
glanced up once, but there were no lights on the balcony and
the princesses could look out through the gauze over the
hanging forest of cut-glass chandeliers without themselves
being at all visible.

The conversation died. The path wound southward, keeping fairly close to the river, so that sometimes they saw the
flash of water through the trees. This area, for centuries the
hunting preserve of the Rajahs of Kishanpur, was typical
dry jungle of Central India. Scrub-covered ridges, rough with
the outcroppings of trap rock, rolled ahead into a distant
smoke-blue haze. In friendly silence they passed through a
bare stretch, then a mile of dwarf teak where the huge
skeletal leaves crackled and turned to powder under the
elephants' feet, then open land again, yellow with coarse
grass and picketed by stunted thorn bushes.

They had covered nine miles from the fort and reached
Kishan Falls. Lady Isobel looked up ahead and caught her
husband's sleeve; Rodney whistled; Geoffrey gasped, recovered himself, and lifted the monocle carelessly to his eye.

A tented city rose on parkland running back from the
high bank of the river. At one stride of their elephant they
passed out of the jungle's neutral greens and yellows into a
brilliance from the past. Mounted sentries, wearing yellow
robes and domed iron helmets and carrying old-fashioned

spears, guarded each entrance to the camp. Tents of many colours stood in long loose ranks separated by wide avenues. Some of the tents were a hundred feet in length by forty feet in width, and rose thirty feet above the grass. Screens of coloured canvas curtained off separate clusters of tents, making cities within the city, so that each rajah could withdraw into his own place and amuse himself in his own way. Here Phillora would fondle the twenty breasts of the ten girls he had brought with him, and dream of the six hundred and forty-four breasts left unfondled in his far-away palace; there Kiloi would smoke opium pipes and listen to zither music; there Purkhas would drink cold water and compose poetic apothegms in classical Persian; there the little boy who reigned in Kishanpur would play with a velvet doll and pull Sumitra's hair.

In the light air the standards and banners flapped close to staffs tied insecurely to the tentpoles. Above all the others, as befitted them, were the primrose of Kishanpur; the dull purple of Jamalpur, as sedate and imperial as the state itself; and the irregular tiger stripes of Lalkot, whose history was a gloomy book of murder, treachery, and tyranny. Above the Commissioner's tent in the British enclave a momentary breeze tugged at the largest Union Jack Rodney had ever seen; he laughed suddenly and nudged Geoffrey: the flag was upside down. The elephant stopped; the mahout called and grunted; the elephant shuffled and slowly knelt. They had arrived.

Later, as the sun was setting, Rodney left his tent and walked through the camp towards the river. A knoll by the lip of the falls overlooked a mile-long stretch of water, and there he sat down under a wild lime tree and let the wind dry his sweat-soaked hair. Upstream the river ran four hundred yards wide between low wooded banks, and looked shallow. Still at that width, it slipped smoothly over a fault in the trap rock to make a hissing green-cold curtain one hundred feet high. Below, the banks closed in at once and crowded the tormented river through a steep gorge. The last of the sun shone on Rodney's face and gilded the mist which hovered at the break of the fall.

Across the river a man worked with a sickle to clear a tiny field slanting down to the cliff edge. That would be his hut, three hundred yards above the falls on the far bank, with a smoke smudge drifting northward from it. He watched a bullock cart creep down and past the hut, and heard the driver's faint "Ah! ah!" as he urged the bullocks on into the water. There was a track there; the cart dragged a dust cloud behind it. He glanced up the near bank—yes, another hut, opposite the other, the sure sign of a ford. It could be passable only for a few of the dry months. He wondered how many men had tried to cross when it was too deep, and been swept down and over the falls. He bit the end of a cheroot and half-closed his eyes. . . .

. . . Commander-in-Chief of the Army of His Highness the Rajah of Kishanpur. Major-General Rodney Savage. Major-General *Sir* Rodney Savage, K.C.B., perhaps, if the Queen approved of his work in Kishanpur. Four thousand rupees. Four hundred plus four hundred plus four hundred plus—it went on for ever. It was too much money, too big a job. He couldn't do it.

Goddam it, he *could* do it, and do it well. He wouldn't have to report to that bloody sodomite of a Dewan, but would be responsible only to Sumitra. Now he had to face it: the people hated her, and the better he did his work the firmer he would clamp her rule on to them. But it was silly to think like that. If the Company was going to support her as Regent—and the Governor General had just announced through the Lieutenant Governor that it was—then nothing on God's earth could upset her rule. He would just be doing his professional duty, on a wider field than he might ever reach in the Company's service. He'd jump about thirty paralytic years of promotion, and have the work while he still had the zeal. It would be a great task, and exciting, and would stretch his capabilities to their utmost: to burn out corruption in a well of corruption—Sumitra could have no

idea of the Dewan's extortions and perversions, or she'd
have sacked him long ago—to make these few thousand
men contented and efficient, worthy of their profession, a
fighting force welded together by comradeship, trust, and
confidence, like the sepoy armies; a force fit to take on any
enemy.

He stopped short and shook his head, puzzled. Kishanpur
need fear no enemies. A century or more ago it would have
been different: the British not established as a paramount
power, India a turmoil of warring rajahs. Then, by God,
there would have been real work for him to do—gentleman-
at-large, adventurer-in-ordinary. Frenchmen, Italians, Dutch,
Portuguese, Irish—they had written their own and their
employers' names all over India. But now the Kishanpur
Army would be a mere showpiece, a typical rajah's toy,
expensive and useless. That wasn't like the Rani. He shook
his head again.

No matter. He could live in splendour and retire in magnificence with her decorations glittering on him—and perhaps
that red ribbon from the Queen.

How would Joanna like it? How would Robin grow up,
removed from all contact with English people in these next
few years before he went home? Rodney could send them
both home, immediately—— He stopped dead in his
thoughts and stared at the water. Joanna didn't want to go
back to England, and he had no right to let himself think
of ordering her off. She would like the money, but she would
hate being the only Englishwoman in Kishanpur. He fidgeted
uncomfortably; the Rani wouldn't mind if Joanna never
came.

And there was Robin without English playmates. And he
himself would never serve with the 13th Rifles again. He
could make something out of the Kishanpur troops, but he
he could never make them the 13th Rifles. That settled it.

"Captain Savage, I wish to talk with you."

He started, looked up, and suppressed a desire to swear.
Caroline Langford, dressed in russet brown, stood by

the tree. He made to scramble to his feet, but she shook
her head and sat down near him. As he had done, she looked
slowly round at the bright tents, the green falls, and the red
afterglow in the sky.

She said, "Was the Field of the Cloth of Gold more beautiful? But that's not what I want to talk about. Yesterday
Major de Forrest and I absented ourselves from the Installation and instead visited the city. We went to Sitapara's
house."

Rodney locked his arms round his knees and rested his
chin. Sitapara was the woman at the second-storey window
the night of the riot; he'd found out her name the next day,
for everyone knew her as the madam of a high-grade whore-
house. On Saturday evening, when relating the story of the
riot, he had mentioned her name but not her profession.
Still, de Forrest at least must have guessed what sort of
place he was taking this young lady to.

Miss Langford continued. "Of course I'd heard of her
when I was here before, but hadn't met her. We asked the
way and reached her house with no trouble. A little man
followed us, looking worried, but did not try to stop us.
Sitapara is a very striking woman—and she did not seem
surprised to see us. We talked in French, of a sort."

"French!"

"Yes. She was a harlot in Chandernagore for a few years,
Captain Savage, will you please stop pretending to be
shocked. I am a grown woman and I spent two years in a
hospital at Scutari. The soldiers came in from the Crimea
with wounds, but half of them stayed with venereal diseases
they contracted in Turkish brothels. I am not *going* to talk
round any subject, and I *will* make myself clear. Sitapara
used to be the mistress of the French Governor of Chandernagore, and her French is as good as mine. I went to her
because I hoped she could prove that the Rani and the
Dewan murdered the old Rajah."

Rodney stared at the dark water and thought, Does this
have to come? Already, fifty hours after greeting the other

British guests, murder seemed a dirty crime—whatever its motive—and in his bones he knew the Rani had committed murder. He had not faced it in his thoughts about taking the post of commander-in-chief. His mind had accepted other grounds for deciding to refuse; anything not to have to reach down to that, drag out the ugly thing, and look at it.

He mumbled, "Why go to all this trouble? Why stir up filth? No one cares, and the Company are going to support her."

"Because the old Rajah was my friend! Because you told us on Saturday that you'd seen the wall-eyed man who shouted to you in the riot hanging on a gibbet three days later. Because the Dewan tried to shoot Sitapara. Because the Commissioner gave me no satisfaction about the Silver Guru and what he said to the crows. As for the Company, they would not dare to support her if I can prove that she is a murderess."

He kept his head turned away; it was nearly dark and he could no longer see across the river. She caught her breath and went on less vehemently, "Unfortunately, Sitapara had no legal proof."

"Why did she say she *knew*, then?"

"Partly because she knew the old Rajah exceptionally well; he was her father. I'd heard that too, and Sitapara confirmed it. Her mother was a famous courtesan. The Rajah fell in love with her as a young man—and she with him, Sitapara says. At all events, Sitapara hears a lot, or her girls do. She has a dozen of them, and all the court officers go there, get drunk, and talk too much to prove they are in the inner circle at the fort. One of them saw the Rani push her husband off the roof walk. What no one understands is why she murdered him. She had great power, through him. Her little boy is the only heir the Company could possibly recognize. Sitapara's suggestion is that she is a loose woman, really promiscuous—the kind that must have scores of lovers —and the Rajah found out."

Rodney hunched his shoulders and blurted before he could stop himself, "I don't believe it!"

She kept her voice flat and unemotional. "Nor did Sita-para, in her own mind. And that leaves the assassination, and all the judicial murders which followed, quite pointless —unless the Rani has such an insane lust for personal power that she did it for that."

Rodney sat holding his knees, thinking miserably of Sumi-tra and the golden weeks since January the second. Above the falls the water was a sheet of dull steel; bats flickered by, and the river grumbled below in the blackness. He said, "What else did you find out?"

"Sitapara could tell us nothing about the Silver Guru. She agreed with me that he must have known something, but she insisted he's a true holy man. She couldn't think of any reason which would make him work with such people as the Rani and the Dewan. There's nothing big enough, she says. Then she told us that weird things have been going on since the New Year. Everyone is on edge. People whisper of stars falling, dogs running about headless in the streets, vultures flying in threes across the moon—things like that. No one knows where the rumours come from. And"—he heard her turn to face him directly—"a young officer said one night in her place that one of the top three here—the old Rajah, the Rani, or the Dewan—was bribing Mr. Dellamain, and had been for a long time."

That he could believe, especially since a chance fall of light had uncovered for him the fear behind the Commissioner's imposing manner. If they had been bribing him for a long time, the murder might have been long-planned, and the bribes the price of Dellamain's support for the Rani in official quarters. It made a big difference exactly which of the three was giving the bribes. But again, why the murder at all? Who benefited? The bribes could be for something else. There was the salt monopoly to encourage smuggling; rajahs did slip jewels to British officials who "forgot" to apprise the Governor General of their more outrageous vices and extortions. The girl had uncovered a real dungheap in her determination to drag Sumitra down. And what could she know of all the circumstances to be so self-righteous?

Turning to watch her face, he said with malice, "The Lieutenant Governor was in Kishanpur till yesterday evening. Why didn't you tell him?"

The near-darkness softened the firmness of her bone structure, and she looked less ruthlessly self-assured. She answered slowly, "I did consider it. My uncle, Lord Claygate —Lady Isobel's father—is an important man. The Lieutenant Governor would at least have to listen to me—and if I had evidence, he would have to do something. But everyone knows that I'm unbalanced! Unless I have proof, he'll do nothing. And proof I am going to get! Sitapara is as determined as I am. She's promised to send me a message if she hears of anything definite enough for us to act on."

"Us? You mean you and Major de Forrest?"

"Major de Forrest? Oh, he just said he'd come to the city with me. I meant anyone who will help me."

She meant him. She meant to drag him into this crusade, with herself cast as Peter the Hermit, the madam of a knocking shop as Walter the Penniless, and the Rani and the Commissioner as the infidels.

Of course, if he became commander-in-chief of Kishanpur, he could probably find out—and destroy Sumitra, who had offered him the post because she liked him. Joanna would have a fit at the idea of spying on Dellamain. Even if he did unearth a great scandal he would only be marked down as an interfering busybody. The Company was too big to know everything, and too powerful to relish having the fact underlined by one of its own servants. Anyway, he wasn't going to accept the Rani's offer, and if Miss Langford thought such a lot of de Forrest, let her use him. Damn it, nothing could happen until Sitapara sent word, and then he'd have to judge the facts and see what was his duty.

She said suddenly, "It is your duty, sir."

He shut his mouth with a snap. After a moment he said coldly, "I am not prepared to spy on the Commissioner or on Her Highness. May I escort you back to camp?"

She said nothing. He rose to his feet, pulled her up, and walked at her side away from the river. After a few yards they all but cannoned into Victoria de Forrest; she must have been near enough to hear at least the mumble of conversation, and to have seen them under the tree. Her eyes glinted oddly as he bowed and apologized. Heavens, did the stupid little tart think he was flirting with Caroline Langford? If it had been light enough to see the expression on his face, she would have known different!

# 7

FRIDAY, February the twenty-seventh, was the fourth and last day of the hunting. Many tigers had been killed, and the arrangements for their slaughter were by now little more than a drill. At four o'clock each morning the naked beaters trooped off in hundreds to surround the appointed square of jungle. At seven the cavalcade of elephants began to form up in an avenue between the tents. At that hour dewdrops trembled on each blade of grass, the tents stood knee deep in a lake of mist, and the sun touched the bright flags.

At half-past seven the procession moved off; by seven thirty-five the trees had swallowed the hiss and rumble of the falls. Thirty or forty minutes later the hunters reached the starting line and spread out along it; then the drive began.

This day Rodney rode with Geoffrey Hatton-Dunn on an elephant near the centre of the line. The mahout, naked but for turban and loincloth, sat below and in front, astride the great neck. A shikari, one of the state's paid hunters, crowded into the howdah with them; he wore a patched black coat and a loincloth, and stank of garlic. Twenty yards to their right the Maharajahs of Tikri and Gohana shared the next elephant; beyond them were de Forrest and Caroline Langford. Twenty yards to their left the Rani, Mr. Dellamain, and the chief shikari of the state rode on Durga, the Rani's favourite elephant. Beyond in both directions the line stretched away through thin forest, the khaki and grey of the hunting howdahs patterned by the gaudy colours of the princes' coats. The elephants were dull black, the trees green and yellow, the shadows warm blue.

Rodney murmured, "Wouldn't Julio love this!"

Geoffrey drawled, "He'd go wild, old boy—prob'ly shoot the mahout."

The chief shikari glanced at the sun and listened for a moment to the silence ahead. The beaters should be well in position. The Rani spoke a word; the old man cupped his hands, his goatee beard waggled up and down, and he sent a shrill call quavering across the roof of the jungle. "My lords—forward!"

Each mahout grunted, kicked with his bare heels, and brandished his ankus. Each elephant heaved one slow foot forward, waved its trunk, and began to move. The yellow tiger grass swirled along their flanks; the teak branches swept overhead and tugged at the howdahs; the carpet of teak leaves crackled like a pistol battle. Rodney stood in the front of the narrow howdah, tense and alert, gripping his favourite rifle, a double-barrelled ten-gauge that fired a spherical ball. Geoffrey, similarly armed, stood in the back. Between them the shikari carried two spare rifles, both loaded; powder flasks and canvas bags were slung across his shoulders. Rodney caught the Rani's eye, and she smiled briefly over to him. He'd have to see her tonight and tell her. He'd managed to put it off so far, but now it could not be avoided. He'd tell her tonight.

A confused noise broke out somewhere ahead; that was the beaters, beginning to move. He wondered whether there would be any tiger left by now, then remembered that the shikaris had been trapping for weeks before the hunt began. There would be tigers, crouching in pits, angry and hungry; there would be men up trees with ropes to spring the traps and let the tigers out. Then the tigers would run away from the loud noise of the beaters towards the faint noise of the elephants. The State of Kishanpur would ensure that its illustrious visitors went home satisfied. After all, they had come a long way, just for this.

The elephants swayed forward in irregular line. In front the shouting increased, and a boom and clangour as the beaters banged metal pans and struck the tree trunks with sticks.

Durga stopped. The mahout jabbed the point of his ankus into the hide behind her head; Rodney saw the man's set teeth and the sweat shining on his shoulders, and the Rani's blazing eyes. Durga took three slow paces and stopped again. She curled up her trunk and her head wove from side to side. To right and left of her the mahouts halted their elephants to keep in line.

Behind Rodney, the shikari muttered, "Whore of a great sow. Can't think why Her Highness keeps her. She's played up every single day."

There was no wind, and the jungles smelled hot and dry. Ahead the ground fell away for a hundred yards, then tilted up in a long even slope. Up there the sun momentarily picked out the white of a beater's loincloth among the trees. The shikari muttered urgently, "Sahib, sahib, look—there!"

He thrust forward, pointing with his chin. Geoffrey raised his rifle and set his face in an expression of boredom, his monocle swinging free at the end of its ribbon. Half-right, at the foot of the slope, a deeper gold moved in the yellow grass and was gone. Rodney's heart beat painfully. He gripped the stock of his rifle and stared into the grass. The shikari cried, "There! There!"

A Royal Bengal tiger—ten feet long, male, heavy, and white-ruffed—ran crouched past a tree trunk. It ran with head and tail down, elbows up, and stomach close to the ground. The waving grass swallowed it. All the elephants fidgeted, catching fear from Durga as she fought to turn round, oblivious of the ankus hook driven through her ear. As the mahout tugged at the flesh, she curled her trunk up and over in an S, opened her jaws, and trumpeted. All the mahouts jabbed and bawled; all the elephants sidled back and trumpeted. The appalling thunder screamed along the line; it filed the hunters' nerves and crackled in their brains so that they lowered their heads to it and screwed up their faces. Away to the left a rifle exploded with a heavy boom —and another. The echoes sprang back from the trees. Rodney, leaning over the howdah and searching the grass, saw a black bar move in the shadow of bushes, and lifted his rifle.

The tiger burst from a patch of thorn. The sun burnished him, made him a rippling glory of black and gold, and turned the white ruff at his jowl into a golden halo. He stretched his stride and came on like a river in the sunlight, his head high and his jaws half-open. Geoffrey whispered along the stock of his rifle, " 'Tyger! tyger! . . .' "

Before he could fire, the tiger swerved and ran under their elephant's belly. Geoffrey swung round to face the back of the howdah. The tiger sprang up from out of sight, dug his foreclaws into the hide over the spine, and jerked with his hind legs at the loose folds of the elephant's fork. Opening his jaws wide, he roared so that the blast of fetid breath hit them with the quake of the sound. As he hung, he roared again, and his yellow eyes glared at them in a fire of fury; his hind claws sliced long raw strips of meat from the elephant's loins.

Geoffrey put his rifle to the tiger's chest and fired both barrels. The tiger coughed, choked, and dropped away. The mahout yelled and swung the ankus with all his might, but he could not keep the elephant facing the front of the line.

It ducked its head and swung round, while the howdah rocked. It jabbed down with its blunted tusks at the dying tiger and trumpeted. Then it hurried half a pace forward, and dropped its eleven thousand pounds of mass squarely on to its fore knees. The tiger's breath boomed out in a harsh groan. The howdah bounced, and they clung to the framework while canteens, packets of sandwiches, and both spare rifles showered down past the mahout's head on to the tiger's corpse.

Geoffrey wailed, "The skin! Mahout, save my skin!"

The mahout could do nothing. He hung with his knees locked in behind the huge ears while the elephant trumpeted and squealed and kneaded the black and gold radiance until it was a pulp of fur and flesh, until blood ran out from the tiger's nostrils and over its teeth, and the entrails spewed from its fundament.

The elephant squealed at last in triumph and stood up, again facing the front. Rodney scrambled to his feet and looked round, feeling seasick. No one had noticed their adventure. He saw tigers everywhere, running up and across the slope, half a dozen of them. The hunters were in a pandemonium of excitement.

A slim tigress ran out of the grass, raised her tail, and charged straight at Durga. Rodney took aim—no, that one was Dellamain's; he waited in the aim. Dellamain leaned over, his big face white and crumpled. The rifle shook in his hand, and he fired.

The tigress's snarl grated under the shots, trumpets, squeals and screams. She sprang up, all claws extended and jaws wide, and landed high on Durga's forehead. The mahout rolled sideways to the ground and ran. Durga shut her eyes, lowered her head, and charged a tree thirty feet off. As her forehead smashed against it the tigress released her hold and flung clear. The tree cracked, splintered, broke apart, and keeled slowly over. The howdah fastenings burst; the Rani, Dellamain, and the chief shikari tumbled in a heap to the ground.

The tigress went mad. She sprang vertically twelve feet up, fell back, rolled over and over, bit at her spine, and bellowed. She bit the earth and attacked the fallen tree. Splintered wood and shattered boughs flew through the air in a cloud of dust. Rodney steadied his aim, but she was a whirling demon. He fired. The bullet smashed her across the broken tree as though she had been a kitten, but it did not kill her. Durga lumbered round and ran, the howdah bouncing and rattling beside her on the end of its tangled harness. He had his finger squeezing the trigger again when she passed between him and the tigress. The trailing howdah knocked the Rani down, and when he could see again the tigress was out of sight. From the corner of his eye he saw Dellamain throw down his rifle, turn, and run. The chief shikari writhed on the leaves, held one knee, and groaned. The Rani climbed slowly to her feet.

The tigress crouched in a dip of land behind the broken tree. He could see nothing but her lashing tail, and Sumitra stood too near his line of fire. Her hands hung at her sides, the sari draped her shoulders, and her head was up. She must have looked straight into the tigress's eye, for they were less than ten feet apart.

Rodney put one hand on the edge of the howdah and vaulted out. Geoffrey's cry faded in his ears. A long, long fall, watching the tigress all the time; he must land on his feet, he must not stumble for a fraction of a second; he must land on both feet, balanced, the rifle in his shoulder and his finger on the trigger. Ten feet to fall—not to look down, to watch the lashing tail. While he fell the tail rose. The earth smashed up under his feet, the rifle came into his reeling shoulder, the yellow eyes sprang out. The eyes passed Sumitra, still as a silken statue, and came on. He did not hear the roar, for all of him was in the sights—in the V of the backsight, the bead of the foresight, the expanding eyes. He fired in her teeth. The recoil knocked him on his back, and the eyes and a quarter of a ton of gold fur somersaulted on to him. The sun went out, and it was painless, dark, and without breath.

The sun on his eyelids . . . a whirlpool of light in his head . . . men grunting. They dragged the tigress off him, and each breath stabbed a spear of ice into his lungs. Sumitra was there, her hands at her sides, exactly as she had faced the tigress, but now she was looking at him. Suddenly she grasped at a tree, and men ran to help her.

Geoffrey's arm was under his shoulders, helping him up, and when he stood the arm supported him. He felt his bones and moved his limbs and laughed unsteadily. His ribs ached, and that was all. The princes crowded round him, touching and murmuring; Lady Isobel limped up and kissed him; Geoffrey stammered incoherently. The Rani thanked him with a sudden stilted formality, but did not meet his eyes. Sir Hector Pierce strutted through among the awed whisperings and wavings and stopped a yard from where Rodney stood between Geoffrey and Isobel. Sir Hector was wearing checked trousers, a brown frock coat, and a tall beaver hat. He swept the hat from his head and spoke in a small lilting voice that yet enforced silence with the effectiveness of a pistol shot.

"Captain Savage, the hand of the Almighty guided you and kept you." His mouth shaped a prim smile; the skin crinkled round his eyes, and Rodney felt the force of an overwhelming personality embrace him with its approval. He found himself blushing like a girl as the general continued, "I am privileged to have made your acquaintance, sir."

He replaced the ludicrous hat, clasped his hands behind his back, and walked away. No one smiled.

From the edge of the crowd de Forrest muttered a phrase of congratulation. Caroline Langford caught Rodney's eye but said nothing; he thought she was crying. Lady Isobel definitely was. He patted her shoulder and said, "I'm all right, Isobel, quite all right. There's no need to cry now."

She sobbed. "I know—but we're all so proud of you."
Then they took him back to camp.

He slept till seven, and awoke stiff and bruised but well.
The Rajah of Mamakhera sent his barber over to massage
him, and while the man was at work Geoffrey sat on a canvas
chair beside the camp bed and told him the news. Mr.
Dellamain had taken to his tent and given out that his
ankle was seriously injured. He had in consequence already
received many straight-faced messages of condolence from
the princes. The Nawab of Purkhas composed his in the
form of an elegiac Persian quatrain. The Dewan had had the
head elephant keeper's right hand cut off, and intended to
proceed in the same manner, a member a day, till there was
nothing left.

Rodney sprang up, swore, and scribbled a scornful note
to the Rani. Rambir went off to deliver it; Geoffrey left;
Rodney ate a meal and dozed off again.

Lachman the bearer was shaking him. *"Sahib, ek admi
a-gya."* Rodney propped himself on one elbow, saw the lamp
was lit, and looked at his watch—eleven o'clock. He said,
"What sort of a man? Damn it, it doesn't matter, tell him to
come in."

The visitor was a Kishanpur court servant. He sidled
into the tent behind Lachman, salaamed, and said, "Sahib-
bahadur, His Excellency the Dewan asks if you can spare
a minute to talk with him on urgent business. It is about
your sepoys."

Rodney slipped out of bed and pulled on the black suit
and white shirt which Lachman had put out. He couldn't
imagine what had happened to the company. They were still
in the river camp downstream; Narain was in command and
sent a messenger up every other day; the reports so far had
been that all was well. On the other hand, anything might
have happened—fire, rifle accident, man run amok, someone drowned, cholera—oh, God, not that, not so soon. He
hurried after the servant through a maze of tents until the

man stopped at the end of a canvas alley outside a big marquee. Only then did it strike him that the Dewan might have had the consideration to come to him instead of sending for him at eleven o'clock at night. He paused, drew himself upright, pushed back the flap with a curt swing of his arm, and strode into the marquee.

The canvas walls and roof were dyed the same shade of red-brown as the stones of the fort. A few small tapestries decorated the walls, and Tabriz carpets in grey and blue patterns covered the grass. A lonely black and gold figure sat with crossed legs and upright back on a profusion of scarlet cushions. It was the Rani. He slowed his stride, putting his heels down less emphatically.

She sat in an amber pool of light under the highest point of the roof. The lamp was on a table beside her, with a carved metal box, an enamelled vase, and a bowl of jasmine petals floating on water. In each corner of the canvas room a charcoal brazier stood on bare grass, making the air warm and slightly acrid. She was watching his face as he came on towards the light; her expression was drawn, but he could not interpret it. He realized that his mouth was set in the hard lines it fell into when he was angry.

Now he was here he'd tell her of his decision—but not just yet; he'd have to choose his moment. If he spoke now she'd think from his face that he was annoyed with her, and he wasn't. He relaxed the muscles of his face, smiled, and stopped beside the table. Looking down on her, he said lightly, "Well?"

She dropped her eyes. "The Dewan did not send a message to you."

"That I had already begun to suspect, ma'am."

"I sent the message. I wanted to thank you. I was afraid you would not come unless I said it was about your company."

"That wasn't necessary, ma'am. I had to come and see you sometime anyway, to——"

She swept her hand up to rearrange her sari and knocked

the metal box off the table. It burst open, and a few rings and loose gems—emeralds and rubies—rolled out on the carpet.

"Oh! How careless! Let me help."

She swirled off the cushions and knelt beside him, picking up the stones and putting them back in the box. While Rodney still knelt, peering about for any that had been over-looked, she said, "Will you have some peach sherbet? It is cold. I think this tent is hot? And I have sweetmeats, and brandy to drink your health. Please sit down."

He lowered himself to the cushions and arranged his legs beneath him. The Rani clapped her hands twice, and waited. No one came. She shrugged carelessly. "A woman without a husband is always badly served. I will bring them myself."

She went out at the far end of the marquee and glided back almost at once with a tray of gold and black Jaipur enamel work. The brandy was still in its labelled Courvoisier bottle; the sherbet flagon, the two goblets, and the sweet-meat dish were of honey-coloured Venetian glass. An opened but full box of cigars stood on the tray. He saw that they were the Burma cheroots he usually smoked, and took one. She moved quickly, poured a mixture of brandy and sherbet into each glass, put the filled glasses into his hands, brought him a live coal in tongs from the brazier, held it to his cigar. His hands were full, and his mouth stopped by the cigar; he could not move or speak, and did not much want to. Warmth, inside and out, smoothed his aches and doubts.

At last she sat down, not very near him, and took her glass. She had not met his eyes once since he had first spoken. He felt a constraint of shyness, knowing what he must say to her.

Still looking down, she idly swirled the mixture round in her glass. "How would an Englishman thank a person for saving his life?"

"Well—usually he'd say, 'That was uncommon civil of you.' Perhaps he'd shake the person's hand. It rather de-pends on whether the two had been introduced."

"Then I suppose I had better do that. It was uncommon civil of you to save my life today, sir. Is that right?"

"Perfect, ma'am."

"Thank you. And if it was an English lady, what would she talk about when she had said it? If she had been introduced to the person."

"Herself. Or possibly the weather. She'd say, 'Haven't we been having a lot of weather recently?—for, of course, the time of the year.' She might discuss the servants."

"I have talked about the servants already, have I not? Myself—I have nothing to say. The weather——" She held the empty glass in her lap, and turned away to refill it. When she faced him again he looked for an instant into her eyes and saw tiny lines of strain at the corners and by her mouth. It must have been a terrifying experience to face the tigress, unarmed. She looked away. "What can I say about the weather?"

"Oh—'It's unusually hot—or cold.' "

"Is that what I say?"

"It's customary, ma'am."

"Very well. It is unusually hot—or cold—this evening, is it not, Captain Savage?"

"No, no—one, but not both."

"It is not true. It is very good, between hot and cold. That is why we have the tiger hunting at this time of the year. Your orderly brought your note to me, about the Dewan. I told him to stop what he was doing. I had not heard of it."

"Of course I knew that, ma'am. Sumitra, I've been thinking about——"

She jerked up her hand, turned her head, and said sharply, *"Shh! Sunta nahin?"*

He listened but could not hear anyone trying to get in. He whispered, "I can't hear anything."

"I can. I will look."

She walked silently to the entrance and pulled back the flap. He saw over her shoulder that there was nothing there in the alley between the tents; the stars rode through blue-white clouds above the trees. A draught of cold air tugged at the flame of the lamp. She closed the flap and came back to the cushions, shrugging.

"Nothing. I am sure I heard a noise. Please have some more of this. It is good brandy, I think? It is imported through England." In pouring, she splashed several drops on to the table. "It is from a shop in London. The Rajah bought from them. The Commissioner who was at Bhowani before Mr. Dellamain told him about the shop—that was Mr. Coulson. I met him once. He was a small man with pale hair, and I think his manners were coarse, but he was liked by the Rajah. Do you think the brandy is good? It is easy to make a mistake when you do not know exactly. Our tastes are different. Miss Langford tried to tell me about gold ornaments and carpets and too many pictures, something about taste, but I did not understand her. She is of a great family, and related to the lady who limps, you said. But she is not a clever woman, and not beautiful. These glasses—we ordered them direct from Venice. The Commissioner before Mr. Coulson was——"

"Sumitra, I have——"

The flow of her words turned off. The nervous animation drained from her face and left it utterly empty, the huge eyes hungry. In one motion she flowed off the cushions and knelt in front of him. He looked down on her bowed head, where a line of red lead marked the parting of her hair; she smelt of sandalwood and jasmine water. She brought her palms together in front of her face and moved them up to her forehead and down again in the gesture called *namaste*. Reaching out, she touched his right knee and foot in turn with her right hand, supporting her right elbow with her left hand as she did it. These were the signs that acknowledged overlordship, and Rodney's eyes clouded. The sunlit dream had gone on too long; the incident of the tigress had thrown her off balance.

She raised her head. "My lord, I cannot act any longer.

I am not English. I cannot even thank you for saving my
life. You are my lord and can save me or leave me as you
wish. Only look at me kindly."

His bruises ached. He slowly set down his glass and cigar
and put a hand under her chin. "Sumitra, don't speak like
that. I can't——"

*"No! No!"*

She flung herself on him. He twisted his head, but her
mouth was wide, soft, and wet, and a spasm contracted the
muscles at the base of his spine. He put out his force,
tightened his arms round her. She arched her back over
and struggled open-mouthed for breath. She had given in,
collapsed in a second from a queen to a woman. Had she?
Had she not won a victory? There was pure joy and relief
in her sigh as he relaxed a little the strength of his grasp,
and deliberate abandon in her body curved back over his
arms. Love him or not, at this moment she was using her sex
for some purpose other than its own satisfaction. Angrily
he recognized it from Joanna, and that six months ago—
what the hell was it she'd wanted that time?

He crushed with sudden brutality, so that Sumitra gasped
and opened her eyes. His mind grated in fury. When she
was a jelly of desire he'd let her go and bow and say coldly,
"Was there anything you wanted of me, ma'am?" No one
should use him. Damn Joanna, damn, damn, damn.

She writhed in silence to break free, but he held her. With
a desperate effort she jerked back an inch and tried to speak.
Her breath heaved out in short gasps, and her eyes shone
hugely luminous and black. Before she could say a word
he slammed her back into his arms, closed her mouth with
his tongue, and fought her to the cushions.

She went soft, and even in his anger he knew that this
was not the other deliberately clinging softness. This was a
helpless, moving softness, shivering and moaning under him.
This was a composite of all women east and west, and of
all female need. Sandalwood, jasmine, a sharpness of musk,
and a flame of brandy. He drew back quietly and looked

into her eyes. This was Sumitra, and she loved him. Here
were the keys to unlock power, power so flooding and full
that he had to be gentle. He slipped his hand inside her sari,
cupped her breast, and touched the trembling rigid nipple
with his finger. He kissed her eyes and knew that she was
pulling at the skirt of her dress. Her bare thighs were warm,
and her hands were on him. She turned up her face and
whispered, "My lord, I love you, I love you. I did wrong—
you don't know, but go on, go on. I love you."

The love in her voice caressed him. He stroked his cheek
against hers and could not speak for the welling up of tenderness. He wouldn't harm her, sweet Sumitra who loved him,
sweet tender tigress with her claws gone. With the bound-
less power she'd given him, he had to be gentle, had to be
gentle.

Near three o'clock he awoke. She was coming into the
tent, walking as though pleasant weights dragged at her legs,
and smiling to herself. He caught at her as she passed, and
she sat down beside him and stroked his hair. Neither spoke
for several minutes, till he said, "I ought to apologize,
Sumitra—but I can't."

She kissed his ear. "Silly! I am a queen, and you are my
king. Who are we to make apologies?"

He held her wrists and looked up. Her face was so happy
now—fulfilled, and relieved.

He said suddenly, "When this—when I came in, you had
something on your mind. What was it?"

"I was afraid you wouldn't come back to take all the things
I want to give you. I was a fool, but these last weeks have
been awful, unbearable, to love you so much and treat you
so formally. But I'm glad now—now I know that you love
me, and you will come back to me."

He stared at the shine of black cloth on his knees and
could not speak. When she had first knelt down, he knew
that she loved him, whatever she was trying to make him do.
He knew, too, that he admired her and liked her and felt

sexual desire for her—but he did not love her. He wasn't sure that he knew what love was, except that this was not love. In a sudden realization he saw that they had flown down from planets far apart in space, met, and for an instant joined on the scarlet cushions. She was a queen of the East. She loved, and thought he did. That was all; that was enough. Wife, child, profession—all would bow to her, take their new places, and be honoured. He was an Englishman, a married captain of Bengal Native Infantry. Surely she must know that this was a point of time, wonderful, but isolated and secret for ever? That here their touching wings must part? He was frightened that he, who admired her so well, and thought he knew India, could have been so blind. She lived in another room.

Sunk in unhappiness, he said, "I do not know whether I love you or not, Sumitra. But I cannot come back."

The words came out flat and final. Her hands tensed, and he felt her fighting to control herself. Exhausted with the giving of love, she could not do it. She collapsed on the cushions and lay still while tears ran silently down her cheeks. The fight continued; Rodney watched miserably and admired. He knew that hell; Joanna used to have the power to send him down into it.

Suddenly Sumitra lifted her head, seized his arm, and almost screamed, "My lord, Rodney—you must, you must come; you must, you must! I must have you here—and your wife and child, everything you love. Oh, God's cruelty! Everything has gone too far to stop. I can't stop it!" She rocked in an agony. "My lord, you *must* leave Bhowani and come to live in my fort, now, before—— Now! I will give you all the money you want, all the money your wife can possibly use—ten thousand acres of land. You need never see me again except in public. I will submit even to that, and I am a queen. Do you not believe me? Does this prove anything?"

She ran to an iron-bound chest standing against the canvas, rummaged frantically, and pulled out an ivory silk bag. She hurried back, breathing hard, and spilled a cascade of diamonds and pearls into his hands so that they overflowed and rolled across the carpet in glittering streams of fire. Rodney felt her panic scrabbling at his sanity; he knew there must be something appalling, because he knew she was fearless. In a moment he too would start to pant in terror, and not know why. He set his teeth and clenched his hands on the jewels: this wasn't real, it wasn't English. No one behaved like this, no man could possibly mean as much as this to any woman—not the jewels, but the mad panic.

"Take anything, ask anything, but promise!" She knelt, dropped her head on his knees, and sobbed.

He smoothed the wreck of her hair and said hoarsely, "Sumitra, I'm a swine. That's all I can say. I didn't understand how much—I didn't know that—oh, Christ, I'm a swine. I can't ever see you again."

She looked up, and he saw that he had condemned her to live in a nightmare. He would never understand how it could be so, but he saw that it was. She climbed to her feet and stood unsteadily over him. He waited for the storm of her fury to burst. He wanted it, for that would be the real, proud Sumitra he knew. Perhaps he could believe then that she was not in reality so deeply hurt. He wondered if she had a knife on her.

She spoke in a low relaxed voice. "Very well, my lord. It is a punishment for trying to use you. The gods twist straight trails under our feet and spread nails. I can see that my love means as little to you as the dancing girl's body. She was lucky; she'd have no breasts now, or nose, if she had succeeded in doing what I told her to do."

"Did you—were you watching then?"

"Of course. I watch the mating of my mares and stallions; I watch the men dying on my scaffolds. That was only Friday —a week ago. And even then, God save me, I would not admit I loved you—an Englishman! I wanted to admire you; you were the good commander I needed for my army. It had to be something else—not love. I prayed the girl would settle it for me—I am jealous—but she could not. Then this week, talking to the princes——" She broke off suddenly and shivered. "You will never know what I have passed through." Her voice dropped. "It is all over now. Forget I love you, but keep this to remember today—the tigress, and Sumitra."

She pulled from her finger the ruby ring which he had first noticed the night he met her on the battlements. She pushed it on to the little finger of his left hand and pressed the hand against her wet cheek.

"Keep it on always. And, one night, if you have time, remember I offered you much else. I know it is useless—but remember the post is open for you to accept at any time. Wait. Say goodbye to my son. It is all for him."

She slipped out and came back carrying the young Rajah in her arms. The boy was asleep; Rodney ran his fingers gently through the dark straight hair and bent to kiss one cheek. It was petal-soft, like Robin's; the child was about the same age, but not as chubby.

He saw her eyes were burning and thought her mother-love was beautiful, but she said, "When he is a king, I will tell him what sort of man it was that I murdered—for him."

The words shocked and hurt him. She didn't have to throw her murders in his face. But she was crying again, relaxed and wide-eyed, like one who has given up all struggle. Suddenly he felt completely drained of all emotion and all strength. He stumbled weakly across the carpet, diamonds and pearls hard under his boots, and went to his tent.

# 8

ON THE road back to Bhowani he let the sepoys open their collars. Marching on foot at the head of the company, he moved his shoulders uncomfortably. There had been a nostalgic sheen in his early weeks at Kishanpur, even while he was living them. Kishan Falls had been different, an explosion of feeling. The vivid scenes there—intensely delicious, intensely bitter—overlaid the earlier sweet melancholy. He could blame only himself for the scorn weighting his shoulders. He would do better to forget all about Kishanpur, if he could; but his thoughts would not be checked and, as he marched, played over every incident. The red road stretched ahead.

Before he began to feel tired it was one o'clock and they had reached the halfway stage at Adhirasta: twenty-five miles done, twenty-three to do. Before dismissing the company he glanced at the sepoys to see what shape they were in. They were hot and sweaty but carried themselves with the careless flexibility of men who are not tired: they'd like to get back to their barrack huts. He ordered that the march would begin again, after a rest and a meal, at nine p.m. and continue through the night. The sepoys fell out and scattered under the shade trees, grinning and chattering and idly swinging their rifles. The red flowers of the flame-of-the-forest stippled the jungle, and the sky was blue and clear. He gave Rambir his belt and sword, took off his boots, lay down at the foot of an isolated *sal*, and forced himself to sleep.

At nine they were on the road again, heading west. He felt the hard, sure rhythm of their marching as a current of satisfaction in him; they were fit, and so was he, and to that extent at least he had done his job. The tramp of boots and creak of accoutrements lulled him. Out in front, where he was, clean air dried the sweat on his face; behind, they tied handkerchiefs over their mouths and the dust made the bottle-green uniforms a paler brick-red in the starlight. The moon was in the first quarter and gliding high. He marched in the removed trance of the professional infantryman, his thoughts miles from this business of swinging one foot ahead of the other. He watched the wheeling stars, savoured the night smells, thought of Robin and Sumitra and money, and wondered what the sepoys were thinking of; but another part of him knew where the hands of his watch pointed, and caught every break in the rhythm, every drag at the step.

Shortly after one o'clock he decided to cut south-west off the road and travel instead along the cart trails criss-crossing the jungles. The dust could be no worse, and the bare earth would jar their spines less than the metalling which had been put down on this section of the main road. Within an hour he began to recognize features of the country and knew they were approaching the village of Devra. There the forests straggled to an end; beyond lay crop lands and eight flat miles to Bhowani.

The moon was low ahead in the west. To his left the shadows flickered, some distance off. His brain snapped alert, and he peered into the thin jungle as he marched. The flickering took form, and he saw a man running under the trees, running with an easy lope, passing from moonlight into blackness and out again. He was coming in on a converging trail and had not heard the dulled tramp of the sepoys or seen the moonlit dust haze they raised. The event was bizarre, for villagers seldom traversed the jungles at night, and it was mysterious that the man should run. Rodney stopped and held up his hand. Behind him the soldiers jostled in silence to a halt.

The man, coming on with head bent to pick his way among the tree roots, ran straight into Rodney's arms. He screamed shrilly and collapsed to his knees. His eyes rolled up and round at the sepoys, immense and threatening under the tall

shakos, and he gabbled a Hindu prayer. Rodney had thought
he might be a district mail runner whose bell had lost its
clapper, but the man had neither letter pouch, badge, nor
bell. He was just a man in a loincloth, his face and body wet
with sweat. In his right hand he clutched a pair of the thick
discs of unleavened bread called chupattis.

Slowly the terror died from the man's face as he recognized
them for sepoys with an English officer. Strained anxiety
replaced the fright, and he scrambled to his feet and made to
wriggle away. Rodney and a couple of sepoys in the front
rank caught and held him.

"What's the matter, brother? Can we help? Is there a tiger
after you?" Rodney laughed and nodded down at the
chupattis. "Surely the one in your house can't be so hungry
that she makes you bring her bread, at this pace, in the dark
of the night!"

The man tried to hide the chupattis behind him. Rodney
secured his grip on the scrawny neck, snatched the discs,
and stared at them suspiciously. This got odder and odder;
the ordinary villager would have been volubly eager to talk
about his errand, his flocks, the rain or the lack of rain, and
anything else that would pass the time.

"What have you got in these? Stolen jewels?" He felt the
discs with his hand; the fellow might be a dacoit—an armed
bandit—who had murdered some woman, hidden her rings
and gold ornaments in the chupattis, and buried his weapon
till it was needed again. It had been done before. But there
was nothing foreign in the texture of the bread. "You won't
be able to eat them, now I've handled them—unless you're
an untouchable; you're not, are you?" The sepoys took
their hands away in alarm, but the man shook his head
vigorously, and Rodney shrugged. "Well, it's your own fault.
What *are* you doing?"

The man whined, "There's nothing in them. Give them
back to me, sahib-bahadur. I am doing no harm."

"You tell me why you're acting like a robber, and I'll let
you go. What use are the chupattis to you now, anyway?"

Subadar Narain had come up from the back of the column
to find out the cause of the halt and was standing at Rodney's
side. He took the rifle from a sepoy's hand and slammed
the butt down on the captive's bare toes. "Answer the sahib,
clod!"

The man danced and howled, "Mercy! Mercy! I am only
taking these chupattis to the watchman of Devra, for his
village. *Please* let me go on!"

Rodney stared, astonished. "For heaven's sake—leave him
alone, Subadar-sahib—what good are two chupattis to a
whole village? Though I see they are good thick ones."

"I must take them, sahib."

*"Why?"*

"The watchman of Pathoda brought the orders to me."

"And who the hell are you?"

"I'm the watchman of Bharru—it's a little village four
miles east of here. Pathoda is——"

"I know Pathoda; we passed through it on the main road
three or four hours ago. Go on."

"The man from Pathoda came to me early tonight, bringing two chupattis. He said I must make six more and carry
them on to the nearest villages west, south, and north of
mine, just as he had done—two to each village."

"What on earth for? Come on, the whole truth, or we'll
take you with us to Bhowani Gaol."

"I don't know what it means, sahib, but it must be done.
He said Pashupatti baked the first pair—away in the east—
and Yama is in one and Varuna in the other. The wrath of
Shiva will certainly destroy anyone who breaks the chain."
Rodney nodded; that was clear enough, for all the names
mentioned were manifestations or attributes of Shiva the
destroyer—Pashupatti was Fire, Yama Justice, and Varuna
Punishment.

The man went on with more assurance, "When I get to
each village I am to call the watchman and, when he comes,
say, 'Out of the east—to the north, to the west, to the south!'
Then I give him two chupattis, first breaking one into five

equal parts and the other into ten equal parts. And I am to promise Fire, Justice, and Punishment on him and on his village, unless that night or the following night he too makes and delivers six more chupattis—two each to north, west, and south. Let me go, sahib. It is late in the night and I have visited the villages to the north and south of mine. Only Devra remains."

The sepoys shuffled their feet uneasily. Murmuring shivered away down the files as the men in front whispered back what was happening, and the word was passed on. Subadar Narain muttered in a subdued voice, "We had better let him go, sahib. The anger of Shiva is not to be lightly disregarded."

"It will strike *all* who hinder the passage of the chupattis," the runner broke in meaningly.

Rodney made up his mind. He could report the incident to Caversham or Dellamain, but the man was committing no crime that he knew of and would have to be released. The civil might be interested; then again they might not. They'd probably dismiss it as another utterly pointless mystery and forget about it.

He motioned to the sepoys, they let go quickly, and the man slipped away. Rodney watched him run on down the track towards Devra, flickering in and out of the dying moonlight patches. He shook his head, hitched up his sword, and began to march. The company, after a few hesitant minutes, dropped into the familiar rhythm, but the confidence was gone. He heard the mutter in the ranks and knew the runner's story had disturbed them. To them, there would be nothing fantastic about it. Out of the east the god Shiva was sending messages across the earth: he was threatening someone or something with fire, justice, and punishment—and perhaps it was them, the sepoys. Someone, someday, might explain further—or events might make the Destroyer's meaning very clear.

When they reached the lines, in the last of the night, he was glad to dismiss them and stood watching as they broke ranks and wended to their quarters. They were tired now and dragged their feet. He was standing with Rambir by the corner of a hut; the men came out of the fading darkness like greenish dust wraiths, shuffled past, and went their ways.

At the other corner of the building a sweeper stumbled unseeing into a sepoy. The sepoy swore, picked up a stone, and shouted, "*Hut!* Low-caste ape, lump of defilement!"

The sweeper dodged the flung stone and jeered. "Low-caste ape? Lump of defilement? Listen to who's talking! Why, you have no caste left yourself, licker of cow's fat!"

The sepoy swung up his rifle like a club, and Rodney darted forward. "Stop it at once! Come on, we're all tired. Go to your cots."

The men separated sullenly. When they were gone, Rodney sent for Boomerang, mounted, and rode up the Pike towards cantonments.

He'd have to speak to the Native Officers tomorrow and issue an ultimatum about this squabbling; quarrels like the one he'd just seen were becoming frequent. He must find out, too, what the sweeper had meant and try to protect him. It was an accident, but the poor fellow would have to do unimaginable penance for defiling the sepoy unless the latter could be persuaded to pretend that it had never happened. Who was that sepoy? Ramlall Pande—Brahmin, eight years' service, a poor shot, home in a village near Cawnpore. He might have eaten some cow's fat or flesh by mistake somewhere and the sweeper come to hear of it. Rodney himself would have to feel his way with care; if he went and kicked up a fuss he might uncover a scandal everyone was trying to gloss over and do a lot of damage. The sweeper's behaviour was odd, as odd as that of the runner in the night. A sweeper was the lowest of the low, outcast, untouchable through life, dedicated by his birth to the disposal of human ordure. The sepoy was a Brahmin, twice-born, highest of the high. It was all but unthinkable that any sweeper should raise even his voice against any Brahmin.

Rodney shook the reins impatiently; he didn't want to upset the foundations of society, but he would do all he could to help the sweeper. The general goodwill and good sense of the men made the Bengal Army work—but no thanks were due to the caste system. He'd often seen Native Officers and N.C.O.'s of middle caste grovel before a Brahmin sepoy; Brahmins were never put on a charge unless a British Officer saw the offence and insisted; even then, everyone was uncomfortable. The sepoys were still unhappy that the Brahmin caste had been subjected to the ordinary criminal laws and could be tried and hanged like anyone else if they committed murder. Then there was old Mehnat Ram, the retired subadar-major, who trotted out to make obeisances to his juniors—that had been the early morning of January the first; today was March the third.

What on earth was the meaning of the chupattis, and why break them up—one into five pieces, one into ten? He passed under the gold-mohur tree at the entrance to his drive, saw his bungalow, and put the worries from his mind.

He slept all day, disturbed only once, by the clamour of the ladies assembled for Joanna's mid-morning coffee salon. Then he bathed, ate, played with Robin, accepted the greetings of Jewel and Harlequin, inspected the stables, conversed with the butler, and could find no more excuse for putting off a talk with Joanna. He had tried, and failed, to think of a reason that would justify him in keeping the Rani's offer a secret. Acceptance of it would have altered his life and his wife's, and there was no way out of it; he had to tell her.

His father's Bokhara rugs were back on the hall floor. In the drawing-room an embroidered screen hid the empty grate, and the double doors in the east wall were opened on to the dark verandah. A mosquito whined in his ear. The hot weather had begun. He felt shy and guilty and did not know how to begin, so he poured himself a drink. Joanna sat opposite, knitting; the compression of her lips showed that she had noticed the size of his peg.

He said in a sudden rush of words, "Joanna, the Rani asked me to be commander-in-chief of the state army at four thousand rupees a month—and a major general. I refused."

The click of needles stopped. She slowly laid the knitting in her lap. "You refused? You threw away four thousand a month and a major generalship? Rodney, you're joking!"

"I'm not. There are a lot of disadvantages which aren't so obvious until you think about them a bit."

She picked up the wool with an unconscious movement, still looking at him, and held it in her hand. "We could have had another carriage, and all the clothes I need—I've hardly got a stitch fit to wear—and invited the Commissioner as often as we liked, and served the best champagne. Robin could go to Eton. I would take precedence everywhere."

"Charterhouse. And I don't know who you'd precede, dear. There aren't any other English people in Kishanpur, and the high court officials there are a great deal richer than we could ever hope to be."

That was not quite true. He remembered the fantastic wealth the Rani had offered him: if he changed his mind he could be the richest man in the state.

Joanna said tearfully, "Rodney, surely she'll let you change your mind? She can't have got anyone else yet. She didn't ask Geoffrey, did she? That would be too much, with all they've got already. Or Major de Forrest? Rodney, don't be so silly. I know what you're thinking of—that it would be bad for Robin, that he'd have no one to play with. But he and I could live in Bhowani, and you could come over lots of times. There can't be much work; she just wants to be able to order a white man about—and I'd be expected to kowtow to her if I went; I wouldn't like that. But everything's all right if I stay here. Rodney, you *must* tell her you'll go."

He felt himself cornered and fought to keep hidden the reason which must make his refusal final.

He snapped, "You want me to accept so that you can spend April to September in Simla, and September to April here, basking in the sunshine of your precious coward Della-main! Do you mind telling me whether you share a bungalow with me because you want to, or just to stop gossip?

You didn't let me have you for four months before I went off, not even on my last night. Do you want to leave me? If so, say it right out."

"Rodney, shhh! You're disgusting. I—I'm frightened of having another baby. You know how Robin tore me."

She burst into tears, but he would not stop for them now, as he used to in the early days of their marriage. "*I* didn't have the baby, so I don't know. But I know the doctor said it wasn't serious. And I know you've said since Robin was born that you wanted more children. Oh, God, what does it matter? I apologize. How the hell did we get here? I refused the job, and I'm not going to change my mind."

He could feel Sumitra's arms round his neck, and her warmth enwrapping him, and see the happiness in her face. He stared at his wife, his eyes glittering. It wasn't true that he had given up everything for her; Robin had counted most, and the regiment; but he had at least thought of her wishes, and she wasn't worth even that.

Joanna in turn lost her temper. He saw her search for things to say that would hurt him.

"You beast, you won't go because you want to be here with that dreadful Langford girl! You want to spite me by letting me think of all the things I need and now I'll never have! *You* told that black woman not to invite me to the tiger hunt! And I'd had two costumes specially made because I was sure she must ask me when you were there on duty, and I told everybody, and I felt such a fool when she didn't, and Mrs. Caversham gloating! It's all your fault!"

Langford? Caroline Langford? What on earth had she got to do with this? He stared at Joanna in astonishment. Suddenly he remembered Victoria de Forrest by the falls. He jumped out of his chair and seized her shoulders.

"Shut up!" He shook her hard. "Listen! Caroline Langford pesters me with some damned tommy-rot about the old Rajah and the Silver Guru, and I can't stop her. That's all! I'm not interested. I don't like her. Besides, you must have heard de Forrest has attached himself to her."

She looked at him slyly. "It's no more ridiculous than your nasty hints about Mr. Dellamain. And he's not a coward; he sprained his ankle."

"I believe he did." Rodney laughed sourly. "But not till he'd thrown away a rifle still loaded in one barrel and run a hundred yards in exceptionally fast time for a man of his age and weight."

"And why did *you* have to be such a hero? You wouldn't have done it for me. What sort of pension would I get if you'd been killed? Nothing! I'd have to work as a seamstress. And what about Robin's future? You're always restless; you don't think of your responsibilities. And why are you wearing that ridiculous great ruby? Did she give it you? I hear she was always ogling you."

"That spiteful little vixen again!" This was nearer the bone, but nothing would make him take off the ring. Controlling his voice, he managed to speak gently. "You can't have it both ways, Joanna. If I'm supposed to be so charmed by the Rani, why didn't I accept the job—especially as you're so keen to leave me alone with her in Kishanpur?"

"Ah, but you didn't know that when you refused."

He let go of her and stood up. With a great effort he stilled the trembling at the corner of his jaw.

"Joanna—I don't know what's happened to us. Let's try to——"

"I know what's happened! You'll never grow up, and I've found it out. And you drink too much, too. Everyone's talking."

His anger flowed away, leaving him limp and exhausted. He flopped back into his chair. "I'm sorry, Joanna. I know I'm restless. Sometimes it's all right, when I can persuade myself that all this routine and stuff is worth while. Other times I suddenly feel that I'm bogged down in a slough of pettiness, and I'll never get out. That's why I drink, I suppose. I didn't drink much while I was in Kishanpur, because I had a big job to do, and it was all—well, exciting."

"What excitement is there in Kishanpur that there isn't

here? And if you found that job big enough, why did you refuse a much bigger one?"

"I had to."

He wanted to say still more, blurt out all that he had done and thought, flay himself before her and expiate some of the hurt he had caused Sumitra. But he would only hurt Joanna as well if he did, without helping Sumitra. Joanna would think he was telling her to humiliate her by flaunting his infidelity.

He went on. "As for Miss Langford—well, look at her."

Joanna bridled, and some of the discontent left her face. A voice in Rodney's head was shouting, "Swine! Swine!" Caroline wasn't as plain as that; she was just not chocolate-box pretty, her symmetry was in her bones, and she'd be a wonderfully impressive old lady. But she was outside this quarrel, only dragged in by Victoria de Forrest's gossip. Joanna was the woman he must live with for the rest of his life, and make happy if he could. Any weapon was permissible which would help him clear up this sordid tangle. "Why, she's almost ugly! And I've got you—sometimes. I've told her I'm not going to have anything to do with her nonsense. I'm finished with it, and with Kishanpur. I'll try and settle down, really I will."

"Oh, Rodney, promise? And will you *please* be more respectful to Mr. Dellamain? He can do so much for us. Darling, I'm tired. Shall we retire?"

She put out her left hand, and slowly he stretched out his right to cover it. A dark flush mantled his neck, spreading up to his face. He raised his eyes to hers, praying, begging that there be no more punishment in them for him. And if there were any sort of genuine love, even genuine physical desire, it would hurt, because it was too late, and he had gone from her for ever. He bit his lip and turned the light out quickly. It was all right. Behind the deep swimming blue of her eyes there was—nothing.

# 9

AFTER ten days Kishanpur seemed a thousand miles away, and it was a hundred years ago that someone of his name had killed a figure there and lain with Sumitra on scarlet cushions. He saw little of the Hatton-Dunns and nothing of Caroline Langford. The torpid current of cantonment life carried away Victoria's gossip about him, and newer fresher scraps floated down to replace it: de Forrest's attentions to Caroline, Victoria's affair with Hedges, Geoghegan's new Indian girl, Two-Bottle Tom's recovery from the D.T.'s, his daughter Rachel Myers' claim to have seen an angelic vision.

The heat increased. Officers and sepoys sweated through the heavy serge of their tunics, staining their belts and cross-belts with black wet patches. White trousers of coarse cotton drill replaced the thick cold-weather pattern in all three regiments. The 60th Cavalry took out their peaked caps and white neck-curtains. For the seventh year in succession the two infantry regiments tried to get the new white Kilmarnock caps to replace their heavy shakos—and for the seventh year were told that none was available. Parades began earlier, afternoon siestas lasted longer, and it was difficult to get to sleep before midnight. The Club was a sunbaked mausoleum until five or six in the evening, when nearly every day the cantonment gathered to gossip and play whist, cribbage, or croquet. At this season, especially, the ladies practised their archery, for the Club's annual Hot Weather Tournament of Toxophily (Ladies' Section) would take place on Saturday, April the fourth, beginning at four-thirty p.m. (sharp), and Mr. Dellamain had undertaken to present the Silver Arrow to the winner.

Rodney and Joanna reached the Club the afternoon of the

tournament at a quarter past four. A cup of tea had not altogether dispelled from his mouth the foul taste of afternoon sleep. The shadows had begun to slant away from the trees, but the lawn was still a hard glare and the air dry, hot, and motionless. Grey squirrels scurried along the branches of the trees; from somewhere across Clive Road a coppersmith bird, like a faulty metronome, beat out the rhythm of the hot weather: *dong dong dong—dong dong—dong dong dong dong dong*. The Club marker pottered round the far line of targets, his turban on the back of his head and a ball of twine in one hand. A dozen or so English people stood in groups in the shade of the front verandah, talking and unlocking bow cases.

Victoria de Forrest, in the nearest group, hardly bothered to acknowledge Rodney's short greeting; the girl had a new and rather unpleasing assurance these days, presumably due to Hedges' continued attentions. He was there with her now, and so was Anderson, the second-in-command of the 13th. Rodney listened with half an ear to their conversation behind him while Joanna took out her bow and began to wax the string.

Victoria was saying, "My dear Major, I'm *sure* I shall have to abdicate as my father's hostess soon. Someone else will be supervising the Sixtieth's entertainments."

"And is Eddie here going to get himself a hostess too, in competition, eh? Ha!" That was Anderson; without looking, Rodney knew he would be scratching his upper lip and screwing up his small eyes.

"Now don't be a tease, I *do* think Father should be more careful of the proprieties, even in India. These unchaperoned rides—oh, yes, they're out now, didn't you know? At least, Father went riding, and I can't think of anyone else he would go with."

"Where do they go, Victoria? and"—the major's voice dropped—"how long do they stay out, eh?"

The girl giggled. Dirty-minded little slut. This story of de Forrest's rides with Miss Langford was news to Rodney.

Joanna's catty remark at the ball, that the two would make a suitable match, seemed to be coming true.

Victoria continued. "I'm sure *I* don't know where they go. Father never says. They ride out at two, in the worst of the heat, and come back at seven, or eight, or even later. Yes, a groom goes with them, but I'm not in the habit of getting familiar with servants."

"Aren't you, dear? I thought you had such a way with ayahs."

Rodney bent his head and chuckled; that was Lady Isobel, cold and cooing. She could cut when she wanted to, and she certainly wouldn't tolerate Victoria's spreading prurient gossip about her cousin. A clean, beautifully delivered cut, heard by as many people as heard Victoria's chatter, all of them knowing that Victoria talked with ayahs to ferret out the gynaecological, obstetrical, and matrimonial secrets of Bhowani.

Victoria was silent. Rodney glanced around covertly and saw that her flat face was sullen and scarlet. Lady Isobel limped by heavily, a smile for him in her steady eyes. Joanna laughed, a silvery laugh. It was a mistake, for Victoria had to Joanna no such sense of inferiority as that imposed by Lady Isobel's character and title.

Victoria said in a clear voice, "Shall we go out now, Eddie? Though really we shall have to shoot impossibly badly if the Commissioner is to give the Silver Arrow to the right lady."

Joanna tightened her lips, jerked the bow viciously, and slipped the loop of the string over the upper notch. That petty dart hurt her; it hurt him too, that she should have made herself vulnerable to it. What a place, what a pack of vixens! He kept his head down while fastening the straps of the leather bracer on her left forearm, and at once hurried behind her down the steps and on to the parched grass.

Soon Eustace Caversham called out politely, and the shooting began. Joanna's first flight did not look good; the others would indeed have to shoot badly if she kept this up. They waited till the westward-shooting members of each pair had shot their flights; then Caversham's reedy voice called, "All finished? To the other end, please."

Rodney was wearing a wide-brimmed straw hat and a pale grey suit with a long coat. He undid the coat buttons, tilted the hat forward over his eyes, and leisurely followed Joanna and her partner, Mrs. Bulstrode. The arrows flew; the contestants and spectators proceeded back and forth. If only the grass sprang thick and richly green, dense from centuries of scything; if Thames or Avon slipped by at the foot of the lawn, and trout hid there under a Roman bridge, and an English cathedral rode an English sky through English clouds!

They walked to the east, and the quiver belts marked the compression of the women's waists, made wider the billow of their skirts. The arrows flew, *clunk,* into targets of padded straw. They walked to the west, and the feathered arrows stuck out sideways and upwards from the quivers on their right hips. The arrows flew—and the women should have had jaunty little hats with curled brims and curled feathers, but they wore big sunbonnets which got in the way of the bowstrings; and the Sindhya Hills rolled down like a rumpled carpet into the haze over the plains, and the coppersmith hammered monotonous rivets into the copper-plated sky. And the women talked.

"I hear Captain Hedges is as good as hooked."

"Oh, dear, Mrs. Savage, I wouldn't put it like that, would you? Victoria is young. I'm sure she'll steady down when she finds Mr. Right."

"You misunderstand me, Mrs. Bulstrode. I think Captain Hedges *is* Mr.—the right man. He deserves nothing better."

Another mistake: Mrs. Bulstrode admired Eddie Hedges for his very wildness and to-hell-with-everything attitude. Perhaps that was how she remembered the George Bulstrode of thirty years before. And even she could defend herself against Joanna. She spoke across Joanna to Rodney. "That is a wonderful ring you wear, Captain Savage. I've so admired it. The Rani gave it to you for saving her life that day, didn't she? We were *so* proud of you!"

Rodney muttered, "Yes," shuffled from one foot to the other, and quickly excused himself. He strolled away with careful nonchalance, while Joanna sparred for an opening to strike back at Mrs. Bulstrode.

A little farther up he stopped behind a tree five yards from the row of targets and lit a cheroot. Nearby Mrs. Atkinson was shooting, watched by her partner, Mrs. Cumming, and by two spectators—Louisa Bell (née Caversham) and her mother. Harriet Caversham, he knew, thought archery unladylike, and Louisa Bell had given birth too recently to take part in the competition; she was looking tired and pale. She was a fool even to come out so soon; but then she was a fool, just that.

Mrs. Atkinson was speaking. "The twins are in wonderful shape again. Tom's taken his pony over walls at least two foot six high." She paused. *Twang—whirr—clunk.* "Bother! A black, I think. And do you know, the groom had the impertinence to demand an extra rupee a month for teaching him, and he gets five and a half as it is."

"Your husband didn't give it to him, I hope?"

"Certainly not, Mrs. Cumming. There! that's better, a red. I hear"—she dropped her voice, but not very far—"that Mrs. Herrold is expecting a little companion for Ursula in December."

The match burned in Rodney's fingers; he calculated quickly. December—early April now. It wasn't possible! Tom and Ruth Herrold could hardly have got out of bed before these women were talking about the child conceived in it. He tried to work out the channel of information: the Herrolds' sweeper of course would know first; he'd tell the other Herrold servants; the ayah would tell the Atkinson ayah; and she'd tell Mrs. Atkinson. What a country! They might just as well live their most secret moments in the middle of the Pike. He threw away the match hurriedly. Mrs.

Atkinson had raised her voice, for the rest of her news was not exclusive.

"Dotty van Steengaard's is not kicking much. Mr. McCardle says he thinks it will be a breech. He is going to try and turn it in three weeks' time."

"Oh, no!"

"Yes, Mrs. Bell. It is a most distressing and embarrassing experience. I had it done before Billy was born—good! A gold!"

Louisa Bell said, "I can no more hit that gold circle than get gold hair!"

"Archery is not difficult, Mrs. Bell, if one only perseveres." That was Mrs. Cumming.

Mrs. Atkinson cut in. "It is for some people, Mrs. Cumming, however hard they try. It's a knack, like—oh, riding for example."

A murderous silence, and Rodney backed out of earshot. The lawn was the site of two separate competitions, one with wooden, the other with verbal, arrows. The score in the first was easy to reckon up: Mrs. Cumming had shot a flight of three arrows into the target—one black, one red, one gold—nineteen points. To assess the value of the hits in the other, poisoned, competition you had to know Bhowani. Louisa Bell had started it by her remark about gold hair (Mrs. Atkinson was widely believed to dye her hair)—a little cheap; score it a black for Louisa—three points. On the instant, Mrs. Cumming had shot under Louisa's guard; but to appreciate it you had to know that the leaders of Bhowani society thought the Bells a dilettante and affected couple, too much given to facile enthusiasms—say five points. Recovering herself admirably from Louisa's original tally, Mrs. Atkinson had promptly struck down Mrs. Cumming in an indirect but none the less effective way. ("Captain Ernest Cumming of the Eighty-eighth B.N.I. is your husband; we all know he just cannot ride a horse with grace, however hard he tries. Riding, however, is an accomplishment—or knack—that all gentlemen are born with; therefore your

husband is not a gentleman; therefore you are no lady.")
Excellent, and so quick—and worked off, too, on someone
who was attacking her attacker and therefore entitled to
gratitude rather than insults—a golden nine points all the
way. Mrs. Caversham hadn't scored yet; but she would,
she would!

At the end of the line of targets he caught at the sleeve
of a short, hurrying, sandy-haired man and cried, "John
McCardle! Stay and talk to me. You never gossip or swear,
you're always serious and careful what you say, and I love
you."

McCardle had a square face and the uneven freckled
complexion which often goes with sandy hair and eyebrows.
His freckles stood out now like the scabs of a disease against
the drawn white skin of his face.

"Let go, Rodney. Ah've bad news. Ah can't find de
Forrest. Ah'm luking for Gosse. It's nae gude trying to keep
it secret any more. Julio's deid."

Rodney's hands fell slowly to his sides. "Julio? *Dead?*
John, he can't be. We were out fishing together a few days
ago. I heard he'd gone to visit Father D'Aubriac."

"It was a lie, man. He's deid. Hydrophobia."

"Jesus Christ have mercy!"

"Aye, He's the one that's done it—but He had nae mairrcy.
Rodney, will ye promise to get hog-stinking-blind drrunk wi'
me tonight? Ah've never had a drrop in me life. Stay on
here after the competeetion."

"But, John, how did it happen?"

McCardle stared at him in a kind of stony anger. His blue
eyes were frightened. "How the bluidy hell do I know?
Julio's dog is fine. The poison can lie low for six months, a
yearr. Any one of us may have it in us now. Any dog in
Bhowani may have it. Didna your Jewel have a fight wi'
a jackal in January? It cude ha' been herr. We don't know.
And there's nae cure."

He talked fast, as if he could not stop, hardly moving his
lips or teeth. "So Julio's deid. D'ye remember him as dull

and nairrvous when ye went out fushing? And couldna
stop talking? Aye, that's the beginning of it. We brought
him into ma little hospital secretly. He didna froth at the
mouth, tha's all balderdash. He lay wi' a headache, getting
worrse and worrse, luking out the window—it's bare there
and hotter than hell. He was mad tae drink but couldna; it
choked him, and then he'd go crazy mad for a five-ten
minutes. Whiles he'd vomit, black stuff, and whiles he'd have
a convulsion, but when he came rround he knew exactly
wha' was happening to him, and it tuke me and Miss Langford and five orrderlies to holt him doon—Christ, tha' girl
was an angel, but there's not one bluidy thing Ah cude do—
Christ, Rodney, Ah sent a man running for ma pistol, but
Ah've nae more courage than a snivelling rabbit, and Ah
couldna do it. Rodney, he near brroke his back, arrching
over more and more each time till—he deed in a parroxysm,
and couldna speak. But he knew! *Knew!* Ah'm going to
get drunk, Ah'd cry on Miss Langford's shoulders, only that
she's exhausted, near deid."

McCardle walked, like a man already drunk, over to
Captain Gosse. Rodney heard a shivering sob beside him
and looked round into Rachel Myers' agonized face. He
caught hold of her and yelled for help. Mrs. Caversham
hurried to them; the marker ran to fetch Mrs. Myers from
her target. The archery stopped, and a cluster of women
gathered round. Sick at his stomach, Rodney pushed his
way out. Behind him he heard Rachel's moans. "He said
terrible things—I didn't understand—oh, how could he?"

He clenched his teeth and walked aimlessly away. Mc-
Cardle, who never swore; the dour Scot who held his peace.
Murderous, torturing India; to gouge out the dregs of his
bitterness in filthy words! Lucky Rachel, to be lost in her
adolescent visions of the Beatitude. Poor John McCardle!
Julio—days in hell, days. Was Christ there? Only the nosy girl
Caroline Langford. Why had no one sent for him, Rodney?

Lady Isobel was beside him, her hand on his arm. "It's
happened?"

"Julio's dead. Hydrophobia."

"My dear, I know. Caroline's been nursing him for two days. Julio made Mr. McCardle promise to keep it secret, for all our sakes, so that the archery could go on—so that we wouldn't have to think about what was happening to him —and for your sake especially, Rodney, because he didn't want you to know till it was over."

She crossed herself and stood a minute in silence. He felt her compassion supporting him. But—Caroline Langford had travelled the hardest road with Julio, where it was his place; she hadn't been out riding with de Forrest, at least not for the last two days. He was jealous of her.

Isobel said, "I'm afraid we're going to have a bad hot weather. There's cholera up the Pike already, and a case of smallpox in the Bells' servants' quarters, I believe."

Suddenly anger flooded him so that he trembled. "Smallpox! And Max and Louisa have the nerve to come here today, goddamn their eyes! I'm sorry, Isobel, but what do they mean by it? *They* might get it, or have it already, and we'd take it back to our children! Robin might get it!"

She faced him directly. "Rodney, I know how you feel, but those are risks we have to take. We would go insane, we would want to commit suicide, if we shut ourselves up in our bungalows whenever any disease was about."

He slammed his hands into his pockets. "I suppose you're right, my dear—as usual. Where's Joanna? I want her to hurry back to the bungalow. It's silly, I know. There's nothing we can do. But there it is. I've got to look after John McCardle; we'll both be drunk as beasts tonight. When I think of it, I want to—I don't know what I want to do— and he's a doctor!"

He pressed her hand and hurried through the whispering crowd, avoiding their eyes. He'd get a bottle of brandy into John right away, and another into himself. The women, the backbiting—bestial pettiness. But it did not seem so petty now, somehow. They were armouring their minds against this filthy country, sticking pins into human dummies to exercise the unspeakable things that crouched in every corner of their real lives. They had homes, husbands, babies, servants; and every pet they kept, every green thing they ate, every drop of water—the sun in the sky, the beggar in the road, the air they breathed—might tomorrow destroy it all. God, Caroline Langford had guts.

In his mind he saw Robin, his baby Robin, lying on a cot. The child's back arched over and over, more and more; his small white teeth ground together; black vomit spilled over his nightgown. Under Rodney's feet a twig snapped; Robin's spine snapped.

He ran round to the front drive. Joanna, pale and frightened, was getting into the victoria. He seized the coachman by the arm and whispered fiercely, "Mangu, tell Rambir to shoot Jewel—yes, and Harlequin—at once, as soon as you get back. D'you hear? If they're not dead and buried in half an hour, I'll shoot *you*! D'you hear? Joanna, I'm not coming to the Gosses' for whist tonight—if they're still having a party. Tell them I'm drunk—again."

He hurried up into the Club and found McCardle in the bar. A bottle of Exshaw's No. 1 brandy, already half empty, stood in front of him, and he was stone-cold sober.

# 10

ON MONDAY morning the officers were already gathered for the officers' weekly conference by the time Rodney reached the Orderly Room. All Mondays were bad, and this one was going to be very bad after Julio's funeral yesterday. He saluted, took his place, and glanced round. Lieutenant Colonel Caversham at the head; then—clockwise from him—Major Anderson, the second-in-command; three captains—old Sculley, Geoffrey Hatton-Dunn the adjutant, and himself; two lieutenants—Atkinson, and Sanders the quartermaster; three ensigns—Torrance, Simpkin, and Neville. King, the sergeant-major, and Toombs, the quartermaster-sergeant, completed the circle. Surgeon Hackett was on leave and not due back till the end of July.

That added up to ten infantry officers present, where there should have been twenty-six. While the others chatted, waiting for Caversham to put his notes in order, Rodney quickly ran through the regiment's roll as it lay open in his mind's eye. The 13th was grossly understaffed in British Officers; the majority of those on the roll had been assigned by Leadenhall Street to duty elsewhere, and had not been replaced in the regiment. He knew that the 88th and 60th—every Native regiment in the country, for that matter—were just as badly off.

When in this mood, he wondered how the Army managed to achieve any kind of efficiency. A regiment of Bengal Native Infantry was supposed to have twenty-six British Officers—call it twenty-five, because the colonel was hardly ever present. Of that number not more than seven were supposed to be away from the Colours—so the pack of money-grubbing civilians in Leadenhall Street let it run with ten, misappropriated fifteen, and so saved themselves the expense of paying non-military men to do the non-military jobs. The sepoys became dizzy keeping track of their officers, who should have been as immutable and comforting as the old shade trees in their villages. It seemed impossible to persuade the merchants who ran the Company that an infantry officer must serve with his regiment in peacetime to build the trust between man and officer that makes victory in wartime. They failed to appreciate, or deliberately ignored, another factor peculiar to India—that the Indian sepoy did not care whether his officers were good or bad, but demanded only that they should stay with him a long, long time.

Caversham was droning on—something about band subscriptions. Rodney fiddled with his pencil and drew a circle on the sheet of paper in front of him. Tattered cobweb threads dangled in the corners of the bare whitewashed walls; dirty water filled the cracks between the flagstones. The room had been cleaned but, as usual, not thoroughly cleaned. The grimy windows hung open, and flies buzzed in and out. He could just see a row of sepoys—orderlies, clerks, storemen—squatting on their heels farther along the verandah. A long lath hung from the ceiling on three iron hooks; a cord, attached to the centre of it, led out through a hole high in the wall; a deep strip of cloth was nailed on to the lath and hung down above the table. This was the punkah. Only the punkah-boy's turban was visible through the window; he would be nine-tenths asleep, squatting with his feet against the wall and rocking slowly on the cord like an oarsman on his oar. Inside, the hooks squeaked, the cord creaked, the cloth swished; these were the sounds that accompanied all hot-weather thought and conversation. He had a headache. . . .

"Are there any objections?"

He'd half heard. The colonel had proposed to increase band subscriptions from officers, because the bandsmen needed new dress uniforms and a few instruments had to be replaced. That sounded all right; he had no objection. He glanced across the table at Simpkin. The ensign's chubby face was pale, but he wasn't saying anything, and he kept his eyes down. Rodney wondered if Caversham knew that the boy, who was only twenty-one now, had married a barmaid of thirty-five before he came out to India and sent most of his pay home to her. Rodney had found him one afternoon in his bungalow, looking at a pistol on the table. Then, under promise of secrecy, the boy had blurted it all out: he'd said, of course, that he'd never think of committing suicide; it would be unfair to his wife. "It's my duty as a gentleman to support Emma." Caught and plucked before his feet were clear of the shell! Rodney caught his eye, shrugged, and smiled. With an effort Simpkin managed a painful smile in return.

Atkinson, the legalist, coughed importantly. "Has it been decided, sir, what fund should pay for the wood and oil used in burning the corpses of sepoys who die of disease contracted in military service, but not in the field?" Rodney had already given his views to the quartermaster and sank back into another reverie.

Corpses—Julio's funeral, the worst he'd ever been to. He hadn't got to bed all Saturday night, and John McCardle hadn't got drunk. Marching up from the lines at seven a.m., the muffled drums thudding in front, he'd thought he was going to vomit. There was no church in Bhowani, only a large cemetery surrounded by a high wall. All the living English were gathered there, round the hole in the earth, but still they made a lonely cluster among the gravestones. Two troopers of the 60th had ridden forty miles to fetch Father D'Aubriac from his desolate mission hut, and he was there. His home was Saint-Flour in the mountains of the Auvergne; he was short and round, black-bearded and steady-eyed, and Rodney liked him. Two or three times a year he left his dwarf aborigines and rode up out of the southern jungles to drink in the Bhowani Club and complain about the cooking.

John McCardle was there—though Rodney had implored him not to come—and was sick under the wall of the cemetery before the service began, and swore at God and Father D'Aubriac. No one heard what the priest said to him there in the corner, but he staggered home, and Father D'Aubriac smiled after him.

At the graveside Rodney stood between Rachel Myers and old Gosse. A few yards back was one of the many short mounds in the cemetery, and he had seen the headstone's inscription: *Sacred to the memory of Elizabeth Gosse, departed this Vale of Tears on the 9th day of June, 1850, in the ninth year of her age. R.I.P.* Of course everyone knew that Gosse's only child lay here, but the known fact struck him with a new force then. Gosse was bald and fattish, with watery eyes; he kept glancing across Rodney at Rachel and half-smiling. Rachel hated the way he pawed her. The child under the stone would have been fifteen too.

Then Hedges stumbled under the coffin, and the other bearers let it fall. Rodney happened to know that Hedges had summoned the most expensive whore in the city up to his bungalow the night before and was probably cross-eyed from his exertions. Ordinarily it wouldn't have mattered, but this was the hot weather, and the lascars had worked so hastily that the box broke open. Thank God the winding sheet did not unwind. Joanna and Mrs. Bell fainted, and the long white roll lay there in the flat light, and a troop of mynah birds squabbled cheerfully in a cotton tree.

Rodney carefully drew an equilateral triangle in the circle on his sheet of paper. Riding down to the lines this morning, he had seen a big crowd under the Silver Guru's peepul. The Guru was intoning threats of ruin and destruction— something to do with the chupattis, and a need for prayer. A bespectacled merchant was there on the outskirts, his fat legs almost meeting under the belly of his stunted pony. The fellow had caught Rodney's eye and smiled with immense superiority, as if to say, "These superstitious yokels! You and I know better, do we not, sahib? For we are educated people." Rodney knew the type well enough, and in general did not like it. This specimen was from Bengal proper, probably Calcutta, and would be here battening on the local moneylenders, who in turn would batten on the villagers and —if the British Officers were not watchful—on the sepoys. However, the man closed his umbrella, scrambled awkwardly off the horse, and salaamed low, politely enough. Rodney had acknowledged him with a nod and a half-smile; somehow he could never ride past such salutes in the cold, unseeing majesty proper to maharajahs and British Officers. He had even said, *"Ram ram, babu-ji.* You're a long way from Calcutta, aren't you?" The fat man's gestures were no more than those ordinarily volunteered to any minor Indian

landowner or illiterate petty squire, and they were certainly
due to a commissioned officer of the Company. Yet there
had been something discordant about the performance. That
sneer on the man's face, if a shade more pronounced, would
have included him, Rodney, with "These yokels."

Whose voice was that, reedy but loud, and pitched to
cause alarm and despondency? He hid a grin: Eustace
Caversham, proving who was the commanding officer of the
13th Rifles. Harriet Caversham bullied him into this performance once a week. The effect was that of a rabbit in a
leopard skin. The lieutenant colonel thumped the table; the
flies buzzed in alarm.

"The days are past when officers in the Company's service
might properly conduct parades, or indeed military business
of any kind, while lying in bed on their verandahs. Besides,
it is a Madras custom and has never been general in this
Presidency. It does not look well, and *I will not have it*!"

Anderson sniffed loudly; the shot was aimed at him. He
dealt with defaulters from his bed, and he would continue
to do so. The blare in Caversham's voice cut out, and when
he spoke again it was with his usual unsure politeness—
something about barrack furniture and hutting money. The
quartermaster was making an aggrieved denial.

Rodney listened with half an ear. He'd known in his bones
that the chupattis would disturb everyone. He'd reported the
affair to Geoffrey, and eventually it reached Dellamain, who
then sent for him to discuss it. Rodney hadn't seen the Commissioner since the debacle at Kishan Falls and expected to
find him particularly pompous. He'd been wrong, for Dellamain was interested, and his interest overcame his unpleasant mannerisms. He told Rodney that the chupattis
might be very important, and he was going to investigate
further, meanwhile reporting to the Lieutenant Governor.
And that had been that—until this morning.

Before coming to the conference, Rodney had tried Sepoys
Ramdass and Harisingh, charged with returning five days
late from leave. They were types, wildly different but in-

separable—Ramdass a sly, talkative little townsman from
Bareilly; Harisingh a bovine peasant from a foothill village
in the Kotdwara district—the one always leading the other
into trouble. Harisingh pleaded guilty and offered no excuses;
Ramdass spun a rigmarole which Rodney would not normally have believed—but he did this time. Ramdass said that
the two of them had been returning from a visit with Harisingh's father's cousin in Cawnpore, and reached the Jumna
ferry at Kalpi in good time. The boat wasn't there, so they
and a crowd of other travellers waited on the bank for three
days.

At last the ferrymen poled the boat back and said they'd
been hiding. Why? Well, a village watchman wanted to take
some chupattis across and demanded a free ride on the
ground that he was for the moment a messenger of the god
Shiva. The ferrymen refused; the watchman argued, so they
threw him in the river and he drowned. Then they hid,
because Shiva would be extremely angry. Waking up still
alive three days later, they thought Shiva might have forgotten about them and rather nervously returned to their
work.

The sepoys finally crossed the river, and spent two more
days praying at a roadside shrine in case Shiva thought *they*
might have had something to do with the death of his
messenger.

Rodney had ordered that each forfeit five days' pay, and
when they were gone sat back in his chair, wondering. So
the chupattis were travelling across the Ganges-Jumna plains
too. They might be all over India.

He snapped to attention. The colonel was saying, ". . . outbreak of arson in Barrackpore, particularly in the lines of the
Thirty-fourth B.N.I. It seems extraordinary, but General
Hearsey there believes that the incidents spring from an
altercation which took place in January between a sepoy
of the Thirty-fourth and a low-caste coolie employed in
the Dum-Dum ammunition factory. Apparently the coolie
taunted the sepoy by saying that the cartridges for the new

rifle are greased with a mixture of pigs' fat and cows' fat. As it is customary, of course, for the sepoys to bite off the end of the cartridge and pour the powder into the barrel, the story has spread with great rapidity. The grease would defile Hindus and Mohammedans alike—in other words the whole Native Army—if the story were true."

"*Is* it?" Rodney exclaimed. That might explain the sweeper's jeer at the sepoy the morning they got back from Kishanpur. A few of his men had been given the new Enfield rifle and cartridges at the end of December, and by now they all had them. Barrackpore and Dum-Dum were just outside Calcutta, but news of that sort travelled fast and might have been whispered among the men here within a few days. What an unbelievable folly to commit! It could easily be true. He could just see some goddamned accountant —probably sent from England with orders to do something about the well-known inefficiency of Anglo-India—adding up his sums and reckoning he could save the thousandth part of a pice on each cartridge.

The colonel rebuked him. "Kindly do not interrupt me, Captain Savage. Thank you. As I was about to say, commanding officers have been instructed to assure the men that the grease is not defiling and that the rumour is untrue. It is suggested that sepoys be permitted to break these cartridges open by hand, instead of biting them, or even grease them with their own materials, until the matter has been thoroughly thrashed out."

"I hope they are thrashing it out, sir," Rodney said. "It's the sort of thing that could be very serious. And the suggestion about letting the men grease the cartridges themselves won't be of much use to us. The ones we have are greased already; they'd just be spreading their ghi, or whatever they'd use, over the top of the other stuff."

"Damned tommyrot!" Major Anderson cried. "Johnny Sepoy will do what we tell him—always has, always will. If anyone's raising trouble, they're agitators, probably in the pay of the Russkis or the Frogs. Make 'em all use the cartridges, *and* like 'em, according to regulations. Shoot any-one for mutiny who refuses. That'll bring out the agitators."

Caversham mopped his face. "Mr. Sanders, there are plenty of the old-pattern cartridges left, I expect?"

"No, sir, there is none, and they are no use, besides, with the new rifles—and the annual musketry practice is due to start at the end of the month."

"Dear, dear, that's a pity. Are you sure we have none of the old?"

"Certainly I am sure, sir." Munro Sanders, though as Scots as McCardle, spoke the pure, accurate English of a man who has learned it in school. He was a big Highlander, the son of a Caithness farmer, and his voice had the Gaelic lilt.

Caversham crumpled his handkerchief into a ball and raised doubtful eyes. "What do you suggest, Major?"

"Get on with the musketry, Colonel. Swear that the cart-ridges are not greased with this fat, if we must—but after that, by God, insist on discipline. It doesn't matter what happened in the Thirty-fourth; *this* regiment's sound."

Rodney could no longer contain himself; he leaned for-ward to attract the colonel's attention. "May I speak, sir? I think this is important. In the last few years the sepoys' world has been shaken up a lot. Oh, for instance, when they took away the field allowances the garrisons of newly con-quered territories used to get—that is still being talked about. Right or wrong, it was a custom to give them, and you can't play with custom here. Every year the Company creeps for-ward somewhere. The regiments are stationed farther and farther away from the men's homes."

He took a deep breath and to his surprise found that he was on his feet and almost shouting. The hot weather had got him already. The others were looking down at the table, ashamed for him. He raised his voice. "And apart from these Army things, they're affected by the same things which worry other Indians of their class and caste: suttee for-bidden, female infanticide forbidden, Brahmins made subject to the criminal laws. We think those are good and just ideas, but the sepoys don't. They used to talk and try to understand our point of view; now they don't. In my company the men are jumpy and have been for several weeks. I know other company commanders have noticed the same thing, where companies have British Officers. Of course our regiment won't do anything rash, but I don't think any more strain should be thrown on them. Can't the musketry wait till after the rains, when this cartridge muddle will be cleared up? It's only ten rounds a man, anyway."

"If your men are jumpy," Anderson said venomously, "it means you're not looking after 'em properly."

"I am!" Rodney snapped. "And I do not command them from my bed, either—sir!"

His temper rose; he'd *make* them understand. He'd spoken to Narain and Godse several times, and he was determined to transmit to Caversham the unease he'd felt. Narain had stroked his drooping grey moustaches and looked at his captain with old, careful eyes. Once or twice something close to his heart had almost found release in speech—but never quite. He'd said it must be the heat; the sepoys were content; he couldn't think of any cause for discontent; he'd ask again if the sahib wished. Rodney had tried speaking to individual sepoys, but they retired politely into a separate room and shut the door—Caroline Langford's phrase.

"They've got other worries too, sir. You remember the chupattis? That's unsettling them. I had another instance only this morning."

"What have chupattis got to do with cartridges? Nothing at all!" Anderson snarled. "Captain Savage is making a mountain out of a molehill, as he's done before, sir. You've given your orders. Let's get on to more important things." Caversham had not yet given any orders, but Anderson knew well enough how to force him into a decision.

Rodney made a last effort. "And then, you know, Major Myers takes a Bible down to his lines when he's—well—not sober? And tries to convert the men to Christianity and rants at them about the wrath of God? Just by chance I happened to overhear one of my sepoys ask Narain the other day if it were true that we were going to force them all to become Christians. That could be really serious, if they believed it."

"For God Almighty's sake, Savage! Major Myers is a fool, but he's in the Eighty-eighth." Anderson was beside himself. "What he does is Colonel Bulstrode's look-out, not ours."

"Kindly do not blaspheme so frequently, Major Anderson."

"I apologize, sir—but really! Is it true, sir, that the pay of field officers is going to be raised forty rupees a month? It ought to be——"

"And what about captins? I 'eard——"

They were off. Rodney sat back, hard mouthed, and looked down at the table. The waves of petty controversy surged round him while he jabbed angrily at the paper and at last broke the point of his pencil, Sculley, Geoffrey, Sanders, Atkinson, Torrance—one after the other, round and round. They were all good fellows; why couldn't they see? Don't they believe him? Did they really think he was too excitable, an alarmist? Tripe, twaddle, inconsequential piddle. He listened furiously.

"As your adjutant, sir, it is my duty to report that some officahs are allowin' their men to use bazaar polish on theah leathah, instead of . . ." "My store will soon become too small for the quantity of equipment I am asked to keep in it, sir. I must have another building. The end hut of Number Two Company now, that will . . ." "I need all the hutting space I have. The quartermaster doesn't appear to understand that . . ." "Mr. Atkinson does not understand . . ." "How many days' leave may I grant men during the Holi, sir?"

And on and on and on—till his tunic clung to him, his head drummed and quaked, and the punkah's steady squeak hurt like a rusty screw turning in his skull. Everyone was pale with nervous anger but far from speechless. They were worse than the women at the Club, and with less reason.

The conference at last ended, nothing settled. Rodney flung out of the room, mounted, and spurred Boomerang into a split gallop up the Pike. The road glared back into his eyes, and the dust grated between his teeth. Nothing settled—except that the sepoys would have to use the new cartridges. Most surely there were too many separate rooms and too few windows.

There was the affair of the little carpenter to prove his point—no, damn it, Caroline Langford's point. This morning, after he'd given judgment on the two sepoys late back from leave, Piroo the lascar had been brought up with a request. The man was a fixture in the company, and a good enough carpenter; Rodney did not trust him because he never held his head up, never looked anyone straight in the eye, but whined and grovelled and crept round the sides of rooms and huts, hugging the walls. He was always bare above the waist; under a thin mat of grey hairs scars latticed the shiny dark skin of his chest. His ears were large and stuck out from his head, seeming by themselves to support his untidy turban; his eyes were dark, ruminant, rheumy, sunk deep under a bony and receding forehead; his Adam's apple bobbed up and down in his sinewy throat. He sometimes wore a loincloth, and sometimes rolled-up green trousers cast off by a sepoy and two sizes too large for him. The corner of a clean black silk handkerchief always peeped out at his waist, and seemed a useless and incongruous ornament, for he never used it, but blew his nose with his fingers like any other Indian. He was a follower—carpenter, odd-job man, noncombatant—and of low caste.

Today, after minutes of crawling abasement, Piroo had asked for leave to go home and rebuild his house, which had fallen down. That was interesting on two counts. Count one: the man must have rare cheek. Every sepoy's and every follower's house "fell down" once a year, in the big rains of the monsoon; accordingly every sepoy and every follower asked for leave at that time to go home and rebuild it; so much was rigid tradition. But to announce that your house had fallen down, and ask for leave on that account, when there had been only a few mango showers—that was cheek! Count two: Piroo said his house was in Devra, eight miles away, and he owned land with it. Rodney had seen in Narain's expression that the subadar was as astonished as he to hear this. The little man was a whining low-caste lascar in the regiment, but outside the regiment's back door he might be lord of a hundred acres, and no one know it.

Everyone had a room of his own; and each liked his room and kept it locked and thought secret thoughts in it.

Faster! To hell with the heat and the dust. Drunk on Saturday with McCardle, he'd be drunk again tomorrow at the 60th's guest night—dead the day after, like Julio. Or Robin might be dead, everyone dead in a welter of petty spite. Faster! Faster!

Boomerang reached out with frantic strides; Rodney spurred him on and swore continuously. The passers-by dived for the shelter of the trees when they saw them storming up the Pike, and put the ends of saris or turbans over their mouths until the dust settled.

# 11

AS SOON as he walked into the 60th's mess, he sensed that the night would be long and hectic, but not genuinely cheerful. Julio had belonged to this regiment; as clearly as if it had been an order shouted in his ear, he understood that this night they were all to join in determined, furious gaiety to dull the edge of memory, to disperse the cloud of bad temper hanging over Bhowani, to exorcize the smallpox at the Bells' and the cholera up the Pike.

White covers assuaged the burn in the anteroom's leather sofas, and the 60th's grey and silver shell jackets helped to temper the impression of heat. But the look of coolness was an illusion; what air moved through the opened double doors and windows was hot, and the men were flushed, sweaty, and already partly drunk. It was six o'clock and dinner would not be served till eight, an hour ahead of the usual hot weather routine. Rodney liked this room—high and white, Georgian, carelessly elegant with the dash that cantered in the very syllables "Bengal Light Cavalry." Fox-hunting prints hung, widely spaced, on the walls, and between them standards and guidons captured in Lake's campaigns in Central India. Standing in the doorway, he eased his shoulders and, while looking for his host, automatically checked to see who was here.

Everyone knew everyone in Bhowani. All but one of the 60th's officers were present: Gosse, Russell, Hedges, Willie van Steengaard, his host, Long, Bates, Smith, Waugh, Geoghegan, the veterinarian, Herrold the surgeon—the man who was going to become a father in about nine months' time. Only the regiment's present commanding officer, Major Swithin de Forrest, was not here. In the same sweeping glance Rodney noted the other guests: Sanders of his own; Bell of the 88th, drinking warily (wife Louisa and mother-in-law Harriet Caversham would give him hell whatever he did, so why didn't the fool drink up?); and a tall fresh-looking boy of about seventeen with excellent teeth and curly auburn hair. The boy was wearing the 88th's scarlet with white facings, and Rodney did not recognize him, so he must be young Myers, Rachel's hero brother, arrived yesterday from Addiscombe.

Anyway, as the 60th had no colonel or lieutenant colonel —and de Forrest must be dining at home—Gosse was senior dining member. He searched again for the bald head, walked over, bowed, and said formally, "Good evening, sir."

"Evening, Savage. Hey, Willie! Here's your guest. Let's all have a drink."

Rodney relaxed. They were off.

Outside on the lawn the band, dismounted, played English and Irish airs. Liveried mess servants scurried about with silver buckets and silver trays. At first it was an effort to talk, a strain to laugh; but the champagne fizzed cold on his palate, and soon he found he could talk about anything. He argued and swore vehemently and waved his glass, and the champagne kept coming—jeroboams of champagne, nothing but champagne—the golden bubbles—Bengal Light Cavalry!

Dinner at last, and the grey and silver were swimming together in his brain. Life was a sheen, shimmering with music. The regiment had a long table, made of ebony and well polished. A row of Doric candlesticks, severe as the columns of the Parthenon, marched down the centre of it; silver and crystal and white damask floated on it, and their reflections wavered under its surface. The candlelight, rather than the dim walls and distant ceiling, curtained off this place where he was. The score of servants in the room stood outside that magic of golden light; they broke in, like genies, with a plate or cradled bottle, and stepped back and did not exist. Out there it must be dark and silent, and perhaps cold; the clattering and the uncontrolled laughter in the candle circle must die there where the light died. Outside, they looked in and watched the mystical communion. Here the officers partook of the continuing body of the regiment and of the blood spilled in its battles. The parade ground and the offices were for work, mere mechanical efficiency; but here union with a common past linked the officers, so that together they faced the cholera, and Julio's ghost, and would face together the future's unrevealed enemies.

A silver trumpeter, the table's centrepiece, galloped over the ebony's fathomless black, his head turned round and back, his silent trumpet shrieking to the rafters. His stallion's long tail streamed in the wind of his imagined passage; his dolman flew out behind him. He was jumping a broken, up-turned gun; two gunners sprawled dead across barrel and trunnions. Behind him, Bengal Light Cavalry had charged in the glory of battle—they were the glory of battle; but they were not here, even in silver—only the inspiration of them, and its reflection in the faces of the officers round the table. The boy trumpeter galloped alone, as he had at Laswari.

Rodney leaned forward to peer at the inscription on the low plinth: *In memory of Trumpeter Shahbaz Khan, 60th Bengal Light Cavalry, killed in action on November 1st, 1803, on the field of Laswari.* The words blurred—he had read them many times—and he concentrated on a scarlet blob opposite. Scarlet—not Bell—must be young Myers; face scarlet too; boy'd be under the table soon, sunk in a grey and silver sea.

By eleven o'clock he was drinking brandy in the anteroom and flinging himself into the violent games customary on guest nights—wall racing, high-cockalorum, cockfighting. The moon shone on the lawn, the band played, everything was forgotten except the delights of wine, resilient muscles, and fellowship. The servants smiled at the immenseness of their lunatic energy.

Near midnight glass shattered, and a confused banging and yelling broke out. Rodney heaved up from under a pile of bodies, the wreck of a round of high-cockalorum, and called, "Look at this!"

Eddie Hedges was riding around the anteroom on a frantic band-horse. It sidled and fretted and knocked over chairs and tables. Hedges put the inevitable hunting horn to his lips and blew the racketing *Gone awaaaaay!* Then he yelled, "C'mon, get a horse each—midni' steeplechase!"

"Good old Hedges! Trust the Buck to think of a good idea."

"To horse! Out, you lazy pack of buggers! Out! Out!"

The hunting horn screamed. They tumbled, yelling and whooping, on to the lawn.

"Hi, stop! Where in thunder are we going?"

"I don't know, Willie—whassit matter?"

"Hi, hi, *listen*—le'ss go up the Pike to the ol' temple. D'you all—all—know it? Then roun' the well in Bargaon— then back here!"

"Whassat? Sic—six miles? Drummer, hold that bloody horse still—hup! *Achcha, chor do!* My God, the Infantry are coming. Ha, ha!"

"Of course I'm coming. Have you heard 'bout the cavalry officer who—who was so stupid that—*all the others noticed it!*"

Rodney laughed at his own joke till the tears ran down his cheeks. They were all mounted by now, except Sanders and old Norman Gosse, who watched staidly from the veran- dah. The bandsmen laughed in the shadow of the trees; a flying fox, disturbed by the racket, flew angrily out of the branches and flapped across the face of the moon. They had taken off jackets, waistcoats, and spurs for the games in the anteroom, and most had their shirt tails out. Geoghegan had lost his trousers and wore no underdrawers. "Ready, you buggers? Go!"

The white shirts flapped across the lawn. They leaped the low wall in a mob, and swung, whooping and screaming, towards the north. Gosse and Sanders turned back into the mess, and the thirty-seven bandsmen picked up their instru- ments and began again to play for them.

At first the riders were bunched together. They yelled to each other and shouted hunting cries, and woke officers and their wives asleep under mosquito nets on the lawns. The hoofbeats echoed back from the trees lining the cantonment roads. A few minutes later they galloped past the hovels on the northern outskirts, near the 60th's lines, and reached open country. They began to spread out.

One after the other they turned off at the Pike at the old temple, and the pace slackened. As Rodney rode across the moon-bathed fields some soberness began to dim the clear beauty of his exhilaration. This was hellish dangerous; these fields were a maze of pot-holes, unfenced wells, sunken tracks, and wide thorn fences. He dropped back, fighting to dispel the woolly cloud in his brain, and began to concentrate on riding. White shirts fluttered dimly ahead like spirits hurrying home to the graveyard at cockcrow. The night air rushed by, drying the sweat on him, and seemed cool; it smelled of horses and saddlesoap and good Indian dust. The horse's powerful rhythm helped to clear his head and settle the sliding queasiness in his stomach. He was still young, and he would not die like Julio, not yet. He laughed aloud at the madness; it was lucky that no one was expected to explain why he did what he did on guest nights. Rodney remembered he had not seen young Myers on a horse, or on the verandah with Gosse and Sanders. The servants would probably find him under the mess table when they came to clear it up; then they'd carry him home, hand him over to his bearer, and pretend it had never happened. That had been his own introduction to the Bengal Army.

At the Bargaon well he knew that only Hedges, Willie van Steengaard, and Jimmy Waugh were in front of him. He was thinking that he would not disgrace his regiment, or infantry in general, if he kept his present position, when hoofs drummed up on his right and Geoghegan dashed past, swearing and singing. He had torn off his shirt and rode stark naked except for his boots. Ahead, the hunting horn screamed fainter and fainter.

Rodney slowed to a hand canter and peered round. He must be about a mile east of the cantonments, with the Benares Gate of Bhowani City not far off to his left. Bending low over the horse's neck, he saw housetops silhouetted against the sky, and knew he was right. Any moment now he'd be on top of a narrow, slightly sunken lane which ran through the fields hereabouts. Standing in the stirrups, he saw the lane and saw something moving in it.

The moon shone on the white canvas awnings of bullock carts, ten or twelve of the rare four-wheeled pattern, trailing along one behind the other, each pulled by four bullocks, the noses of each leading pair of bullocks an inch from the tail of the cart in front. He grinned, gave a wild yell, and urged the borrowed band-horse into a gallop. At the near edge of the track he bent forward, pressed hard with his knees, and yelled again. The horse gathered itself and lifted in a wide arc over lane, bullocks, carts, and all.

The monstrous shadow flew across the moon, and the bullocks in the leading cart snorted, flung their shoulders against the yoke, and dashed up the side of the lane. They thundered away across the field, the cart bouncing and rattling, and Rodney cantered after them, still laughing. The cart driver seemed to be awake, which was unusual, and well seated; he shouted at the maddened bullocks while the cart tore on over the rough surface. At the end of the field there was a dense thicket, and the bullocks, swerving to avoid one tree, jammed the cart heavily against another. The front wheel on the left side broke off and flew away from the axle. The yoke snapped, the driver rolled forward over the struggling bullocks, and the cart turned on its side. Half a dozen wooden boxes and barrels spilled out and spilt open, and a man was catapulted through the canvas top to sprawl cursing in the undergrowth.

A broad column of moonlight shone down through the trees and glinted back in little curved arcs among the bushes. Rodney stared—shells, not solid roundshot but modern explosive shells, probably for twelve-pounder cannon. He leaned forward quickly. Near the shells powder trickled from a big keg. The man in the thicket scrambled to his feet and searched frantically with his hands for something on the ground. Though he wore the plain white clothes of a middle-class townsman, he was the Dewan of Kishanpur.

Even as he noticed these things Rodney had been starting to urge his horse forward. It was a childish prank that he had played, against people who couldn't protest, and he was ashamed of himself. He had no money on him and was planning to take the driver back to his bungalow and pay him there for the damage, plus a little something.

But when he recognized the Dewan, he checked. Simultaneously the Dewan found what he sought and stood up.

A pistol was in his hand; the driver beside him had a pistol; bare feet pattered across the field from where the cart convoy had halted. What sort of men were these, all armed?

The Dewan stared up with eyes narrowed, trying to see who was the white shape on a grey horse in the dark. When he raised his pistol and began to move forward, and the driver moved with him, Rodney swung the horse around. Stretching out along the withers, he galloped for cantonments. No one shot at him as he went.

He'd better ride to the Commissioner's bungalow and report at once. Then he could act as a messenger if Dellamain asked for cavalry to be turned out.

He lifted the horse over the low cactus hedge bordering Auckland Road, the eastern boundary of cantonments. Two people on foot were right under him, coming in the opposite direction. He saw the flash of the moon on their clothes, jerked savagely at the reins, and forced the horse to curve its spine and land jarringly off balance. He yelled, *"Hut! bahin ka chute!"*

They would be servants, sneaking out to the city on some shady errand connected with the approaching Holi festival. He dug his heels into the horse's flanks, but a woman's voice cried out in English from the foot of the hedge. "Captain Savage? Quick! Did you see Shivarao—the Dewan of Kishanpur—out there? We must catch him."

Caroline Langford stepped forward, and, a little behind her, Swithin de Forrest. Rodney dismounted and told them in brief sentences what he had seen, eyeing them covertly, for they were dishevelled and flushed. De Forrest wore white trousers and shirt, Caroline a low-cut cotton dress and an elbow-length cape. De Forrest shuffled his feet, kept his head down, and gave no sign of interest in the story.

Rodney finished. "I'm on my way to the Commissioner. I've never seen an armed bullock-driver before, and the Kishanpur Army is not allowed explosive shells, or cannon bigger than six-pounders. I found that out when I was there —it's a clause in the treaty, and they thought it was insulting.

But the carts must be going to Kishanpur. I can't imagine
what they think they're going to do with them. I'd better
hurry."

De Forrest did not speak. Caroline held up her hand. "It's
no use going to Mr. Dellamain. Whatever it is, he's in it.
You remember about Sitapara promising to send me word
if she heard anything? Sitapara the courtesan? A man came
in after dark with a message from her—word of mouth. I
was to watch the Commissioner's bungalow tonight."

"Oh. Is that all she knew?"

"That's all she said. Please don't interrupt; we haven't got
all night. We—Major de Forrest and I—hid in the bushes
in the Commissioner's garden. About three-quarters of an
hour ago a man crept in round the side wall. He looked as
though he might be a servant, only he waited under a tree
until the watchman passed on his round, then he slipped
forward and tapped on a window. Mr. Dellamain came out
at once—I saw him in the moonlight—and the man handed
a thing like a small bag over to him and went away quickly."

"And the man was the Dewan?"

All this explained at least why de Forrest had been absent
from his regiment's guest night. Rodney wished the man
would speak instead of standing there like a withered tree.
He was the senior; this affair had obviously become official;
he should take command.

The girl answered Rodney's question. "Yes, it was the
Dewan. We followed him carefully, but lost him lower down
Auckland Road. I was going to give up, and then we met
you."

Rodney remembered his promise to Joanna. There were
several courses he could follow; none of them would be
"respectful" to Mr. Dellamain, and any of them would
involve him again in Kishanpur and Caroline Langford's
obsession about a mystery. He wished he knew what Dellamain was frightened of—but he hadn't time to think about
that now.

He turned to de Forrest. "Obviously it's no use going to

Dellamain, sir. If you agree, I'll turn out a troop—or a squad—of your regiment, catch these people, and take them straight to Colonel Bulstrode as station commander. Then he can hold the evidence in military custody until the Lieutenant Governor sends someone down from Agra to investigate."

De Forrest looked up. The sweat gleamed on his face, and on Caroline's as she watched him. He spoke with a collected, flat, lack of emphasis. "No, Captain, I will not agree. I have not seen the Dewan of Kishanpur tonight, or Mr. Dellamain. I have not, therefore, seen anything handed over to Mr. Dellamain. I am returning to my bungalow now, and my advice to you is to do the same. Good night. Good night, Miss Langford."

He turned and walked silently up the road. Rodney watched until the shadows absorbed him. The girl was drawn and tense, and her voice suddenly harsh.

"Never mind, Captain Savage. I'll explain later. Can't we catch these people ourselves, if I get a horse and a pair of pistols?"

Rodney glanced at her in admiration; now she was almost beautiful in her determination. With a man's eyes he looked at her as he replied, "It's silly to do that, Miss Caroline. We must go to Colonel Bulstrode." She frowned, and he added, "Really we must. The colonel's a great deal shrewder than he looks, you know."

She pulled the cape tighter across her chest, and the curve of her breasts showed clearer through the material. The silly girl didn't know what she was doing. "All right. If we must. Hurry."

She refused to ride the horse, and Rodney led it by the reins. They walked fast along the shoulder of the road, her slippers scuffing in the dust. She'd have to say something about de Forrest soon, but he didn't see how he could help her.

Without warning she brimmed over, the anger bitter in her low voice. "You think I'm doing this for the pleasure of destroying the Rani, don't you? There is no pleasure in it at all for me. I believe that our duty to God's principles— justice and truth—is more important than our duty to people, or any particular person, especially oneself. We aren't in this world for our own pleasure, but to further God's principles. The old Rajah was my friend, but I hope I'd have the strength to do what I'm doing even if he had been my enemy. I had to get help. I asked Major de Forrest because he showed interest. He wasn't excitable like you, and that was right—I'm not crusading against people, or human enemies, but against falsehood, and there is no need to hate anyone. He just did what I asked him to." She broke off and muttered, "How much farther?"

"A few minutes."

She slowed her pace, and he slowed with her. She had to unburden herself of this, and a few minutes would make no difference in catching the carts.

"This evening he suggested we should get married—it was in Isobel's garden. I couldn't believe my ears; I'd never thought of it. I've never met *any* man I wanted to marry. I was too surprised to speak. Then I answered 'No, thank you,' and he said perhaps I was right. A little later the messenger came from Sitapara. I didn't see what difference the proposal made, so I asked Major de Forrest to come with me—and he refused! I asked him whether he had only helped me in this as a necessary preliminary to a proposal, and he said yes. He said that he had thought we could live undisturbed lives together because I had outgrown the stupidity of emotion. He said that he saw from my reaction to this message that he was mistaken—he said that I merely got inflamed by ideas instead of people. He said that would outweigh the benefits of disposing of Victoria as a house-keeper. That's what he said!"

Rodney cleared his throat. "We're getting near. I think there's a light on."

Why did she tell him all this? To make him believe her story of the mysterious incident at the Commissioner's, by

showing that de Forrest had a motive for lying? That was
unnecessary, and surely she knew it. Was she trying to
explain her association with de Forrest, and so kill the
gossip? She wasn't a person who cared much about gossip;
nor did he care whether the gossip was true or not, and she
knew that too.

"I've nearly finished. When he said that, I was so angry
that I lost my temper. He'd thought that *I* was like *him*—
incapable of feeling. He was going to use me, so that he
could get rid of Victoria and replace her by an efficient
housekeeper. He does have one feeling—he hates Victoria.
But the message was so important that I had to make him
come with me, just this last time, and I did. But it was all a
lie still, inside him. You heard what happened."

They turned into Colonel Bulstrode's drive. It was past
one in the morning, and Rodney quailed at the thought of
the reception they would get if the old man were sleeping
off a mountain of curry and a gallon of beer. The girl walked
unspeaking at his side round the curve of the drive, and
the band-horse's hoofs clicked evenly on the gravel.

"He was going to use me." Did she realize that de Forrest
would think she had tried to use *him*; that ordinary people—
including Rodney himself—resented being treated as mere
tools with which she could more efficiently uncover the
beauty of a divine principle? And there was something else,
even more interesting. The tone of her voice at one part of
the story had quivered with plain female fury; she was not
merely grieved because de Forrest was so numb to abstract
principle; she was angry that he had thought of her as an
unexciting woman. She didn't know herself as well as she
thought she did, and he liked her the more for it. Besides,
the real she was much more interesting than either the one
she pretended to be or the one she hoped to be.

The light they had seen was on Bulstrode's verandah. The
drive curled round the front of the bungalow, and they saw
the colonel sprawled in a long wicker chair under his carriage
porch. Half a dozen empty beer bottles littered the gravel

around him, and a servant squatted on his hunkers at the
edge of a flowerbed nearby. Bulstrode was wearing sandals,
filthy white trousers, and a dress shirt—the latter unbuttoned
and not tucked into the trousers. He grunted when he saw
them but did not attempt to get up, and showed no surprise.

"Ha! Good morning to you both. *Chokra,* tie the sahib's
horse to the tree, and bring beer. Miss Langford, you take
beer? Good girl! Now, you haven't sense enough to know
this is the best time for paying friendly calls, so—what's the
matter?"

He shifted slightly in his chair, and the little eyes glinted
towards Rodney. Hesitantly at first, then with increasing
assurance, Rodney told his story; when he had finished,
Caroline filled in the gaps.

The colonel listened intently and did not stir except to
bury his face from time to time in his mug of beer. At the
end of the tale he wiped the froth from his beard and
moustache, hawked noisily, and spat the phlegm accurately
at a red-and-black moth perched on a pillar of the verandah.
He started scratching among the jungle of hair on his chest.
"First things first. No one's to go haring round in the middle
of the night after these fellahs. They're slow—got forty-
seven miles to go—catch 'em tomorrow if we want to. The
Dewan won't be with 'em when we do. He'll have a horse
meet him somewhere in the jungles. Right. Now, Dellamain's
certainly taking bribes from someone. Known that for two
years. Why? Because he wants to retire, go home, buy himself a seat in Parliament. Wants to finish his book—*Fiscal
Policy and Land Tenure,*" some name like that; knows a hell
of a lot about it—well, I suppose someone's got to. Fellah
dreams day and night of seeing his name in *The Times*—
The Right Honourable Sir Charles Dellamain, P.C., etcetera,
etcetera. Would, too, in politics at home—very capable
fellah, straight as a corkscrew." He transferred his scratching
to the rolls of fat on his stomach. "I don't like him—don't
care a damn about bribes of course, but he's an oily, gutless
four-letter man. Proved it at Kishan Falls, eh? Beats me

how he's got into this. Take a few diamonds to wink at rajahs' little vices—burning wife alive, running boy brothels —that's one thing. Help fellahs run guns, that's another, and damned dangerous. Should've thought it'd have given him the wind up. Anyway, he won't have the carts chased if he can help it, fear of what might come out. If I ask him to, he'll choke me off somehow, make his own inquiries later."

He broke off and stared intently into the flowerbed. "See that little snake, just moving down there—earth-snake, called *murari sanp*. Lots of superstitions about him; fellahs throw him up in the air to kill him, then bash him with a stone, call it *suraj dekhana*—'show him the sun.' The Gonds eat him, farther south; so do I; very tasty dish. Another thing: Dellamain may be busy on something official and secret. Government here's an underhand business sometimes—has to be, to earn any respect. I've been out thirty-nine years, learned to leave civils and politicals wallowing in their own plots, if I can."

He paused again and eyed the snake.

"Fellahs swear he comes into houses at night, takes milk from women's breasts. Don't believe it, miss. Where was I? Oh, yes, let 'em wallow. But this time I can't. Too serious. Right! I'll order de Forrest have a squad of the Sixtieth at your disposal, six a.m., at your bungalow. I'll tell him to keep his mouth shut—you too, please, miss. Savage, you take the squad out, tell 'em you're after dacoits. The troopers are Mohammedans, don't celebrate Holi, but they get a day or two's holiday for it, so try and bring 'em back quickly. You ever seen the Holi, miss? Don't. Disgusting business; I like it. And Savage, you must *not* take the squad into Kishanpur, or there'll be hell to pay.Got it? Report direct to me when you return. I'll fix your commanding officer. Now go to your bed—I mean beds, ha!"

He nodded, chuckling wetly, and called for beer—one bottle.

Out in the road again, Caroline Langford said, "I can get home by myself now, thank you. I insist. One thing; I meant to tell you why Major de Forrest and I went riding. It was to find out where the chupattis came from. I heard the story, and it seemed eerie, like the Silver Guru's words to the crows, but worse."

"I fear you were wasting your time, then. The thing starts somewhere far beyond riding distance. I had a case yesterday which proved the chupattis are coming into Kalpi from the east—and that's a hundred and fifty miles north-east of here."

"I didn't know that. But did *you* know that recently the watchmen have been carrying handfuls of raw meat instead of chupattis? Three pieces of goat's flesh, with the skin still on them and the hair and outer layers scraped off, so that they're shining white on one side and raw red flesh on the other. One piece is always large, one a little smaller, and the other very small. It's unearthly—to meet a man after sunset, running with red hands, not knowing what he does or why, driven on by a threat from nowhere. Major de Forrest said he'd tell the Commissioner, but I suppose now I'll have to make sure he has. Thank you and—good night."

She turned brusquely away. Rodney said good night to her back, swung into the saddle, and trotted home. He wanted to talk to her about Julio—perhaps he didn't. Anyway, she'd gone.

A white glimmer on his lawn showed where a mosquito net covered the double bed. He hoped Joanna was asleep and wouldn't wake up. He'd have to waken her early enough and tell her he was off after dacoits. That might be difficult; she'd probably think he was being punished for something by being sent out to work over the Holi holidays which began today. In truth, the odd thing would be that he, an infantry officer, was taking out a cavalry patrol. She wouldn't notice that, but others would. Well, it was Bulstrode's affair now.

He gave the horse to his night watchman, with orders to arouse a groom and have it taken back to the 60th's lines. Sher Dil, who slept the light sleep of old men, doddered into the house a few seconds later. He shook his head grumpily as Rodney told him what must be made ready for the morrow, and at the end muttered, "Dacoits, thugs, five o'clock in the morning—just like Savage-sahib. Why don't you go on the staff and settle down, Rodney-sahib?"

He shook the old butler's elbow gently and whispered, "All right, all right. I know you want a scarlet cummerbund. Where's Lachman hidden my nightshirt?"

The tick of the clock in the drawing-room sounded through the house, and somewhere out in the fields a pack of jackals set up their insane yelping chorus. He pulled on his boots as protection against snakes and scorpions, and tiptoed out to see if the disturbance of his arrival had awakened Robin. The cot was on the north verandah, with Ayah's string bed at the foot; Ayah was asleep, completely rolled in a sheet, and Robin was asleep. Rodney tiptoed down the hall and across the grass of the lawn. Joanna was asleep.

He stretched carefully beside her and hoped the jackal pack would not come into the garden. Back in Monghyr, in '51, Gerry Curtiss woke up one night, heard a noise, pulled up the mosquito net to investigate, and stuck his face into a jackal's. The jackal bit him on the nose—'50 or '51, it was— damned lucky not to get hydrophobia—Julio. He went to sleep.

# 12

"*H*UZOOR, *huzoor, panchh baje, panchh baje.*"

Quarter-light, Lachman's round face, the trembly aftermath of champagne, and five o'clock it was. He picked up the cup of hot tea, his hand shaking a little, and listened to the starling-chatter of the mynahs in the trees. Life went round in circles—but this day's work promised more than a routine march to Kishanpur. Today he might really gallop with the fate of an empire hanging on his skill and courage. He turned and shook Joanna. She was sleepy and grumbly, as he had expected. He swung his feet out of the mosquito net, found his boots, and walked across the damp grass into the bungalow.

At five to six the squad of cavalry jingled up the road and halted outside his driveway. Boomerang stood under the carriage porch, and Rodney checked quickly that all was in order: cape and blanket rolled behind the rear arch; food for himself in the wallets; nosebag full of grain, and its mouth well secured; canvas water bucket, picketing pegs and ropes, spare horseshoes. On himself, sword, sabretache, pistol, cartridges, canteen. Money? No Englishman ever carried any in India, but he could hardly ask for food in some jungle village, eat half a dozen chupattis and a bowl of curried vegetables, and then give the man a chit redeemable thirty miles away at the Bhowani Club. He might have to buy food for the troopers too. He told Sher Dil to bring him twenty rupees in small change.

He saw, out in the road, that he knew the Native Officer in command—Jemadar Pir Baksh, a clean-shaven dark man with thin shoulders and a long body. He called the officer to one side and told him the agreed fable about dacoits. The Jemadar listened with unusual intentness, several times glancing up sharply. Rodney could not be sure that he accepted the tale at its face value, but he went on at once to work out with him on the map how far the carts could have gone. He decided to split the squad into two parties of twelve each, one under himself, the other under the jemadar, and allot areas of search to each party. At last, having fixed an afternoon rendezvous, he gathered the troopers round and explained to them the circumstances and the plan. They listened woodenly, appearing to find nothing remarkable in the story. The two parties rode off at twenty to seven in the morning, and almost at once separated to follow different paths.

The rendezvous was for four p.m. in the village of
Mornauli, twenty-five miles east of Bhowani. Mornauli was
a cluster of wooden huts squatted in a jungle clearing, and
Rodney rode into it a few minutes after four, his troopers
trotting wearily in half-sections behind him. He saw that
the other party had already arrived. He had never in his life
been hotter and dustier, or needed a long cold drink so
badly; his throat was swollen and aching. He croaked the
orders to dismount, water, feed, and rest, and flopped on his
back under a tree near the village well.

Jemadar Pir Baksh walked over, stiff-legged, to report that
his party had found nothing. Nor had Rodney's; he sat up
and tried to think. Where could the brutes have got to? He
and his troopers had covered nearly fifty miles of jungle
trail, asked at every village, and examined a hundred bullock
carts even though only a handful had been four-wheelers.
Pir Baksh shook his head and said grimly that he himself
had done the same.

Rodney pulled out his watch. "No move before five,
Jemadar-sahib. Orders in half an hour. Don't unsaddle;
loosen girths, and get some rest."

The jemadar looked as if he were about to protest; Rodney
waved him curtly away. He knew the men were exhausted
and the horses foundering; all day the temperature had been
about 105 in the shade—and the dwarf teak gave little
shade—but the carts *must* be found. He was near dead himself, and his face was on fire. He drank from his canteen,
refilled it at the well, and sat down again, leaning back
against the trunk of the tree. Two naked little girls and a
long-horned black buffalo came out of the village to inspect
him, stopping three feet off. He threw the children an anna
each, and opened a packet of curry puffs.

He must concentrate. The Dewan and his people knew
that a stranger had seen the shells when the cart upset. They
might therefore lie low in the jungles for a few days, and if
they did he could never find them. But it was dangerous for
them to hide, because sooner or later they'd have to cross

the Kishan, and pickets could reach the crossings before them. They were more likely to hurry the carts on, make all speed to get across the river into Kishanpur State. Rodney had directed the movements of his little force on that assumption, and for a minute he worried afresh as to how he and Pir Baksh could possibly have failed to connect with the carts.

He chewed furiously. He *had* failed, so now the Kishan was the best place to intercept them. He pulled the map from his sabretache, spread it on his knees, and began to calculate. The carts had left Bhowani at, say, one a.m.; they had forty-seven miles to go, and were not capable of more than two and a half miles an hour. If they made no stops, they would reach the Kishan in about nineteen hours—eight o'clock tonight. But it was physically impossible for bullocks to do that distance in this heat without rest, and water and fodder. They must stop for at least three hours, which would make it eleven o'clock before they could reach the Kishan.

He began to scribble in the margin of the map. He was in Mornauli—twenty-two or twenty-three miles to the river, depending on which route he took. With men and horses in their present state, he could not do better than six or seven miles an hour; it would be safer to calculate on four hours for the distance. If he set out at five-thirty with the troop, he'd be there at nine-thirty—perhaps a little earlier. That should be in good time to catch the carts.

The next problem: where would the carts cross the Kishan? The map showed only one ferry—on the main Bhowani-Kishanpur road—and no fords.

A memory nagged him. He stared crossly at the map and remembered. Kishan Falls: two huts opposite each other, a bullock cart creeping down a dusty track and into the river. That was a ford, unmarked; there might be others. He'd have to risk it; perhaps he could ask when he reached the river whether there were any other crossing places; the villagers here wouldn't know. But would the carts use the ferry or the ford? The ford, tucked away in the deserted

jungles of the hunting preserve, was surely better suited to
the secrecy of this affair.

He made up his mind; he would send Pir Baksh's party to
the ferry, and go to the ford himself—both parties to set
out at five-thirty.

At eleven p.m. he reached the ford. Sweat and dust were
caked on his skin and uniform; his head hurt, and a towering
anger possessed him. Once he had lost direction and ridden a
mile southward before he gathered his wits, looked at the
sinking sun, and turned off on an eastward track. That was
his own fault and no one else's. But the other things—the
mishaps which made the ride a bungled nightmare—those
could not all have been his fault, unless the gods hated him.

It began when a trooper complained that his horse had
contracted a severe girth gall; Rodney left the man behind
and told the daffadar to ensure that he was put on a charge
for neglect. Another trooper's horse cast a shoe; after a little
delay, Rodney left that man behind too. The same thing
happened again, and he decided to wait while they cold-
shoed the animal, for his party was becoming depleted and
he did not know how many armed men there were with the
carts. Then the daffadar's horse threw him, and it took ten
minutes to revive the daffadar and catch the horse. Rodney
could not be sure, in the gloom of the jungle, but suspected
that the daffadar was not so badly hurt as he pretended,
and certainly no bones had been broken. Twice after dark
the troopers shouted out that so-and-so was missing; the
horses crashed about among the trees, the strayed man was
gathered, and they rode on. Once Rodney suddenly realized
he was alone, and that the whole lot of them had disappeared; after twenty minutes' galloping he collected them.
Then he lost his temper and blistered them with curses, and
that did not help. Certainly the men were very tired, but
that was no excuse for acting worse than a mob of recruits.

When the roar of the falls dinned in his ears, he peered
at his watch—five to eleven. He rode straight to the hut

he'd sighted on this bank that distant February day. Leaning down from the saddle, he banged on the low door, and after a minute a frightened little man came out.

Rodney longed to bawl and scream, but that would only petrify the man. "Don't be frightened, brother. We are Company's cavalry, from Bhowani. I want to know whether a string of bullock carts have crossed the ford here, in this direction, in the last hour or two. Most of them were four-wheelers."

He bent forward anxiously. The man's mouth was open, and he was staring slowly round the circle of troopers. Rodney fought down an impulse to let off his pistol by the fellow's ear, and waited. At last it came.

"Carts, sahib? Deshu from up the road crossed at sunset, with his woman. But he was coming from Kishanpur, see? The other way, see? And—yes—Parmanand a little later, with a load of straw. But he was coming from Kishanpur too, see? The other way, see? And their carts are two-wheelers; you couldn't hardly call them a string either, could you, because they only have one each, see? And then thirteen long 'uns just now, four-wheelers, going to Kishanpur, see? I don't know who they are—foreigners, see? They always cross here. Then there was——"

"Thank you, brother. Here"—Rodney threw down a rupee —"and don't tell *anyone* we came asking questions, or we'll put you in Bhowani Gaol, see?"

He snarled the last words, but the joke died in him. That was the convoy he wanted; "foreigners" meant only that they didn't live within walking distance of the speaker's hut. He turned wearily away and slumped in the saddle. That was that. He hated defeat—caused by these miserable troopers too—but that was no excuse. He was in command, and he had failed. His brain would not stop.

The carts, being now in Kishanpur State territory, might turn off to some secret arsenal; nevertheless it was a better chance that they would head for the fort. He could swim his half-squad across the Kishan and intercept them on the road—perhaps at Monkeys' Well—but that would get Colonel Bulstrode into serious trouble. Or he could go over by himself; he was armed now, and not afraid of the Dewan or his mysterious carters. That was an idea; his tactics should be to find out exactly where the carts went, then report it to Bulstrode.

He urged Boomerang into a fast trot. An hour later he knew from the configuration of the bank that he was opposite his old riverside camp. Halting, he motioned the daffadar up alongside.

"Bivouac in here, out of sight of the river. I'm going over alone. Don't tell anyone where I am. If I'm not back by this time tomorrow night, return to Bhowani and report direct to Colonel Bulstrode. Understood?"

He dismounted and handed over Boomerang's reins to a trooper, took off spurs, shako, belts, and tunic. The pistol belt he refastened around the waist of his trousers, and prayed that the water would not affect the cartridges. He slipped into the river. The water was warm, but it flowed cool and wonderfully soothing across his overheated skin.

He was more tired than he thought, and at the far bank lay for a few minutes on the grass. The whiteness of his shirt worried him, so he plastered it and his face with mud. Then he walked through the strip of thin jungle, which he remembered well; his tents had been here. Ahead, the seven tall trees at Monkeys' Well stood up dark across a field. He bent low and worked towards them on the blacker side of a thorn hedge.

Close under the trees he moved more slowly. There was no wind and no sound, and in the moonlight the ruined well seemed the shadowy altar of a vanished people. He placed his feet carefully, peering at the ground; the hamadryad ruled here. The monkeys—he'd forgotten them—set up a sudden shriek and gibber, and crashed from bough to bough. Leaves and twigs showered down from a pandemonium in the darkness overhead. He hurried the last few paces and dropped to his stomach; it was lucky no one was here.

Slowly he let the breath out of his lungs and began to relax. Water dripping from his shirt made tiny noises on the earth.

Someone was here. As a face leaps suddenly out of a puzzle picture, the figure of the Silver Guru sprang out of the trellised shadows by the well coping. Rodney half-rose, for the cold eyes looked straight at him. The chest did not seem to rise and fall; the trunk was upright, and the legs crossed. The figure was like a statue; the splashing light made leprous spots where it fell.

Rodney sank down and lay breathless. He could not believe that the Guru did not see him. Tautly concentrated, he saw nothing but the still shape opposite, until a noisy panic once again disturbed the treetops. With infinite care he turned his head. The Dewan, on horseback, trotted into the grove from the direction of Kishan Falls.

Rodney almost sighed with relief; this was better, more what he had expected. He eased the pistol forward in his hand.

The Dewan slowed to a walk and peered from side to side as he came on. He was muttering in a suppressed and angry voice, "Where are you, you damned charlatan of an Englishman? Stop playing the fool!" The horse shied violently. "*Hut!* You gave me a start; you look like a snake yourself. Fornication! These monkeys are making a filthy row."

He dismounted, and the Guru said quietly, "They have done it several times tonight. The hamadryad is about, so mind where you put your feet. You seem excited, Excellence. What is the matter?"

"Matter! One of your compatriots, swine-drunk and capering about at midnight outside Bhowani, upset a cart and saw what was in it! They sent cavalry after us; I suppose Dellamain couldn't prevent it. Luckily it was the——"

"Not now, Excellence. At three."

"That's the time, is it? I'll be there. The carts are on their way to the lake, but the girls are making a fuss. I'll have to arrange for them to be moved on at once, and the other stuff. By God, I shall be happy when this is all over. I want the killing to begin. My fingers itch."

He mounted, sawed at the horse's mouth, and cantered away towards the city. Rodney lay still and watched the Guru. So he was in it, something that would end in killing, and he was English. Leprosy and exposure to sun and wind had effectively disguised the colour of his skin. The part under the loincloth he had probably stained in some way; then there were the ashes with which he usually covered himself. His eyes could have given him away, but many men from the extreme northwest of India had those pale eyes. He'd travelled reasonably fast to get here, for on Monday he'd been under his trees in the Little Bazaar, talking about chupattis, when that fat merchant was there listening.

The carts were "on their way to the lake"; that might be anywhere, for many small lakes and big ponds dotted the state; Rodney certainly couldn't find them tonight. But he could follow the Silver Guru and gather a little more information for his report to Bulstrode. The references to "the girls" and "the other stuff" he did not understand.

Five minutes later the Silver Guru rose without a sound. Carrying the wooden begging bowl in his right hand, he strode down the middle of the trail towards the city. When he was only a tall shadow in the moonlight, Rodney stood up and followed him. The monkeys screamed; the fields lay ghostly grey on either side.

Soon the fort cut a black square out of the lower sky to his left, and a confused murmur from the city ahead throbbed in his ears. That would be the Holi celebrations; they might help or hinder him. The bulk of the people would gather in the square and the main streets, leaving the lanes in the slum districts empty; but gangs of revellers would stray everywhere and might run into him. They were unlikely to molest him, except in an excess of drunken playfulness, but they could make him lose touch with the Guru.

The shadow ahead passed the first shacks of the city, and
Rodney closed his distance. The alley here had no lights,
and the central gutter overflowed with slops and garbage.
Close to the houses a thick layer of dust and dried cow-
dung deadened the sound of his boots. A rank smell permeated the air. Once a drunken peasant lurched from a
house as he passed and cannoned into him; Rodney held his
breath—but the man was too full of toddy to notice or care.
The noise in front grew louder. At each turn he waited until
the Guru was well round the next, then he scurried forward
and waited again.

Peering round the corner of an empty shop, he saw that
thirty yards ahead the alley widened out and was flanked
by three-storeyed houses. At the end there was bright light,
and a host of people shouting and blowing horns; there the
alley ran into the main square. He remembered the night of
the riot. As he was looking now, Sitapara's house stood
somewhere to his left, the temple to his right.

When just into the wider part, the Guru turned sharp
right and disappeared. Rodney slipped forward and found
the place where he had gone—a narrow slit between blank
walls that must lead to the back of the temple. He waited;
he dared not follow the Guru yet, but where he stood he was
in full view from the square and protected only by the
uncertain light.

A knot of revellers broke from the mob in the square
and surged yelling down the alley towards him. They carried
brass jars full of water dyed red, brass syringes, and bags
of red and blue powder. As they ran they splashed and
squirted red water over the house doors and over each other,
in the rite symbolizing the bleeding of women; and they
shouted obscenities, because in legend a demoness had once
been frightened away from a village by the villagers' rude
words. The leading man had a wooden phallus two feet long
strapped round his waist; with one hand he held the
vermilion-daubed knob away from his chin, and in the other
brandished a small bell. Rodney pressed flat against the

wall and hoped that they might pass by him unseeing, for their eyes were glazed with toddy, opium, and lust.

All together, they tried to force into the narrow part of the alley. They could not, and doubled their yelling as the red water and coloured powder flew, and lifted their torches so that sparks showered up. At the flank a coolie woman in a dark red skirt and brief separate bodice leaned back in giggling stupor against the wall. A man stumbled by and sloshed the whole of his jar of red water over her. She collapsed across Rodney's feet and spread her knees; the man dropped the jar and, as he bent swaying down to rip her bodice open, fell forward on top of her. His head hit Rodney's thigh, and he looked up, hiccoughing. "Out of the way, friend. I'm going to have this one!"

Then he saw. Rodney watched the bleared, half-focused eyes travel up—from his trousers to his shirt to his face. The man shouted, "It's an English sahib! Sahib! Sahib! He's come to our Holi!"

He meant no harm; Rodney thought for a second the man was going to offer him first go at the woman. But the mob heard and turned, and the torches flared in his face. He pushed the drunk hard and dived into the lane after the Guru. The mob rushed screaming behind him, led by the man with the phallus.

Forty yards down the lane the houses on the left gave way to a plot of waste land. Across it was a big building, and he recognized the architecture of the temple. The Silver Guru had vanished; he must have gone in there. Rodney vaulted a low wall and ran for the nearest door. Pushing it open, he burst through, slammed it shut behind him, and leaned panting against it.

The smoky little room was full of men. There were ten or twelve of them, in loincloths, cotton shirts, and turbans, and they were all staring at him. There was something familiar about them.

He did not think the mob outside would have hurt him, unless he had drawn his pistol. They were drunk enough to have done anything then. But it had been unpleasantly exciting, and his heart leaped when he realized why the men in the room seemed familiar. There was Naik Parasiya of his own company, one or two others of the regiment, a big old fellow he knew to be a subadar of the 88th. Rodney did not know them all by sight, and they were not in uniform, but his first quick glance told him, by the way they stood, that every one was a sepoy, N.C.O., or Native Officer of the Bengal Army. He smiled and moved towards them.

They were moving towards him. They came on slowly together across the floor, like men concussed. Their mouths drooped slack and open. Their muttering was a sibilant hiss.

"It's a sahib, it's a sahib, it's Savage-sahib . . ."

# 13

A DOOR in the far wall flung open and the Silver Guru strode into the room. He called out, "*Rescue* the sahib! Block that door! The madmen *outside* want to kill him!"

Rodney looked at him in surprise across the heads of the sepoys. The mob had not seemed to be in so dangerous a mood, but it was impossible to tell, when people were drunk. The sepoys stopped in their tracks; Naik Parasiya stared round at the Guru, then suddenly echoed his cry. "*Rescue* the sahib!"

Most of the men turned away; a few ran past Rodney to the door. One of these, a squat long-armed man with an undershot jaw and wide nostrils, opened it a fraction and shouted through the crack, "Go away! There is no sahib here."

"But we saw him go in. He is defiling the temple!"

So their temper had changed after all. The ape-man quelled them with a hoarse bellow. "No sahib is here! Dismiss, you drunken owls. *Hut!*"

The chief Brahmin of the temple waddled in. His forehead was marked with a red line down the centre, the sacred thread looped diagonally across the rolls of fat on his bare stomach, and his face was grey with fright. He whispered to the Guru.

The Guru turned to Rodney. "Come with me—this way. The passage is open to the main square, but no one's taking any notice that side. Keep on my right."

Rodney had a hurrying vision of the market-place—red-splashed faces, swirling spotted clothes, the far housefronts shaking in the irregular light. It was a Brueghel canvas sprung to life. Shadowy dwarfs shouted and ran about in droves, some with the gigantic wooden phalli strapped to them. Bonfires glared sudden unearthly colours as men threw powder on to them; rockets rode vivid trails into the sky; bells rang; conch horns quaked. Oblivious of it all, a humped white bull urinated on the steps of the temple and chewed the heavy garlands of zinnia, canna, and jasmine drooping around its neck.

They passed through an open door, and the Silver Guru bolted it behind him.

The room was about twenty feet square. The floor and walls were of red stone blocks; black and yellow designs were painted on the ceiling. Six pillars stood out in high relief from each wall, and there were two doors—the one they had entered by, and another, open, facing the plot of waste land at the back of the temple. The drunken gang there had dispersed, and the stirrings of the hot air brought in only the muted noises of the crowd in the market-place.

Round above the pillars ran a stone frieze depicting the adventures of the god Shiva in his home on the Himalayan peak of Kailas. A foot-high phallus of red sandstone sprouted from the floor in the centre of the room; the sculptor had carved the face and body of Shiva into the stone, and someone had daubed the whole with vermilion paint. Cotton wicks burning in earthenware bowls of oil diffused a smoky light. There was one in each of three corners of the room; in the fourth corner, the lamp was on the plinth of a small statuette of an eight-armed god. The god sat cross-legged, knees and thighs flat, and with two of his arms grasped the minuscule figure of a woman. Her geometrically rounded breasts pressed against him, her arms and legs twined round him, and the stony carving of her sexual parts engulfed him. Jasmine petals and dried cow-dung littered the floor; the sacred bull had been here too.

Rodney leaned against the wall and wiped the sweat from his forehead. He saw with disgust that his clothes were splashed with red and blue dye. Looking up suddenly, he said in Hindustani, "What are those sepoys doing here, out of uniform?"

The Guru had subsided to the floor and sat in his usual upright position. "They can get leave of absence during the Holi, can they not? This is a famous temple of Shiva and caters well for the holy lusts of the flesh. I do not know why they are out of uniform. It is more sensible to ask, what are *you* doing here?"

Rodney remembered now giving Parasiya leave. The others would have got it too, from their own company commanders; they'd probably clubbed together to hire a couple of pony traps for the journey. There was nothing strange about it.

He eyed the Guru and began to collect himself. Half an hour ago, intent on the affair of the carts, he had thought and acted like a British Officer of the Honourable East India Company. Now the dishevelled wreck of his clothes, the atmosphere of exploding desire, the sexual riot of this night under a full moon, all conspired to make him forget that he was an Englishman and stood here by right of blood and conquest. But he must remember, for he was on duty.

He spoke in English: "Guru-ji, I was the drunken com-patriot of yours capering about at midnight outside Bhowani —but I was not too drunk to see the shells. I am acting on orders. You will explain to me at once, and truthfully, the whole scope of the plot in which you, Mr. Dellamain, and the Kishanpur government are engaged. And speak English."

He wondered what he would do if the Guru refused to speak—force him out at pistol point, perhaps, and with the sepoys' help take him back across the river? The Guru turned so that his eyes, which always looked straight forward out of his head, focused on Rodney's. Rodney stared back grimly, and the two pairs of light eyes, one blue, one grey, glinted in the guttering flicker of the lamps. When the Guru began to speak Rodney looked away. He had won.

"I will tell you, and what you do about it afterwards I do not care. It began when the Rani murdered the old Rajah. I had foreknowledge of that, but at the time it was none of my affair and I did not try to prevent it." His English was uncertain, as from long disuse, and had no accent of class or locality.

"Why did she kill him?"

"Fear—and lust. She is one of those women with a fire in the loins, and will certainly be burned by it in hell hereafter. In this life it takes many men to damp such a fire. The Rajah found out. At first he would not believe—as I see you do not wish to believe. Then he had to. So she killed him."

Rodney watched the smoke curl up from the lamps. Clamped on the god, the stone woman did not move, but her desirousness pervaded the shadows.

"Go on."

"The Dewan saw a chance to regain a power which all his family once had—you know he is a Bholkar, of the Bholkars of Goghri? He began to prepare a revolution which would overthrow the Rani and leave him as real ruler of the state, with some Rawan as puppet Rajah—perhaps the boy."

"But he hasn't had time to arrange all this, and get the guns imported from overseas and brought here, since January the first."

The Guru paused perceptibly. "His plans were laid before-hand. He knew the Rani would do it sooner or later. And not all the weapons come from overseas. There are many secret stores in Maharajahs' palaces and forts up and down India."

"So the Rani and her supporters will be murdered! That's the killing the Dewan's looking forward to? You can't *kill* her!"

"Why not? What is death? What is it to me of all people?" He held out his scaly arms and laughed with a clear tinkling sound that was gruesomely out of place and terrifying. "She'll die. So will you—one day." He forestalled the question on Rodney's lips. "Dellamain-sahib—*Mister* Dellamain I should say in this language—is in the Dewan's plot too, but not of his free will. Since long before the murder—for over three years—the rulers here have been bribing him to let them smuggle opium, salt, and children of the harlot tribes through his territory. It has always been a main source of income to the state—Kishanpur is the clearing house for Central India. Nowadays the state pays 'protection' to a British official instead of a Mogul satrap. That money—in diamonds—was paid to Mr. Dellamain by various hands, but always on the authority of the old Rajah—and now of the Rani. The Dewan is simply smuggling his arms in with the same convoys that bring the opium and the girls. He black-mailed Mr. Dellamain by threatening to reveal the original bribery and ruin his career for good—and he added a bigger bribe on his own account."

"You mean Dellamain's collecting a bribe from the Rani to wink at her smuggling, and at the same time allowing the Dewan to use her convoys to destroy her?"

"Yes. Mr. Dellamain put one foot wrong and has been pushed the rest of the way. However, there is one point which helps to prevent him rebelling. He knows, and I know, and many others know, that the Governor General will weep no tears if the Rani is murdered. Lord Canning would never tell Dellamain to have it done, as a Mogul would—we are a hypocritical race, sir. The reason? She is very unpopular with the people. A palace revolution is better than a people's revolution, because it does not alarm other rajahs. If you think, you will see what I mean."

Bitter at heart, Rodney saw, and nodded his head. If the people here in Kishanpur rebelled and threw off the Rani, they would then ask the British to rule them in her stead— for they would never, of course, imagine they could rule themselves. The British would be forced to take over to avoid anarchy. And nothing would persuade other princes that the British had not planned the whole affair from first to last with precisely that end in view. The Dewan's plot on the other hand could end only in a palace revolution, which would neither alter the relation between state and Company nor disturb other princes.

He saw that it was only too likely a situation. Nothing could excuse Dellamain's personal bad faith with the Rani, but the circumstances might easily decide an ambitious and nervy man like that to lie quiet under this novel combination of blackmail and bribery. Bulstrode also would have to walk delicately after he had received Rodney's report. Only one factor seemed unaccounted for: the Dewan was as much hated as the Rani, and just as likely to be overthrown by the people. But presumably first things must come first. None of it was pleasant to think about.

Rodney turned on the Guru. "How do you know so much about it? Who are you? I know you're a fake holy man, and on the way to be a murderer—but who were you?"

"A private of Her Majesty's One Hundred and Twenty-Fourth Foot—only it was still His Majesty King George the Fourth's when I deserted thirty years ago, about the time you were born. You are surprised that I do not have a common person's accent, I see. Not all private soldiers are the scum of the gutter—didn't Wellington call us something like that once? I was born a gentleman—perhaps a little more than that. For many years, too, the only English I have heard is from officers speaking it by my tree in Bhowani. My

tongue is rusty, but I talk in English with myself, inside my
head, and imitate what I hear. I was a good soldier once.
You would find it in my record of service if I told you my
name, which I will not. And I was young—younger than you
—and whored and drank in the cities at night with other
lads. One day—this."

He stretched out his hands.

"A spot—here. And the same day fifty lashes for over-
staying late pass. I deserted. India had touched me—here—
and I belonged to her."

"But you're a Christian!"

"What is a Christian? Or a fakir, or a sadhu? Is not
leprosy a religion? For two years I lived with a sweeper's
widow in the slums of Benares. For five years I travelled
the roads as a beggar and learned the fakirs' lore—oh, the
crows were real, and so are other frightening things I could
show you. I read sacred books, and argued with holy men in
the dust outside temples and mosques and Sikh gurdwaras.
The leprosy grew worse. For four years I studied alone at a
shrine near Badrinath in the Himalaya. Then I came to
Bhowani and sat down under the peepul tree—nineteen
years ago."

"Why did you join in this filthy plot? How do you benefit?
You must realize you're doing nothing but evil."

The Guru stared at the wall and did not answer for a long
minute. His voice was gentler than before. "Captain Savage,
I know you. I have seen you galloping down the Pike, and
laughing and joking with your brother officers and the
sepoys. I know that you dream of romantic adventure. I
know that duty did not compel you to swim the Kishan
and follow me here into this temple. Your blood drives you.
Don't you think I might be the same sort of person? I have
island blood too, and in those years on the road I found
that I could not master it. I am cast out from my own
people." He lifted his hands again and slowly lowered them.
"I must grub about in dung to find my gold. It is pure gold
to me to be a leper under that tree, and from a leper's world

—which is himself alone—burst out into other worlds. This is not my first adventure—plot, whatever you like to call it—but I think it will be my last. I am getting old."

Rodney paced uneasily up and down the floor. At one end he looked out on the waste land and the low wall; at the other on the god and the woman locked in stone embrace. The wind of his passing tugged at the flames so that they guttered and puffed in the bowls while distorted shadows crouched across the ceiling. Incense and wood smoke burdened the hot air, and the throb of chanting. From one end he saw the Guru's straight back and matted hair, and from the other end stared into the man's eyes.

They were North Sea eyes, grey English Channel eyes, and indelible on their retinas thirty years of this—fecund squalor, diseased and germinating dust, circling vultures, grey glowing sky, hot rain, and rioting lust, and a silver skin. He was a fresh-faced boy like young Myers, a tall young man in scarlet serge who drank strong rum with a thousand others like him of his regiment, and ate salt beef, and swore monotonous soldiers' oaths. India touched him, but not with her hot hand of death. That laid the body under a slab in a walled cemetery—distorted, shrunk, discoloured, preserved for ever in its English thoughts. *Here lies Private X, H.M. 124th Foot, died of the cholera, on such a day, 1827, in such a year of his age*—such a young year. Rodney had seen hundreds of them.

Those dead were English and would remain English for ever under the Indian sun and the Indian tree. At the end of "for ever" they would be remembered with the men in the sea and the girls under the Devon hill.

But this tall man would not, because India had touched him and turned his white to silver. Selecting him, she branded him and drew him ashamed out of the English room into the darkness and the glare. After that he could have no master or servant or lover but her, and, because she had caressed him and he carried the mark, her people revered him.

Rodney felt tears close behind his eyes. The light glinted down the Guru's back, and a harsh shadowline edged the bony shoulder-blades. India had taken him, given him no choice. As an Indian he was sane and wise and perhaps merciful. Rodney blinked and grated his teeth together; as an Englishman the Guru was perhaps mad, certainly cruel. They were going to kill Sumitra. She had lost control of herself that night in the marquee by the falls and babbled words without meaning: "It's gone too far, I can't stop it." He understood now. She had known about the plot, and by refusing her he had condemned her to death, and her little boy.

"The Rani asked me to command her army. She knows about your plot. Why doesn't she get another Englishman instead?"

"She may know something about it, but she is helpless. At one time she would have taken any Englishman. Now she still hopes that you will change your mind—for reasons which perhaps you know of."

Rodney swung once more up and down the room and came to his decision. "Very well. I will now tell her everything that I know. If she wishes, I'll escort her to safety in British territory. I don't care what she's done; she's not going to be murdered by a bloody little rat like the Dewan. I'll report to the officer who sent me, of course. If we want you, we'll get you, wherever you go."

For a quarter of an hour something had nagged at the back of his mind, something important to him personally. Now he got it. Every prince in India knew that he owed his own present subordination to the discipline and skill at arms of the Company's native armies, for without them the British spearhead would have had no shaft. Presumably those qualities would fetch a high price from men plotting to overthrow a prince.

"Those Native Officers and sepoys—are you people enticing them to desert, to help in your revolution, promising them special privileges—loot, high pay, and so on?"

"No, sir. They are here in the combined pursuit of sex and salvation, as I told you. They would never desert. You know that."

It was true enough. He had seldom heard of a sepoy deserting to take up service in a state, though men pensioned off or for any reason dismissed could usually find a rajah keen to employ them.

The Silver Guru's eyes had gone out of focus. There was nothing more to be done here. Rodney had to find the Rani, give her his warning, and swim back across the river. He said, "I'm going, and—can't I get a doctor to look at you, in Bhowani?"

He knew no doctor could do anything; the Guru did not answer. Rodney stared helplessly at the scarred back and at last went out on to the waste land. A dog nosed about among the garbage; a man slept, rolled in a sheet, under the low wall. Glancing at the stars, Rodney slipped over into the lane and hurried back the way he had come. The alleys were empty and in themselves silent, but murmuring with diffused noise from the marketplace. Moon shadow painted the walls of the houses dull blue; red bonfire light, reflected from the sky, tinged the roofs and cornices. The marks of coloured water lay red and blue on bolted doors and shuttered windows.

He walked quickly in the dust under the walls, looked back often, and stopped at each transverse lane. There was no need to be cautious now, but he was on edge and would have liked to run. It was a little before three o'clock; he tried to think what words he would use to Sumitra. Near the edge of the city he paused at a corner and wondered whether he should turn right for the fort.

A white shape swept round the corner and bumped into him. He gripped tight with his arms, his nerves and muscles contracting. The thing gasped and he saw it was a woman, enveloped from head to foot in a burqa. At once she snapped upright and whispered fiercely, "Let go, you drunken sot!"

He knew the voice and the authority in it, and the black glitter behind the coarse netting of the eyepiece. At the same moment she recognized him. He tightened his hold on her elbows and dragged her into a doorway.

She said softly, "Well?"

"What are you doing here, Sumitra?"

For a moment longer she stared at him. He felt her brace her shoulders. She motioned at the splashes of red on his shirt. "It looks as if I am on the same errand as you."

"What do you mean?"

"The Holi, fool!" She trembled under his hand. Her voice hardened, working itself into a quivering anger. "Are you a child? Must I explain in simple words? If you wanted a brown woman, why not me? If I'm not expert enough, if you like the gutter, why didn't you change your suit? I do."

He jerked out his pistol and came to the edge of vomiting. This tender flesh submitted to him—and to every shame of the night. This, that had been jasmine and sandalwood, crept by choice into the darkened temple chambers. Under the burqa she'd wear the dress of a dancing girl, a hereditary harlot, and in the dark no one would see her face.

He snarled and rammed the pistol into her stomach. Tears watered the blackness of her eyes as his finger itched on the trigger.

He gritted his teeth. "Tonight—don't go to your filth. Your Dewan and the Silver Guru are planning to murder you. They have a secret store of arms and have probably suborned your army. Go back to the fort, take your son, and escape into British territory as quickly as you can. There, that's my duty. You meant something to me, a lot of courage and brightness. I thought I'd behaved like a swine to you—you murderous bitch."

He stepped back. As he gauged the distance he saw her eyes were streaming and heard her moan. He smashed his open left hand with all his strength into the side of her head. She fell into the gutter, and lay spread-eagled, crying hopelessly. He tugged the ruby from his finger and flung it at her.

He turned and ran, his boots echoing in the lane. Images crowded in on him: she lay on the cushions and smelled of musk; she crouched in a darkened temple room, the revellers came, slipped money to the priests, and went into the room; they fumbled at the femaleness of her. Twenty times between now and dawn—the hands, the seeking, the sweaty struggle; peasants hog-drunk and acrid from the plough, syphilitic officers of her army, strong coolies, fat merchants, sepoys. She lay there in the dark and wriggled.

He panted with the effort of running and the struggle to force down the images and forget. Let these animals drown in the ordure they wallowed in—plot, counterplot, treason, treachery, vice, procurement, murder, dope, sadism. It would end in half of them being disembowelled while the others watched with savage sexual pleasure. Then they'd begin again.

Where the lane debouched into the fields he met a fat man in white robes. He'd seen him before too; it was the Calcutta merchant who'd been in Bhowani on Monday morning—on his way back east, hurrying now to the temple and the women, and Sumitra. Rodney flung past and ran on, noticing the man's suddenly taut expression—of course, the pistol was still in his hand. He put it back into the holster.

Let them all wallow. The red splashes would stain his skin for life. He longed only to get to his bungalow, to burn his clothes, and be again an Englishman, happy and unseeing.

# 14

"AND HERE are the three copies of Captain Savage's report, sir."

Major Peckham, immaculate in scarlet and white, fumbled to untie the ribbon binding the roll of papers. Bulstrode waited, his hand out and his little eyes examining the major; he too was wearing the white trousers of hot-weather full dress but he had not put on his tunic. Suddenly he said, "Third button upside down, Major. Don't let it happen again. Thank you."

He took the papers with a flicker of the eyelid at Rodney and sank grunting into a long chair. The others sat down around him—on his left Rodney and the flushing Peckham, on his right Caroline. As the colonel began to glance through the pages of copperplate script, he bawled, "Prunella!"

The small mouselike noises inside the house stopped, feet scurried down the passage, and Mrs. Bulstrode trotted on to the verandah. She came to her husband's chair and stood by it, head bowed and hands folded. "Yes, dear?"

Without looking up, he said, "Breakfast; have it cleared away. And the steak—overdone. Give someone hell."

"Yes, dear." Mrs. Bulstrode hurried back into the house, looking more nervous than ever but not at all ashamed or angry.

Bulstrode read on, tugging at his ear, while Caroline stared at him, an angry sparkle in her eyes. The bearer took away the dirty dishes; Rodney guessed from the remains that the colonel had breakfasted on mulligatawny soup, beefsteak with devilled kidneys, and a bottle of claret. Mrs. Bulstrode appeared to have had a cup of tea.

He stared at a bowl of ferns suspended by chains from the ceiling over his head. Screens of coir matting hung down all

round, and water dripped from them on to the flags. Outside
the sun glared on a dozing garden, but in here there was a
dark light, like that of a crypt, and it threw no shadows. A
thickness in the air dulled the noises—the swish of water as
the watercarrier drenched the screens, the squeaking of a
punkah inside the house, the tapping of a woodpecker at a
tree. Bulstrode's shirt was wet and drops of sweat formed
on his bald head and ran down his face into his beard; a
servant boy stood behind his chair, fanning him with a hand
fan made of plaited grass, wafting the rank smell of his
shirt over the others; the bearer reappeared and put a plate
of Nagpur oranges on the table. Bulstrode laid the papers
aside and began to peel an orange.

"Feeling better, Savage? Dead beat yesterday, weren't
you?"

"I was tired, sir."

Today was April the eleventh, a Saturday. After his en-
counter with Sumitra at the edge of Kishanpur City, he'd
reached the half-squad in their jungle bivouac at four on
Thursday morning. He'd slept most of that day, set out for
Bhowani at four in the afternoon, and arrived at three
o'clock on Friday morning. Four hours later he had come
here to Bulstrode's bungalow to make his report, and the
colonel had sent for Caroline and Peckham to hear it too.
He'd been tired all right then; he had ridden a hundred and
thirty miles in temperatures between 90 and 105 in the shade,
besides swimming the Kishan twice. But it was not physical
fatigue which made his face in the mirror haggard and set
lines of strain round the corners of his mouth. He'd explored
an underworld of emotion, and he carried the marks of his
experience. He had thought the others would not notice, but
Bulstrode's eyes were always shrewd, and the girl had unpredictable flashes of sympathy; they had both detected his
exhaustion of spirit. That was yesterday; today he felt less
tired, but more apathetic. Action was over; Bulstrode had
spent a day and a night thinking what he should do. Now
they were gathered at his bungalow to hear his decision.

Bulstrode said, "You were more than tired, boy. You did well, spite of disobeying orders. About this report—you sure the Rani understands those fellahs are after her blood?"

"Yes, sir."

Yesterday he had said only that he had warned the Rani of her danger; he had not mentioned the place and other circumstances of their meeting. He did not meet the colonel's glance, and noticed that in this light the blue veins were very prominent on the back of Caroline's hand.

"Good. Don't want to feel we murdered her. Now she can stew in her own juice, or stew t'others in theirs, hey? Probably strung up a few score of those fellahs already, if you ask me."

A servant came out and picked the pieces of orange peel off the floor, where Bulstrode was throwing them as he ate. He went on, between chews.

"Pity you didn't get a chance to talk with Purshottam Dass—head Brahmin of the temple there, the fat fellah with the red line down his forehead. They're Shaivas in that temple—that is, credit Shiva as chief power of creation and reproduction, as well as destruction; have a wonderful old illuminated copy of the Shiva Purana—lists a thousand and eight names of Shiva. See the frieze of demons, the Pramathas? Best piece of carving between Delhi and Nagpur; the stone damn well moves as you look at it. Pity! Still, I s'pose you were busy. Right.

"I've read that report carefully. Situation is this. Either Silver Guru, or Private Whatever-his-name-is, is lying—or he's telling the truth, eh? Let's say he's telling the truth. Then we go to Dellamain. He'll swear it's all official and aboveboard, but far too secret to explain to women and clods of soldiers like us—and, by God, he may be right. Often these fellahs—commissioners, collectors, residents—have to guess what policy is, and act on their own initiative and judgment. If they guess wrong—worst of all, if they ask too many questions upstairs and force the fellahs above 'em to do the Christian thing—then they get a pat on the back and a twenty-year stretch as Collector of Rumblebellypore. Remember Dellamain must have one miscue chalked up against him already, or he wouldn't be in this hole, with *his* brains.

"What that comes to is this: leave 'em all alone if we possibly can. We're soldiers, just the business end of this damn great engine; keep our fingers out of the guts of it or God knows what'll happen. I don't care a damn if Dellamain takes bribes from here to doomsday—and that Rani deserves to be murdered!

"My duty is to make sure Dellamain knows the facts, and to pass report on privately to the general. Then Dellamain can do what he likes—competent to take any action he thinks fit. Don't forget this territory is leased; there's never been a Resident at Kishanpur, so the Commissioner here does a job that's normally two different people's. The general can do what *he* likes; may write a note to the Chief, to the effect that he hears something funny's going on in Kishanpur. You can see what happens then—note goes across to Lieutenant Governor, down to Dellamain, all very guarded. Answer—a lemon. Right. That's all on the assumption that the Guru's telling the truth.

"Now let's say he's lying, that the guns are not for the Dewan's plot. This we have to think about, because Dellamain wouldn't know. They could lie to him just as easily as to you—easier. Then who in God's name *are* the guns for? Only one sensible answer: the state, the Rani, the Dewan in his official position. What for? Three answers: one, face; two, fear; three, ambition. Face—the bigger a rajah's guns, the bigger the rajah. But they all know it's too damned dangerous these days to smuggle in guns just for prestige. So that's out. Fear—who are they afraid of? Us. A few piddling guns won't help. Another state? They know we'd never allow states to have private wars. So that's out. Ambition —who are they going to attack? Another state? We won't let 'em. Us? It's fantastic. Goddam it, all the states in the Presidency couldn't stand for five minutes against the Bengal Army, and they know it. Any of those things are possible,

but they're so unlikely that the Silver Guru's story is almost
certainly true. Don't forget he's English—mad, of course, but
if any of these other theories are true he'd be aiding and
abetting treason. No Englishman in India can be a traitor,
however mad—never has, never will be. Another point: they
didn't try to kill you, Savage. They would have if there'd
been something as important as treason to shelter. . . ."

Rodney thought back. Only once had he felt the presence
of personal danger—when he first went into the temple—
and that was obviously an infection caught from the Silver
Guru's panic. It could not have been anything else, because
by then he'd recognized the sepoys, and he knew that with
a dozen of them he could calm or disperse any crowd. Bulstrode was still talking.

". . . Several things not clear still. Why did the Guru make
that remark about the death of a tyrant, the one which
worried Miss Langford here and started all this off? Only
possible reason is face—fellah must be vain as a peacock.
It worked; word got round, and he's treated as a major
prophet now. Then Sitapara's message to you, miss, telling
you to watch the Commissioner's bungalow. Remember she
was on the lookout for stuff connected with the murder of
the old Rajah. You acted on the message, uncovered a bribe
to Dellamain, and gun-running. Can't make it out, quite.
Perhaps I will later." He looked up suddenly at Caroline
Langford. "De Forrest, miss. Is he in it?"

She must have been expecting the question, for she answered without hesitation, "No, Colonel, I am positive he
is not. He saw all that I saw, but I am sure that his only
motive in denying it was to be left alone again when——"
She stopped short.

"When what, miss?"

"When I refused to marry him."

"H'm, you didn't tell me that before. Well, that clears him
anyway."

Rodney appraised the girl's pale face; was she sorry that
she had let out de Forrest's secret? Was she angry that he

had not allowed the Rani to be sacrificed on the altar of justice? Was she thinking how she could yet drag Dellamain to judgment?

Bulstrode stared up at the ceiling with unseeing eyes. "I haven't got any morals, miss—don't believe in 'em—but by God I know this country. Those chupattis and bits of flesh —far more disturbing than this Kishanpur nonsense. They really worry me. Been devilling the Commissioner to find out. He's doing his best, I know, but he gets nowhere. Then there's my drunken coot of a second-in-command, Myers, and his goddamned God. I've told him I'll have him court-martialled if he talks religion to our fellahs again; they've got a perfectly good religion of their own. The new cart-ridges—don't like that either, but I'm trapped, same as Della-main but different. Either I say they're unclean, and as good as announce that the Company's just tried it on to see whether the sepoys'd notice—or I say they're not, and tell a lie which'll be found out, because by God I believe they *are* unclean. Don't like any of it. I know these people, and they're in a damn funny mood. Never seen anything like it."

He brought down his eyes and fixed them on Miss Lang-ford. It was clear that he was exerting himself to convince her. Peckham and Rodney were soldiers; they would merely receive his orders and obey.

"Now miss, you're a private person. If you don't agree with me there's only one thing for you to do—go to Mr. Colvin, the Lieutenant Governor, in Agra. If you do that, you'll be doing it for one of three reasons: ruin the Rani for murdering the old Rajah; ruin Dellamain for taking bribes; air this plot because you think there's treason behind it. First two things are up to you; the third I've told you —you may be doing England a great deal more harm than good. What about it?"

Caroline looked down into her lap. "Can't we help Mr. Dellamain escape from this circle of bribery and blackmail somehow?"

Rodney started in surprise; Peckham shot her a friendly look; Bulstrode's face was expressionless.

"Not without getting him broke, miss. Anyway, now the cat's out of the bag over there in Kishanpur, the Rani and the Dewan may come to some agreement. That'd settle the blackmail part."

She thought for a few seconds, and said, "It is hard. I do not like it, but I will abide by your decision."

"Right. I'll be ready in a minute."

The colonel heaved himself upright and waddled into the bungalow. Peckham gathered up the papers and pretended to read through them again. Caroline remained in her chair, her eyes on the floor. Rodney got up, hitched his scabbard into his hand, and walked slowly down the verandah. She was trapped now, for here her abstract idealism became practical vindictiveness. She had turned out to be human after all, like everyone else, and she was very unhappy about it. He wished there were something he could say. It didn't matter—one unpleasant hour with Dellamain, the hour whose shape ahead had made him uncomfortable all morning, and it would be over.

Bulstrode came out, pushing the matting aside, and jammed on his shako. "Come on. Got those papers, Peckham?"

At the Commissioner's bungalow the doorkeeper wore scarlet and gold livery and a scarlet and gold turban, and a whistle of office hung from his neck on a silver chain. He led them along the verandah, past a row of salaaming Indians, and into the drawing-room. They sat in a semi-circle of chairs, not speaking, and waited. A profusion of mahogany furniture filled the huge room; a triple punkah creaked overhead and hardly seemed to disturb the dust. Bulstrode spread his legs and dozed off. Rodney avoided Caroline's eye. The Commissioner was going to make them wait, perhaps to impress on the Indians outside that he was the master of Bulstrode and the army too.

Several visitors had been dispatched when the door-keeper announced that now the Commissioner-sahib would be pleased to see the Colonel-sahib, the Major-sahib, the Captain-sahib, and the Miss-sahiba.

Dellamain was standing behind his wide desk. He wore a formal dark grey frock coat, white trousers, white shirt, and thin black tie. Rodney saw afresh that he was big and intelligent, and afraid. Still, the Commissioner had full control of himself and greeted them jovially, though he must have guessed this was no ordinary call.

"Miss Langford, Colonel, Major, Captain; I'm delighted. Please take chairs. Cigars, gentlemen? I think Miss Langford does not object to the weed. No? I must apologize for keeping you waiting, but I had much business to transact. The secret with an Indian visitor is never to sit down; then he cannot. I'm sure you make use of that principle, Colonel?" Bulstrode grunted and clanked his scabbard against the chair leg. Dellamain's smooth flow continued. "Did you notice that last pair? They're surveyors for the resettlement I have persuaded Government to undertake in this territory—at last!"

Caroline interrupted. "What is resettlement?" Bulstrode frowned, Rodney bit his lip. It was a disease with her—find out! Then he saw in her face that, in part at least, she had spoken from a wish to make this interview less frightening for Dellamain.

The Commissioner was delighted. "Resettlement, Miss Langford, is a process of land survey which has as its object the reassessment of the land's agricultural capacity, and hence of the revenues to be collected from it in the way of taxes. In the process of settlement or resettlement we discover and record many facts concerning the ownership of land. It is a long, long task—this territory comprises six thousand nine hundred and eighty-three square miles—and will not be completed until long after my retirement. But it is essential. We are still working from the records taken over from the Rajahs of Kishanpur, and they are unbelievably inaccurate. We have to find the character of the soil, and assess the value of improved communications and irrigation. When we leased this territory from the Rawans in 1809 the old irrigation works were in decay, for instance; we have put some of them in order and begun to build better ones. Account must be taken of all these matters, and hundreds more, in the resettlement report. It is interesting. Look."

He spread his hand out on the wall map, dropped suddenly into natural English, and in a few crisp sentences made clear the complicated laws of land tenure, revenue, and inheritance, as they ruled in the territory at the time. He was brilliant and brief, and even Bulstrode had to nod his appreciation. The effect on Caroline was not quite what Rodney had expected; she was interested enough but she was also, he thought, a little jealous. She understood completely and wanted to use her own brain on problems as big and important as this; and she knew she was more hopelessly trapped than Dellamain. He could go to England —when he had made his money—and earn recognition on the wider English stage. One day Palmerston, Gladstone, and Disraeli might acknowledge him, but she could not change her sex, or the traditions which manacled a woman's capability.

Bulstrode collected himself, shuffled his papers, and belched. In the silence he said, "Sorry to interrupt, Commissioner. Got an important report to make. Miss Langford, you begin."

Dellamain sat down rather suddenly. As though a hand had been passed over it, his face assumed an air of judicial command. For the third time in the week Caroline told her story. Rodney followed, looking away from Dellamain as much as he could, because he did not like to inflict hurt in cold blood or see the wounded squirm.

The Commissioner paled slightly during the recitals; at the end he flushed a mottled red and raised his protuberant eyes to Bulstrode. He spoke slowly. "And you, Colonel, you permitted this? You ordered out cavalry behind my back?"

George Bulstrode sucked his teeth and swivelled his bulk round to face the Commissioner. "Yes."

In the long harsh silence Rodney examined his toes. It was obvious now what Dellamain would say. After the long pause, he said it.

He spoke with firmness and conviction. If his plump fingers had not fiddled with a round ebony ruler on the desk; if his voice had not gathered that canonical richness; if Bulstrode had not forecast his story so exactly, Rodney would have been glad to believe him. Caroline was right in seeing that he needed help. Bulstrode was right in seeing that the bribery was unimportant. Charles Dellamain was administering the Bhowani Leased Territory better than anyone else could have; the inner, frightened Dellamain somehow knew the land and the people. These myriads that he ruled did not care what bribes he took; he protected them and gave them peace and justice. What did it all matter compared with the resettlement, the tasks of building confidence and prosperity?

Dellamain did not speak long. He denied that he took bribes or that he had ever countenanced smuggling of any kind. As to the details of the gun-running, he said he was well aware of them; that they were connected with a political matter so delicate and secret that it could not even be committed to paper. He was indeed surprised to learn from them that the Silver Guru was English; but he was glad to know it, because the Guru was an important link in his negotiations, and he, Dellamain, could now be more sure that his trust in him was not misplaced.

At the last, he turned to the attack. He looked from Rodney to Caroline, ignoring Peckham, and spoke with heavy authority. "You two, abetted by Colonel Bulstrode, have been like mischievous urchins playing with gunpowder. Your amateur muddling interference might have endangered the British position in India, no less. I did all I could to discourage you, short of explaining to you things which you should not be allowed to know. You, sir"—he glanced at

Rodney—"are a military officer, and less blame attaches to you than to your superior. But it is clear that your own lack of balance led you to fall in the more readily with his plans. And you, Miss Langford, must be regarded as the instigator of this foolishness. I have attempted to dissuade you. I have dropped hints to your cousin Lady Isobel, which must have reached you. I have appealed to the faith, integrity, and common sense I thought you possessed—in vain. Your faith is reserved for Indian rajahs; you blundered relentlessly on. Colonel Bulstrode, your conduct leaves me with an impression that you lack the sense of proportion appropriate to your high rank. Now"—he had regained full assurance as no one spoke or contradicted him—"let us all forget and return to our respective duties. I should not like my last six months in the Company's service to be marred by ill feeling and mutual recriminations over this unfortunate affair."

"You're retiring in six months? I didn't know that."

"You do not, if I may say so once more, Miss Langford, know everything. Yes, I am going. I have been privately in touch with certain parliamentary figures at home and intend to devote myself to politics there."

He had not altered his voice much, but the last sentences carried the unmistakable plea: *I'm so near escape from this labyrinth. Be kind.*

Bulstrode, who had closed his eyes during the Commissioner's upbraiding, slapped a wad of papers on the table. "My official report to you—two copies. Sign one as a receipt please, Commissioner, and give it back to me."

Dellamain seized his pen and scribbled angrily. Bulstrode glanced down. "Time and date, please, Commissioner."

When they had been added he handed the signed copy to Peckham and rolled out of the room with a parting nod. The others followed. The Commissioner of Bhowani sat shrunk in his chair and stared at the sheets of white paper littering his desk.

Bulstrode and Peckham went towards the station commander's office; Rodney and Caroline walked slowly north through cantonments. Men were out scattering water from goatskins to lay the dust in the roads, and the smell was clean and fresh.

Caroline said, "It goes down, layer below layer, each worse than the last. I wish I could believe, really believe, that we've uncovered the lowest layer of all. But I can't. Can you?"

He knew he could not. Down there in the depths were emotions and wisps of suspicion he could not even identify; he knew only that they made him uneasy, and ashamed.

He did not speak, and the girl went on, her voice detached and sad. "I hear the Governor General has a big Georgian house in Calcutta, and the drawing-room is white and gold. I see him, poor man, sitting at a desk, looking out on the garden, and worrying over what will happen if there's a rebellion in Kishanpur—not for long; he has too many things to worry about. He might know Mr. Dellamain's name, but he wouldn't know *him*."

Rodney nodded. The Governor General would know nothing of the nature of this Charles Dellamain who served him—the ability, the banked fires of ambition, the bribes.

"Then the Rani plots, the Dewan plots, the Silver Guru plots. Mr. Dellamain puts a foot into one whirlpool and is dragged into another. Below, other little people plot and bribe."

And below again—what? She hadn't been down that far; she didn't know that down there it became impossible to separate good from evil. In trying, you met an eight-armed god and were of a sudden touched with his desires, ruled by his code of values. The humped white bull licked with a rough tongue; the night smelled of women and dried urine; smoke drifted across a frieze of endless copulation; there was a man in a bright coat, and he had a hawk and a knife, and others threw red and blue powder on him. Where was right, in this?

"There are not two standards for us, for the English—only one. We must keep our standard, or go home. We must not, as we do now, permit untouchability and forbid suttee, abolish tyranny in one state and leave it in another, have our right hand Eastern and our left hand Western. It is not that India is wicked; she has her own ways. If we rule we must rule as Indians—or we must make the Indians English. But we do neither; we are like Mr. Dellamain. We have one foot in a whirlpool. Sometimes I am sure we will be dragged into another and drowned. God will punish us for compromising. As He will punish me."

She turned abruptly into the Hatton-Dunns', and Rodney walked on alone. She was wearing a pale blue dress today and a wide-brimmed hat. Her wrists were too fragile and her shoulders too thin to support the weight of her concerns. Now that he had studied her face more often he did not know why he had ever missed its beauty; perhaps because it was strong and always serious, especially the eyes. She must not lose that quality of seriousness—he knew too well how barren was a human being completely without it—but she must learn to stand away from it sometimes, and laugh. She had no right, at her age, to throw away her sense of humour and flay herself unrelentingly for the furtherance of God's purposes. Didn't God create laughter too? But she was so much kinder than she pretended; he wanted to help her.

Cantonment life lay in wait to enfold him, as on his previous return from Kishanpur. Then he had for a time resisted the cushioning familiarity; now he would welcome it. Parades, drills, the Club; they would be again what they had always been—the dull, strong fabric of living.

April the eleventh. April, the mango showers and a lifting of the air at dusk. May, the blinding noon of heat; in May the sky was clean and blue, shading to iron-grey in the heat of the early afternoon. May was a breathless night on the lawn and the mosquito net flimsy as the veil of a ghost; or an evening dust storm, and they would sleep on the verandah while the watchman threw water, all night long, on the matting screens; or a stirring of the air at midnight when the earth under the trees cooled and the flower petals nodded. May was drought, parched throat at noon, 115 in the shade, the sun striking the parade ground and lashing back up into the eyes.

In June the air would day by day become more humid, while heavy clouds passed overhead from southwest to northeast. The monsoon would reach Bhowani after the middle of the month—June the twentieth last year, June the nineteenth in '55, June the twenty-third in '54, June the eighteenth in '53. He remembered, as everyone did, the exact date of each annual rescue. There would be electric storms for a few days beforehand—high winds, thunder and dust, a heavy drop or two of rain. Then, on the first day of the monsoon, a tremendous storm of rain, lasting for hours; half a day's pause—another storm; pause—another. When it rained, large drops fell slowly, then faster and thicker until they were almost a waterfall. It fell too fast for the earth to swallow it; it laid the dust, filled the rivers, and spread a surface of slippery mud on the hard earth. Later it slackened but fell still, a few hours at a time, all through July and August. Between the storms, white cumulus clouds sailed in a blue sky, the temperature was not much over 90, the air was washed clean and felt heavy with more rain and the sound of running water.

In September the rains drizzled to an end. Water stood in the roads and fields, and every disease of India flourished. The earth was soft deep down, and replete; the little streams full, the big rivers overflowing, twenty, thirty, sixty feet above normal, depending on the shape of the banks; the formerly brown grass green, the roof of the jungle green, the night awhirr with moths and flying beetles.

October and November were a golden sun and a cool night, wood smoke, fragrant evening; in those days a patina of calm overlaid the routines of barrack and bungalow and lent them grace. The cold weather: December, January, February; English warm clothes, a fire in the grate, and the punkahs stilled; manœuvres, tents in a mango grove; sunny afternoons, raw nights, and snapping dawns; duck and snipe, and the leopard in the jungle.

He'd heard a rumour that the regiment was to change stations in January and would go to Dinapore—four hundred miles. They'd take six weeks on the march, and what an upheaval there'd be after five years in Bhowani. The regiment would march; women and children, furniture, pets, and toys would travel in pony traps and bullock carts.

Meanwhile, the embrace of secure monotony. Musketry practice with the new cartridges; his birthday at the end of this month; children's party at the Club in May—the last outdoor function until September. What was it Sumitra had said to him one long-ago day? "You will die in England as Lieutenant Colonel Savage, B.N.I., retired—dried up and worn out. I have heard what it is like. They will laugh because you eat curry, and laugh when you try and tell them what *this* means." She had swept her hand round the shimmering jungles. "They will say you are unhappy because you have no black servants to order about."

That was right; that was how it went. There'd never be a great thing to do, and if there were his countrymen in England would laugh at it when it was done.

# 15

THE WHITE Club building slept in the dense blue shadow of its thatched roof. As Rodney went in, George Bulstrode's purple face and congested eyes swam out of the gloom of the centre hall and floated towards him. On Saturdays the old man customarily ate a late tiffin here, after drinking in the bar from ten till two.

"Hullo, Savage. You on duty? H'm, yes—damfool children's party. Well, bed for me." He turned and bellowed down the passage, *"Koi hai! My horse!"*

The door slammed behind him. Rodney's eyes became accustomed to the semi-darkness, and he glanced idly at the papers pinned in overlapping profusion on the notice board. One, on the surface, read:

> *The Committee of the Bhowani Club has selected Saturday May the 9th (at 4:30 o'clock) as the date of the annual hot-weather children's party. New members are requested to note that it is not customary for ayahs to accompany children, nor should infants under 2 years of age be brought.*
>
> W. O. Ransome-Frome.
>
> *February 13th, 1857*          Honorary Secretary

He pulled out his watch: two o'clock. He had plenty of time. He called for a servant, shouting *"Koi hai!"*

Nothing happened. A pulse stirred rhythmically in his temple. The silence caught and imprisoned his shout. Out at the back of the Club the beaten earth of the compound glared like white fire. A lean dog scratched its mange for fleas, got up, and limped away. Rodney tugged at the collar of his tunic, yawned, and went to look for the duty waiter. He found him stretched on the stone flags under the bar, asleep and breathing noisily through his mouth. Rodney leaned over and snarled, *"Koi hai!"*

The waiter blinked and struggled to his feet, obviously disliking the taste in his mouth. Rodney felt a sullen sympathy with him—to be on duty at two of a Saturday afternoon in May! He yawned again. "Has the fatigue party from the Thirteenth Rifles come yet?"

It took time for the question to penetrate the heat-fuddle in the man's brain. "I think they are waiting outside, huzoor. Shall I fetch the jemadar-sahib?"

"No. I'll go to them."

He walked down the steps, winced, and plunged into the

trembling furnace of the open air. The sepoys stood in a
loose group under the trees at the far end of the lawn.
Seeing Rodney, the jemadar in charge of them gave a command and strutted across the brown-green grass to meet
him.

"Sir! Jemadar Godse, two naiks, nineteen sepoys, one
carpenter, reporting for fatigue duty—present and correct,
sir!"

Rodney returned the salute with a gesture of his hand
and moved in under the shade. The men made way for
him.

"Stand easy, if you please."

Godse repeated the order, and Rodney pulled out a
cheroot. "Well, how are we going to arrange things? Have
you brought the gear?"

The jemadar pointed to a pile of wooden poles, planks,
canvas, and rope.

"Good. Now, what about it?"

They stood side by side, looking at the lawn, the hap-
hazard trees, the beds of dirty marigolds and sickly zinnias.
Godse cleared his throat. "Last year we put up the swings
under that far tree, and the awning over there. Shall we do
it the same way this year?"

The sepoys stood wooden and silent around, and Rodney
tried to make them smile. He said lightly, "And what did we
do in 1805, Jemadar-sahib?"

It was not a good joke, but ordinarily it might have
amused them. He glanced at their faces and wondered what
was on their minds. The carpenter Piroo stood apart from
the sepoys and bowed low as Rodney caught his eye.

He waved his cheroot. "Very well. Do it like that. I'll get
the Club servants to carry out chairs. Make sure the awning
is near the end of the verandah there, so that the conjurer
can stand under the tamarind. Perhaps he'll want to make
something appear out of the branches, eh? Is that understood? Oh, and keep the croquet pitch clear—all those little
iron hoops."

The group dissolved as the men dragged the planks out into the glare; Piroo the carpenter trailed after them, carrying a hammer and a bag of nails. For a minute Rodney stood alone in the shade and watched them. Then, feeling impelled to share at least in part their martyrdom to the heat, he followed them across the grass. The nearest men had begun to make the framework for the swings, and were working hard.

They were talking in low voices and did not see him come up. One of them, holding a post upright, said, "Naik, is it true that the Silver Guru has taken a vow to fast in silence?"

The N.C.O. was Naik Parasiya, who had been in the temple at Kishanpur that night of the Holi. He was stooped down, fastening a guy rope, and Rodney heard him answer, "It's true."

"How long is he going to do it for? And why?"

"He said 'Until the destruction promised by the gods overtakes the wicked.'"

The naik stood up as he spoke, saw Rodney, and muttered, "Quiet. Get on with your work."

Rodney's brain ticked over idly. The tunic glowed across his shoulders, and the top of his collar burned where it touched his neck. He wriggled uncomfortably, wondering what the Guru meant. One day, a week or so after the Holi, the leper had reappeared in the Little Bazaar, which meant presumably that they had all settled their affairs in Kishanpur without bloodshed. Perhaps the Guru had given up his intrigues altogether. These remarks about destruction and the vow to fast sounded like phrases designed to attract attention and increase his reputation in this other life of his, the one he lived under the peepul tree in the Little Bazaar. Other things pointed the same way—his intervention in the matter of the greased cartridges, for instance. It was no use fretting about it now.

Rodney saw that all was in hand, and turned up into the Club. A quiet glass or two of brandy, with plenty of cold water, would pass the time; the fatigue wouldn't be finished for a couple of hours, and then the English population of Bhowani would begin to arrive, every last one of them—except Curry Bulstrode, snoring in his bungalow. Rodney's own tiffin of crumbed mutton chops, mango food, and beer lay heavy in his stomach.

He stood in the gloom of the bar, holding the brandy in one hand while he cautiously tested the chairs with the other. Sometimes, at this hour and season, the greater comfort of the leather armchairs made up for their greater heat, sometimes not. He shook his head; today it would have to be a cane chair. He sank back, put his glass in the hole in the arm-rest, swung out the pieces which extended into leg-rests, lifted his boots up on to them, and stared at the ceiling.

A minute later he got up and riffled the leaves of the English periodicals, all four months old, littering a table against the back wall. He did not want to read any of them; he had read them all already, twice each. He sat down again.

A brainfever bird opened up from a tree in the compound: higher, higher, higher, higher—break, pause, begin again; *pippeha pippeha pippeha pippeha, ha ha ha, pippeha pippeha* —higher, higher. The heat seeped in through the thick walls and tight-shut windows, and the air seemed to glow in the darkened room. He took a long drink and licked his lips. Better be careful of that stuff; he liked it. Better still, find some task that would engage his whole interest and capacity; that was the real answer. A soldier's trade ought to have adventures enough; it didn't though, and nowadays an officer couldn't tie a lady's glove to his lance point and ride out looking for them.

That wasn't quite true. Somewhere in a bureau drawer in the bungalow there was a square of paper. A man in peasant clothes had handed it up to Rodney as he was riding through the Little Bazaar a week before. The man had already dissolved in the press when Rodney glanced up from the note. It was in English, a large black script: "Post still open. *Please* come, at once. S." *Please* was underlined three times.

She had a nerve to pretend that the night of the Holi had never been. He was not going to answer it.

There was something the matter with the world. Away off to the east the 19th B.N.I. in Berhampore had refused to receive their percussion caps. They'd been disbanded and gone off peacefully to their homes, even cheering old General Hearsey. He was a fine old warhorse. But that was a terrible end for a fine regiment. It was impossible to persuade the men these Dum-Dum bullets were all right. Damn it, everyone ought to know better what went on inside other people's heads, muddled or not. Thank God the musketry had gone off all right here. A word from the Silver Guru, and all is well. God in heaven, who commands this regiment—Anderson or the Guru? Not Caversham, anyway.

He moved his head irritably so that a trickle of sweat ran down into his left eye. Of a sudden the buzzing of the flies infuriated him, and he yelled, "*Punkah wallah!* Wake up and do some work, God damn your eyes!"

He heard the slight noise of the boy awakening; overhead the ramshackle framework began to creak, and the hanging strip of cloth to swing. Dust showered down, with a faint hot draught.

He awoke to the sound of men laughing, and opened his eyes slowly. Abel Geoghegan was leaning back against the bar and laughing at him. Alan Torrance stood beside the veterinarian, a small grin on his face. The two men were dressed so fashionably as to be all but foppish—Torrance in tan trousers, a flowered green waistcoat, a single-breasted tan coat reaching nearly to his knees, and a huge black cravat polka-dotted in green; Geoghegan in black and white dog-tooth-check trousers, double-breasted grey frock coat, and thin yellow tie. Torrance's youth and floridly Byronic handsomeness suited the style to perfection; Geoghegan looked like a prosperous racecourse tout, an impression strongly reinforced by the hoarseness of his voice.

"See there, Torrance, me boy. Behold the Garrison Captain

of the Week, on duty! Now there's the way to success in this Bengal Army—and he with a mouth like a barmaid's arm-pits, I'll wager."

Rodney sat up. "Be quiet, you noisy bogtrotter. You're hellish early, aren't you?"

"It's nearly half-past four, y'know," said Torrance. "The ladies will be heah any minute. Mrs. Caversham made us promise to help at the swings."

"More fools you. Here, let's all have a drink. *Koi hai!*"

The world stretched and began to arouse itself. The building creaked, the leaves shook on the trees, bare feet padded in a distant nowhere. A spurt of energy throbbed in Rodney's muscles, and he swatted quickly at a fly.

Geoghegan shook his head. "It's no use, Rodney dear—but we've only fifty years here, at the most. Aha! an' I'm goin' back on leave next year. You can think of me a-sniffin' the Liffey smells—ah, the brewery of Mr. Guinness!" He wrinkled his nostrils. "Perhaps I'll not come back, too; no more dust, no more de Forrest—och, the man's no better than a snake with the piles the way he looks at me when I'm tellin' him a horse must be cast——"

Rodney said, "I'll wager you do come back."

"Sure, I'll have to come back. *You* know how 'twill be—unless me dear old great-aunt passes on. I can't afford to live at home in the style to which I accustom meself—no horses, no young lady of me own, me boy."

Rodney thought, I bet you'll long to be back here from the moment you reach Dublin. But why spoil the fun? In India the secret was to live a year, ten years hence, in some ecstatic future, and when that future came and was no ecstasy, but a dull present, to look forward again. No one lived their "now" properly, except perhaps Caroline Langford, and she was a visitor; certainly Rodney didn't himself.

Torrance said, continuing Rodney's line of thought, "For me, ten years, ten solid endless years."

"Oh, you're a chicken, me boy, and why should you be worryin'?"

"My flesh creeps when I think that in ten years—in eighteen *sixty*-seven—I shall still be heah, or in some Club exactleh like this, drinking brandeh on a May afternoon. Why, I shall be——"

"My age," said Rodney with a grim smile. "You won't feel quite decrepit, take my word for it. When you're twenty-one, ten years stretch away for ever in front of you, but when you're thirty-one they look like nothing at all behind you."

Geoghegan stroked his thin ginger hair, and his mobile Irish face assumed an exaggerated gravity.

"An' there's the Cardinal-Archbishop's last words." He grinned cheerfully, showing uneven tobacco-stained teeth. "But listen to this. Have ye heard the latest? 'Twill be *the* hot-weather campaign this year in Bhowani for sure."

He gathered their eyes with the infectious enthusiasm of the born raconteur and launched out. "Ye know old Mother Myers had the colic three, four months gone? Of course! Well perhaps ye didn't know she borrowed a bedpan, in private ye understand, from the hospital stock of our little assistant-surgeon man, John McCardle. It's a shamin' thing for a big fat lady like her to be a-thinkin', ye see, of everyone else a-thinkin' of her squattin' on a bedpan like a great grampus, now isn't it?"

"I wouldn't dream of imagining the circumstance," said Torrance, reddening.

"Wouldn't ye now? But plenty would, I'm tellin' ye. Well now, she recovers from the colic and forgets all about the blushful bedpan. A month later who should have a small go of the dysentery but Mrs. Nose-in-air Cummin', no less—an' *she's* so hoity-toity she doesn't want even our little John McCardle to know about it. So she sends her bearer over to borrow the bedpan direct from Mother Myers, which he does an', Mother Myers bein' out, just takes it, an' no one tells her it's gone, only later she hears where it is. Now me boys, d'ye see what a wonderful arrangement we have here to keep the ladies happy through the rest of the hot weather an' the rains?"

"I'm dashed if I do." Rodney watched the lizard as it
darted six inches up the wall and flicked out its tongue at
a fly.

"Well of course John McCardle is verra verra seeerious
an' Scawts, an' last week he wants his bedpan back so's he
can count it properly in his inventory. An' Mother Myers
says she hasn't it but she *hears* Mrs. Nose-in-air Cummin'
has stolen it away. An' wee John McCardle doesn't believe
her an' asks, very stiff, who gives *her* permission to lend *his*
bedpan away. An' Mrs. Cummin' hears of this an' becomes
in a tearin' panic for no reason at all, an' denies she ever
seen the blushful thing, an' sends her bearer out in a black
midnight to bury it under a bush at the bottom of her garden,
an' swears every one of her servants to secrecy with passin'
of money an' bloodcurdlin' threats."

From the gravelled front drive the clop of horses' hoofs
echoed through the Club. Women's voices rang clear and
high on the verandah, and a child's excited yipping. Torrance
shifted his feet uneasily; the set of his rather sulky face and
the pout of his full lips showed his resentment of Geoghegan's earthy gusto.

Geoghegan mopped his brow with a large linen handkerchief. "Here come the petticoats. We'll have to be goin' to
our duty, Torrance, me boy. Now don't ask me how I come
to hear about the bedpan hurroosh——"

He winked; Rodney remembered with distaste that the
brown fifteen-year-old girl who lived in Geoghegan's compound was said to be the daughter of the Cummings' butler.

"—but isn't it perfect? It's a feud ready-made-to-order,
it'll last for ever, an' already the ladies are gatherin' their
forces. They've even forgotten about Dotty van Steengaard's
breech, an' the poor filly's expectin' any moment now. Ye
see, the married women all know about the bedpan but they
don't have to tell their husbands because it's on the dis-
gustin' side—and that's perfect too, because the menfolk
might settle it in three minutes. *But*—an' this is the cream
of it—every man will be in one camp or the other, dependin'

on what invitations he accepts in the next two, three weeks, an' he'll not be knowin' a thing! It's *all* perfect! Now don't breathe a word. I haven't told a soul but you two, so sit back and watch the ladies get to work. Come on, Torrance, me boy!"

He smacked his lips over the last of his brandy and walked out, chuckling, Torrance smiling self-consciously at his side. Rodney swished the liquor round in his glass and shook his head. It was funny, but it was tragic too, for he knew that Geoghegan was right. The ladies of Bhowani would worry at the ridiculous incident for months, and be secretively happy, like dogs with a hidden bone. It would be the most important event of their year, the candle which would long hence light the memory of 1857.

The fatigue party should have finished their work by now. He put on his shako and narrowed his eyes against the glare. The sepoys were waiting to be dismissed, standing and squatting in the same loose group under the same trees where they had been when he first saw them. Godse called them to attention; they stiffened. Rodney gestured in salute and moved in under the shade.

"Stand at ease. Thank you, Jemadar-sahib. It seems to have been well done." He glanced round. "Tell them I said so, please."

The irregular succession of carriages swept round the curve of the drive. Godse gave a curt command to fall in. As the sepoys stood in the ranks Rodney looked closely at their dark wet faces and saw that their eyes followed the carriages and the children. Their expressions were unusually taut still, but he knew they loved children and they loved a party, and to have the two together would be bliss.

On an impulse he said, "Jemadar-sahib, any men who want to stay and watch the party may do so—but they must keep out of sight, round the end of the lawn here. March off the rest, please."

They shuffled their feet, and Rodney repeated the permission, adding with a smile, "Come on, my sons. There'll be some toys left over for your children." Several men moved to leave the ranks then, but others were as anxious to dissuade them. Jemadar Godse compressed his lips and said nothing. Naik Parasiya, bursting out with an odd suppressed passion, urged them all to come back to the lines because here they would only get in the sahibs' way. In the end four or five fell out; the rest marched off at the superquick step of a Rifle regiment, their white trousers jerking away left-right into the fading heat, their knees always a little bent in the Indian manner.

Rodney turned and heard the carpenter's whine at his back. "Your Majesty, Your Highness, you are my father and my mother . . ."

"What is it, Piroo?"

"Your Honour is a mighty hunter. Would Your Honour be graciously pleased to come and shoot a tiger out at Devra tonight?"

The words were set in the form that custom demanded, but the tone of voice carried an urgency and, more than that, almost a rasp of command.

Rodney stared at the wrinkled gnome. "How do you know there's a tiger near Devra? Oh, of course, you own land there, don't you? But tonight? I can't possibly. Next time he kills I'd like to, Piroo."

"Come tonight!"

Piroo spoke harshly, using neither honorific titles nor polite forms. In all the years Rodney had known him it was the first time there had been no grovelling abasement in his voice. He blinked in astonished anger. "It's impossible. Dismiss!" He nodded curtly and walked away from Piroo towards the carriage porch.

There, at the head of the steps, the members of the ladies' reception committee were receiving the station, greeting with marmoreal formality people they had seen nearly every day for years past and would see every day for years to come. Mrs. Bulstrode wore russet brown, and the rims of her eyes were as usual a little red. Mrs. Caversham glittered in an electric blue which emphasized the bony angles of her body; as usual her lips were pursed, and as usual she looked like a soured schoolmistress. Victoria de Forrest stood with them, by right of being her father's housekeeper. A virginal white dress accentuated the overblown ripeness of her figure. The gossip about her affair with Eddie Hedges was growing virulent, and she held her head up defiantly. All three wore poke bonnets, and lace quilling framed their faces with varied effect. Mrs. Bulstrode fiddled nervously at a brown silk reticule.

As Rodney approached, Captain and Mrs. Ernest Cumming of the 88th stepped out of their victoria and slowly ascended the steps. They were a nice, rather shy pair, he thought, who were turned in on each other by their childlessness—but she *did* carry her nose in the air, now that he looked at it. Perhaps she did it because her husband couldn't ride a horse like a gentleman; perhaps, if he had been a superb horseman, she would not have acted so foolishly in the matter of the bedpan.

Strange currents stirred the reception committee. Mrs. Caversham froze and stared gelidly at the Cummings as though they were little children detected making a mess in the corner of the classroom. Mrs. Bulstrode scurried forward, stammering an involved and overly warm greeting. Victoria de Forrest opened and shut her mouth, like a voluptuous cod stunned and thrown on the floorboards of a boat. Rodney smiled wryly. By God, Geoghegan had been speaking the unvarnished truth for once; already the sides were drawn up for the Battle of the Bedpan.

The six-year-old Atkinson twins, Tom and Prissy, rushed up and seized his arms. "Uncle Rodney, Uncle Rodney, when's Robin coming? We want to play with Robin."

Their eagerness cheered him; he was not related to them, but in India all English children called all English grownups Uncle or Aunt. They had adopted Robin as a wonderful new kind of animated doll. Rodney laughed down at them.

"He'll be here soon. Let's go to the swings; that's where he'll come."

"Ooh! Did you put up the swings, Uncle?"

"The sepoys did, Prissy. I—er—told them what to do."

They pulled him through the scattered groups forming on the grass. Two-Bottle Tom was there, shiny white of skin, atremble and ill, walking a little behind the matronly bulk of his wife. Mother Myers, flushed with pride, hung on her son's arm and plainly wished he could have been in uniform, like Rodney. At the swings Rodney handed the twins over to Geoghegan and flopped in a chair to watch. Rachel Myers was here too. She stared alternately at Torrance and Geoghegan, and each stare was loaded with soul-force. Only an expert could tell that Torrance basked in ethereal admiration, while Geoghegan wallowed in a bath of mercy and pity. The veterinarian was not an expert; from time to time he glanced nervously at the girl and secretly fingered his clothes to see whether he had left any buttons undone.

The children swung and shouted, and Rodney drooped. Where did that fearful enthusiasm come from? Where along the road from childhood did it vanish? Or did it trickle away all the time, unnoticed, until one day you found you didn't care a damn about anything? Was it a childish thing to thrill to the ripple of a galloping horse? He licked his lips; he'd like a drink.

The carriages rolled to a stop under the porch. Each woman, with the billows of her crinoline, occupied a seat wide enough for three, while her husband and children huddled opposite. The committee greeted them, and then they came out on to the grass, and when they were close it could be seen that their faces were wet and their hands damp and their dresses already a little crumpled. For a minute or two the children would walk primly beside the parents. As the grown-ups stopped to gossip, the children broke free and ran among the flowerbeds, yelling to each other in Hindustani and English, until their shrill clamour invaded every corner of the lawn. No one could tell boys and girls below six apart, unless he knew them, because all wore white dresses and several petticoats, and all had long curls flowing over their shoulders. The bigger girls looked like dolls which might have been made by women of another generation, for they were dressed in the adult fashions of twenty years before; their skirts were shorter and less full than the modern crinolines, and showed their pantalettes beneath.

The bigger boys glowered sullenly as "Aunts" exclaimed over their finery. Peter Peckham, aged seven, wore elastic-sided brown boots, cotton stockings barrel-striped in blue and green, full-hipped tartan trousers ending an inch below the knee, a plaid gingham blouse, and a tam o' shanter with a cockerel's feather; he clutched his mother's hand and frowned ferociously at the grass. Master William Osbert Ransome-Frome, ten, wore a sailor suit and a ribboned straw hat. Master Timothy Osbert Ransome-Frome, eight, wore stockings and kilt of the sickly Dress Stewart tartan, and full Highland trappings, and Rodney found time to wish that the Queen had never heard of Balmoral. Albert Bulstrode, nine, wore a blue Dutch boy's costume; its high-crowned maroon velvet cap, with short peak and long tassel, clashed in anguish with his ginger hair and freckled face.

Joanna came at last and brought Robin down to the swings. She swished off again immediately, saying she had promised to play croquet with the Commissioner. The twins pounced on Robin and brought him dolls. True to his age, he left the dolls and became very busy about the task of moving every twig on the lawn six inches from where it had been before, talking to himself as he worked.

Rodney watched, absorbed; he'd give anything to know, to understand, what went on inside all those small heads. The place swarmed with children; one never appreciated how many there were in Bhowani until they all came together at a party like this. The voices of scolding mothers rose shriller and more often. The Club servants came out carrying trays loaded with glasses of boiled milk, cakes, and mangoes. He saw by the groupings of the women that many men must already have slipped away to the bar.

Lady Isobel put her hand lightly on his sleeve. "Rodney, you go and enjoy yourself. I'll keep an eye on Robin for a while." He thanked her with a smile and worked his way over to the croquet pitch.

A mixed foursome—he thought he'd never seen one quite so mixed—moved slowly from hoop to hoop, tapping in succession at the coloured croquet balls. Joanna and Mr. Dellamain were playing against Mrs. Hatch and Swithin de Forrest. Dellamain played well, with only a small part of his attention on the game. The fingers of his left hand hovered always at the brim of his tall hat, ready to lift it an inch or two in gracious recognition of the salutations due to him. His glance flickered across Rodney's face, and Rodney saluted. The grey hat rose, the full lips smiled, the eyes were sad and worried.

Joanna made a deft shot, and Rodney joined in the applause while she stood in a pretty attitude, resting both hands on the shaft of her mallet. Mrs. Myers rolled by, making a heavy bow; Joanna contrived to smile at Mr. Dellamain and simultaneously to rake Mrs. Myers with an icy stare. Rodney glowered as he followed the players to the next hoop. If he had to take sides in the bedpan battle he would prefer to be in Mother Myers' camp. Swithin de Forrest played an expressionless and fairly efficient game, speaking seldom and then only to give his partner, Mrs. Hatch, a word of cold advice. Rodney saw that Joanna was behaving as if Amelia Hatch had no part in this game, was not in Bhowani, did not exist; she was boiling with bewildered secret pique that Dellamain had invited a sergeant-major's wife to play with them; she hadn't learned yet even how to condescend graciously.

"Mrs. Hatch presents an unusual spectacle, does she not?"

That was Caroline Langford's voice, strangely stilted, from just behind him. At a party ten days ago she had tried to talk to him about Kishanpur; but there was nothing to say. He had known she wasn't satisfied then, and here she was again. She'd bring up the old subject unless he could stop her. He said, "She does."

He would not turn round; he would concentrate on Mrs. Hatch and the problem she represented. Each Native Regiment had, besides its British Officers, one British sergeant-major and one quartermaster-sergeant. They were the only Englishmen here not of commissioned rank and so, by definition, not of the upper classes. And of the six of them in Bhowani only Tom Hatch of the 88th had married a white woman; the rest kept Indian girls. Work kept Hatch busy, while Amelia had nothing to do but sip gin and fume over the wasteful incompetence of Indian servants. She'd never had servants before, and knew she could do the work better herself if she were allowed. She hated alike the loneliness of her bungalow and the condescension shown to her at such parties as this. She longed to gossip, and cut a fine figure, yet sometimes weeks passed without her talking to another Englishwoman. The gawky half-grown Hatch children were rolling their hoops apart from the rest even now, though Lady Isobel was trying to bring them into the games, and their clothes were as clean and smart as anyone's.

Mrs. Hatch had spared no effort in her determination to dress up to the officers' ladies. Her snub-nosed cockney face glowed brick-red above a maroon pelisse of frilled cashmere. Her crinoline dress was made of lilac satin and was monstrously skirted. A tiny poke bonnet of lilac satin, profusely decorated with artificial flowers, was held on the back of her head by a broad maroon ribbon tying under her chin. Wisps of hennaed hair, grey-brown at the roots, straggled over her ears and forehead, and under the bonnet half of her bun had worked loose. Large black buttoned boots thrust out from underneath her dress. Even where he stood Rodney caught the gin on her breath; that explained how she was managing to enjoy herself.

She moved erratically from hoop to hoop, flushing, giggling, curtseying frequently to de Forrest and Dellamain, eyeing

Joanna ferociously, and swearing under her breath. He grinned suddenly to see her play off Joanna's own trick against her. While simpering at de Forrest, she managed to say in a voice of boreal hauteur, "Ai don't know, Ai'm sure, wot the position in ehr contest is, Mrs. Sevvidge."

It was no good; Caroline still stood there behind his shoulder. He had nothing to say to her. He would not face her. She said in a voice pitched so that anyone nearby could hear, "I am leaving Bhowani on Tuesday, Captain Savage."

He turned in surprise and looked at her. He didn't see why she wanted to go rushing off suddenly. If only she'd relax she could be a wonderful person to talk to. He said, "I'm sorry to hear that."

Lightning flashed behind her eyes and died. She said, "You are not!—I apologize. I believe you are."

A small hand tugged at his tunic, and he glanced down. Robin, bored with playing, had come to find him and stood now with his face shyly pressed against Rodney's trousers. Rodney put down his hands and caressed the boy's shoulders.

Caroline said, "If I have made any trouble for you, I am sorry. Perhaps it's all over now, as Colonel Bulstrode said. But I'm running away, really—which is stupid, because I cannot escape from myself."

He smiled, trying to bring out some lightness in her. It was difficult to smile though, because she was very slight, and very hurt; and because he was wondering if she could find in the whole world any place, any way of life, where she could fulfil herself; and because he did not think she could until she learned to laugh. She was so much his opposite that way. He could make her smile if he had the time—it didn't matter now, because she was going.

And that was just as well. Really, she'd been nothing but a damned nuisance. A man couldn't survive here without his blinkers and she kept tearing them off.

Joanna came up, her game finished. Pretending not to see Caroline, she stooped over Robin and cooed baby words into his ear. Caroline's deep eyes glowed with the strangest grey fire as she looked down at them. Instinctively Rodney tightened his grip on his son's shoulders and bent his brows on the girl. She turned and left them standing there.

He swore silently and went up into the Club and through to the bar. It was full of men snatching a quick one before returning to their duties as husbands and fathers. On this special occasion, as on Christmas Day, the sergeants were allowed into the Club; they were all here, and the officers of their regiments were standing them drinks. Tom Hatch's pleasant square face beamed shyly round; he was half drunk. Rodney called for a brandy and retired into a less crowded corner.

A hand clapped him on the shoulder and he looked up angrily. It was Major Anderson. "Well, Savage. You see, the musketry went off all right, didn't it?"

"Thanks to the Silver Guru, sir." He eyed the Major's face, a few inches from his own. "I spoke to my company beforehand, reminded them how long we'd known each other—was it likely that I or any of us was going to try to destroy their religion?—asked them to trust me. But I found out afterwards they'd asked the Silver Guru, too."

"Insolence! And what did he say?"

"He told them to obey orders—pointed out that if the rumours were true there would certainly have to be justice and absolution." Rodney swirled the brandy around in his glass and averted his face; Anderson's breath smelled sour. That affair, the Silver Guru's intervention, was incongruous; but the man could hardly be expected to discard half a lifetime's role as a religious oracle just because one or two people knew he was an Englishman and a part-time political intriguer. Angry again, Rodney looked up and said deliberately, "It wasn't necessary, anyway." That was what really annoyed him. The musketry could so easily have been put off until the air cleared. There was no need to bite the cartridges, because they could be torn open by hand; the movement was already out of the drill book.

Anderson wagged a finger in his face. "It *was* necessary, boy. You'll learn. Give in in one place and you'll never be able to stop. I was glad I was there to make you. So will you be—one day."

He sidled away through the crowd, and Rodney returned to his drink. Fragments of conversation floated into his ears. "The Derby? Tournament—fours. Gleesinger a thousand to fifteen, Blink Bonny twenty, but you'd throw your money away on a filly." "Our lines are a *disgrace*. They're not fit for pigs to live in, let alone sepoys of the Company. Why doesn't . . . ?" "We're going to Simla nex' year. Mrs. Sculley insists, and 'oo is Thos Jos to contradict?" "I assure you, Hedges, I wouldn't serve with Queen's troops if they paid me double. Five-and-twenty years I've been out here, and I assure you Johnny Sepoy is . . ." "No trouble at all. Except a couple of fools in Number Four. Curry B. clapped 'em in the quarter guard. Court martial Tuesday. What? No, no nothing to do with the grease as far as I know. These two just refused to accept their percussion caps yesterday morning. Have a drink." "A bedpan? There's no need to whisper about it, I fear. You're lucky, sir. *My* wife picked someone else's flowers once, and great heavens . . ." "If Janki Upadhya is the next senior naik, then he *must* be promoted. Rheumatism's got nothing to do with it. There's no way round the regulation, and a dashed good thing too."

Rodney, moodily gulping his brandy, glanced up and intercepted an odd look of sympathy in Willie van Steengaard's eye. Willie! *His* wife was due to have a baby any moment. Didn't he have troubles enough of his own? Rodney scowled at his friend, set the glass down with a crash, and elbowed out of the room.

The conjurer was near the end of his show. His ingratiating voice rattled on in Hindustani and broken English. The children looked peaked and pale; how could the poor little devils pick up stamina in this filthy climate, on this disgusting food? The conjurer waved his hand, and three pigeons flew out of his turban. Some children squealed, some cried fractiously, most stared glumly at the pigeons, now sitting in a row on a branch.

Robin said very clearly, "Pigeon going do *maila* man's head."

The pigeon did. The audience dissolved in near-hysterical laughter, and there were tears and threats of thrashings. The flocks of ayahs waddled round the corner of the Club, quacking stridently. "*Sarhe chhe, baba, ghusl, nini, sab hogya, baba.*" Half-past six, baby, bathtime, bedtime, all finished, baby.

Robin was lead away, monotonously chanting, "Pigeon do did *maila* man's head." Rodney followed them to the victoria; he'd call for Boomerang in a minute and ride after them. He glanced up and thought they were in for a dust storm, for the sky had turned dark and the leaves were very still. Joanna came, to tell him that she wanted to stay and talk with Mrs. Cumming about a sewing bee next Wednesday, and would he leave the carriage for her. Ayah could wait too. That was fine; Rodney would take Robin back on his saddle-bow.

The Atkinson twins and little Ursula Herrold found the four sepoys who had stayed to watch the party, and danced round them hand in hand, begging pickaback rides in a last desperate ruse to escape from their ayahs. Naik Parasiya had returned for some reason, and watched with a tortured face and pinched nostrils. Rodney thought of ordering the man to report sick, he looked so ill.

But suddenly he was stiff and tired and did not care. Everyone had enjoyed himself after his own fashion, and it was time to go home. The excitement of the Kishanpur affair had not died with the meeting at Dellamain's, as Rodney had persuaded himself it would; as long as Caroline Langford was here he half-expected some new vivid mystery. She was the thread running through it all—even in his weeks in Kishanpur he had been trying to prove to himself that she was wrong; so she had been a presence looking over his shoulder all the time, staring down even into

Sumitra's gaping face to see if there was murder there.
He had seen her for the last time now, and the thread
was broken.

He hefted Robin on to the front arch of Boomerang's
saddle and swung up behind him. Crooking his right arm
round his son, he felt the thin shoulders wriggle ecstatically.
This was the joy that is perfect because it has no memories.
This child, this joy, was two; and he was thirty-one. Time to
go home, time to relax and let age come, time to sink into
the secure infinity of cold weathers, hot weathers, rains, as
the sun was sinking into the hills of Lalkot. But the sun
would rise again and make a million bright mornings. The
weight of the unseen years settled briefly on him, and he
shivered.

# 16

*THE SUN sank as a dark red disc from which ragged
pennants of green, gold, blue, and saffron trailed
across the lower sky. The glow died out of the dusty
heat haze, leaving the air dead. The dust storm passed by
to the south, but the threat of it made the twilight black and
electric. Then the word passed. It was not even yet an exact
word, but a curse and a warning:* This is the night. *The word
ran across the plains, leaped wide rivers, and raced through
the jungles as a fire races under dry leaves. A woman tapped
on a city wall and whispered it to her neighbour. One man
cried it to another as their bullock carts passed in the fields.
It set out at sunset from every place where sepoys were
stationed; it travelled in every direction; and before the
morning of Sunday, May 10, 1857, it had crossed and re-
crossed itself many times. People hurried home when they
heard it, or bolted their doors, and waited. They did not*

*know who was threatened this night, but it might be they.
Some prayed; some shrugged; few went abroad.*

*Shivarao Bholkar, Dewan of Kishanpur, held the queen of
spades in his hand, but revoked by playing the king of
diamonds. Suddenly he said, "I can't play any more. This
is the night." Prithvi Chand grinned and said, "Night for
what, Excellence?" and began to sing softly that Pathan
love song which is called "The Wounded Heart" and whose
words begin:* There's a boy across the river with a bottom
like a peach. . . . *The Dewan threw the cards in his face,
and he stopped singing. The Dewan jumped to his feet, stood
near the light, and stared down into Prithvi's face, saying,
"This is the night. Do you mean you never knew? We've
succeeded better than we hoped. I'll tell you. Tonight
the English are going to die, all of them. The sepoys are
going to mutiny and kill them. Tomorrow the name Kishanpur will mean again something it used to mean—something
India's forgotten, yes, even you've forgotten. No one will
sneer behind my back after tonight. Perhaps I won't stay
awake at night. Perhaps I won't think of my mother every
minute of every night. I've prayed for this, and now—God,
I want to be able to sleep." Prithvi Chand's fat face quivered,
and the puzzled expression dissolved from it. He began to
shake all over and said in a cramped voice, "All of them?
The women and children? Captain Savage? Murdered in the
dark? Oh, India! India!" The Dewan said, "Tonight, I know
what you feel like. Tomorrow, I won't." He walked slowly
out of the room; Prithvi Chand bowed his head over the
scattered cards and began to weep.*

*The Silver Guru waited until he could no longer see the
steps at the edge of the river, close to his left hand. No crowd
was gathered under his peepul, and the Pike was deserted,
north and south. The air was so still and the land so hushed
that he could hear the Cavershams and their guests singing
"Drink to Me Only with Thine Eyes" in the cantonments
up the road. He rose, picked up his bowl, and strode due*

*east across the fields, looking to neither the right nor the
left.*

*Piroo the carpenter lit a lamp in his tiny hut. He moved
with purpose and twice glanced out of the only window, a
grimy square of glass in the back wall. He took off the old
green trousers and tied on a dirty loincloth. His legs were
long for his height, and very thin. He tucked a black silk
kerchief, nearly three feet square, inside the loincloth so
that only an inch at one corner showed. He pulled a wooden
box out from under the string bed, unlocked it, and extracted
a small pickaxe, oiled and bright-clean, with a light straight
two-foot helve. He put his hand on the bolt of the door
and in that instant cringed and became another man—the
man the sepoys knew and never noticed. This man opened
the door and shuffled across the square, across the Pike,
and on due east across the fields, looking to neither the right
nor the left.*

*At ten o'clock the word came to Mehnat Ram, once a
subadar-major of Bengal Native Infantry, now retired. He
was ninety-three years old, and lay on a cot in the front
room of his house by the road from Bhowani to Kishanpur.
His skin was brown, shiny, and paper-thin, and knots stood
out at every joint; he was naked except for a pair of cotton
drawers. A man, late in from the city, ran by and whispered
the word to the old man's granddaughter. She was fifty, and
lived here with her husband, tilling the land she hoped to
inherit. The subadar-major heard too, for he was not asleep.
He lay awhile trying to think, but always after ten or fifteen
seconds his thoughts would go off on a foolish tangent—his
cows . . . seed for the winter sowing . . . oil for his pyre . . .
the handful of parched lentils he'd shared with the little
Ensign-sahib by the breach at Turkhipura. What a night that
was! Couldn't remember the Ensign's name—Eshmit,
Eshmoot, Eshmyte, something like that. This is the night.
He got up and fumbled into his old scarlet uniform coat;
the trousers had long since rotted away, but his white drawers
would have to do; no boots either—slippers with turned-up*

*toes. His sword hung on the wall below a steel engraving of
Lord Lake. One of the sahibs in the regiment had given it to
him when he retired—a tall thin sahib. Couldn't remember
his name. This is the night, serious work afoot. . . . The black
calf, something wrong with its near fore—bitten by a jackal?
By the gods, he couldn't help that now; they'd want someone to guard the barrack stores and perhaps the women and
children while the sahibs led the young sepoys off. No one
would care about his low caste at a time like this. . . . Priests,
money to the priests or they'd never burn him properly. He
pushed off his granddaughter's arm. "Fool girl, stay here
with that other woman you call your husband, and guard
my estate. Man's work afoot tonight!" He hurried west
across the dark fields towards Bhowani. Might be Lalkot
cavalry vedettes on the road, or those dogs from Kishanpur
—high time they were all wiped out. He knew the fields as
he knew his veined hand; he felt fine. . . . Sholingur, Bhurtpore, the frowning might of Gwalior ahead, Lord Lake;
Cuddalore, and the dark 24th and the white English soldiers,
storming shoulder to shoulder—young blood, rivers of fire,
the glacis' slope and the rockets' glare.*

*The word passed through the lines of the regiments. It had
started there, but few knew that—except, in each company
and squadron, one or two knew. The sepoys gathered in
barrack rooms where the lights were out or dimmed and
the windows covered by sacking. No air moved, and the
night temperature was 105. They strained sweating against
one another and whispered, "What's happening? What's
happening?" The fear and the heat melted the barriers of
rank. In the dark ovens they did not always recognize who
it was that talked and took the lead, but in each gathering
one man did—among others, Jemadar Pir Baksh of the
60th and Naik Parasiya of the 13th. The speaker's voice was
always taut and urgent; the hearers were afraid already and
became terrified. The voice said, "This is the night. Shiva—
or Allah—has promised destruction, and this is the night.
The Silver Guru said, 'Until God's promised destruction*

*strikes the wicked.' Who are the wicked? We are the wicked because we have not defended our gods. The English have hanged Brahmins, stripped our princes, attacked our gods in their temples—and we have done nothing. We have helped them. Now they are going to kill us. They do not need us any more. They are going to kill us, for only we can protect the old gods they despise. We've whispered it and warned you, and you would not believe. Now they've started—yes, yes, they've started, haven't you heard? They disarmed our brothers at Gondwara last night and blew them to pieces with the guns, and the English soldiers shot them down. That is why the word is out. The guns are coming up the Pike now, and the English soldiers, coming up for us." The hearers jostled and muttered to each other, "I'm going mad in this heat. I can't believe it. Gosse-sahib? Savage-sahib? Caversham-sahib? Going to kill us!" "It's true, I tell you. Step by step they've trodden us down. They will make us sail the Black Water, they will take away all our old rights as they took away the field allowances. You must believe or you will die, all of us die, die defiled. Remember Mangal Pande. They lied; we know the cartridges are greased with defilement; we know. They killed Mangal Pande and hunted his comrades down. They have two of our brothers in the Eighty-eighth's guardroom now. They will kill them when the guns come, and scatter us in the fields and murder us with the guns. Can't you read the messages? Kill or be killed. Do you want to die sewn up in a pigskin, and spat upon? Kill or be killed. The guns are coming up the Pike now, galloping all night. Can't you read the messages? A chupatti in five parts, signifying the fifth month. A chupatti in ten parts, for the tenth day. Flesh, white-skinned on one side, raw on the other—a big piece for a sahib, a smaller piece for a memsahib, and a little piece for a child. On May tenth kill all the white skins—or they kill us!" . . . I'll die, lower than a sweeper, defiled, hopeless for eternity. I've been in here for hours and I'm going mad. I sweat and tremble, and a hundred eyes roll, and we gnash our teeth. The guns are galloping up the Pike. Out of here, get out of here, for any sake get out!* "We are the masters. Remember the snows in Afghanistan and the way we died, though they led us. Remember Chillianwallah. They are not gods. Get them together. We will burn the court to get them out, and kill them there. Kill the others in their bungalows. Kill the sahibs you do not know, that pity may not stay your hand. Pity—and die. Remember Mangal Pande. Haven't we wives and children? Who is not with us is against us. Arm yourselves. Run, run to the court. This way. Come with me; you to the court, you to this bungalow, you to that. Be silent and hurry. Remember Mangal Pande. That will be the sign, listen for it, wait for it—'Remember Mangal Pande!' "

Rodney awoke at midnight from a light sleep. The threatened dust storm had decided them to sleep inside the house. Beyond the open windows his garden lay breathless under a full moon. By the far wall the leaves on the two peepul trees stirred, and their shadow was a patterned carpet across lawn and flowerbeds. Inside the room each piece of furniture shimmered in the half-light.

Joanna lay beside him under the sheet. Her mouth was open, and her hair spread in a yellow aureole over the pillow. Her face glistened with sweat. The moonglow, reflected from the white walls and high ceiling, smoothed out the lines of self-pity drawn in her face, and softened the pout of her lips. He looked at a ghost, pale, ethereal, and remote from all human passions. The quick shallow intake of her breathing raised her breasts under the sheet. This was his wife for ever, Robin's mother, a woman asleep, and he did not love her.

He lowered his feet to the floor, found his slippers, and poured out a glass of cold water from the earthenware jar on the table. Robin might be awake; when the moon shone he sometimes lay in his cot and stared at the walls or out at the trees.

Rodney walked quietly along into the next room. Ayah was there, asleep on her bed, her head wrapped in the end of her sari. He stared at the shapeless white bundle; she wouldn't stir if the house took fire over her. He bent smiling over Robin's cot. The eyes came round, huge baby eyes still, and stared back briefly; then turned away and up at the ceiling, and the mouth smiled at a secret joke. His father kissed him, and he closed his eyes at once.

Rodney went back to the big room and slipped into bed. Sweat trickled down his back and between his thighs. The moon shone like a night sun—not clear and cold but thick and living. Robin had been good at the party. He'd never been to a big one before, and considering the rumpus he'd done very well not to get over-excited or throw a tantrum. He'd made a consul's triumph out of that homeward ride on the saddlebow, bouncing up and down, laughing, shouting in Hindustani to his friends the sepoys as they passed along the cantonment roads. The men usually gave him a grinning mock salute, and said *"Salaam, buddha sahib,"* but they hadn't this time. They'd been too busy stiffening into a real salute for Rodney. *Buddha*—"old." Sometimes the child did behave like a miniature patriarch; that was the pet name Rambir had given him when, as a baby, he used to wear such a puckered and care-worn frown.

Suddenly a sick emptiness of love ached in the pit of his stomach—for his son, who was two and had a halo round his ash curls; to keep the lights for ever in his hair and in his eyes, to have him live for ever, and for ever be a little boy riding his father's horse in the crook of his father's arm.

The sheet burned and he could not sleep. He lay still while his thoughts wandered. In the evening he had mentioned that Caroline Langford was leaving Bhowani. Joanna had said, "Of course. She's seen she can't get de Forrest, and she can't get you." When he asked her what she meant, she said, "Didn't you see her face when she was looking at you and Robin? She's a wicked, jealous woman."

He tried again to recall the girl's expression; it had been

strange, and frighteningly hurt—but not jealous, for God's
sake. He wondered suddenly about Caroline's body, her
thighs. Breathless, he turned over and held the sheet in both
hands. Christ, Christ, the sword was in his loins; was this
to be his punishment?

He looked out of the window. The garden sprawled in
the heat of the moon. Below Joanna's breathing he could
distinguish no other separate noise, and yet the night shuddered and a pulse of sound made the leaves tremble. He
closed his eyes.

Joanna. She was not perfect, but nor was he. He believed
there was an Eternal Witness, and tried to live as a man
should. She called him unstable and hairbrained, and cried
that he would never amount to anything. He'd never be the
sort of husband she had grown to want—nor she the wife.

Robin would have to go home in '60 or '61. Joanna's
mother had a room for him in the house outside Balham,
but he'd be all right in India for another three years, no
more; he looked pale. Joanna could take him up to Simla
next hot weather, or there was that new little place he'd
heard Max Bell mention—Almora; that would be much
cheaper. Then, if he borrowed more, or went on the staff,
he could take them both home when he went on furlough in
'60 and leave them there when he came back. Eighteen-
sixty. That would make thirteen years in India without a
break. His father had done forty-four and died here, burned
out. Forty-four years was too long. His father could have
taken furlough several times; perhaps forty-four years passed
in a flash when you were crusading as he had against the
Thugs. Perhaps you thought of nothing but the task in front
of you, and it concentrated you and kept a fire burning in
you, and you were happy. *Me Lords, Ladies, h'and Gennel-
men—Colonel William Savage, the Destroyer h'of Thuggee!
H'and 'is son, Captain Rodney Savage, the Meddler of Kishanpur!* He chuckled to himself.

He wanted to sleep. Long ago the Native Officers and
sepoys of his company had arranged an open-air party for

tomorrow, the tenth, and had invited him. Their caste laws forbade him to eat with them—they didn't even eat with each other for that matter—but he would come later, in time to watch the amateur juggling and listen to the stories. They'd smoke rolled-leaf cigarettes and hookahs, and talk about crops and cattle. All parties in the lines had a pleasant sameness, and he knew already that he would sit sedately on a hard chair at Subadar Narain's right hand and listen and nod. The sepoys would be full of chupattis and lentils, and content. Rambir, his batman, who had never hurt a fly, would tell again how he strangled the huge Sikh gunner at the battle of Chillianwallah, and everyone would laugh because they liked old jokes the best. Narain would talk about the Afghan War of '39 when he had been a mere three-striped havildar; about the snow in the northwestern passes in '42. He would relate what he had said to General Napier, what General Wellesley said to his father, how his grandfather lost an arm at Plassey fighting against the British. Plassey, June 23, 1757, where Clive established the foundations of an empire—and Jonathan Savage with him —almost exactly a hundred years ago.

By heaven it was hot, and no longer still. The night pulsed insistently. A reddish light wavered on the lawn . . .

. . . and the wavering of the walls. As to the shock of cold water his mind sprang up and the muscles at the corners of his eyes contracted. He stared intently across the room, then up at the ceiling cloth. On the ceiling, on the walls, on the floor, the unsteady light had a crimson tinge. Waves of red, pale and dark, moved across the bed and the hump of Joanna's body. The solid substance of the room crawled. For a moment longer he lay tensed, watching the broad bands writhe and coil. The moon had gone; crimson patterns were traced in a black sky.

He jumped out of bed, struggled into boots and trousers, and ran on to the verandah, a white shirt in his hand.

Outside, beyond the bulk of the peepul trees at the edge of the garden, men ran in the dust of the road. The throbbing separated out and he heard the distinct sounds: bare feet—pad-pad in the dust; boots—a heavier thud-thud-thud; metal—the clink and clash of steel on stone and steel on steel; horses' hoofs—running. They knew where they were going, running steadily through the murk, and made no other sound. No one shouted or coughed or called. The smell of burning tingled sudden and acrid in his nostrils.

Above intervening bungalows and trees the roof of the 88th's mess stood up in square silhouette against the shaking sky. Something beyond was on fire, in the direction of the courthouse and gaol.

The tautness in him relaxed. Everyone knew what to do about a fire, and he wondered how he had not heard the bugles and trumpets blowing the fire alarm. The 88th's quarter guard stood across the Pike opposite the court building. He must go; better go on foot; a horse would only be a nuisance at a fire. He ran back into the bedroom and shook Joanna. The watch on the bedside table showed half-past three—in the morning of Sunday, May 10, 1857. Joanna stirred heavily and sat up, mumbling, "Wha-what is it?"

"There's a big fire—the court, I think. I'll have to go."

"Are we safe here? Why d'you have go?"

"Yes, quite safe, and I'm Garrison Captain this week, you know that."

She spoke petulantly, still half asleep. "Well, hurry'n come back. Don't li' being lef' 'lone here at ni'—all these blacks. An' if Robin wakes, he'll be fr'n'd."

He snapped, "Pull the curtains in Robin's room. Wake Ayah and tell her what's happening. I must run."

At the door he glanced back, to see her face a shiny dark pink in the fireglow. He knew she wouldn't get out of bed. As he went she rubbed her eyes, frowned, and settled back on the pillow with a sigh.

Tongues of flame licked up from behind the mess and into the sky, and the bougainvillaea on his verandah was bathed in thin fire. The crackle and mutter echoed from wall and tree. He heard men's voices for the first time, shouting faint and far from every part of the cantonment and the city. To his right the hoofs of galloping horses rang metallic on the Deccan Pike. A scorching wind from the plains rattled the leaves and shook the flowers and blew on the back of his neck. The wind, the men, the horses, rushed in towards the fire.

The runners in the road had raised a dust so dense that he could not see more than five yards. They were mostly troopers of the 60th Light Cavalry, on foot, but some were men of the 88th B.N.I, and a few were of his own regiment. He wondered briefly how they came to be running this way —to the south—for the 13th's lines were down the Pike and beyond the fire. They all ran with tunics buttoned and shakos straight on their heads. They came out of the haze, the light glistened red-black on the sweat of their faces, and they were gone. They ran with knees lifted high, and they all carried weapons—rifles and bayonets, pistols, sabres, carbines. They did not turn their heads to look at him, but the starting eyeballs swivelled towards him and quickly away again. To right and left the officers' bungalows lay quiet, each in its small estate of trees and lawns. In some a light burned or a shadow moved across a screen.

The three buildings of the court group formed a hollow square on the other side of the Pike from the 88th's quarter guard. The court building itself was parallel to the Pike and set well back from it; the other two wings jutted forward at right angles from the ends of the court—the clerks' offices on the south, the gaol on the north. The offices were on fire from end to end. Flames rippled up the walls and whooshed through the skeletal roof. Ladders of sparks climbed into the sky. The smoke pillared and rolled slowly to the north. The air smelled sweet with the fragrance of wormeaten rafters and musty files. These were the Commissioner's records burning, the distilled labour of many men over many years, all the words that dead farmers had spoken, all the plans that dead officials had made.

The fire in the court was not so far advanced, but its windows glowed like tigers' eyes and smoke streamed out under the eaves. The gaol was untouched, and the firelight from the other buildings played over its bleak walls and barred windows; the prisoners must have been taken out already.

Here, west of the fire, Rodney saw the whole scene clearly. It reminded him of a pageant setting, torchlit and complete with excited spectators. For the sepoys were doing nothing to put the fire out, and many were not looking towards it. They surged together in thick eddies on the Pike and gabbled under their breaths. He swore when he noticed that here too they all had arms. No one had brought axe, pick, shovel, or crowbar—the tools they were supposed to carry to a fire. Some fool of a bugler must have blown the Alarm instead of the Fire Alarm; that had happened before, three years ago, and he grinned momentarily at the memory: eight hundred excited sepoys, armed to the teeth, gathered uselessly round a burning hayrick. They never allowed Bugler Birendra Nath to forget it, and still nicknamed him the Alarum-wallah.

The lamps on the verandah of the 88th's quarter guard were pinpricks of yellow light, diminished by the fire glare. The sepoys of the guard clustered in a loose group, armed and accoutred, and looked down at the crowd. The sentries stood passively at ease on their posts, one at each end, bayonets fixed. The jemadar in command walked back and forth, fingering his sword knot. A few other British Officers had come and were shouting orders, each one trying to get a grip on the part of the crowd nearest him. Nothing happened.

A hoarse bellowing drew Rodney's attention and he tried to see between and over the shakos. He saw a mottled face and unbuttoned scarlet tunic surging through the haze up the Pike. Below, the waler rolled its eyes, flung back its head, and fought to be free of the bit. The mutter in the crowd died to a shuffling whisper, and the fire crackled louder.

Bulstrode forced the horse on and called out to men of his 88th by name. Again Rodney smiled, for this was a familiar and dearly popular scene with officers and sepoys alike—the Curry Colonel exploding in purple apoplexy.

"Govindu Ram, get those men back behind the Pike and await orders. Rudra, take twenty and fetch buckets. Pyari Lall, form a cordon. Owl's pizzle! No! Out *there*! Where the devil's Mr. Dellamain? This is his fire."

He fixed his bloodshot eyes on Captain Bell. "Bell, order the quarter-guard bugler to sound the Stand Fast. Why hasn't that pig's arse of a jemadar had it done already?"

Men coagulated into groups under Native Officers and N.C.O.'s, but at once eddied back into the still-swelling mob. Order appeared in one place and vanished in another. Rodney had never seen sepoys behave so stupidly. They turned their heads this way and that, as if looking for somebody; their faces shone in the irregular glare, and were dark and frightened. They had become strangers, Hottentots, and there was no way of making contact with them. The last shreds of Colonel Bulstrode's temper broke. He trumpeted like a bull elephant and lashed their shoulders with his riding crop. Rodney pushed savagely at the men nearest him and yelled at them to get back across the Pike. It was useless, and for the first time in his life he struck a sepoy. He hit him in the face with his fist and the man did not notice, any more than the others noticed Bulstrode's whip.

There was something eerie about them—about the fire too. He looked at the court, by this time ablaze and drumming from end to end, and wondered suddenly if it could be arson. The smoke drifted away and laid a black canopy over cantonments, its under-surface crimson-lined.

He turned as another English voice shouted something from behind him, and saw Geoffrey Hatton-Dunn forcing slowly through the mob on a polo pony. Geoffrey swayed in the saddle as he came, and his hair fell in wet streaks across his forehead. A dirty dark blotch stained his shirt, and his monocle swung free on the end of its ribbon. He was babbling words, but Rodney could not make any sense of them. The sea of shakos nodded; above it the white shirt —stained at the back too—drew closer to Bulstrode's scarlet tunic.

Twenty yards away, the left-hand sentry of the quarter guard lifted his rifle. Every man of the crowd, the men with the scared and roving eyes, saw the movement—everyone except Hatton-Dunn and the bellowing colonel.

On the high verandah the sepoys of the guard watched their comrade. He held the rifle in the aim a moment, steadied the sights, and squeezed the trigger. His shoulder jerked back to the kick of discharge. The glare of the fire swallowed the orange flash. The powder smoke puffed back from the muzzle. A new blotch, lower and more central on the shirt, spread out across Geoffrey's stomach. His long body sagged forward on to the pony's withers, and his fair hair tangled in its mane. The sentry reloaded with quick calm movements. Rodney watched dully; the new cartridges —very efficient. The sentry aimed, steadied the sights, and squeezed the trigger. Rodney's legs would not move; no one could move; the men in the line of fire did not move.

Geoffrey fell head first into the crowd. Rodney saw his face as it went down. It tried to speak in death, but could not. The pony danced and screamed, and a hundred hands clawed up. They were dragging Geoffrey down—no, no, they were breaking the body's fall. He shook his head violently, and his heart pounded. The sepoys' mouths opened wide and stayed open, showing red inside down their throats. The crowd wail caught up and drowned the separate screams.

A vivid flash on the gaol roof forced his attention to it; that had taken fire at last. In the light from the burning offices opposite he saw faces pressed to the bars, and arms writhing through. The convicts had not been released after all. He turned back.

Colonel Bulstrode swung the waler on its haunches. He snatched up a cavalry sabre from the crowd, leaned forward, and rode at the sentry. Rodney found his head nodding in agreement. All this was detailed in orders; everyone knew what to do. George Bulstrode knew, and was doing it.

*When an armed native soldier runs amok, he will immediately be shot or cut down, without parley, lest others should suffer from his madness.*

The jemadar and those armed men on guard duty knew the orders too. But the mere presence of lunacy seemed to deprive the sanest Indian of his sense. It was infectious; beneath their stolid surfaces some of the others up there might be as overwrought as the sentry.

Bulstrode hurled the waler up the steps by main force. His bald head shone, and the muscles were knotted in his neck. The madman held his rifle up in both hands and did not try to defend himself. He cried, "Remember Mangal Pande! Remember! Remember!"

Bulstrode whirled back, the sabre-arm rigid. The seams burst at the back of his scarlet coat. The horse stumbled on the top step, and twenty stone smashed down behind the steel. Bulstrode followed the blade through, diving to the stone flags with a crash that shook the building. The sword's edge struck where the sentry's neck jutted from his high collar. His cries choked out in a whistling shriek. His head jumped off and up and out and twenty feet over the crowd. A fountain of blood spouted from his neck. The rifle clattered, the knees gave, the trunk folded and rolled over and over down the long steps.

Who was Mangal Pande? Rodney knew he'd heard the name recently—the sepoy of the 34th in Barrackpore who ran amok and murdered an officer, the case that was supposed to be something to do with the greased cartridges. And this poor devil of a sentry, brooding over it, had gone mad too. The guard here was behaving almost as badly as the 34th's guard that day, and there were two sepoys in the cells for refusing to accept their percussion caps. He looked anxiously about him and wished he could collect a bunch of his own 13th; then he'd be ready for whatever happened.

Bulstrode grabbed a pillar, dragged himself upright, and glared at the jemadar. The murmur in the crowd grew louder, the men swaying this way and that like tall crops in the wind. It was scalding hot, about 130 here in front of the fire. The fire—now suddenly it sprang to life. Flames poured through the gaol roof and roared up into the sky. All together, the convicts shrieked; Rodney remembered the writhing hands. He braced himself, shoved desperately through the crowd, and ran forward.

The heat from the fire beat at him, scorched his face, and charred his whiskers and eyebrows. The air burned in his lungs, and the smart of it wrinkled his eyes. He ran on, knowing that other men had joined him and ran blindly beside him with hands on his shoulders. He knew too that they were green-jacketed sepoys of the 13th who drove with him into the flames. He glanced quickly at them: Ramdass and Harisingh, the inseparables.

He searched along the wall for the keys. Sparks volleyed among the rafters, flame burst in his face, smoke choked him. He found the key ring on a nail near the far end, and knife-hurt hot to the touch. He jabbed key after key into the door of the cell nearest the court while Ramdass and Harisingh fought with the rusty bolts. At last a key fitted; the three leaned coughing against the door. It swung open, and five half-naked men stumbled out. Rodney ran on burning feet to the next cell, found the key quicker this time— four more convicts. Then the next . . .

Behind them the roof of the court building collapsed and sent a flat sea of flame roaring over them. For a second it bathed them, but they were at the last cell. No key fitted its door, but they beat insanely on the wood with their hands. The faces inside pressed against the grille and yowled. Ramdass put his rifle to the lock and blew it in. A score of tattered scarecrows fell out—murderers and dacoits, still manacled and dragging leg irons.

Out on the cool-seeming Pike, Rodney staggered into a Native Officer of cavalry, and recognized Pir Baksh. He gasped an order to collect the convicts again and guard them. Pir Baksh saluted and did nothing. Rodney's head swam. He croaked angrily, repeating the order. No one was listening to him. Jemadar Pir Baksh and all the men around stared down the Pike towards the 88th's quarter guard.

The beams of court and gaol exploded like volleys of cannon shot. The wind backed sharply and hurled a torrent of sparks and whole burning splinters of wood across the Pike. The bright shower flew over the crowd to settle on the roofs of the quarter guard and of the magazines and storehouses behind it. Not for thirty seconds could Rodney hear, under the other noises, the bang and rattle of rifle fire.

All the 88th were firing—the sepoys in the crowd and the sepoys on the guardroom verandah. Their scarlet coats stood out among the dark green of the 13th and the french grey of the 60th. He saw a naik shoot Colonel Bulstrode in the back. A spatter of shots struck Cornet Jimmy Waugh, and he knelt down and died. A scarlet octopus of arms pulled Max Bell off the verandah. The arms rose and fell, the bayonets flashed. Others fired in the air; all shouted an incoherent, crazy chant.

"Remember Mangal Pande! Mangal Pande! This is the night of the raw flesh. . . . Kill! The guns are coming. Kill them all! Kill or be hanged! Remember!"

He was right; the 88th had mutinied. He saw that nearly everyone round him wore the 13th's rifle green. His collar rasped his raw neck, but he shouted with relief. He called out to them by name.

"Manlall, Badri Narain, Thaman, Vishnu. To me! To me! The Eighty-eighth have mutinied. Thirteenth, to me!"

He thanked God they had brought their rifles after all. The fighting passion, like a river of fire, burned out his pain and weariness. His fierce pride of regiment sent him shouting and exalted above them—pride in the memories, pride of the stubborn shared endurance of Chillianwallah, pride of the meteor charges, side by side, into the icy dawns of the Punjab, pride of the men who followed him into the fire.

Together, in equal and matchless loyalty, they had for a
hundred years rolled like a flood over all enemies.

"Thirteenth Rifles, to me, to me!"

Their faces turned slowly towards him; they were the faces
of strangers, lost and blind-eyed. Their lips moved and their
fingers twitched on the triggers.

Beside him Alan Torrance whispered under his breath,
"They've gone mad. Lord Jesus, they've all gone mad."

The green strangers pressed closer. An inch from his ear,
a rifle exploded. The ball smashed into Torrance's appalled
face, blew off his nose, and ploughed up between his eyes,
into his forehead, and out at the top of his head. The Byronic
boy squirmed gobbling in the dust, and spouted blood and
brains. The strangers closed in. Feet stamped, bayonets
searched, the sounds faded. Insanely they tried to kill it,
but they could not altogether stop its whimpering.

Rodney's heart turned over and swelled and burst. His
pride drained out in a sweeping groan and left him empty.
He was sweating cold, and sick. That was Sepoy Shyamsingh there, his face twisted and his eyeballs glistening—
Shyamoo the quiet peasant, Shyamoo with the farmer's dry
humour, Shyamoo, who snarled like a dog and thrust his
bayonet into Alan's bowels.

Rodney felt no fear for himself. In that second there was
no room for anything but disgrace. He stood among them
and sank into a slimy lake of shame. All that he was had
failed. The English in India had failed England; the Bengal
Army had failed its faith, his regiment its glory; he had
failed these men; they, who were a part of him, had failed
themselves.

Robin. All the women and children alone in their bungalows. Joanna. He knew what Geoffrey Hatton-Dunn had
tried to say. He lifted up his arms and in disgrace and shame
and horror cried out in English, his voice breaking, "Stop
it! In the name of God, stop it!"

It was useless to cry for mercy or call them by name.
They were only more angry that he knew them, more intent

to kill, so that none who had seen this moment should live
to tell what he had seen. But he had to live, he had to rescue
Robin. Panic choked his throat. The dark faces closed in.

The night split apart and the fire darkened. A violet flash
leaped out and up to all horizons and the sky. Solid white-
hot air thudded against his eardrums and pressed him without pain into the dust. Long rocket streamers, vivid sparkling
scarlet, streaked up into the smoke clouds. A noise began
and roared and quaked without cease, and the earth shuddered. Bricks and stones crashed among the crowd. Bulky
shapeless things droned overhead and splintered distant trees.
The upper half of a sepoy's scarlet-coated torso squelched
by his side and skidded away towards the gaol. The magazine had exploded.

*Tom and Prissy Atkinson awoke with a start, together.
Tom's voice trembled. "Ayah, kya hogya?" Big dark
shadows moved about their room, and Mummy had gone
to help the stork who was bringing Auntie Dotty a new
baby. There were bangs and flashes outside, and big ugly
things in the room, smudged and vague through the mosquito net, and Ayah didn't answer. Prissy began to whimper:
the bogey man had come to get her, the bogey man with
the purple face and the black hat and the steel claws. She
screamed in a hiccuping crescendo, rhythmic, hysterical.
The mosquito net ripped.*

*Victoria de Forrest lay awake, naked and uncovered, on
her bed. A drowsy tenderness made her face lovely, and she
touched her skin with the tips of her fingers, and her tongue
moved. Eddie Hedges, asleep and naked, lay with his back
against hers, and his lips, which she could not see, curled
in a thin sneer. She looked at the shape of his head in the
darkness. His clothes were scattered in an untidy heap on the
floor. Her father would never come in, but perhaps Eddie
had better get back—there seemed to be a fire somewhere,
and a disturbing, whispering noise. He must marry her, she
loved him so; but he said his debts were so great, and he*

*was so keen on his work. He'd be famous, and the old sticks who had such a down on him would be jealous. No one knew him as well as she did. She'd wait; this was worth all the world and all the sneers—this. She stirred and felt the warmth of fruition, here, and here, and here. She didn't care. He'd have to marry her if it was true, and she knew in her womb that it was. She'd be the best wife in the world, for him; and she'd look after him; and he'd settle down and never want to roam any more. . . . The noise came suddenly close, right outside, there on the verandah, shots and shouts. Armed men burst in and fired before she could move hand or foot. Eddie was sitting up, naked, the sneer hard on his face. He fell back, and she fell across him. One sepoy turned them over with his bayonet; another spat on the floor and said, "Harlot! But he was like a good wild hawk, wasn't he?"*

*Major Anderson, second-in-command of the 13th Rifles, was a bachelor and lived alone. When something awakened him he sat up, pulled the mosquito net aside, and pushed his head out. He fumbled in the dark for the matches, snarling, "What the hell's all this row? Who are you? What's the matter?" He struck a match. Eyes glinted in the sudden light, and he saw ghostly grey and silver uniforms. A trooper raised his carbine and stepped forward. The breath choked in his throat. He was alone, and his heart cried out,* Not me, not me. You can't! *The match burned his fingers. Alone with a tiny light, alone among crowds, alone in the grave, alone for ever in the whistling desert of eternity. He loved no man or woman or child. The match went out, and the trooper fired.*

*Moti, the Savages' ayah, had not slept. The word passed at dusk, and she lay trembling, her head wrapped in her sari. She heard Rodney come in and look at her.* This is the night. *She didn't want to die. The gods had found out that she mixed the ergot to give Savage-memsahib a miscarriage last year. They'd told the sahib. It was wicked, and the gods would kill her now, or the sahib would. The dark-*

*ness quaked, and her teeth rattled. In her village there were vengeful spirits and ghosts and hobgoblins. The sahib didn't kill her that time. He'd come to make sure she was there to be killed as soon as he was ready. When the fireglow lit the room she rose silently and scurried out of the house. In the fields she turned south and stumbled towards the city. She'd stay with the corn chandler's wife. If it was all right tomorrow, she'd come back. She'd tell the memsahib she'd had an attack of malaria and lost her memory.*

*Lady Isobel Hatton-Dunn clenched her hands until the nails cut her palm, and lay still with eyes closed. She screamed continuously, but not too loudly. She and Priscilla Atkinson had come straight from the party to the van Steengaards', to await the arrival of Dotty's baby.* Almighty and most merciful God, give me strength and mercy. *It was dark, and Priscilla lay in the corner, crumpled, half-naked, raped, and dead. Assistant-Surgeon Herrold was dead. Their blood ran sluggishly across the floor and under the bed, where Dotty hid. She hadn't had her baby yet; the waters had broken an hour ago, and travail had begun. If she, Isobel, could make noise they wouldn't hear Dotty's groans. She kept up her screams, not feeling the man who grasped her and sweated to his climax.* Scream again, carefully, just right. Let another sepoy replace the first—no, the fourth, that was. Make a noise carefully, just right. Geoffrey must be dead, Willie dead, Priscilla dead, Rodney dead. Scream, but not too frantically, just right, so that they will keep on, and not kill me and drown my cries. *She opened her eyes suddenly. They were dragging Dotty's grotesque body out from under the bed. Lady Isobel cut her scream short and began to fight in desperate silence. The man rolled off her and did not fight back. All struggling stopped, and they watched a baby's birth. She lay panting and tried to hope. The sepoys' faces were tender. They were farmers, and their faces became shining and alight. One knelt to help the struggling girl. Another sprang with tormented eyes out of the shadows. He swore, kicked the helper aside, fired*

*his rifle, and stamped with his booted feet. Isobel watched
the muzzle come round on her, and felt the bayonet point
slide in.*

Subadar Narain lay half stunned among the crowd outside
the courthouse, quite close to Rodney. He watched Rodney
get up and run, and lifted his pistol, then slowly lowered it.
Turning, he looked straight into Naik Parasiya's angry eyes.
The naik's teeth were clenched; he said, "We have to kill
them now, Subadar-sahib. Anyone who is not for us is
against us." The Mohammedans of the 60th were running
together; they dribbled at the mouth and screamed, "Din!
Din! Din!" The subadar climbed shakily to his feet. Madness. What could he do if this was happening all over India?
He'd wait and see, and try to get control of them again when
they calmed down.

Fifty yards away Ensign Horace Simpkin died quickly. His
clothes were blown off him, and flash burns covered the front
of his body from forehead to feet. He was blind and dying,
and the Union Jack waved somewhere above in a lightning-
shot murk of pain. When he saw that the 88th had mutinied,
he had run to blow up their magazine. That would take away
their power; the 13th and 60th would have time to come to
the rescue; he'd save Bhowani for England. That was what
he meant to do. But a piece of Indian timber, whirled by
fire, did it a second earlier. The magazine blew up in his
face. He was dying, and he remembered his debts. It was his
duty as an officer and a gentleman to repay the moneylenders what he had borrowed, and the interest at twelve
per cent per month. Captain Savage had lent him fifty rupees.
He wouldn't leave an estate big enough to pay them. He
wriggled on the ground and groaned. Emma—it was his duty
to support her, and she said she was starving. The Union
Jack blurred until it was only the blood-red St. George's
Cross of England, flying above the winds of agony, fluttering
and whipping at the staff while black smoke boiled round
it.

Harriet Caversham woke to a smell of burning. She sat up,

*sniffed and nudged her husband sharply. "Eustace, some-*
*thing is on fire. Go and see about it at once." Lieutenant*
*Colonel Caversham was singing an aria in a golden tenor,*
*while the thousands who filled the mighty hall wept and*
*applauded. He heard and obeyed, still three-parts asleep, his*
*mind singing. A line of flame ran across the ceiling cloth,*
*and he saw that the thatch above was on fire. Blinking, he*
*guided his wife out before him on to the verandah, so that*
*the sepoys among the trees shot her first. She fell back dead*
*into his arms. He stared down at her and out at the lawn.*
*The flames silhouetted him and made him a perfect target*
*but it took them three more shots. To the last he had no*
*faintest notion of what it was that kept smashing into his*
*stomach and chest.*

*Two-Bottle Tom Myers was in his own room. His wife*
*and Rachel slept in the next room and sometimes one or*
*the other would come and sit with him, but he was alone*
*now. He lay fully clothed on his bed, gripping the wooden*
*frame and watching the ceiling. God the All-Terrible ad-*
*vanced on him in cloud and fire and a wrinkling spread of*
*grey, lined with scarlet. God the punishing Father came like*
*a scorpion, and the scorpion crawled over his head, curled*
*its tail, was large and larger, grey and black, and lined with*
*scarlet.* Let there be no mercy. Let my sweat run and my
blood come, and the silent scorpion stride down with giant
strides. I have sinned against heaven, and in Thy sight, and
am no more worthy to be called Thy son. Others see me and
follow me, and I do not die. Strike. *The wrath of God struck*
*down in light. The brilliance blinded him and seared him.*
*The hand of God came out of the violet light and pressed*
*him down and smothered him. His bladder and bowels*
*emptied, he jerked once, and closed his eyes with a smile.*
*The sepoys, creeping into the stench a minute later with a*
*lamp, did not touch him for he was clearly dead. There was*
*no secret leader here, and they muttered prayers and ran*
*out of the bungalow. Mother Myers and Rachel huddled*
*together in the next room, listening to the silence.*

*Lachman the bearer ran fast through cantonments, the cook's carving knife in his hand. He thought fast, too: the goldsmith in the Street of the Metalworkers had a room at the back to shelter them for a few days, and could get a horse somehow. Sher Dil hadn't been a bad old man—for a Mohammedan—but he'd really been showing his age these last two years. He presumed too much; it wasn't right or dignified that the great Captain Savage-sahib should be called Rodney-sahib as if he were still a baby. Now that the sepoys had killed the old fool, Savage-sahib would certainly promote him Lachman, to butler. Then he could serve the sahib for ever, and be near him, and the work would be most properly done. The sepoys—treacherous swine, they'd catch it when Savage-sahib was able to get back at them. But Lachman had to find him first and help him to escape, or they'd murder him. He'd thought of everything: knife, money —all his own savings and all his wife's gold trinkets—hidden pistol, ammunition, set of native clothes. He'd get the sahib away all right. Sepoys stopped him from time to time, and he always answered, "I'm looking for my sahib. I want to kill him, or at least stick this into his corpse, the bullying white swine!"*

*Ursula Herrold held the sides of her cot and giggled. She loved the shakos and the dark faces—nice hard hands to lift and swing and tickle, much better and harder than Ayah could, nearly as nice as Daddy. Gurgle and shout. This always made them laugh and lift her up when she was out for a walk with Ayah and met them. "Cummany! lef-righ- lef-righ!" She stamped her bare feet in time with her own shout, and crowed down the muzzle of the rifle.*

*The Rani of Kishanpur stood on her battlements in a hushed night. A dust storm had raved about the fort at dusk, whipping the trees in crazy fury, and it was cooler. She faced west, gripping the edge of the stone and feeling its rough- ness with her hands. She saw nothing out there and knew she never would see anything except the silent river and the jungle. She swallowed from time to time and waited there until the sun came up behind her. Then she ran down to her son on his cushions and hugged him, and did not leave the room all day.*

The battering pandemonium stopped. Rodney heard men shouting "Din! Din!"; others near him lay breathless and open-mouthed against the earth. He scrambled to his feet and ran round the back of the court, northward through the gardens. Behind him the crowd breathed, all together, like a huge animal, but there was no pursuit. He did not think anyone had seen him go.

He worked towards his own bungalow as fast as he could, stumbling, climbing awkwardly over walls, dodging past servants' quarters. He had no weapon; one thing at a time —get to Robin and Joanna. His head ached fiercely and his eyes brimmed over; shock and strain were physical hurts, as definite as the agony of his burns. He knew a sudden reasonless certainty that on this night all India had exploded into smoke and fire, that all its millions would be his enemies and he would find no pity or shelter in all its miles of plain and jungle. To right and left the bungalows burned, and outside each one men moved about in silhouette. Some of them were shouting excitedly and firing rifles; in others the first panic of fear had gone, so that they stood about in whispering knots.

And, kneeling in the shallow irrigation ditches, lying face down across the well copings, spread-eagled in the flower-beds, crumpled in the dusty paths, lay the broken and the dead. There were white and brown, master and servant and sepoy; a disjointed body at the foot of the Sculleys' garden wall; a girl in a nightgown, armless under a jacaranda; a sepoy across her, bayoneted; bright flames from a bungalow, and shrieks, where a woman burned alive and troopers waited, carbines ready. That was the Cummings'. Isobel would have been with Dotty van Steengaard; Caroline too, perhaps. He checked his pace—but he couldn't stop now. A ripple of insane expectation changed his pain to pleasure.

He'd split a sepoy apart with a steel edge, drag his entrails out slowly, by hand, while the man still lived. His eyes flared in his blackened face, and blood ran out under his fingernails.

At the lower wall of his own garden he saw that the bungalow, the servants' quarters, and the stables were on fire. He heard the horses screaming and the beating of their hoofs against the walls and doors. Something in white lay on its back near the carriage porch; straining his eyes, he thought it was the corpse of Sher Dil. Ten or eleven sepoys of the 88th wandered around the garden, searching aimlessly. The flames picked out their scarlet coats, white trousers, white crossbelts, and immensely high black shakos, and twinkled on crests and buttons. He had seen them a score of times like that, round campfires. He ran straight forward on them, his hands open.

The cry choked in his throat and he knelt quickly. Beneath his feet a face glistened dark and wet in a bed of canas. The dull scarlet flowers were crushed down, and beside the face there was a white bundle. He put out his hands and touched them. His batman Rambir, shot in the throat and chest, lay on his back with his hands crooked up. His son Robin lay beside Rambir, face down in his nightshirt, the back of his head a black and clotted blur. Rodney felt the skull gently and thought it was not broken. Blood still trickled under the fair hair and dripped on the earth. They must have held him by the ankles, dashed him once against a wall or a tree, and thought they'd killed him. Rodney gathered him up and pressed him, kissing the round face and purple eyelids. The boy breathed in quick shallow gasps. The sepoys still moved about the lawn.

One of them stopped by the banyan tree across the drive and looked up into it. At once he shouted in triumph to the others, and they all ran together under the tree's drooping air roots. The first man scrambled into a fork and on up out of sight. The leaves shook, a woman screamed. Joanna crashed through the branches and fell sideways on the hard earth. Rodney held his son tighter and slipped slowly over the edge of reason. He must go to her, and his son was alive in his arms. He must go; his arms crept down, he could not make his muscles obey; slowly he laid his son in the flowers. He climbed to his feet and lurched forward.

At the first stride a blow smashed against the side of his head and he reeled into the earth. He fought to hold consciousness, fought murderously to get on, his legs still running, his eyes forward. The thing behind hit him again. Heavy bodies pressed down on his back. A hand that smelled of smoke and sweat clapped over his mouth. He closed his jaws on it, tearing at the flesh until the bones grated in his teeth.

Two sepoys dragged Joanna round the lawn by her ankles. Her hair trailed on the grass, and her embroidered white nightdress rode up over her thighs. She shrieked and moaned as they bayoneted her in the breasts and belly and face.

He was on his knees again, running on his knees, bursting towards her. A third blow exploded in his head, and the world expanded; he could just see her a hundred feet away, spread naked and dying under their bodies. A man sobbed into his ear, "Lie still, lie still. Do not look."

He could not close his eyes. A harsh voice cried, "Enough!" She must be unconscious and nearly dead—Joanna, whom he had sworn to love and protect; Joanna whom he did not love and had not protected, his wife and Robin's mother, who had not liked to be left alone with Indians.

"Lie still, sahib, or we'll all die—the baby too. They are like mad dogs."

Blood filled his mouth. The hand lay crushed and placid between his grinding teeth.

Her raw body quivered no more. A sepoy bent over with his rifle and put the muzzle to her ear. Still Rodney could not shut his eyes. At the explosion waves of fiery darkness engulfed him.

Later everything was the same, but reasonable. Men straddled his back and held him to the ground. That was fine; he was quite comfortable. A mangled hand lay in his tight-clenched mouth; it tasted sweet, of blood, and he let it drop. It was a beautiful night, hot, but beautiful and red-lit. Someone had burned his face with a torch. The buildings crackled merrily, and sepoys stared at the lovely light. Joanna had chosen to sleep out naked on the lawn. He knew by the stirring in the trees that dawn was near. He re-called an aimless bustling in the night, but now all was in order. He heard the familiar rhythm of marching men and the sound of a trumpet call—the Rally—blown twice from somewhere in the 60th's lines. It was indeed a beautiful smoky scarlet night.

One of the men on his back was muttering urgently, some-thing about the dawn coming; the other grunted. Rodney recognized the voice and the grunt now—that cocksure little beast Ramdass, and dear gloomily silent old Harisingh.

He said, "Ramdass, Harisingh, what are you doing here? It's long after Last Post."

Tears splashed warm on his neck. . . . Ramdass's voice, whispering, "Shhh! Look."

A pressure on his head. . . . He peered round into the gloom. Behind his feet Robin and Rambir lay together among the cannas. His teeth chattered and he struggled to get up, but the two on his back held him down.

"Lie still. It's all over. We couldn't let you be killed. We followed you after the explosion."

Ramdass talked for both of them, and Harisingh grunted softly in agreement. Rodney lay with his head on the hard earth.

Ramdass whispered, "Take Rambir's uniform, sahib. We will find a sack."

Rodney did not answer. The hoarse whisper continued.

"And, sahib, we did not believe what they said. Re-member us when the madness has passed. We will take off our uniforms as soon as we can, and go to our villages. But now we will be killed unless we behave like the others. Do not give us away. Remember us."

They slid off his back, and Ramdass helped him to crawl into the black shadow of the peepul by the corner of the wall. Harisingh hauled Rambir's corpse in by the arms, so that its dragging boots clicked together, and then went back for Robin. Ramdass eased off the batman's black leather belt and dark tunic. Harisingh, nursing his bitten hand, searched among the flowers until he found the shako. Then they rolled the body under the wall and spread earth and leaves over it.

Ramdass whispered, "He had no other equipment. Here, he was using this pistol of yours. There was a little ammunition in his trouser pocket. Do you want my rifle too?"

Rodney shook his head dumbly; he'd have enough to carry. The birds had been cheeping and croaking for some time, disturbed by the false dawn of fire. He had no watch, but he knew the light would come soon.

The two sepoys crept along in the shadows for thirty yards, stood up, and walked slowly forward. When they came close to the others he heard a shouted greeting, and, very distinctly, "Did they kill Savage-sahib?"

Harisingh's deep voice spoke for the first time. "I think so. At the court building."

"Anyway, we killed the dam and the pup here, didn't we?"

The speaker laughed raucously. For a few minutes the group of sepoys followed Ramdass and Harisingh, asking questions about the affair at the court building. Rodney could not hear how they got rid of them, but soon the others dropped away and the two green coats trailed into de Forrest's compound and out of sight. He saw that de Forrest's bungalow had not been burned.

He began to struggle into Rambir's uniform. The wet patches on collar and chest were cold to his skin, and the batman had been fatter than he and a little shorter, so that the tunic bagged in one place and stretched in another. When he had finished he drew up spittle into his mouth and spread it on his face among the burns and dust. Then he lay down, listened to Robin's breathing, and stared at the white blur of Joanna on the grass.

The two sepoys slipped back over the wall near him; in a bar of light between the trees he saw the burns on their faces and the charred ruin of their coats. Ramdass carried a bulging canvas sack, a military kitbag, over his shoulder. He put down the sack and walked on at Harisingh's side; in a second they were gone. Rodney emptied out the straw they had put into the sack, and saw that the metal eyelets at the mouth would give Robin air. He had been numb, and thought he dreamed. Looking at the little holes through which his son would breathe, he was gripped by a terrifying urgency, so that his hands trembled. He lifted the boy and eased him carefully into the sack. The shape was recognizably human, particularly the head. He filled the spaces and rounded the bumps with straw, loosely roped the mouth, and prayed Robin would not cry. He slung the sack over his left shoulder and made sure the pistol at his belt came easily to his right hand. Daylight began to paint livid green-grey streaks on the underside of the smoke pall over Bhowani.

He forced his brain to think what he should do next, where he should go. One thing at a time. The Cheetah River was to the west; he could not swim it with Robin, and dared not risk the ferry. To north and south bands of mutineers would be roving the Deccan Pike. He must go east. He had no choice.

In this earliest promise of a scorching day the green of the trees was yet fresh, and some of the night's dust had settled. His stables were level with the ground and his horses roasted alive. His bungalow was a black and crackling-red ruin, and the bougainvillaea had burned with it. The goldmohur by the entrance pillar of the driveway scintillated in a cold brilliance of orange and gold and scarlet against the rack overhead; when the sun touched it, it would hurt the eyes, it was so bright. Stooped under the weight of the sack, he climbed the wall and crept along the side of de Forrest's compound. He threaded east through the gardens, a lonely

sepoy with a dark and bloody face, murderous eyes, and a
sack of loot. Those who saw him did not interfere with him.

Here in the overcast morning pallor he saw clearly what
had been half-seen in the tumult of the dark. To right and
left smoke rose from the shells of bungalows, and the
nauseous-sweet smell of burned hair and flesh clung in the
dust. Broken sofas and chairs strewed the lawns, their covers
ripped and the horsehair stuffing dragged out. Children's
toys littered the roadsides among cups and clocks and torn
clothes. A few low-caste followers grovelled drunk under
the trees.

A gang of sepoys of the 88th marched by, dragging the
body of a white woman by the heels. They did not recognize
him, and he did not recognize her, for she had no head. The
head that swayed in triumph on a bayonet's point at the
tail of the group, severed by a hundred blunt sawings at the
neck, was the head of a man—Major Swithin de Forrest of
the 60th Bengal Light Cavalry. His mouth was set in the
same dead sneer he had worn through life, and below the
powder burns on his forehead the eyes were contemptuous.

The jackals were out. Usually they hid themselves by day
and ran about the cantonment by night, shrilling a maniacal
chorus. They had kept quiet through this night, frightened
by the noises and the light of fires; even now they were not
sure that all the new dead were really in their power. Their
sense of smell would reassure them as the May sun climbed,
and already they were out of their earths, sniffing and wondering. They ran from bush to bush or cringed grey and
hang-tailed among the cactus and crept closer to the bodies
lying in field and garden and lane and street and courtyard.
Vultures sat in rows on the branches of the trees, stretched
their naked necks, and waited.

The Silver Guru might help him—but that would mean
going close by the city and into the Little Bazaar. And
perhaps they had discovered his race and killed him too.
Dellamain must be dead. The Commissioner's bungalow was
next to the court buildings. Surely the mob had burned it

and killed him. Where had Lachman run to, and Ayah? Where were Simkin, Anderson, Sanders, Caversham, Isobel, Dotty, Caroline? There were too many to think about. Kishanpur lay east, in the direction he was going. Kishanpur, where all vices slithered in coils about each other, where the shadow of the fort lay like a corruption. Sumitra had melting flesh and huge eyes. Had he touched a clean fire in her once, so long ago? Was it all gone, all pretence? He couldn't face her again. There must be somewhere else. Robin had to have rest and shelter. The kites dropped one by one out of the barren sky, the wind soughing in their wings. For him there was no place.

He'd saved her life. She'd help him. He had no other hope, no choice.

He passed into the fields and tramped on, skirting the common to the north of the city. Flat ploughland, dotted with mango groves and clumps of stunted thorn, spread for eight miles ahead to the low rock ridges of the Sindhya Hills. There the jungle began and he could hide. The sack bit into the raw flesh of his shoulder. A single bird sang loudly and flew from branch to twig ahead of him.

Once he came upon about thirty sepoys of his 13th, marching from north to south in formation. He lay on the ground till they had passed, but none of them looked round. The crop stalks scratched his chin, and as he watched he knew that the world was mad. Where were they going, so purposefully, to the tap of a single drum? What mad perversion of discipline brought them here, sweating through the cane stubble and wearing the Company's uniform so proudly? He groped to his feet and walked on.

Later he found a body in a ditch and saw that it was ex-Subadar-Major Mehnat Ram, unhurt but stiff and dead. He was dressed in old-fashioned uniform, and his sword was in his hands. Rodney turned the corpse over with his boot and muttered, "You, too?"

Two hours after leaving the bungalow, and four miles across the plain, there were no more sepoys but many signs

that the people fled from a scourge. Avoiding the main road,
they had slipped away on bypaths from the cantonment and
the city, and here the paths began to converge. Each thin
pony and trailing family, each pack-ox and bullock cart
dragged a finger of dust across the plain. There had been
no such terror here for fifty years, but the people knew what
to do and were ready when the word passed; flight and
despair were a part of the folklore they inherited at their
birth. This government, like every other their fathers and
grandfathers remembered, had blown up in murder, mutiny,
arson, and pillage. Sooner or later they would be the ones to
suffer. It had seemed so secure, but they trusted nothing, and
now they knew what to do. Rodney passed close to some
of them and thought it could not be long before they saw
through his thin disguise. Perhaps they would get a rupee
for telling the sepoys—or perhaps two for killing him themselves.

He dared not stop to rest. Robin's irregular breathing was
close at his ear, and faint. His back ached and his hands
kept scraping loose from the crimped mouth of the sack. He
gathered all his strength and will and concentrated them on
one task—the next step forward, then the next.

He tramped heavily out of a mango grove. There were
square shadows here, and a yellow dog snapping at his heels.
The dust swam beneath his feet, and he raised his eyes. He
was in the dirty alley which was the road through Devra,
and he could not turn back. Objects sprang into sharp focus
and as suddenly blurred and were gone. He saw a peasant
family resting in the shade of a well and thought they looked
away as he passed, but could not be sure. He saw a cluster
of people under a tree: the village well. His tongue swelled
and his mouth opened. He saw among the swaying half-tone
curtains a single point of silver brilliance. It was a trooper
of the 60th, haranguing a crowd at the well. His accoutrements sparkled above the stooped colourless peasants. He
was a leader, sober but alert and exalted, and his eyes
flashed over the thin crowd. An old man mumbled a

question, and he cried, "How do you know it's true?" He groped in his sabretache and threw something out. "Here, look at *that*. Isn't that the sign of the raw flesh which ran through your village in the night?"

A man's left hand, tightly clenched and cut off at the wrist, fell in the dirt at Rodney's feet. He recognized the heavy gold signet ring on the little finger, and the red hairs curling behind the powerful knuckles.

The listeners murmured and twisted around to stare at the hand. The trooper called across their heads. "*Jai ram, ji,* brother. Here, come and help me persuade these yokels to kill any English they catch. A few escaped. And give me back the Englishman's hand. It is the fat Colonel-sahib's."

Rodney dragged on. He muttered with averted head, returning the salutation, "*Jai ram,* brother."

The tall trooper flashed through the crowd to block his path, and said hectoringly, "Not so fast, you. Who are you, where are you off to? And what have you got in that kit-bag?" His eyes narrowed. "Looting? *And* deserting?"

Rodney moved out of the tree shade into stabbing sunlight. His face was scorched bronze-black under the dirt, and out of it his eyes crackled old and ice-blue and mad. The trooper saw it all, and the bullet hole, and the wide stains on the tunic front. He and every watching villager read in those eyes the murderous finality of despair. He did not see that this creature was an Englishman, only that it was insane, and he spoke quickly in an altered, more humble voice, "Brother——"

The sack across Rodney's left shoulder stirred, and the child wailed, "Mummy."

A bewildered frown crossed the trooper's face. Rodney drew the pistol out of his belt. George Bulstrode's clenched fist lay in the dust between them. The pistol moved, coming up. Robin moaned inside the sack, and Rodney whispered gently, incessantly, "It's all right, Robin darling, Daddy's here. It's all right. It's all right."

When the barrel lined up with the emblazoned belt buckle in the centre of the trooper's stomach, he pulled the trigger. The buckle disappeared, blown through a gaping hole in the flesh. The trooper coughed once and held his stomach. His eyes were tight and amazed; his frown deepened, and blood gushed between his fingers. His knees folded and he slipped silently to the road. Still talking gently. Rodney put the pistol back in his belt. He picked up the Colonel's fist, stuffed it in his pocket, and stumbled forward again. The villagers made way for him.

At the edge of the jungle the trees stooped over him, the ground slid away, and he fell down.

When he recovered consciousness he dragged Robin out of the sack and laid him in the shade. The sun was not yet high, but the temperature was about 110 and the sky already turning from blue to the lead-grey of extreme heat. He was on a low rise of land where the trees began. He knew the place; it was a favourite lying-up spot for the deer that came out to eat the crops at night. Near here he had met the night-runner with the chupattis. Near here his father had ridden under the mango trees and waited for the terrified villagers to come out and whisper news of the Thugs.

He had no present and no future, only a past. His past sprang back, beyond the conceiving of him, to the first Englishman who had come to this land, and linked him for ever with India. He looked out to the west through eyes too crusted-burnt to close. He put his head in his hands and looked at the stones. He had no money and no food. Countless millions of Indians crouched ready to kill him. The sea was six hundred miles away.

He grated his teeth, scratched among the stones, and buried Colonel Bulstrode's hand. He'd rest first, and then see. He'd creep down into the village when the men were out, kill a woman alone by her hearth, and steal food and perhaps a bullock cart.

One day, one hour, at a time. He'd die if he didn't sleep soon and obliterate the memories. He looked across the level and saw the blue smudges of village cooking fires. Beyond them the plain lay under a pall of smoke touched by the silver glint of the river. Here, in the quiet edge of the jungle, shrieks dinned in his ears, he heard trumpets and bugles and marching men, and smelled blood. He lay down beside his son and stared up through the branches at the leaden sky.

# PART TWO

# The Running Together

# 17

H E KNEW he had not slept long—or had he been unconscious, open-eyed?—but could not for a time realize where he was, or why he came to be here. He lay on his back under a tree in the heat of noon, and saw that he was wearing white uniform trousers—could it be manoeuvres? A sepoy's shako was near his hand, and the place smelled of hot rock and dried leaves. Then he saw Robin and still could not shut his eyes. He was alone with Robin and they had no food. His eye caught a glint of metal nearby. He jerked upright, the pistol in his hand and his teeth bared.

Nestling among the roots of the next tree were two pots full of milk, a plate heaped with rice, a bowl of vegetable curry, and five mangoes on a big dark leaf. The vessels were of chased brass, and the sun shone brightly on them. His tongue swelled and saliva flowed under it and dribbled down his chin. He saw feet near the pots—two brown and hard, two white and bleeding—and raised his eyes higher.

To the left, Piroo the carpenter squatted on his heels above the food; he was mixing something in a brass bowl over a tiny fire. Caroline Langford sat farther away, to the right, leaning against a tree; she was wearing a cheap sari; her face was calm and exhausted and her eyes shut.

Piroo looked up. "Put down the pistol, sahib. It's not loaded anyway. There is much to do if you are all to escape alive."

Rodney nodded vaguely. That made sense. Piroo had an air of quiet authority—of course, he owned land here. Rodney giggled as the carpenter carried food and drink to his side—the little rat might have poisoned it. He loaded the pistol, his hands shaking, and when it was done took a wary sip of the milk.

Caroline opened her eyes. He watched her swim up from a black deep, as he had done, and realize why her feet were torn. He watched her fingers tighten while she fought down a rush of panic; then her mouth was calm again, and her eyes steady. She smiled a little, stretched, and walked over to Robin. Blood stained the stones where she put her feet; Rodney kept on sipping.

Robin's breath came in fluttering whispers and there were purple hollows under his eyes. She took off his nightdress, spread it on the earth, and stretched him out face down on it. She took the child's left wrist and drew a sharp stone across the vein. The light blood flowed evenly, at first in a trickle, soon more strongly. Rodney held the pistol in his wavering right hand and glared at Caroline over the muzzle; with his left hand he continued to stuff food into his mouth. No one should hurt Robin, no one; he would trust no one. One false move . . .

Caroline did not look up. She watched the blood run for a minute or two, then pressed with one thumb to stop the flow. Piroo gave her the bowl he had been stirring, and she dabbed steamy paste from it on the cut; with fingers and teeth she ripped a piece off the nightdress and made a tourni-quet. Piroo said, "The head too. It's good stuff." Caroline hesitated, looked again into the bowl, and then, without cleaning off the clotted blood, slapped paste thick over the wound on Robin's head.

The boy's cheeks had sunk, and after the bleeding his face was green-white. She sat him up in her lap and held a jar of milk ready in her right hand. He stirred and moaned, but when she trickled milk between his teeth he swallowed it. She did it again, and in ten minutes he had drunk a quarter of a pint. When he vomited the milk over her knee and coughed weakly, she waited a minute and began to feed him again. When the little jar was empty she put it down and held him cradled in her arms. A long time passed and he did not vomit. With her feet she pushed herself to the tree, leaned back against it, and looked up into the muzzle of the pistol.

He had forgotten it was in his hand, for he had been studying a new softness in her face as she worked. He lowered the pistol, keeping his eyes on her, and felt over the plates with his free hand—all gone, he'd eaten everything. The mango stones lay around him, chewed clean, and his mouth was full of the last piece of fruit. Caroline was giving Robin to Piroo. His mind fumbled at a curtain; reality was on the other side, but it would be too harsh there, on the other side, and he was glad he could not get through. He tried to stare her down. He couldn't; let her fight.

"Lie down."

He whimpered as she eased his eyelids down and spread paste over his face. It was hot, and smelled earthy, of worms and herbs. He writhed and clenched his teeth, but it cooled quickly and set to the consistency of dough. The jabbing needles shimmered away into a ventral ache that wrinkled his skin. She eased the tunic off his shoulders and opened his trousers and pulled them down round his ankles. He shook his head and mumbled, "Only the burns. Nothing else wrong."

The edges of darkness crept round him. Oh, God, they had put something in the food. God, God, God. They had lulled him and drugged him. She wanted to kill Robin. She was jealous. Joanna had said so. He stared up at the weary face and could not move. Loose strands of her hair brushed his forehead. She wore a sari; she was an Indian in disguise; she'd planned it all. He strained to reach the pistol, but he could not move. Tepid lead filled his veins and weighted his muscles. His eyes would not stay—would not stay open. . . .

He awoke silently to full consciousness, and knew this time where he was and what had happened. It was dark; the

sky twinkled with stars, and the moon hung low—east or
west? He looked at the stars again. East. May the tenth,
moon two days past full, rising; it must be early in the night.
He had to kill someone. His pistol was gone and he sat up
trembling. Caroline's voice was low and strong in the darkness near him. "Are you ready to move now?"

The sari framed her face, and the moonlight painted it
with calm so that it was beautiful. She was in her old
position, her back against the tree, and Robin slept in her
arms. Piroo stood beyond her; beyond him again there was
something big and white among the tree trunks. Rodney
recognized the shape of a two-wheeled bullock cart fitted
with a low-domed canvas roof. Two white bullocks stood
in the yoke and blew through their nostrils. The boughs
creaked and a small breeze stirred his hair.

He said, "I want my pistol."

Piroo gave him the pistol and he tucked it into his belt.
Caroline tried to stand up, clinging one-handed to the tree
until the strength came back into her legs. She must have
sat there through the crawling hours of the afternoon heat,
and never moved. She lifted Robin into the cart, and Rodney
followed. Blankets, felt rugs, and a litter of pots and sacks
covered the rough floor. She laid Robin along one side, and
sat at his head; Rodney curled up on the other side.

Piroo fastened the canvas flaps front and back and whispered in through a tiny crack, "You can look through here,
sahib, but don't shoot until I say so—on no account."

The frame creaked as Piroo took his place, squatting in
the open on the back end of the shaft. They heard him prod
the bullocks' haunches with the goad. The cart heaved and
settled back, heaved again, rode heavily over a tree root,
and began to groan and squeak through the jungle.

After an hour it dropped into a rutted track, turned left,
and moved faster down a forest alley.

The night passed. Rodney dozed twice for short periods
and each time awoke in frantic terror. He must have cried
out, for Caroline had put her hand across and was holding

his arm. Each time he stilled the trembling and shrugged her off. Twice he heard Robin whimper, and after it Caroline's soothing murmur. In the dawn she passed him a mango, and he lay chewing it and watching Robin. The boy's eyes opened to stare up at the canvas, where the light filtered through and made the dust a cold dancing fog. The eyes were blank; shivering. Rodney scrambled over, kissed his son's cheek, and muttered incoherently in his ear. The child's blue lips stirred, then he closed his eyes and went to sleep again.

The cart turned off the track and passed through uneven rock-strewn jungle. After a while it stopped, and Piroo opened up the flaps. They climbed stiffly out into a clearing, where the rocks of a dried stream bed held a pool of black water. Piroo unyoked the bullocks, and propped up the shaft by turning the yoke bar through a right angle and jamming one end of it into the earth. The bullocks lay down where they were, and he flung them a few handfuls of chopped straw. Then he crept under the cart without a word, lay down, and in a minute was asleep.

The air was hot and fresh, and there was no dust. Caroline brought out a blanket and put Robin down on it; Rodney listened to the sounds of the jungle awakening. Twigs snapped a long way off, a deer called, voiceless birds stepped through the leaves. He did not want to know anything more; he would go to sleep.

He heard her speaking. "Piroo knew something bad was going to happen. But he didn't know what. He says he tried to make you come away, but what could he say? Even if he'd known everything, no one would have believed him."

Rodney grunted. Believe Piroo, if he'd announced on Saturday that the world was coming to an end? He didn't believe it now, on Monday. It hadn't happened.

The girl's voice pressed him, pleading. "We have to get well, and fight for ourselves. We owe it to Piroo; he's risking his life. He picked me up in the fields, found a sari for me.

I tried to get to Isobel at the van Steengaards'. I tried to get to you. There were fires everywhere and——" Her voice trembled. "A goatherd from Devra told us where you were. We *must* fight, for Robin's sake."

He grunted again, shut his eyes and ears, and burrowed down into sleep.

A thin waft of smoke, sharp in his nostrils, roused him to the familiar panic and set his heart thumping. Piroo was cooking over a fire; Robin was conscious, and Caroline was fanning him with her hand. Rodney rolled over on his side and watched the red ants crawling among the leaves. Fight? What was there to fight? They ate and slept, and Robin lived; they ate and slept and moved. Moved. Where to?

He raised his head. "Piroo, where are we going?"

"Bombay."

Rodney frowned painfully. Something wrong there—something wrong. Bombay was—eight hundred miles southwest as the roads ran. Eight hundred miles in a bullock cart, two and a half miles an hour. That made—too many hours. He drew his brows together. Too many miles, too many moths fluttering big black wings behind his eyeballs. If he could concentrate they'd go away.

Bombay. The only alternative was Kishanpur, and why did that make his spine tingle? Not reason—something lower, something that would make Jewel's hair rise and roughen along the back. Jewel was dead. Shot to death for being a dog. A dog's death.

He dared not see Sumitra again. What a chance she'd have to pay him back for that night of the Holi! She might even have him killed, by accident. Who'd know? And Robin with him.

What was Caroline waiting for, so compressed? In plain reason, they had no choice. The old fool Piroo couldn't take this wreck of a cart to Bombay, across a score of great rivers, through a country in flames—and the monsoon coming in four or five weeks! And who knew that Bombay Presidency hadn't fallen too? And Madras? Robin couldn't survive the journey. Only a lunatic, or a scoundrel, could suggest going to Bombay. It was a trap.

He said, "Go to Kishanpur. We have to go to Kishanpur."

When Piroo tried to argue Rodney screamed furiously, "Kishanpur, Kishanpur!" A drumming pain rattled his teeth, and he watched his hands fidgeting with the pistol. He'd have to kill someone.

Caroline spoke in her slow accurate Hindustani. "He's right, Piroo. I hate it, I don't know why—but the little boy must rest. We have no choice."

Piroo shrugged and turned away with a curt, "It's all the same to me." Rodney looked keenly at his back: this wasn't the same man as the carpenter of Bhowani; this was a dangerous man, not to be trusted. One hour at a time. If he kept to that and was alert, he'd save Robin, and himself.

The decision made, he sank under a weight of depression and could not sleep but stared all day at the ants and talked to himself.

As the sun dipped into the hot red blaze behind the trees, they climbed into the cart. In the twilight they were threading through the jungle; at dark they dropped into the ruts of the track and the motion became smoother. The dark bulk of the trees passed over in a silent procession. Piroo swayed in silhouette against low eastern stars.

The night ended, the cart stopped, and the second day passed. Here there was no pool, and Piroo dug with his pick-axe to uncover a brackish trickle two feet down.

In the evening, as they set out, Piroo said, "We will cross at the ford by the falls. There may be other carts on the trail. Men travel by night in this season. I do not think we are in great danger, but keep hidden; and remember, do not shoot unless I say the word."

There were other carts moving through the night. Piroo whispered that one, going in the same direction, was close ahead; shredded tendrils of dust from its wheels hung under the trees still. Twice carts creaked past in the opposite direction; once a group of men trotted by, bunched together and singing to frighten off wild beasts. Beside a deserted shrine there was a sepoy; his rifle was in his hand and he was getting up from sleep.

The sound of the falls swished against the canvas, and the bullocks splashed into the ford. Rodney, peering out, could recognize now each ridge and plain of the hunting preserve: there Sumitra saw a paradise flycatcher, that branch nearly knocked Isobel's hat off, here the Silver Guru had sat by the Monkeys' Well and waited for the Dewan. The monkeys crashed and chattered overhead. The cart turned off, moved through the grove until it was out of sight of the trail, and stopped. The monkeys fell silent.

Piroo slipped down and whispered. "You did say that shako's too small for you, sahib? It looks like it to me."

He answered dully, "Yes. Rambir had quite a small head."

Piroo disappeared, and for ten minutes nothing happened. At last they heard muttered voices and the crackling of leaves. Rodney put his eye to the slit.

Piroo was coming back, and in front of him the sepoy they had passed on the other side of the river. His stained green coat showed that he was of the 13th; he threaded wearily among the trees with the rising sun in his face, and Rodney saw that he knew him. It was Shyamsingh of his own company. Shyamsingh the quiet farmer, Shyamoo who snarled like a dog. His feet stumbled, and he looked sick. Rodney dragged the pistol from his belt and aimed at Piroo's chest; he'd get it first.

He saw that Shyamsingh's rifle was slung across his back, and heard Piroo's whining voice. "Here's the cart, your majesty. The broken place is round the front."

The sepoy said, "If you can't mend it, Piroo, what can I do? You're a carpenter. Anyway, I'll look." He had the face of a lost and frightened child, and there were bloodstains and clots of liver on his bayonet. His voice was thick, and wherever his mind was it was not here by the Monkeys' Well. He moved towards the front of the cart; Piroo followed, whining, and Rodney could no longer see them. Silently he twisted round, while Caroline put one hand on Robin's forehead and held the other near his mouth.

The low sun projected the shadows of the two men on to the canvas of the hood. In front was Shyamsingh's angular bulk—the towering shako, the long bayonet; behind, Piroo's small head and hunched back. Rodney raised the pistol.

Piroo's arms moved, pounced up and over, jerked back and clear. A straight black bar of shadow linked them to Shyamsingh's neck. It was a shadow play, and the hairs crept on Rodney's scalp. The sepoy's fingers clawed up at the bar, his shako toppled and fell into the dust, his body rocked. After a minute of fearful soundless straining he began to fidget and his boots to dance a noisy little jig, clicking together. His bigger shadow subsided slowly, and still the rigid bar connected the two marionettes; the other moved its hands, the bar curved in the middle and opened out. Shyamsingh fell, his head crashing against the cart wheel.

Rodney jerked open the flap and saw Piroo, sweat starting out in pimply drops on his forehead, tuck the square of black silk back into his loincloth. Shyamsingh lay on his side against the wheel, his face purple-black, his eyes half out of his head.

Piroo looked ten years younger as he turned excitedly to Rodney. "Did you see that, sahib? Did you see, miss-sahiba? *Very* good, that was. Of course he's known me for ten years and trusted me, but still—I did it single-handed. And—let me think—twenty-five years and a few months since my last. I'd reached eighty-four then. This is my eighty-fifth." He was squatting by the corpse, unfastening the belt. He looked up, and a childish pucker creased his cheeks. "But I can't really count him, because we're not on a proper expedition. I haven't been blessed or anything."

He dragged the body away by its arms towards the well, shaking his head and muttering to himself. Rodney climbed out and stowed the rifle, bayonet, and belt into the cart. He felt better; the sight of Shyamsingh's corpse had made spittle run into his mouth, and his eyes sparkled.

Caroline was looking at him, and he hung his head, pretending not to see. She said slowly, "What does it mean? Who is Piroo?"

"Mean? He's a Thug, a professional religious murderer—retired. My father probably made it too dangerous for him, and he got out while he could. And he's been a carpenter in the regiment, my regiment, for over twenty years!"

He laughed silently. Piroo returned, and Caroline said, "Why did you kill that man, Piroo—lure him in here and kill him?"

The carpenter turned his head and peered down in surprise. "The sahib needed a bigger shako, didn't he? The sahib's father nearly had me hanged, didn't he? Oh, he was a great one, the sahib's father. So of course I'll get a hat for his son. It's a privilege. It's fun, too. Well! we nearly forgot it after all that!"

He handed Shyamsingh's shako through the flap, took the other and threw it carelessly into the bushes.

Caroline said, "But—but—he wasn't going to harm us."

Rodney snarled. "Look! See those marks? That's Alan Torrance."

He thrust the bayonet close under her nose and held it there a second. When she dropped her eyes he put it in the scabbard and called through the canvas, "Get on, Piroo." The rough wheels rolled again.

After a quarter of an hour the cart stopped and Piroo spoke back to them. "Sahib, I won't go up to the gates. We're two hundred yards away. I'll go to Sitapara's. Yes, I know her. I'll be there if you want me again."

He unfastened the flap and Caroline got out, carrying Robin; Rodney followed. Piroo turned the bullocks and the cart creaked away. The sun glare struck back from the road into Rodney's eyes. Screwing them up, he saw the fort gate, the sentries there staring down towards them; there was safety, and four walls, and a place to sleep. He walked slowly forward beside Caroline. Step by step his strength ebbed, and the nervous force he had so strainingly held in. Caroline's feet were bleeding, but Robin was comfortable in her arms and she had the strength to carry him. The fort swam and his knees were buckling so that he had to hold on to Caroline's shoulder. At the gate the sentries in their primrose coats barred the way, and their havildar ran out. Rodney knew the man and tried to draw himself upright, while the N.C.O. stared as at a ghost.

He said thickly, "Greetings, Gurbachan. Send word to the Rani. We ask for shelter."

In through the dark of the entry port, leaning more heavily on Caroline. The fountain splashed in the courtyard and she sat down suddenly on the edge of it, where Julio had sat and showed his book of birds to Prithvi Chand. Robin awoke and cried; she soothed him and drew her fingers across his forehead while Rodney swayed. He must stay near her, or he'd fall down.

The Dewan came, with three or four courtiers. Rodney hung his head. They gasped and looked at him and muttered. They took his pistol away. They grasped his hand and led him somewhere. He shook loose and clung to Caroline's elbow. He could not see well. They crawled along dark passages where his shuffling boots whispered and each stumble echoed and re-echoed and currents of cool air stirred the hangings. Up, up, up; he forced his knees to bend and stretch, and held tight to Caroline. Sentries in the corridor— what for? They saluted—drill as ragged as ever—one of them pushed open a heavy door. He went in. The door clanged shut.

Three wide window embrasures were cut at a slant through the outer wall, and a large divan stood under the centre one. Isfahan rugs in pale colours covered the floor, and it should have been a light and luxurious apartment, high in the palace and overlooking the river. He stared round at the string beds ranged against the bare walls, at the litter of cushions and soiled rags. He had been here before; there had been an ormolu-encrusted table in the window at the right, and revealing shadows on Dellamain's face. Now there was a smell of sickness and weeping, and people drooped like unstuffed dolls. Tears trickled down through the stubble on his cheeks as he turned from face to face.

Father d'Aubriac stood by one of the windows, telling his beads. Mrs. Bulstrode sat on the floor and stared at a wall. Louisa Bell crouched on the divan, listlessly giving suck to her baby; her filthy nightdress hung round her waist, exposing her narrow shoulders and swollen breasts. The Myerses were grouped by one of the string beds; Rachel lay on it. Mrs. Myers sat on the edge, and young Myers stood at the foot. Mrs. Hatch and John McCardle were by another bed where a man lay with bandaged eyes and twitching fingers; Rodney knew by the straggly hair that it was Geoghegan. Dellamain's features swam into focus; the man's mouth opened and shut but Rodney heard nothing; he saw that the riding trousers were torn and the heavy face shrunken.

One by one, as he met their eyes, they had acknowledged that they knew him. Father d'Aubriac smiled, Mrs. Hatch exclaimed loudly, but none of the others spoke. A flicker of something passed over, and then they were again as they had been—wide dry eyes, slack lips, taut cheeks. His head nodded and he tried to think what ailed them, and himself. Not fright —only Dellamain's always-moving eyes showed fright. He looked again, and this time saw, mirrored in the refugees, his own shame. They were naked in their minds, stripped of faith and trust by the same blast that had destroyed wealth, family, and position. Naked, they did not want to see or be seen.

He walked slowly to a vacant bed and lay down. Caroline glanced at him and carried Robin over to John McCardle. He heard them talking; the tiny whispers boomed in his head.

"Mr. McCardle, can you do anything for Robin—Robin Savage? He's bad."

"One moment. We'll finish wi' Mr. Geoghegan here." A long silence. "Now, miss, wha's this muck on the child's heid?"

The whispering faded. Robin whimpered, and Rodney gripped the frame of the bed while sweat sprang out on his face. He'd have to leave it to Caroline, because the ceiling was floating away and the darkness coming. He shut his eyes.

# 18

THE SUN shone level through the grilles and traced a geometrical design on the wall above his head. The aura of despair had lightened; the room was not cheerful, but he heard a murmur of talking, and the refugees moved about as men and women move, instead of dragging themselves like ill-handled puppets. Caroline was at his bed; she gave him a cold chupatti and milk from a brass bowl. He ate and looked at her, and followed her with his eyes when she went to help Louisa Bell with the baby and afterwards came back. Robin was asleep.

Dellamain was talking to someone in a dark corner; Rodney heard a few words. ". . . ghastly disaster . . . dastardly scoundrels . . . troubles over now, my dear lady . . . every reason to believe the outbreak was confined to Bhowani . . ."

The Commissioner's voice had recovered its fruity timbre; that meant he wasn't sure. He couldn't be, because his words made nonsense, and he must know it.

Rodney munched the chupatti and muttered to Caroline, between mouthfuls, "He knows, but he pretends not to. We'll never sleep again. We'll never trust a soul. What did *he* see? Oh, God!" The moths were fluttering away with his sanity. He put his hands to his head and rocked to and fro. "Shyam-singh's face. Thaman, Vishnu, Thirteenth Rifles, to me!"

He laughed, and Caroline was there, holding his shoulders. *She* knew, *she* understood; he stared up at her. She was appraising him for some reason, seeing how strong he was, testing whether he was broken quite into little child-pieces. He sat up and said quietly, "Well?"

Something was coming which she must force herself to say. He jerked round to see if Robin had died in his sleep, but the boy's chest rose and fell regularly.

To stop the shaking in him he folded his arms and stretched out his legs. She was bending over him, and in the shifting windows of his mind her breasts were tight and her thighs perfect, smoothly shaped. He looked at her in dumb anguish. It was God's punishment to thrust that piercing-sweet desire into his wonder of her. She was his elder sister and his mother; she would protect him and guide him. Robin was hers, not his, because he and Robin were equally children and equally helpless. She looked down at him through a rent in the veil; he could for the instant touch the sanity of her world, and know it was cold and shadowed. She had taut pointed breasts, and he could have kissed them, but she was weighing him like a little boy to be told bad news. He saw her as once in a long time, out of nowhere, without words, a little boy sees his mother and is bowed by the weight of her anxiety and holds her hand to comfort her. Wondering, he touched her fingers.

Sister with the fragile neck and blue-veined wrist, what have I to do? Shall I tell you a story? . . . Of a Jack-a-Manory? Shall I kiss it and make it better? When I was a little boy, and my mother was worried, and I saw it and was very good for her sake—she cried. I don't understand.

She dragged her words up one by one. "Robin is a little better, but—the Silver Guru was in the courtyard as we came in. He moved away. It was too late. I saw him."

He said, "He escaped? I was afraid they might find out he is English."

She braced herself once more, and her voice was sharper-edged.

"Listen. I can understand how the Rani had to make peace with the Dewan when you uncovered the plot against her. But she had no need to forgive the Silver Guru. You know her better than I. Is it likely she would? If the Guru is here, the Rani has no quarrel with him. So the guns were not for a revolution against her; they were for rebellion against us. Colonel Bulstrode did not say it was impossible; he said it would be ridiculous, because the Bengal Army could crush all the princes put together."

Rodney giggled suddenly.

She went on. "And now I have seen the one thing that we were never to see—that you must have been so near to seeing the night of the Holi, the night the Silver Guru lied to you. You saw all the people who were supposed to be plotting against each other—the Rani, the Dewan, the Guru, the ringleaders of the sepoys. It must have been a terribly important meeting, perhaps their last, the one where they confirmed their plans. And you came so close. A few minutes later and you would have seen them together, not separately. They would have killed you, I suppose. Captain Savage—Rodney—we must not be blind again. Please, please see. O Almighty Father, please not again, not too late again."

He listened to her urgency and struggled to encompass and acknowledge the meaning of the phrases. He mumbled, "We're all right. Silver Guru's an Englishman. Lots of reasons he could be here—may've run for his life like us, come to make his peace, come to preach. Sumitra wouldn't harm us. I saved her life. Anyway, it's not true!"

She wanted to believe him, and the glow in her eyes died to an unwilling point of grey flame. Robin babbled something; Rodney turned towards him. Bandages enswathed the small head and hid the fair hair.

When Rodney looked back, Caroline's lips were hard set; he cowered under her harsh whisper. "There is no rest. We're exhausted with horror. We think we can't face any more of it. We're sick from shame and horror. Mr. Dellamain's useless, he's trapped by his past, he's blind! He thinks he has a hold over the Rani, but it's the other way round. We're prisoners; there's a guard on the door. You and I are the only ones who know enough to see the truth. And you've given up, like the child you are. You're not *going* to lie down and get better, not this time. *You* killed them all in Bhowani because you wouldn't see the truth about the Rani. You don't care about Robin, but you're not going to kill me. Get up! Self-satisfied prig, lazy lecherous cad, baby!"

The words rattled round his ears: sister, telling him to be a man, failing to coax, desperately trying to prick his little boy's pride. But he wasn't a little boy any more. He stared at Robin's bandaged head and knew she was right. He was possessed in that moment by the exact and terrible shape of the demon beyond the curtain. He snarled, "Shut up! Go away! Leave me alone!"

He sprang off the bed and walked aimlessly across the room. Damn, damn, damn her! Prisoners. His eyes glittered; the walls were thick, the room sixty feet above the river. Another slaughter—in here; blood soaking into the carpets; perhaps it would be in the dungeons with the bats. Sane, cold clear sane. He'd have to kill someone—people—the more the better.

What if these fears were fantasies? The Rani *might* harm the refugees; flight would certainly kill most of them. They were frail and battered, and at this burning season half of them would die, including Robin. Disease swept the fields and travelled the roads; they'd die in the jungles, foodless and without shelter.

The others were looking at him strangely. He stopped his pacing and cried, "I'm going to see the Rani."

"I'll come with you."

He heard the gasp of relief in Caroline's voice. He twisted the iron ring of the door handle and when the door did not open tugged harder, hammered with his hands on the wood, and shouted, "You outside there! Open the door!"

Feet approached leisurely down the passage, and a man called through, "What do you want?"

"Open this door at once. I am Captain Savage. Miss Langford and I wish to see Her Highness at once."

Bolts slid back and the door opened. A pair of armed soldiers stood outside, and though he knew them both they would not meet his eyes. They said, "Wait please, sahib," and one called down the corridor over his shoulder. Rodney sat on his bed, trembling and staring in front of him.

Mr. Dellamain came over and said heavily, "I do not wish to intrude, Captain, but as the—ah—senior British representative here I feel communications with Her Highness should be made through me. Perhaps I can carry your message at my next meeting with her?"

Rodney answered shortly, "No." After a while the Commissioner went away from him while the people in the room muttered to each other and Caroline whispered something to McCardle.

Ten minutes later the Dewan came; his sharp dark features were lighted by a fire behind the skin, and Rodney thought he had been drinking, or doping, or both. The twilight from the windows bathed his pitted face; the pupils of his eyes were black points. His tongue caressed his lips as he glanced round the room; his eyes rested for a long second on Rachel Myers' half-dressed nubile body. He said thickly, "Come with me, please. Her Highness is busy but has been kind enough to grant you an interview."

Rodney and Caroline followed in silence along the passages and down the spiralling stairs. Heavy yellow curtains hung over the doorway of the small throne room.

They stopped outside, and the Dewan cried softly, "Your *Royal* Highness. Miss Langford, and Captain Savage of the

Thirteenth Rifles, Bengal Native Infantry, in the service of
the Honourable East India Company!"

The words were loaded with sarcasm, and he leered at
Rodney as he said them. Caroline pulled aside the curtains,
lifted her head, and walked in. Rodney braced his knees and
followed her.

The Rani sat on a pile of cushions, alone in half-darkness.
A dim lamp, on a round ebony table behind her, silhouetted
the smooth shape of her head. They stood side by side,
looking at her, and she looked only at Rodney. No one spoke,
and he scanned her face for a sign. There was triumph or
pride in the carriage of her head—he could not be sure
which. It was difficult to see her features against the light,
but he thought there was no glow of happiness in the flat
brown texture of her skin, and saw that the eyes were sad.
He watched her make a slow careful inventory of his torn
clothes and burned face. Had he met her in a city lane, and
believed her noble lies? Had she sat on cushions like these,
with a light like this, in a tent by the falls of a river? He
didn't remember. She had turned from him to stare at
Caroline, and her mouth had hardened. He was conscious of
the wills stepping out to meet each other. Prithvi Chand was
right; they were alike.

At last the Rani sighed and compressed her lips. "What
is it?"

He forgot what it was that he had come to say. She had
helped to organize the mutiny. The Rajah had been an
honest old man, one who held the given word above everything, and his father had given the Rawan word to the
English; so she had murdered him. He knew now what the
princes had talked about at the tiger hunt, why they had
been gathered together. How many had said Yes, how many
No?

It was Sumitra's triumph that he stood destitute and
wounded before her. And it was a rage of personal defeat
trembling in Caroline beside him, not any abstract loathing
of treachery or fear for the future. His spirit only absorbed

these things and recorded them. His own fury had evaporated, and he could not fight either of the women. He saw that Sumitra's eyes were pitying and protective when she looked at him. He had nothing to say.

She repeated her question. "What is it?"

His hands fidgeted, and he muttered, "It doesn't matter. My son is badly hurt. We wanted to know whether you are going to protect us. It doesn't matter though."

She leaned forward. "Who doubts it? You, Rodney? Mr. Dellamain?"

"*I* doubt it."

She whipped round on Caroline. "You? Who are you to doubt the word of a queen?"

"You're not a queen. You're a murderess, a harlot, and a liar."

Sumitra leaned back and smiled crookedly. "I see. Something has made our little white miss a woman. You would kill for him now, and like it? Poor little thing. You have not the courage to fight for what you want. I have. I killed my husband for India; I pretended to be a whore for India; I lied, for India. I am an Indian first and woman afterwards. Poor little thing, just discovering you are a woman first— and nothing else. It is bad, the first time, isn't it?"

"It's not true! Don't say it!"

Rodney hardly heard what they said. They were miles from him and engaged in a battle he did not understand—a battle which had nothing to do with the point. Caroline was losing because she could not speak coherently for rage. It was an entirely new girl beside him, and he stared at her in astonished wonder.

Vaguely he realized that Sumitra had turned on him and that she was in a towering fury. "And *you* crawl down to insult me because she orders you to. Blind, cruel, stupid fool! English fool, man-fool! Why should I protect you or your son or this white she-rat?"

He jumped forward; the mad glare crackled in his eyes, and his voice blared. "If you touch a hair of Robin's head,

I'll break your son's skull in front of your eyes. By God, I tell you we're coming back in blood and fire. We'll burn you black bastards alive over slow fires; we'll quarter you, and hang you on gallows, and rip your filthy guts open with steel."

He was panting, teeth bared, and could hardly see her. A red vision blurred his eyes, where Indians writhed, contorted in agony, and his own face laughed madly at their tortured antics.

He stopped, held down a shuddering breath, and said coldly, "Send us all under escort to Gondwara."

The Dewan and two soldiers had hurried into the room when he raised his voice. They stood close behind him now, but the Rani was oblivious of them. She was on her feet, her eyes dilated; looking into them, he saw horror, and heard her whisper, "Shivarao! No, no!" Then anger overwhelmed everything else, and she spat in his face.

"There! I am Sumitra Lakshmi, Rawan, Regent for the twenty-seventh Rajah of Kishanpur, and I tell you that you English are *not* coming back. You will be rooted out of India like the weeds you are. Do you think you will be safe in Gondwara? Gondwara will fall when we are ready, then all India."

Her voice dropped a tone, and the pride went from it; it crawled with a personal venom. "Who are you to plead? I hate you. I would like to see you all killed, but you—*you* I'd strangle with my own hands."

She clawed towards his face. Caroline gasped and threw herself forward. Three long nail slashes sprang out on the Rani's left cheek, and the blood welled up into them. The soldiers caught Caroline and dragged her back. In the silence the Rani sat back and began to laugh hysterically, shrieking and rolling about on the cushions, while the soldiers held Caroline, and Rodney felt the muzzle of a pistol in the small of his back.

The Dewan motioned them out of the room, and in silence they went back along the corridors and up the stairs—first a soldier, then behind him Caroline, then another soldier, then Rodney, and last the Dewan.

Two lanterns guttered on the floor of the refugees' room and threw distorted shadows on the ceiling. The eyes turned as they came in, and the low buzzing of talk stopped. Rodney waited till the door thudded shut behind him, then went quickly to the farthest corner and whispered, "Come here, please. It's important." They straggled over, McCardle leading Geoghegan by the hand, and gathered round him. He saw the set look in their faces, and noticed that Della-main was frowning.

He said, "Listen to me. The Rani's in league with the mutineers. If we don't escape now, we'll be kept prisoners for months—at best. At worst——"

"She'll murder us."

Caroline spoke quietly; she was by his side, facing the others. He looked round on them, one by one; one by one they looked away.

Dellamain seized his arm. "You're insane! How can we escape? If we do, what hope is there for us in the fields, without food and money? What chance of survival will your son have—or Mrs. Bell's baby? It's hallucination. The Rani has treated us well. She'll protect us!"

"Why are we held prisoners in this room then?"

"For our own safety. The Dewan told me. What does it matter? We don't *want* to go out. I tell you, you're insane. The Rani owes everything to the British—it's sheer madness to think she'll harm us. I have a personal knowledge of her and influence with her." He swung round. "Believe me, my friends! I am your Commissioner."

Caroline whispered fiercely, "Mr. Dellamain, the truth is going to come out however much you try and hide it from yourself. You took bribes from her and allowed her to smuggle, and she arranged the mutiny under cover of it. You tied your own hands. *You* were responsible for the mutiny. Oh, let's not be silly. I was responsible, Captain

Savage was, we all were. It doesn't matter now. We must escape."

Rodney cut in. "Caroline and I are going to escape. Who's coming with us?"

Mr. Dellamain made for the door, shouting, "I'm going to tell the Rani. You're mad, you're both mad. You'll ruin everything for the rest of us!"

John McCardle looked once more at Rodney, then called suddenly, "Before ye go, Commissioner, an imporrtant worrd for your earrs." Dellamain hesitated; Rodney ran to the door and stood with his back against it.

McCardle came forward, a short scalpel in his hand, and motioned Dellamain away. "An' ma worrd is this, sir: if Rodney and Miss Langford want tae escape, ye'll no hinder them. Sit doon, man, or Ah'll carrve you in many pieces. Hurry, Rodney. It shouldna be deeficult—an' Ah'll come wi' ye."

He nodded towards the wide window embrasures. Caroline hurried from bed to bed, ripped off the sheets, and began to tear them into strips. The others stood in clusters, whispering and arguing and watching. Rodney ran to the left window and climbed into the square funnel of the embrasure. He caught the patterned grille in his hands and pulled gently; some plaster gave. Crouching half upright, he pulled harder The whole grille came away and crashed on the floor of the embrasure. He peered out and down. Far below, the stars were reflected on the satin-black surface of the river. He leaned out farther, judging the distance—fifty or sixty feet.

"Sahib, do not lean out. It is dangerous."

The voice sounded as if in his ear. He started violently and jerked his head round. Two soldiers hung over the battlements ten feet above him, and stared down into his face. They were armed; the needle bayonets wavered against the sky. He edged back into the room and dropped to the floor.

Dellamain crouched in a corner, his face wet and shining; Geoghegan had taken McCardle's place as guard and silently held the Commissioner by the throat. McCardle worked quickly with Caroline, knotting the strips of linen together. She looked up as Rodney came back, and he shook his head and pointed up wordlessly at the roof. He was thinking fast. He hurried into the bathroom—no good. Surprise and over-power the sentries at the door, break out en masse? Not enough escapers, or weapons.

Caroline's fingers flew deftly from knot to knot. She was kneeling and spoke to him as she worked, without looking up. "Didn't they—murder people—sometimes—in these places—and get rid of the bodies?"

"The chutes? Yes, all these castles have them. I've seen the ones at Agra, and they're probably the same here. But they're in the dungeons, lower down the wall."

"Mightn't they have wanted—to dispose—of an honoured guest—without having—to carry the body—through the castle?"

"They might, but——"

He shrugged. McCardle was listening and interrupted. "Let's not waste time, man. Pull up the carpets, luke under that divan contraption."

The rope finished, the three of them set to work. Mrs. Bell climbed off the divan, holding her baby, and watched with-out interest. As Rodney shoved, he felt suddenly that it was all a waste of effort. There was no way of escape, they must compose themselves to accept whatever came; the Rani might protect them.

Caroline looked at him with blazing eyes, and his mouth dropped open before the force of her. There might be a chute under the divan after all; it was just possible they could escape down it. He flung his weight forward, and the divan began to move.

They dragged back the rugs lying under and around it. One of the newly exposed flags had two iron rings counter-sunk in it; they heaved, and the flag came up bodily. Rodney looked down a black hole narrow and nearly vertical. There was no way of telling how deep it was, or where it ended; the sides were square-cut and rough-hewn. Kneeling at the edge, he stared from Caroline to McCardle.

Caroline whispered, "It's our only chance to beat her."

Her voice trembled; he saw that she was no longer looking at him or at the chute, but at Robin, lying awake on his cot and sucking his thumb. He looked again at the black square. What if there were an iron grille down there now—below the water perhaps? What if the chute came out feet above the river in this dry season, over stones or just-submerged rocks? What if the sheets broke? If they slid down there they would be flayed, broken, burned alive; those who usually took that ride did not care.

He heard Caroline saying, "Me first. Then Robin, then you, then Mr. McCardle."

He started to argue, but she was the leader, by right of will. She went on, "I'll give two jerks when I'm down, if I can. Then you pull up, tie Robin on, and lower him to me."

"All right."

"Ready? No—wait a minute. I can't leave these people." She swung round and raised her voice. "*Please* listen to me. You are in greater danger than you have ever been. We can get down here. We have friends outside."

Young Myers looked from his mother to his sister, and they looked at the floor; Mrs. Bell held her baby tighter; Mrs. Bulstrode giggled; Mrs. Hatch stared at the black hole and swore under her breath.

Father d'Aubriac said cheerfully, "*Je crois que vous avez raison, mon enfant. Mais ces autres ont le corps et l'âme malades.* My place is 'ere wit' zem. *Allez vite, bonne chance, et que le bon Dieu, qui est mort pour nous, vous préserve dans ses mains éternelles.*"

His hand gestured in the sign of the cross; his eyes twinkled and he seemed to savour the words like a fine wine.

Geoghegan turned his head and croaked, "Ah, an' I'd come but I'd hinder ye. . . . Good luck to ye, the luck of the devil." He grinned fiendishly and tightened his hands on Dellamain's neck.

Caroline said, "Thank you Father. Thank you, Mr. Geoghegan. Goodbye—everybody—and good luck. Now!"

Rodney tied one end of the sheet rope—it was about fifty-five feet long—to the leg of a bed, and threw the other end down the chute. McCardle got ready to push back against the bed. Caroline said, "Where shall we meet if we have to separate?"

"Upstream a mile—this bank—my old camp. Know it?"

"I know it."

"Right."

She sat down quickly on the edge of the hole, took the rope in her hands, rolled over on to her stomach, and was gone. He watched the top of her head bob down until the darkness hid it. Twenty seconds, forty, sixty. A faint splash echoed up the chute, and the rope jumped. He pulled it up hand over hand; obviously it only just reached the water. McCardle fastened a loop under Robin's knees and over his shoulders—and that would take off another four or five feet from the length. The sound of a shot, fired on the battlements, boomed in through the windows. If they hit Caroline, Robin would drown. Robin's dull eyes sharpened, and he screamed feebly and tried to pull himself back from the hole.

"It's all right, Robin. Auntie Caroline's down there, ready to hold you."

Then he couldn't wait, and pushed Robin's shoulders down to break the hold of the small fingers on the stone edge. McCardle lowered away, and Rodney could not breathe until his son's pitiful face faded in the dark. After that the screams of his terror shrilled up the shaft, and in the room Mrs. Bulstrode burst into tears.

They came to the end of the shortened rope, and Rodney looked across the hole at McCardle. Robin must be dangling several feet above the water, where Caroline couldn't untie him. They'd have to let the rope go; then he and McCardle would have to slide down. Another shot cracked on the battlements, and a noise rumbled in the passage. Father d'Aubriac pushed two beds against the door and called to young Myers; Geoghegan let go of Dellamain and shuffled over to join them; together they jammed the door while Dellamain collapsed on the carpet and shouted, "Help, help!"

McCardle untied the rope from the bedpost and nodded. They let go. The last few knots slipped down and disappeared. They heard a splash.

Mrs. Hatch waddled forward. "I've never 'eard of such a thing, but by Gawd I don't like this. 'Ere, I'm coming."

Rodney and McCardle stared from her to each other and again at the black square. Sixty feet. Mrs. Hatch's face shone belligerently. "'Ere, roll me up in the Haxminster. Aincher got no bleeding sense?"

She seized a six-foot rug, lay down, and rolled herself into it. They pushed her to the edge of the hole and straight down. Her long involuntary shriek faded; they heard a quickening series of thuds, and a smell of burning wool came up the shaft.

McCardle said, "You next, Rodney—same way. The auld besom had a right gude idea."

He began to roll Rodney into another rug. The door burst open, the beds against it crashed across the floor, and the Dewan and a score of soldiers rushed in. For a second no one moved, and the room was a murk of shadow and yellow highlights. In that instant Rodney, head twisted up, saw Dellamain's slack jaw and plump still hands. He saw the Dewan in the doorway and the frenzy of lust on his face.

The picture broke. Father d'Aubriac's skirts flew as he landed a kick in a soldier's stomach. Mrs. Bulstrode knocked over one lamp with her hand; young Myers kicked the other, and it was dark.

He struggled to get out; he had to help, he had to. Perhaps they could do something against the swine; perhaps he could kill the Dewan. He fought and yelled to McCardle, "Let me out! Let me out!"

The soldiers were firing blindly; the shots crashed and glared, the bullets droned round the walls. Dellamain was screaming, "I'll tell the Governor General, I'll tell the——"

A yellow flash showed McCardle's eyes a foot from his own. The surgeon said softly, "Hold tight, Rodney. Gude luck."

# 19

THE FOOT end of the carpet roll tilted down. He gripped the edges in front of his chin and shrunk his head into his chest. His stomach lurched up to his mouth, and his breath stopped. The tunnel roared, louder and louder. The sides hit him in the head with a hard, fast rhythm, and thundered a stone tattoo against his back and skull. The tearing whistle split his ears and the smell of burning wool seared his nostrils.

The solid stone vanished and he felt himself plunging through the air. Water slammed against his feet and sent the shock up his spine to his head. He gasped his breath out, then in. Water gurgled heavy in his stomach. Struggling, he pushed away the rug, released himself, and struck up for the surface. As he broke water the ringing in his head subsided, breath came, and he was thinking fast; there would be men shooting down from the battlements. He swam under the water for a while with the slow current.

When his lungs ached he raised his head cautiously but heard no firing. He slid downstream, looking for the others, and found Mrs. Hatch first. She was puffing and coughing, held up by the billows of her dress. She saw him and spluttered, " 'Elp, sir, please. I can't swim." He caught her under the shoulders and supported her. A little ahead he saw Caroline; she was floating easily, close under the corner of

the wall, and talking to Robin in her arms. She reached the
bank first and waited in the water until Rodney climbed out
and took Robin from her. The child lay dumb, shocked into
silence; his eyes moved from side to side, and he did not
recognize any of them.

A belt of trees began here, twenty yards from the corner
of the fort, and stretched down for half a mile to the ferry
site; a yellow light gleamed from the ferryman's hut. Rodney
led into the wood, turned left, and moved down in it parallel
to the river until the trees hid the shape of the fort. They lay
down and listened for sounds of pursuit. There was no noise
from the fort; the quiet river was out of earshot; they heard
nothing but the boom of frogs, Mrs. Hatch's grating breath,
and the drip of water from their clothes.

Caroline whispered, "What happened? Where's Mr.
McCardle?"

"Dead. The Rani's had them all murdered. The Dewan."

His teeth chattered but it was from physical chill. He did
not feel any emotion except tiredness; he had a sore head,
and he couldn't stop his hands trembling. He heard Caroline
draw in her breath, then she went on. "They'll find us here.
We must hurry."

He replied, "Piroo. I'll go now and get him. You stay here
till I come back."

"All right, but I'll go. You're very conspicuous; I'm not, in
a sari. I know the way. Don't be silly. We haven't time.
I'll be back in, say, half or three-quarters of an hour.
Where will you go if they come here searching for you
while I'm away?"

She was a speaking shadow near him. In the dim alleys of
the city she would pass as an Indian woman. He hesitated,
trying to see her face and thinking of her bandaged feet.

"We'll go back to the river now, and hide under this
bank. If I hear them coming we'll swim across somehow.
Then we'll move upstream. Same rendezvous, but the
opposite bank. That'll be safer. Caroline, for God's sake be
careful."

She was gone. He listened until he could not hear the twigs snapping, and knew she had reached the fields. Mrs. Hatch lay in a stupor at his feet; he aroused her, picked up Robin, and crept back to the river. The bank here was four feet high, and the lip, bound together by stones and tree roots, hung over the water. The water was waist deep and the river bottom stony. He searched cautiously up and down for a suitable piece of driftwood to support him in case they had to swim, but found none. He looked sideways at Mrs. Hatch; she was good and plucky, and he'd do his best for her. But if she dragged him down, or got in a panic—— He held Robin tighter. The hot night air dried his shirt; the water flowed cool at his waist and tugged gently at his trousers. A bulging gibbous moon rode out from wisps of dark cloud. He wished he could stop his teeth chattering; and only Robin's weight kept his hands still.

Twenty minutes later, to his left, towards the fort, the frogs set up a louder croaking. Mrs. Hatch clutched his elbow and whispered hoarsely, "I 'ear something—foot-marks." He put Robin in her arms, caught her under the armpits, and prepared to slide out into the stream. He listened with teeth set and legs taut—only one man, walking carefully, no torch. It might be someone going to the ferry on other business. He waited; his jaw muscles ached with the effort of holding his teeth clenched.

An anxious voice cried out in the wood, "Captain Savage, Savage-sahib. It is I, Prithvi Chand. Are you here?"

He did not answer. Slippers patted the earth and rustled the leaves; the man spoke again.

"It is I, Prithvi Chand, your friend. I have a message for you from Her Highness. You are safe; she will protect you."

He smiled grimly. It was Prithvi Chand all right; he recognized the voice.

"Come out, Captain, for your child's sake. I have some-thing very important to say. I am alone and unarmed."

Rodney made up his mind; he sidled a few yards upstream, hauled himself over the lower bank there, and lay quiet while

the water drained off him. Searching with his fingers, he
found a big jagged stone and caught hold of it. Prithvi Chand
passed by, a moonlit ghost against the trees, quavering out
the same message. "You are safe. I promise you."

He sprang up, swung his arm with the stone, and smashed
it against the side of Prithvi Chand's head. The heavy body
fell down among the leaves; he hurled himself astride it and
whispered, "One shout, and I'll kill you, you nigger devil!"

Prithvi Chand groaned and groped slowly up to consciousness. Rodney whispered, "Quiet. What is it? Quick!"

"A message from the Rani. She didn't order the massacre
just now, the Dewan did it all himself. Oh, my head hurts.
He heard her say that she'd like to see all of you people
dead, that she'd like to strangle you with her own hands. He
thought—pretended to think—that she meant it, and took
soldiers and did it—oooh! He was going to take you to
her alive."

"Do you think I believe that?"

"It's true. Here." He got one hand free and felt in his coat.
"Here's her ring, the ruby ring she gave you. She's been
crying on the stones in the courtyard and has tried to stab
herself. She said 'Give him this ring and tell him to remember
when I gave it to him first.' Sahib, no one's pursuing you,
but a lot of the soldiers are out of hand—the country's in
turmoil. She says you won't be safe except in the fort.
But——"

"But what?"

"Don't go back. Let me take the two women and the child
in, and you get away. Someone must reach Gondwara soon,
someone who will be believed. The sepoys there are going to
mutiny when our army and the Bhowani regiments are ready
to attack, *but not before*. They'll be trusted by then, because
they have orders to be loyal until then. They'll fight bravely
in all the first battles and the patrol clashes. They'll hand
over a few men who they will say are disloyal. Your general
has so few troops there; he can't afford to disband them
without reason."

Rodney snarled, "Which side are you on, anyway?"

Prithvi Chand, lying flat on his stomach and groaning with pain between his phrases, was a pudgy shape under him. The ring in his hand caught a little moonlight and flashed like a bloodshot eye.

Now his voice steadied and took on an awkward dignity. "I'm on the side of India. I want my country to be a country one day, and be free. But this mutiny is not the way to do it. We should learn from you, laugh at you as we laugh at forward children, treat you as guests in our country even though you did invite yourselves. That is the true India. We could be friends that way, one day. Perhaps you would all go away, perhaps we would ask some of you to stay. This—this is horrible. I did not know anything about it until the Dewan told me on Saturday night."

Rodney began to get up. As he moved, he heard Robin whimper; mingled with the faint cry were Joanna's screams, Geoffrey's babblings, the thunder of the massacre in the upstairs room. He gripped the stone tight in his right hand and the rage boiled in him so that he trembled.

He gauged the distance to the back of Prithvi Chand's skull and said, carefully keeping his voice steady, "Are you loyal to us?"

"I've told you, Captain-sahib, I'm loyal to India, but I think——"

Rodney swung the stone down with all his force. Prithvi Chand's skull cracked, and he beat and pounded at it, his words jerking out. "Filthy—black—swine! Swine! Swine!"

He stopped and felt the pulp at the back of Prithvi Chand's head, and drew down his lips in a crooked smile. This one at least would never give them away to the murderous bitch in the fort. What was it the Borgia said at Sinigaglia? "It is well to beguile those who have shown themselves masters of treachery." That would be an excellent precept to follow in all future dealings with Indians. That, and contempt.

He rubbed his hands on the grass, threw the Rani's ring into the bushes, and dragged Prithvi Chand's corpse after it.

Then he slipped back into the water beside Mrs. Hatch. He muttered, "A fool. I killed him."

He had a clanging headache, but he felt light and happy. This was better. Later he'd do the same to the Silver Guru and the Rani. There'd come a chance, somewhere, somehow. The Dewan would die much more slowly, and there'd be a fire handy. The Dewan—of course; now he understood why the little sod liked killing. It was delicious. He thought Mrs. Hatch was looking at him strangely, but he hardly noticed because his mind had wandered off down a warm and red-lit corridor, lined with streaming flesh.

Piroo's hoarse voice sounded just above his head. "Sahib, where are you?"

He handed Robin up the bank, scrambled after him, hauled Mrs. Hatch out, and followed Piroo through the tongue of woodland. The familiar cart stood at the edge of the fields; he would wander for ever in this cart, but it was better now. He understood all that had happened and recognized his enemies. He climbed in, smiling softly and flexing his hands. Two people were crouched in there already; Caroline was one, the other must be Sitapara. Now they were all crammed into the little space, and Piroo closed the flaps. The atmosphere was thick with patchouli and sharp with the taint of betel. Piroo hissed, and the bullocks tugged at the yoke.

They sat strained against one another and for half an hour did not speak, while the cart creaked slowly through the fields. The three women were tense in their places, but Rodney leaned back, relaxed and comfortable, because he knew no soldiers would be out after them. He couldn't tell Caroline why without telling her about Prithvi Chand, and then she'd look at him and he'd be ashamed. Still, it was for her sake and Robin's, and she'd thank him one day.

The cart stopped at last, and Piroo muttered, "Monkeys' Well. Not a sign of anybody."

Sitapara whispered, "Wait a bit. Get off the trail." She put her face forward, and they leaned in close to her as she

continued in French, "I've told Piroo to take you to Chalisgon. You must rest there until the child has recovered some
strength. I wish I could see him in daylight. Mademoiselle
says he is beautiful. Piroo knows the way. I have friends
there. They will shelter you and care for you well. They do
not love the Rani there any more than here, and you will
be safe."

Caroline, opposite, was holding Robin. She said, "Thank
you, Sitapara; you have been good to us. Don't risk yourself
any more. We have a rifle. You go back to the city, and God
bless you."

"I will go—in a minute. But first, here is some money, a
hundred rupees in Company's silver. Take it, I have plenty.
Repay me when you can, at interest if you like. But the best
payment you can give me is to have the Rani hanged. I was
beginning to suspect what they were doing. There was a fat
Calcutta merchant here. I know him, and know he never
leaves Calcutta except on the very biggest affairs. Then
suddenly, at the end of the Holi, the Dewan put me in the
dungeons. They must have found out I sent you the message
to Bhowani. He let me out on Sunday. Now, remember,
stay in Chalisgon until the child, and all of you, are strong
again—or the country and the heat will kill you more surely
than the Dewan. Hasten slowly! Rely on Piroo, who is
not such a helpless old fool—as I hear you've found out
already."

Rodney fidgeted, and she turned on him fiercely. "*Espèce
de chameau!* Have sense! You will *die* if you do not trust
*somebody*. Trust me, and Piroo, and the people of Chalisgon,
and you will save yourselves."

Rodney licked his lips. Shyamsingh's body lay crumpled
at the bottom of the well a few feet away, and the hamadryad
would be close by. This was an unhappy place, peopled
with ghosts and snakes, and Sitapara belonged here. When
she got out to go back to the city, perhaps he could say he
had to get out too for a minute—follow her out of earshot.
It would be easy and pleasant. She must be in it; this must

be a trap. Piroo would have to go, of course, before they reached Gondwara, or he'd betray them for certain; that little man would have to be watched, he was too damned clever with the silk square—a dangerous man, and deceptive like all Indians. The one vital thing was to get through to Gondwara quickly. Prithvi Chand had spoken the truth there all right; there was nothing but truth in the unsteady tremble of his voice. Besides, no Indian could fool him, Rodney; he had a superhuman faculty of insight and he knew when they were lying, which was always.

Sitapara said, "I think you're safe now. I came with you because I have only to show myself and no Kishanpur soldier would dare to search the cart—in spite of my imprisonment. I'm known." She added the last words bitterly.

She was up and out of the front before Rodney could prevent her. He moved to follow, but Caroline touched his arm; he shivered and sank back.

Piroo and Sitapara mumbled a little outside; he caught a few words. "You know what to do?"

"Yes. *Jai ram,* sister."

"*Jai ram.*"

Piroo knew what to do, did he? So did others. He began to fumble with his belt, making sure that the bayonet frog and scabbard were on it. The cart moved; he clasped his arms round his knees and closed his eyes.

Treacherous, murderous swine. The first and last task now was reconquest. The English were conquerors here, not friends, and it was a ghastly mistake ever to forget it. There must be no peace and no quarter until every last Indian grovelled, and stayed grovelling. A hundred years hence the inscriptions must be there to read on the memorials: *Here English children were burned alive in their cots, and English women cut in pieces by these brown animals you see around you.* DO NOT FORGET. A hundred years would not be enough to repay the humiliation. That old devil Sher Dil was probably shot in a fight over loot; Lachman and the rest must have run away. How had he ever been fool enough to waste a worry on them? There'd have to be Indian servants and Indian sepoys again, but by the Lord Jesus Christ there'd be a difference. The next few months would lay the new foundations, granite and rough and cold. There'd be British soldiers pouring in from overseas. They'd hear what had happened in Bhowani and Kishanpur, and they'd pay it back a thousand fold. Rodney would lead them. He'd find the words to tell them about Bhowani. He'd make them see the blood, hear the screams, feel the chilling horror of treachery.

He was a professional fighting man. It was no use letting the red rage blind his thinking. Victory first, then the long repayment; no victory, no repayment. If there were no foreign countries in the world, and England were left alone, she could crush these people however long it took. But there were other countries; France and Russia would be overjoyed, and could menace so much that England would not dare spare the troops for a complete reconquest.

Prithvi Chand had been speaking the truth; he knew that. If Gondwara had not gone yet, probably nothing south of Gondwara had gone. The Bombay and Madras armies must be waiting to see what happened in Bengal. Gondwara might be the key to India; if it held fast, the rest of India held, and the reconquest of Bengal would not take long. If it turned, the mutiny flooded the rest of India, and England might not be given time for the gigantic task of re-establishing herself. It wasn't only Bombay and Madras, either; he did not know what had happened in the north—what the Sikhs had done, what Lalkot had done. There must be scores of princes sitting on the fence and waiting, and watching Gondwara.

He ran quickly over the British troops in the Gondwara garrison. They ought to be enough to hold it, providing the Bengal regiments were disarmed and all the sepoys shot. If the sepoys were allowed to keep their arms there would be a catastrophe which would destroy not only Gondwara but, in the end, all the little British communities in India. Sir

Hector was new to the country. He was a strange man; perhaps he'd be fool enough to trust the sepoys; perhaps he'd already blown them all from guns. One couldn't tell, with him.

Rodney saw his own road clear in front of him. He had to bring his party to Gondwara, trusting nobody, unsleepingly cunning and ruthless, balking treachery with guile. When he got there he could tell Sir Hector the truth. He alone could do it; messages would be useless—they'd never be delivered, for one thing. And it was no use getting in a panic and killing himself by hurrying. He was weak and ill and had to get strong. It would take the Bhowani mutineers time to organize themselves, collect stores, join the Kishanpur Army, and move south. And there were so many British troops in Gondwara that the sepoys there would be lunatics to rise until the mutineers were at the gates.

Strategically, the enemy's best plan would be to capture Gondwara at, or immediately after, the onset of the monsoon. The rains would effectively hinder British relief operations until sometime in September. By then the rebels could hope to have the whole of India in their hands. Armies could not march through the rains, but treason could, and the Native armies in Bombay and Madras outnumbered the British components nearly as heavily as they did in Bengal.

A picture of the Rani's face came to him, and he was suddenly certain that the centenary of Plassey would mean a great deal to her. On June 23, 1757, India's native rulers bowed to the English: on June 23, 1857, she would try to make the English bow in their turn. And the date fitted in with the strategic factor, unless the rains came early.

He'd see how long his party took to recover, and then he'd make out his plan in more detail. For the time being it was enough to know that there was no desperate urgency to move, while there was a desperate urgency to rest. He'd have to pretend to trust Piroo and the peasants of Chalisgon.

He settled back, wishing Caroline could see that he was smiling at her across the darkness under the canvas. That

was silly; he wouldn't dare to smile at her if he thought she
could see. Her knee was touching his; perhaps she didn't
know whose knee it was in this welter. Mrs. Hatch was
rocking with the motion of the cart and snoring heavily,
pushing out her breath through fluttering lips.

Caroline he could worship. He would plan for her and
protect her; he would kill for her, and never tell her. At the
last, when they were safe, he'd tell her a little something of
what he'd done, and she'd be proud of him. He couldn't do
anything of it, though, without her well of strength; he'd
draw on that and bend his new fierce mind to use it in the
right way, to kill others and save themselves. There were so
many visions—of red flames and reeking flesh. If only God
would keep away the other ones, of her body, and not con-
fuse him. Surely he'd been through enough. That was the
kind of thing that could drive him mad. The link between
him and her was that between a sinner and a saint, not
between a man and a woman. He would earn her sweet
praise, one day, but this other was torture. He concentrated
on thinking of her face as it had been when she carried
Robin up the road into the fort, and at last went to sleep.

# 20

THE DOORS inside the headman's house were open,
and from where Rodney sat in the front room he could
see into the little back room. There Robin sat on the
floor, holding a wooden toy tiger a villager had carved for
him, and played, with quick movements of hands and head.
He was stronger in body now and his wound had healed
over, but he hardly ever spoke, and he whimpered when
Rodney came near him. If Rodney picked him up to caress

him, he hung stiff in his arms, with panic-stricken eyes. He liked to nestle against Caroline's shoulder or on Amelia Hatch's ample lap. Rodney's lips hung down at the corners, and he turned back to look round the front room.

Mrs. Hatch sat on a low block of wood in the women's corner by the empty hearth. She had recovered from the burns and bruises suffered in the chute—how many days ago? Thirteen; that had been the night of May the thirteenth. Each night at dark he carved a nick in the stock of his rifle —Shyamsingh's rifle; today was May the twenty-sixth. Time had passed quickly while they dozed and ate and dozed again. Of the first week here he remembered nothing but sleep. He was sure there was not another firearm in the village or he couldn't have closed his eyes. The villagers were a cowardly lot, afraid of his rifle, and obviously await-ing a chance to dispose of the English refugees without getting hurt themselves. So he ate, and found his strength again, and pretended to be weaker than he really was. In fact he felt well, strong and merciless and master of himself; soon he'd show these swine he was their master too. He knew where the strength came from which quivered in his waiting muscles, and enabled Robin to play with his toy tiger, and animated Amelia Hatch's cockney jokes. They three had slept, but the fourth had not; warm milk held to his mouth, firm hands on his head when he awoke gasping with fright in the night, the eternal eyes. The three of them had sucked her dry, and she was grey-white, hollow-cheeked, and her eyes burned like lamps. He knew and would not forget. He would raise her on a plinth of ivory and worship her the rest of his life. He must not fail her.

Piroo too had been tireless, but of course Piroo had ends of his own for being so smarmy and helpful.

The headman's front room was square and low. Plastered mud and cow dung made a smooth floor. Apart from Mrs. Hatch's log seat and a stack of winking pans and jars in the hearth, there was no furniture. There was no furniture any-where in the house except a large gimcrack wardrobe in his

own room and a few projecting shelves in the room where
Robin and the two women lived. Here the floor and walls
were bare; woodsmoke had blackened part of the ceiling—
there was no chimney—and spidery shreds of soot clung to
the rafters above the hearth. The room was full, as it had
been nearly every evening at this hour when the village
notables gathered to gossip and smoke. He knew them all by
now, and ran his eye calculatingly over the two groups.

In the far corner were the women: Amelia Hatch, Caroline, and the headman's wife—the last a brown version of
Amelia, with the addition of a small gold nose ring and a
caste mark. All three wore white saris. Mrs. Hatch's dress
had fallen to pieces days before and her black buttoned
boots, prominently displayed, were wildly incongruous under
the oriental flow of the sari.

The semicircle of men squatted barefoot on their hunkers
round a smoky tallow lamp hung in a bracket on one wall.
Rodney sat against the wall with the loaded and primed rifle
across his knees. Next to him was the headman, a square
youngish man with a heavy face and dark skin. Like the
other village males, he wore only a white cloth tied loosely
round his loins and up between his thighs, and fastened in
front. Next came Karmadass, the village bannia—general
merchant and moneylender—who was gross and greasy-
skinned; he was the same stamp of man as that other
Rodney had seen in Bhowani and Kishanpur, the one Sitapara thought was concerned in the mutiny; all of that trade
were cast in one mould. Then the priest—bald, flap-eared,
a white caste mark on his forehead and the sacred thread
across his shoulder. Next, two wizened old men almost in-
distinguishable from each other, with bent backs and rheumy
eyes; they were twins, and might from their appearance also
have been Piroo's elder brothers. Piroo was last, against the
wall opposite Rodney; a corner of the black silk square
peeped out of his loincloth.

A low murmur of conversation filled the room; when
speaking among themselves the villagers used a local dialect

Rodney could scarcely follow, but they could also speak and understand a little Hindustani. It was very hot, and the door from the front courtyard was open; out there the headman's animals breathed, champed, and stamped their hoofs, and seemed to be inside the house. The cheap hookah on the floor in the middle of the semicircle had a pottery bowl and a straight bamboo stem which each man swivelled round as his turn came to smoke. The water bubbled in it; Rodney exhaled and drew in his stomach muscles: he felt *much* better. It was time to be going.

He took another puff at the hookah, dragging the acrid smoke through his funnelled hands so that his lips would not defile the mouthpiece. He asked an idle question; the talkative member of the pair of twins replied. The fat bannia said pleasantly in halting English, "You are speaking werry good Hindustani, sahib-bahadur."

He replied coldly in Hindustani. "As good as your English, I expect, babu-ji."

Perhaps the fellow was only trying to make polite conversation, and show off his English. Perhaps, buried in these wilds, he didn't even know that it was an insult to speak English to an Englishman unless the latter first used that language to him—for it implied that the Englishman was a newcomer to India, or had not troubled to learn Hindustani. It didn't matter; the fat slug had better learn manners and might as well begin now. He looked intelligent in a crafty way. He was probably the one who'd sent that young fellow after him when he went out to kill a deer; the meals were endlessly the same—chupattis and curried lentils—so Rodney had taken the rifle and tried to get some venison. Someone must have told the young devil to go with him. It might have been the headman, looking so innocent there, or Piroo the cunning one, Piroo the thug. That didn't matter either, because the young fellow was dead, bayoneted to death and buried under leaves in a bear's cave up the valley. They'd never find him, never know what happened to him. He'd snivelled and begged for mercy, and said he'd only come to point out the game trails—but he'd had an axe, and a nasty treacherous look.

Rodney rubbed his hands, remembering it with suppressed glee. How straight he'd kept his face when he told the headman that the young man had left him to come home, that he had no idea what had happened to him after that, or where he'd gone! "Perhaps a tiger got him," he had added sympathetically, craftily.

The bannia flushed and stammered an apology. The headman said gently, "You are safe here in Chalisgon, sahib, absolutely safe, until you choose to go."

Rodney did not reply. That was a favourite remark of Caroline's, and the headman copied her, saying the same thing when it was quite uncalled for. It was very suspicious; that line of soft talk wouldn't help the fellow when the time came to deal with him. With half an ear he listened to the subdued mutter from the women opposite, obscured as it was by the bubble of the water in the hookah. The headman's wife was leaning back, cackling with soft laughter and holding her sides. He watched her lean forward with another of her eager questions—about English clothes, servants, food, perfumes, housekeeping expenses, feminine hygiene, obstetrics, care of children. The catechism had gone on for twelve days, and no end was in sight. She found a vast humour in every answer; probably she didn't believe half of them, and laughed in admiration of the white women's fabulous ingenuity. She understood Mrs. Hatch's explanations better than Caroline's, though Mrs. Hatch hardly spoke a word of Hindustani; Caroline's English world was on another planet, while Mrs. Hatch's differed only in degree. The headman's wife was, besides, genuinely awed by Caroline and treated her as she would a visiting queen or an embodied goddess.

They were safe for the moment. He'd make an opportunity to get Caroline alone soon and tell her to be ready to move tomorrow night or the night after. She was looking desperately worried these days, and never let him out

of her sight until he was safely into his room and she in
hers.

He'd better pump these people and see if he could find
out the latest news before he made his plan. He said casually,
"Does no one ever come to Chalisgon, headman? Travellers,
tax collectors, agents of the Rani?"

"Sometimes—but we always know at least a day ahead
because there's only the one jungle trail. And the tax man
has just been. He said it was a special levy and ruined us.
There's nothing more to be sucked from us now, so no one
else will come till the cold weather."

"We could all die here," the bannia said, "and the Rani
and the Dewan wouldn't care—except that then there
wouldn't be any crops to confiscate."

"There's not much now after *you've* finished with us,"
muttered one of the old gnomes, while his brother snickered.
The bannia waved his hands and protested volubly. "I have
to live, and feed my family, don't I? My interest's fair, isn't
it? There's a lot of risk in lending money to idle drunken
old men, like some I could name——"

The head man stopped him with a laugh. "All right, babu-ji,
all right; he only meant it in fun. How could we afford to
have proper weddings without you?"

The bannia grumbled into silence, and the priest said
slowly, "I have heard something. The Rani's army and the
sepoys from Bhowani are gathering in Kishanpur. They will
march for Gondwara in a week or two."

A mosquito whined in Rodney's ear. He slapped at it and
pretended to look for the corpse in order to gain time and
steady his voice. With careful nonchalance he asked, "Will
they come through here, do you think?"

"I have heard so. This is the shortest route; the trail comes
out on to the Deccan Pike this side of Gondwara. But have
no fear, sahib; we will hide you well."

Rodney was silent. He must not show anxiety, or the
wretches might summon courage to murder them on the spot.
He wondered why the priest had let out the rumour at all,

but saw on reflection that it was the safer course for a man posing as a friend. It would have been disastrous for his pretence if Rodney had overheard the news elsewhere in the village.

He decided to probe a little deeper, with care and cunning. He'd hardly mentioned the mutiny since arriving here, and the villagers had been careful to avoid the subject. Now he knew what they were waiting for and felt strong enough to risk it; there were things he ought to find out and tell the general. He noticed that the women had stopped talking to listen.

"Tell me, my friends, what do you hear of this mutiny? What do you think about it? Tell me honestly—for are you not the true people of India?"

That was good; his voice had been warm and solicitous, and they would like being called his friends. The headman and the bannia would certainly die the night that he left; perhaps the priest too—perhaps not.

The headman answered slowly. "We hear that the sepoys betrayed their salt and murdered many English everywhere, shamefully killing women and children. It was a curse on them. We saw the chupattis and the flesh pass, and talked about it many nights in this room. We did not know then for whom the curse was intended. Now we know; it was for the sepoys. We dare not think of the tortures they will suffer hereafter. But perhaps they will win in this life, because we hear there are hundreds of thousands of them and few English."

Rodney scowled. "There are hundreds of thousands of English soldiers coming over the sea. There will be blood for blood, a gallon for a drop—and burning for burning, a tree for a twig." But he saw in their faces that to them power had no existence unless it was present and effective. What could they know of the sea? He caught his breath and said quietly, "Do you want the sepoys to win? Do you think it is not right for the English to rule India?"

He used the word Hindustan for India because there was

no other in common use, and because among the educated
it was a convention that it should have that meaning. He
saw at once from their puzzled looks that here *Hindustan*
carried its narrow, true meaning—the upper valley of the
Ganges.

He thought the bannia knew what he had meant, but the
headman said in a surprised voice, "Hindustan, sahib? Why
should you not rule Hindustan, in particular? We hear there
are many lands before you reach the Himalaya or the Black
Water—Bengal, Sind, Punjab, Carnatic, Deccan, Konkan—
we do not know all the names, or where they are. We hear
they are all ruled by foreigners—English here, Mahrattas
there, Afghan Mohammedans somewhere else. We do not
know whether it is right, but that is how it is."

The bannia took up the tale. "It is like this, sahib. Here
we do not care who rules us as long as he rules well. All
men are foreigners to Chalisgon except men born in Chalisgon, as all of us here were. We would like best to be left in
peace, but that is not possible, because the world is full of
tigers and we are poor starving goats. Someone must protect
us and give us peace."

The twins snorted in unison at the bannia's description of
himself as a starving goat. The talkative one continued in
his vile accent. "Someone's got to do it, and we pray it'll be
the English. The villages beyond the Kishan—only thirty
miles away—they're under the Commissioner-sahib at Bhowani. There a man can't rob and murder as he likes even if
his uncle's cousin *is* a friend of the Dewan's."

"Death and taxes we cannot avoid," said the priest, "but
there the taxes are low and regular, and the clerks in Bhowani very reasonable in their extortions."

Rodney nodded. "I understand. You of Chalisgon have
been good to us. What can I tell the great ones that this
village needs most? When we have deposed the Rani you
too will be governed by a Commissioner-sahib."

The headman swivelled the hookah round, drew tobacco
smoke mixed with charcoal fumes into his lungs, and looked at

the ceiling. "Water—like the great Dellamain Commissioner-sahib of Bhowani promised the villages across the river. He has been killed, we hear. Who had not heard of him? Water for irrigation. There is a ruined dam and a silted lake five miles from here up our little stream." He nodded towards the back of the house. "It is called Naital, and the old good rajahs built it—oh, two hundred years ago and more. They made irrigation channels for this village and the ones lower down, and many miles of thorn scrub were then crop land. Now it is in ruin, and we have no water when we need it. The Dewan will do nothing; our taxes go for other necessary things, he says—elephants and armies and the Rajah's splendour in Kishanpur. It is just that a rajah should live in splendour, even as you sahibs do, with many servants—and it is just that we should have some water. Then we would be happy, most of all if the Commissioner-sahib came often to hunt here, or you officers came with your soldiers and made a great show. Then we could see the mighty ones enjoying the proper splendour, and so enjoy it with them. Then we would be happy."

The others joined in; Rodney listened with half an ear and threw in a word here and a question there to keep them talking, just as though their clownish pretences really interested him. All the while he was sharply alert in himself, and thinking competently. May the twenty-sixth today: the monsoon would break on Gondwara about June the twentieth. He'd better allow a week's latitude and get there by the thirteenth at the very latest. The enemy would probably attack on the twenty-third because of Plassey. Since arriving in Chalisgon he had had time to think, and the more he thought the more the importance of the battle to be fought for Gondwara impressed him.

The city was old, rich, famous, and an important religious centre. It was the last city before the border of Bombay Presidency, and it had once belonged to the Rajahs of Kishanpur. It was the site of a ford across the Nerbudda River which could be used all year except during the monsoon;

the Nerbudda was unbridged throughout its length as far as he knew, and the other fords and ferries were not so important.

He looked at his hands, and the rifle in them, the weapon of a common soldier. His trousers were torn, and his shirt dirty; he shaved every day with a piece of glass picked up on the roadside; he had no sword or silver accoutrements or silver blazon; his hands were scarred and thin and the fingernails edged with black. But he rode on a desperate mission; if empires ever hung on one man's skill and courage, this English empire hung on his. He had not thought his great day would be like this, and glowered under his eyebrows at the naked savages round him, and the women, and the smoky ceiling.

To work; he had to think. Here in Chalisgon they were about a hundred and twenty miles from Gondwara. If they set out tomorrow night, the twenty-seventh, they should get there by the third or fourth of June. That would give Sir Hector ample warning, and time to make his plans for dealing with the Bengal regiments of the garrison. The general would be wise to hold his hand until the last moment; then he'd have to root out treason, and disarm and execute them all. It would be a pleasant duty to watch and supervise.

Everything was clear at last. He'd explain to Caroline as soon as he got an opportunity. In the house the headman or his fat wife eavesdropped of course, through the walls. He'd think of some excuse to get her outside.

She had left the other two women and come over to the men's circle; the villagers were used to her ways by now and made room for her. At first they had been so dumbfounded that they lost their faculties and couldn't understand her simplest words. Now they were pretending to be pleased to answer her questions.

She said, "Do any of you know the Silver Guru?"

The priest said, "The Silver Guru of Bhowani? Yes, indeed, miss-sahiba, I know him well. All our people revere him. He is a great teacher and a holy man. He has travelled through here once or twice in the past year."

Rodney eyed them narrowly. They really believed the Silver Guru was holy, and would follow wherever he led. He wanted to shout out that their wonderful Guru was an Englishman and the dirtiest traitor in history; but Caroline caught his eye and very slightly shook her head. She was right of course; what use to tell them when they were already committed to the enemy? He'd do better to keep his mouth shut and pretend he knew nothing.

He'd thought of an idea to get Caroline alone and turned to say politely, "Headman, I'll go out again tomorrow and kill a deer or two for the village, if you like."

They all froze. But he wasn't going to give them another chance to send an assassin with him, and he added quickly, "I won't need anyone to come with me, except the miss-sahiba—if you'll send some men up the stream and across, to drive the deer down towards me."

They relaxed, and the headman said in a trembly voice, "Certainly, sahib. We will be grateful." Rodney saw that he was looking at Caroline. Caroline said evenly, "Yes, it is a good idea. I will be with the sahib, all the time."

Clever girl. Good girl. She'd caught on; she was warning them not to try and murder him alone, because she would be guarding his back. They wouldn't dare to touch Robin or Mrs. Hatch while he was out for fear of what he would do when he came back; he'd have the rifle.

A woman called from the courtyard, and the headman went out. Rodney waited, caressing the rifle, and when the man returned after five minutes scrutinized his face carefully. There had been a long mumbling out there, and he didn't like it. The headman squatted down near the priest and whispered to him. The priest pulled at one protuberant ear, frowned, and shrugged his shoulders.

Rodney could not contain himself; he'd startle them into some admission of guilt. He snapped, "What is it? Why do you look worried?"

The headman glanced at the priest before answering. Then he said, "Cholera, sahib. It started yesterday—the night before last. We have been keeping the news from you because we did not want to alarm you. We hoped it would touch lightly and go quickly, as it sometimes does. But now I think it will not pass from us until we have been severely punished. Three have died already, and more are sick. That was another the woman told me of—my father's brother."

He stared despondently at the floor. The priest got up and folded his arms. "You had all better leave us at once. It will be dangerous here in a day or two. The air will be foul everywhere."

Rodney pursed his lips. Perfect! He could tell at once that they were speaking the truth, though of course he'd look at the burning ghats later and make sure. Perfect! The biter bit! The poor superstitious fools believed that the cholera was a punishment for their sin in plotting to murder the refugees. They'd be glad now to see them go, alive. Now he could lead Caroline, Robin, and Amelia Hatch to safety, and leave the village to a fate more dreadful than even he could have devised for it. After that only Piroo would remain to be dealt with.

He said easily, "I'm afraid you're right. But I'll kill some deer for you tomorrow before we go. No, no, don't think of dissuading me. It is the least I can do for you."

"Thank you, sahib." The headman had tears in his eyes, and joined his palms in front of him in the gesture with which an Indian acknowledges a great favour and kindness. Rodney forced a yawn, although he could have hugged himself with excitement, and got up to go. Caroline opened her mouth, but this time it was his turn to motion her to be quiet. The poor girl looked ready to faint. He said nonchalantly as he passed by her, "Not now. Tomorrow."

Then he was in his room, whistling through his teeth and cleaning his rifle by the light of a tallow lamp. He did the things that had been his routine in Chalisgon every night.

He fitted the bayonet on the end; it was more difficult to sleep with the rifle in his arms if the bayonet was fixed, but much easier to deal with a sudden attack by, say, half a dozen men. He peered into the huge wardrobe and prodded about among the hanging pelts with the bayonet. No one there. He had collected stones from the brook the first day; he arranged them in the bed so that they looked like the hump of a body. He lay down in a far corner. Ten minutes later he was asleep.

# 21

ON THE plateau in the dawn the air was translucent and warm, the greys tingeing to gold as the sun rose. There was a brittle dryness in it, and in the trees, and in the crackle of the leaves under their feet. Caroline did not speak on the way up, but looked at the sky and the trees and smelled the morning air, and walked as though it were her last walk.

Soon he found a rocky outcrop from which they could see both ways but were concealed from the south, the direction he expected the deer to come from. He found a flat stone for her to sit on and settled down beside her. There would be no game for an hour yet unless another herd, or a solitary sambhur, crossed the forest in their field of view. He wetted his finger and tested the wind; the air was moving very gently from them towards the beaters. That was bad, but it usually veered when the sun came up. Anyway it must be so loaded here with human smells from the village half a mile behind that perhaps the deer were accustomed to it. Also, as they had not been hunted much, perhaps they would not be alarmed. He looked carefully around—no one in sight.

He turned on Caroline with shining eyes. "At last. We're in sight of safety. They daren't try to kill us until the Rani's army comes, and we're going to slip off tonight with Piroo and leave them to the cholera. Then, as soon as we're well on the way, I'll shoot Piroo, and we'll be safe. Safe in Gondwara, by the third or fourth of June!"

He smiled down at her; his heart was bounding. She said nothing, but looked at him with huge eyes. He understood; she had been his well of strength and now she was empty, drained by the idea of safety. Safe, safe. He tasted the word and said tenderly, "Cheer up, Caroline. You've been so strong—wonderful—but you can rest now. All our enemies are dead or are going to die. Prithvi Chand"—she blinked and turned her head away—"yes, he's dead, I killed him. And that young devil here they sent out to murder me. There's only Piroo now, and the rest will die of cholera. God is with us, dear. There's nothing to worry about now."

He'd never seen her cry before. Tears crept down her cheek; she looked away still, so that he saw the curve of her cheekbone. The sari lay crumpled on her shoulders; her hair, mat and lifeless, fell in disorder on her neck.

He could not bear it, she was so forlorn and lost. He put one arm carefully round her and comforted her. "There, there, it's going to be all right."

She trembled in the crook of his arm. He felt her muscles tighten, her trembling still. Her head came up and round to face him. "Rodney, do you realize that you are insane? Do you know that when you look at people your eyes are like the Dewan's? Even sometimes when you look at me, or Mrs. Hatch? Anybody—except Robin, or I'd have shot you long ago." Her voice ached but was steady and firm. "You do know it, don't you? You see murder and plots where there is only friendship. No one blames you; I felt the same for a little time. But it's true, isn't it?"

He let his arm fall and hung his head. So she had been deceived too. He'd have to save them all in spite of themselves. He'd better humour her for the moment. His eyes widened in surprise and he said, enunciating carefully, "Now come, Caroline, you know that's a ridiculous notion. You know they're really traitors, all of them. You're just trying to keep me from worrying. But it's you who are overtired now."

She put one hand on his. "Rodney, *don't*. Everyone in the village knows you killed that wretched young man. The dogs found his body the next day. His mother's a widow. She asked the headman to do nothing to you, not even to tell you, because you had been greatly afflicted by God and couldn't help it."

He gripped the rifle and stared into the blurring forest. Why didn't the beaters hurry? Why did her voice ache? Why was it so low?

"They're risking death in that village for us—every man and woman, every day. They've hardly enough food for themselves, and they feed us. Any one of them could be rich for the rest of his life, by telling the Dewan or the sepoys where we are. Piroo's left his land and house for us. Sitapara's risked torture, and you wanted to kill her—I knew it, back there in the cart. Prithvi Chand was your friend. What did he tell you before you killed him? Rodney, Rodney, you are so strong; but nothing's worth the loss of your humanity. Be stronger still, understand that there is love and charity left in the world, and——"

The teak trees swayed and swooped over him. He'd have to knock her down, take her away by force. He lifted alert eyes to her face, ready to strike. Dark grey—the dark grey granite, the liquid shining eyes, the seas, and under them the stone. He couldn't touch her while her eyes were open.

Tonight after dark there'd come a time—the cart waiting by the stream and the village stilled with death. She was too near God to see the sinfulness of man; the radiance blinded her. He alone could save her, and he wasn't fit to touch her.

The rifle lay at his feet, the sun shining on the wooden stock, and the bayonet's needle point buried in leaves. A sambhur belled in the jungle, and again; the clear tones rang down the aisles of trees. A great stag trotted out and across, head up to sniff the tainted air.

She said, "We must stay in Chalisgon and help them fight the cholera."

He was going to protest, but decided not to. He did not want to give her an inkling of his plan yet.

She went on urgently, kneading his arm with her fingers. "I know how important it is to reach Gondwara, especially for you. But that's only military duty—national duty, if you like. The war may drag on, and fifty thousand—two hundred and fifty thousand—people die if we don't get there in time. But that's a guess, and there's no guess about what's happening here in Chalisgon. At Gondwara, victory is a stake; here it's understanding, love. They're more important. They're more important for England too, in the long run. We'll be risking our lives here, as many unknown servants in unknown places have before us. It's not showy. No one will ever hear of it. We may all die. But if we're to be accepted in India it will be because of things like this—not victories or dams or telegraphs or doctors. Don't you see that *this* is the great thing to do, come to our hands? We can leave something here which will live when all the fighting's done, and our palaces are ruins, and we've gone home, as some day we will. We must stay. We must fight for Chalisgon, not because Chalisgon's risking everything for us—we are not tradesmen—but because it is right."

He listened wearily. She wasn't thinking as human beings had to think if they were to live. A great task had come to their hands—to make the fight at Gondwara a victory; to punish evil and show no mercy—not to die here among thieves. He remembered the trust that had linked him to the sepoys, and them to him; that had been lovely and it had been poisoned, and whoever had done it must be punished. The sepoys must be punished for their weakness. The Silver

Guru was at large, and only Caroline and he knew of his treason; he must be punished, and he would escape unless they reached Gondwara. Caroline was a saint and he could not argue with her. Saints did not feel human emotions; they didn't laugh, or care about earthly material things—and so men who weren't saints crucified them. Tonight he'd have to save her. He said, "All right. We'll stay."

He heard distant sounds in the jungle to the south and picked up his rifle. Waiting for the spotted deer, he began to think and plan while Caroline sat silent beside him. Get Piroo to prepare the cart in secret? A risk there, but he'd have to take it and trust to the threat of the rifle. Caroline and Mrs. Hatch—pretend to them that they were being attacked? Set fire to the house? Force or guile, he'd think up something.

In the evening he went early to his room, closed the door behind him, and stood listening in the darkness. They were talking still in the front room but not cheerfully. The cholera hung over them, and each man would soon return to his own house. He heard Caroline and Mrs. Hatch go into their room next to his, and listened to the faint shuffling and slithering as they prepared for sleep. It was burning hot, and he tiptoed to the windows and pushed the wooden shutters a little open—it wouldn't matter tonight. No light from moon or stars pierced the low overcast; outside and in, it was black. The thin sawing of mosquitoes swooped in his ear and penetrated the farthest corners of the room. He tiptoed to the door again, stood with his back to the wardrobe, and strained to listen.

He heard Piroo's voice, muffled but suddenly loud. "I'm off to sleep now."

The outer door into the courtyard had been open when he left and would remain so all night. Piroo slept out there among the cattle and goats. If he valued his life he'd do what he had promised—lie quiet until an hour after the last visitor had gone, then secretly yoke the bullocks into the cart and steal down to the stream. The axles were greased; that Rodney had seen to himself.

He heard the old twins go. A little later the bannia and the priest left together. Afterward the headman and his wife banged about the house and muttered to each other for a minute. The narrow stairs creaked as they climbed up to the roof where they slept.

The blackness and the heat pressed like fingers into his nostrils, and spiders of fear ran webs over his skin.

Not yet, not yet. Piroo wouldn't start for an hour yet. It must be half-past nine. He couldn't go without the cart because of Robin. If Piroo played him false? If a gang waited in the lane with axes and sticks? He couldn't kill all of them. His hands trembled. He'd better creep down and stand over Piroo with a bayonet. The murderers might not wait that long. They might rush this room, and the women's next door, and come in through the windows. There'd be too many of them. He'd kill a few, then they'd heave and sweat together in the dark, until an axe edge bit into his skull. That would finish it—all the sunlight, Robin's eyes, the strength in his hands, the wonder of Caroline. There was a stone inside his left boot, wrinkling the muscles of his instep.

A long time passed and his hands never stopped trembling. He'd had a plan to get Caroline away but he'd forgotten it. He'd trust to luck, be gone before the murderers came. He knew positively that they were coming. When he awakened her, if they had not come by then, she'd smell the murder in the air. If she didn't, he'd beg her forgiveness and knock her out. If he was holding the doorway and fighting for their lives there'd be no need to explain anything.

The velvet heat embraced him and the sweat soaked through his shirt and trousers. His feet were red-hot inside the boots. The stone grated under his heel. It was the size of a walnut and growing bigger.

He sat on the floor and laid the rifle beside him; it made a small metallic noise as he put it down. He began to untie the lace. He had taken the boots off once in two weeks. The cracked leather was stiff in the shape of his foot, and his heel would not slide free. He crawled into the corner, wedged his back against the wall, and tugged at the heel. The boot came off and he began to feel inside.

Because he had practised many nights to know the tiny sound exactly, he heard the door open. The headman's wife kept the hinges oiled, and he had found no way to make them more noisy. When he heard the scrape he put the boot down gently and reached out his hand for the rifle. It wasn't there under his hand. He remembered he had moved into the corner to pull off the boot. The murderer's feet slithered on the floor. Bare floor, bare feet. Piroo, the black square of silk ready?

Mouth open and all his life in the tips of his fingers, he reached out, farther along the wall. He couldn't have moved more than three feet. It must be here, close now, close; not yet, not in his reach. He began to edge sideways.

The feet were silent; at the bed; a rustle and a clop; a hiccough of breath. The death above the feet had found the stones. The feet turned and trod firm and quick, hurrying back to the door. He put out his hand, grabbed the rifle, and overbalanced. Sprawled against the wall, he swung it up into his shoulder—fire when the door opened.

A hinge grated, wood slammed against wood. The trigger crawled under his finger. The door had not moved. He lurched to his feet and lunged the bayonet forward. The point broke against the hard wood of the door, and he jerked it free. A hollow scream, inches away, appalled his ear; death banged and thundered round him. He jumped back and lifted the rifle again, but he didn't know where to fire. He searched forward, jabbing at the screams, hit wood, jabbed, and struck sparks off the wall. The banging and clattering and screaming rose to a climax of hysteria. His nerves tore apart and he burst for the door, shouting at the top of his voice.

"Caroline, get out! Out! They're after us! I'm coming to you!"

A huge square thing, black against black, loomed over and crashed at his side, and bounced and sobbed by his feet. The sounds were a woman's, and he stood in the door searching feverishly for a fuzee. Running feet thudded through the house. They were shouting from the courtyard, from the roof, from the room at the side. In the sputtering glare he saw the wardrobe on the floor. It creaked, and the woman's cries came from inside. It had fallen front down, and hopped bodily with the efforts of its prisoner to get out. Rigid in panic, he stared down at it. People crowded round him, torches flared, Robin screamed in Mrs. Hatch's arms. "What is it? What's happened?" Everyone was shouting.

The distorted noise in the wardrobe was Caroline's voice; he stepped dazedly forward. Piroo and the headman helped him; between them, hauling and pushing, they stood the wardrobe right way up. Its door swung open. Caroline fell out and lay on the floor, sobbing as though her heart would break. She wore nothing but a sheet, and that had fallen up round her waist. He stared numbly at the bare tight curve of her buttocks. Then he forgot what it was all about, stooped quickly down, wrapped the sheet round her, and picked her up in his arms. She clung round his neck and cried desperately into his shoulder while he muttered softly and foolishly,

"You were in the wardrobe, you were in the wardrobe, it's all right."

The knot of watchers in the doorway did not exist. She opened her eyes, looked from him to them, gasped, and slid to the floor, holding the sheet tight with both hands. She stammered, "I—I—I heard a noise, a clink. I was afraid of what you were going to do. I didn't want to disturb you . . ."

Robin's eyes were wide and anxious. The headman's wife was examining the wardrobe; she shook her head and muttered, "We found it on the Pike ten years ago while we were coming back from a visit. It must have dropped off a sahib's cart. It is accursed. I will have it burned."

The headman was trying to pluck the broken bayonet point out of the door, and Piroo was staring from Rodney to Caroline with suddenly shrewd eyes.

Rodney said gently, "What happened then?"

"There were stones in your bed. I was hurrying out to find what had happened to you, and—and—when I opened the door furry things brushed my face, someone hit me on the nose,—and then, and then——"

For the first time she really saw the wardrobe. Rodney's soothing anxious babble at last penetrated her mind. Her voice broke, she looked at her feet, then up at him, and began to laugh. She rocked on her heels, holding his arm to keep her balance. A vision of her fighting the pelts inside the wardrobe sprang into his mind, and his drawn face creased. He smiled, and there was an aching in his belly. The inhuman zealot girl of January, the inhuman crusader of February, the superhuman saint of May—she was human, a silly girl who'd frightened herself into a fit, and he'd roused the whole village yelling fire and murder.

He began to laugh, shouting joyfully. Villagers packed the outer room; over their heads he saw the flare of torches in the courtyard and heard the anxious buzz and murmur— *What's happened what's happened?* Oh, if they could have seen the wardrobe jumping about the floor! He rocked and pumped Caroline's arm, and cried, "You made a mistake, you made a mistake!"

A rushing torrent of relief sent his laughter up from the pit of his stomach. They were wonderful, marvellous people to see the joke. Caroline was a silly girl, and the world was laughing. Her face was wet with tears and she couldn't speak properly. She threw back her head.

"Yes, I m-made a m-mistake—just a little one!"

Piroo's face cracked mysteriously and the small lines deepened round his sunken eyes. Robin caught the infection and chuckled and reached out his hands to them. The headman smiled in a puzzled way and began to laugh, though he clearly had no exact idea what the joke was. The crowd outside took up the laughter, the torches waved, everybody yelled, the cows mooed. Mrs. Hatch stared from Rodney's bootless left foot to Caroline's insecure sheet. She sniffed, tossed her head, and cried, "I've never 'eard of such a thing!"

She carried Robin out, a wink and a broad grin twisting her face. The headman's wife, following Mrs. Hatch's glance, went off into a fat paroxysm. Seizing Rodney's arm, she bawled in his ear, "Sahib, sahib, couldn't you have been more gentle? Virgins frighten easy."

The crowd passed back the joke and the laughter doubled. Rodney sat suddenly on the bed, while Caroline leaned back against the door and recovered her breath. He looked at her with friendly eyes. By God, it was the best thing that had ever happened. He was sane. Caroline was a silly girl— sometimes—and of course they'd stay and help Chalisgan. It would be unpleasant, but he could laugh again, and he'd made Caroline laugh.

He said, "I'm glad you made a mistake, because it's saved me making one."

"Or two," she said, and slipped out of the room, blushing crimson.

# 22

OR THREE, or four. His mistakes had been many, and she was not a prig or an angel, but a young woman and very mortal. This day Mrs. Hatch had driven him out of the room where Caroline lay sick of the cholera, and ordered him not to come back till dark.

He walked with head hung, crossed the stream, and climbed slowly towards the plateau where they had waited for the deer one early morning in another life. Two hundred feet up he turned, leaned against a tree at the break of the hill, and looked down on the village in the valley. A greasy column of smoke pillared up from the flat place beside the stream where the burning ghats were. A few men squatted by the pyres; the evening sun still shone and dimmed the flames; it was not difficult to imagine death as a slow wind, crowding down the alleys, becoming visible in the quiver of air over the pyres.

The village huddled, close-knit, on the rise of land beyond the burning ghat. The smoke of its dead drifted across it, and he saw the community of it, not close-knit by chance but as a strength against disease, famine, wild beasts, and the stunned loneliness of the hot weather. It was cleaner than the villages of the plains; most of the houses were distempered in white, with here and there among them a few terra cotta or pink. Its many-coloured roofs were like a quilt thrown over it—pale squares of level mud, dark gables of weather-worn thatch, pink slopes of stone tiles. He picked out the headman's house by its larger roof and the window openings on this side. Those were the windows he had once tested so carefully to make sure Mrs. Hatch's bulk could squeeze through when the time came. He had been mad indeed; but even if all his fevered dreams had been true their danger was infinitely greater now. After six days of fighting he knew the nature of the enemy, and knew all weapons were toys.

Mrs. Hatch had refused to stay in Chalisgon unless Robin was sent away, so Piroo took the cart and drove off with him into the jungles upstream. They two would hide there until the pestilence had run its course and the fight was over —or until the three remaining here had died. Rodney wondered whether Robin were asleep at this hour. The jungle would be a lonely world to him; perhaps Piroo could make it familiar by telling him the calls of the birds and whittling animals for him to play with. Piroo could take him to Gondwara by himself if need be.

His son was as safe as anyone could be. The children of the village stayed and played, and died. He could see two small foreshortened figures in a lane between the houses, and knew they were naked boys drawing patterns in the dust with sticks. Their shrill calls came up the hill to him. A young girl washed clothes on a stone by the stream, rhythmically swinging her body to knead and pound.

On the farther slope secondary jungle crowded the houses, and the tangle of undergrowth proved that the land had once been cultivated. A thin line, marked by the greater density of the shadows, followed the curves of the hill's contour and traced the ruined water channel. There were foundations of houses in that part of the jungle, and scattered blocks, and square stone-lined pits. It was the same lower down the stream. With the decay of good government a town had surrendered its prosperity to the snakes, the creepers, and the improvident monsoons.

Surrendered? Chalisgon had not surrendered; it had been betrayed, as India had just been betrayed, by men who had power but no love. White or brown, it made no difference here; nothing was "foreign" to India, for India was illimitably varied. A foreigner was a man who did not guard the past and foster the future; above all, a man who did not love. The greater a man's capacities, the wider he must cast the net of his affection. In this little village men fought drought, disease, the sun. They had not the leisure or the learning to know anything outside the village, whether to love or hate. They became foreigners when they walked ten miles. But he and every Englishman need not be foreigners anywhere. The task was plain—to love, as a father his son, a son his father, a lover his mistress, a priest his flock. Any of love's patterns could be accepted, and flaws in it forgiven. Here, where the shadow of one brown man defiled another, English pride of race mattered nothing; India accepted it as she accepted the tiger's perpetual hunger and the ruthless passing splendour of the Moguls.

India had infinite patience, and no meanness. The burden of power here was weighed only by the bearers of it. Without love it was no more than a peacock's feather, and so it was easier not to love. Leaning against a tree on the knees of the Sindhya Hills, he thought that to men of English blood had been given an opportunity such as God grants but once in a thousand years. After the blind selfishness of two centuries, the hour had come. From here they could ruin themselves with power, or step forward as giants of understanding, forerunners of a new world of service.

It was the crude matrix of that love in Mrs. Hatch, a supremely English "foreigner," which gave the village its strength now. She cursed and cuffed them, because she was used to swearing at her husband and cuffing her children. She called them "niggers" because she knew no other word, and shouted at them in English, because her Hindustani was bad and because she believed that English was understood anywhere if yelled sufficiently loudly. The people of Chalisgon knew all this without being told; they also knew that Mrs. Hatch loved life and all who lived. Her way of expressing herself was to them just another of India's three hundred languages, no more harsh or strange than the *glub-glubbing* words and abrupt northern gestures of the Pathan horse coper who had passed through the village twelve years before. Mrs. Hatch had risen, not by race but by the force of her tempestuous affections, and they were all under her orders—Caroline too.

When he awoke the morning after the wardrobe fiasco, he lay awake on his bed for a time, chuckling to himself. Then he'd thought of Mrs. Hatch and steeled himself to tell her that the party must stay in Chalisgon. He had expected to see fear in her face, fear of the cholera if she stayed, fear of Piroo and the lonely road if she went on. There would be shrill anger that he should force such a decision on her after what she had been through, and all for the sake of a pack of heathens. So he had dressed slowly and gone with lagging feet to find her.

When the interview was over he had a new humility to set beside his new-warmed charity. He saw the smallness of his understanding, and was a little depressed. If Caroline had been herself, Mrs. Hatch might not have been; Caroline's exhaustion clearly had something to do with the result. She was there when he braved Mrs. Hatch, and her face was soft but dead white and drained of strength; she had seemed almost to say aloud, "I had one task—to save this man's mind. By accident I have succeeded. I am spent, and ready to die." Seeing her, there in the courtyard, Mrs. Hatch swelled up and became an earthy angel of wrath. She roared that she would do nothing unless Robin was sent to safety in the jungle, and shouted at Piroo until the bullocks were yoked in, the food loaded, and the cart out of sight. That took only ten minutes. Then she compressed herself and hurled her force against the resigned melancholy of the village.

Then, when Chalisgon trembled with her activity, Rodney really saw her for the first time. She was not young; here she could get no henna and her hair was more grey than brown. She was a fat Cockney woman, badly jointed, and tiny red liquor veins straggled across the coarse skin of her face. She could neither read nor write her own language. Of all she had been through, he had heard her bewail nothing except the loss of a certain china teapot. He knew now it was no callousness, but the ugly courage of the London gutters; not lack of imagination, but the wisdom of the oppressed, who fight only where fighting will avail them and dare not waste their little strength against a world which breaks whom it cannot bend.

At that time Amelia Hatch had taken command of everybody; on him she had forced so much work that he had no time to worry about Caroline. For six days he worked until he was exhausted, and slept without dreams and got up to face more work. When his thoughts strayed from the job in hand it was only to fret over other jobs ahead, or jobs done insufficiently well to please Mrs. Hatch.

Early on the sixth day, June the third, yesterday, while bathing a dying man's forehead, he saw Caroline stumble out of the house allotted as a woman's ward and hurry unsteadily down the lane beside it. He stood in the doorway and watched her return; her face was tightly pinched, the lips compressed and colourless, the great eyes deep-sunk and blazing. He called out to her, but she averted her head and ran into the other house without answering. Behind him the dying man muttered. He had turned back to the smells and sights of the male sickroom.

Up here on the slope he could smell it still. It permeated his shirt, lurked in the curled black hairs of his arm, and clung to his skin. The men lay in tight rows round the walls of each of the three rooms. Smoke drifted in from a bonfire in the lane where the sweepers burned the rags they had used to mop up the stools. When the patients came first they were pale but collected; the helpers stripped them below the waist, and they lay down; a Brahmin would loop up his sacred thread round his ear, so that he might not soil the lower end in his motions. In that early stage they had the strength to go out and squat in the yard, and the diarrhoea was still painless. That did not last long. Hour by hour the flux turned to a bloody paste; their stomachs rumbled; they became too weak to get up, and voided their bowels where they lay. Their faces contorted as the disease took hold and cramped their empty stomachs. They shrank before his eyes as the substance was drawn from every part of the body, turned to paste, and pushed out in those convulsions.

A little later a woman had come running. "The miss-sahiba has it." He'd dropped the rag from his hand and run to her. She lay on the mud floor and for the first time he saw resignation in her eyes. It frightened him more than anything in his life. He lifted her up to carry her to the head-man's house, so that she could be nursed properly away from the stink, the splutter, and the dying. She whispered, "In here—not to the house." He took no notice, and she stirred and repeated her words. Behind the faint voice there was still strength, and suddenly the eyes on him were no longer resigned. He had to turn back and put her down in a little soiled space against the wall between a young girl and an old woman. Mrs. Hatch came running, her eyes heavy from snatched sleep, and sent him to his own work.

Through that night, as through the nights before, the procession continued. Some of the faces were familiar to him; most he did not know. They came in, carried or supported by relatives, and lay down. He made them drink, holding his arm under their shoulders; saw them gulp thirstily; saw them, a minute later, vomit up what they had drunk. He watched the cramps spread upwards from the calves, tighten the thin peasant thighs, knot the flaccid bellies. Later, something would constrict the throat, and panic would come into the man's eyes. Seeing it, Rodney felt panic himself. Was that look in her eyes? He would turn dizzily away and take water to another feeble man.

Karmadass the bannia came. Through the night his strong voice weakened, and the sheen on his face faded, leaving it a dull chop-fallen mask. He breathed hard under an oppression of pain; his protuberant eyes receded into their sockets; his broad nose became pointed; his fat cheeks sank in; his greasy skin wrinkled and became dead. His eyeballs turned up out of sight, and Rodney pinched his face to bring them down. The eyeballs moved, but the skin had no resilience and stayed where it was, the pinchmarks still indented. When those signs came, the bannia, like the others, had neither fear of death nor will to live. His body could not find the strength even to rattle at its dying. He died near four o'clock in the morning and lay where he died until the burning party came after dawn to fetch him. He was on his back, and still warm to the touch—knees up, arms raised beside his head, clenched fists resting against his ears, belly muscles hard contracted, eyelids half-closed and encircled by wide blue rings, nose sharp, lips dark brown. There were more who'd followed him, and in the late afternoon Mrs. Hatch came to find Rodney dumb and trembling in the middle of the ward, and sent him out.

It was getting dark. He had been here long enough amongst the clean trees. A blue haze hung over the village, and fires twinkled out in points of gold. The burning ghat was an orange flower against the neutral brown-green of the slope. He walked down the hill and after a minute broke into a run, leaping sure-footed down the dim path and feeling the spring in his muscles as though he would never feel it again.

In the village they told him there was no change. He took an axe and went to hack down trees for the pyres. The fit men were insufficient for the work, and still the cows had to be milked, the land tended, and food cooked for motherless children. Starvation waited always round the corner here, hungry for those whom disease could spare. He swung the axe in bitter blows and swore unendingly. Long after it was full dark he leaned on the helve to wipe the sweat from his forehead. A light was wavering up the hill. When it came near, and he saw the priest's face, he put his hands behind his back and waited, but could not speak.

The priest stopped and held out his hand. "Tell Hatchmemsahib to give her this. It is good."

Rodney turned the small dirty-white lump slowly over in his palm—opium, the only specific known for cholera, and very rare and expensive in this part of India. There would be no more in the village. He looked at the priest; the lamp shone up and made his ludicrous donkeys' ears more prominent; he was grey and pale. The priest wanted to live too, and might have the cholera in him now, or might catch it tomorrow.

He was saying, "Cut it in six parts. Give her one part, with a little warm milk, every two hours. Some she will vomit up, but the rest she may keep. It tends to hold the urine, which is dangerous—but usually it helps. My friend, there is no other hope. Be quick."

Rodney turned without a word and ran down the hill in the darkness. He would have liked to make a speech or let the tears come, but he couldn't. Perhaps she would die, even after this. Even so the opium would not be wasted. Nothing was wasted in these days in this village; each action and thought illumined dark corners of the past, and would throw light somewhere, in some heart, for the rest of time.

Mrs. Hatch knelt beside Caroline on one side, and the headman's wife on the other. The women here, like the men in the other house, were naked from the waist down, but neither he nor they cared now. Mrs. Hatch looked at the opium and snorted. "Wot's that there—dope?"

The headman's wife snatched it from his hand, whispering, "Who gave you this? I did not know there was any in the village. This could have saved—it doesn't matter."

She broke off a piece, called for milk, and crumbled the opium between her fingers into the bowl. Rodney watched Caroline; after these six days he knew exactly where she was on the short steep road. She was more than halfway down, near the edge of the last abyss. From there he had seen a few, a very few, climb slowly back to life; most went over the edge, slithering fast and ending at the burning ghats. Her skin was wrinkled and dead, and her nose pointed; great forces pushed her remorselessly on, great will power struggled to hold her back. The cramps seized her throat and constricted her breathing, but the panic was in Mrs. Hatch's eyes and in his own. She tried to smile at him when he came in; then a spasm contracted her, and he closed his eyes. When the spluttering stopped he looked again and saw that the headman's wife was giving her the milk. She did not want it; her throat muscles clenched to refuse it, and when it was down her stomach heaved to reject it. Slowly, while sweat burst out on her forehead and her eyes started, she forced her will to mastery and drank, sip by sip and drop by drop.

A second battle began, to keep it down. His own face and neck contracted with hers, and when, after two minutes, the milk spurted out and splashed over the floor, he could no longer stand. He stumbled into the yard and sat down in the dust, where he could see the shadows moving across the far wall of the sickroom, and waited there till day.

When Mrs. Hatch came out into the glare of mid-morning and said, "I'm going to sleep now, Capting, like 'er," and grinned a haggard grin, he fainted.

Caroline was almost the last patient in either ward. Three days later the cholera went on its way. The priest said they had burned seventy-eight of Chalisgon's population of three hundred; no one could remember how many more had had the disease and recovered. The day it left them, the dazed villagers lay down and slept. That night, as after a hurricane, there was an instinctive orgy in which the survivors reassured themselves of their wonderful, wild aliveness.

Four faces were absent from the gathering in the headman's front room—Piroo in the woods, Caroline asleep in her back room, Karmadass and the silent twin dead. Rodney, the headman, and the talkative twin passed round a goatskin of toddy; the priest was in his place but did not drink. Mrs. Hatch and the headman's wife cackled hilariously together in their corner, and between times drank freely from another container of toddy. In spite of the empty places and the overpowering heat it was a gay and light place.

In radiant moonlight Rodney went down to the stream for water. The people he passed greeted him with their unfailing courtesy. They bowed low and joined their hands, because he was of a ruling class; but this time they smiled with their eyes too, because he had proved himself their equal. Drums were beating at the verge of the jungle and men singing in the huts by the stream. In the alleys women moved with uneasy sexuality, and men's voices throbbed when they spoke to them. Others, men and women, grovelled drunk in the dirt and sang raucously. They were not throwing coloured powder about, nor were they so riotous as the celebrants of the Holi in Kishanpur, but the atmosphere was the same and for the same reason: the Holi was the spring of the year, this debauch the spring of a new life. A star in the south made him think of Robin, and then of Gondwara. They'd have to move on as soon as Caroline was fit. He would speak about it later.

The headman and the twin broke off a conversation suddenly as he came in with the water. They were both a little drunk; he set down the jar and said, puzzled, "What is it, my friends?"

The headman scratched the skin behind his ear. "Well, it's like this——"

"Go on!" The twin took a swig of toddy and wiped his lips. "Tell him. It's all right."

"Sahib, you have heard us speak of Naital," the headman said, "the place where there used to be a town and a lake, five miles up our little stream? Well, we think the Rani's store of rifles, guns, and powder is up there."

Rodney exclaimed automatically. He remembered what he had overheard at Monkeys' Well. The Silver Guru said then that the carts were on their way to "the lake." It might be this one. He said, "What makes you think so?"

"The direct trail from Kishanpur to Gondwara goes through Naital. It passes not far from here, up there in the jungle. One day, weeks ago, one of our boys was out late looking for a lost goat. He saw many carts going south—but they didn't pass Pipalpani, the next village, twenty miles on, the headman there told me. Then, we've been forbidden to go to Naital or graze flocks near it for nearly six months now. The order said something about a new hunting preserve, but old Lalla Ram, who is dead, didn't believe that and went secretly to see. There are a few soldiers, he said, not many, living in an old temple there."

"Why didn't you tell me this before, if you knew it all the time?"

The headman shrugged his shoulders and was silent. The twin, Lalla Ram's brother, answered suddenly, "Captainsahib, if anything happens to that store the Dewan will burn this village himself, and torture everyone he can catch here. We sheltered you; that was a duty laid on us by the gods, and we would *never* have given you up. But this was different. We know nothing of war."

Rodney smiled. Guns had little place in a world ruled by cholera and famine. He said, "Why are you telling me now, then? Don't be afraid. I won't touch the cannon. It's my duty, I suppose, but I can't—now."

The headman scratched behind the other ear. "Now—we want you to destroy it. We have seen you and we have had time to think. We have heard news. There is blood all over the face of the land, and fire, and killing. The sepoys hunt like dogs up and down from the Ganges to the Indus. Of the village people, how should we know? We think they will give shelter where they can, like us. We hear this, and we talk, and we are foolish; but we think there will be a great battle at Gondwara. We know that the madness will be crushed quickly there, or will linger on. We will help you, and you must be quick, because the Rani's army marched from Kishanpur yesterday, and will be here tomorrow. After that it will be hopeless."

Rodney got up and paced the room, his head stooping under the beams. Turning by the front wall, he saw Caroline in the narrow passage at the back. Pale but smiling, she leaned against the door-jamb, and he crossed the room to her. "Go back to bed, Caroline, and rest. We'll have to leave here at dawn."

She replied, "I heard what they said. I've been lying listening to the music and the singing down by the stream. There's a night bird outside my window, and there's a big round moon again—the Holi, the mutiny, tonight. It's a lovely night tonight though."

"We mustn't get them into trouble. We must slip off and go quickly to Gondwara. We have a duty there—at least I have. What's the date, the seventh? It'll be a close-run thing."

They had been talking in English, but the others seemed to be able to read the tone of their voices.

The priest rose to his feet. "I gave you the last piece of opium in the village, for the miss-sahiba. You—all of you—gave us the last of your strength. But we are not merchants, to balance favours. It is our wish that the cannon be destroyed. The headman will go now and arrange for the whole village to live in the jungles for a time. It will be healthier; and besides, the English government will repay us and repair what damage the Dewan does."

"He may catch some of you, pandit-ji. And we can't bring the dead back to life, however good the cause they died in."

The priest shrugged. "No. Our people don't know much about causes, sahib. Here death is death. But they will not catch many of us. They will be too busy."

The headman paused by the outer door. "There are twenty fit young men in the village. Perhaps some older ones too can be spared. They will all be drunk, or making more men to replace those we have lost—but I will bring them." He laughed uproariously and slapped his knee. "Heavens, there are going to be some rough words said to me tonight. They'll be here in two hours for you to tell them what to do. Say it all many times, for they will be fuddled—like me. We are willing, but we know nothing of war. We can fight, I think. There are quarrels enough, God knows."

He went out, and the priest and the twin followed. The headman's wife looked at her winking pots and began slowly to collect them into a sack. The three English people stood silent in the back doorway and watched her.

Rodney harshly ordered Caroline back to bed and told Mrs. Hatch to go with her. They scurried off like mice, and he went out into the courtyard, sat on the low wall, and tried to think. The oxen champed steadily, and he scratched the nearest one's back with the toe of his boot. In the dark night a wispy cloud formation had begun to blot out the stars; distant thunder muttered under the horizon. There would be no rain tonight, or tomorrow, or perhaps for two weeks, but the monsoon was on its way.

# 23

HE LAY on the wooded ridge west of Naital, the rocks pressing hot against his belly and thighs. In front of him the air shimmered over a narrow valley. Locusts screeched in the dry jungle; each time one of the men moved a twig snapped or a leaf crackled. There were twenty-two villagers in his party, the youngest a boy of fifteen, the oldest the grizzled twin. They squatted in a bunch behind the crest, and each carried an axe, a hoe, or a pointed stake. They were his little army, and he their general. He thought of his torn trousers, his boots with the holes in the toes, his ragged white shirt; perhaps an officer of the 13th had gone worse clothed into battle, but he doubted it. His rifle lay beside him.

He looked at the sun; in another quarter of an hour he'd have to start moving. Each separate villager's face was eager, but as a group they were worried and uncertain. His own purpose firm, he wished he did not know these men so well, or that they could have been professionals. They might die in this adventure, but he was thinking of the headman's wife and her polished brass cooking pots; that was the sort of thing professionals did not have to think about. He began for the last time to run over his plans, trying to see them and judge them dispassionately.

The party had left Chalisgon before first light and, walking in single file on game trails, arrived on this ridge-line at seven. Five minutes later Piroo had come with Robin and the cart through the jungles to join them. Here, where the trees thinned out and exposed the Naital valley, he sent the rest to wait in cover while he studied the scene with Piroo. They were at the head of a slope surfaced with spear grass and reddish stones, and scattered with big round sal trees, oaks, and a few bushes. Less than a mile away across the valley the ground rose again, thickly wooded, to the rolling Sindhya plateau. North and south the Naital stream wound through the hills in a gorge two hundred feet deep; here its valley widened, and at the lower end, where the hills closed in again, the Rawan of that past century had built the dam.

Looking down, he had estimated it was thirty feet high at the centre, where there had once been a weir and perhaps wooden gates to control the outflow. Its farther end rested against the abrupt slope. On the hither side it curved round, shallower and shallower, until after a hundred yards the ground rose up to meet it. It was twenty feet wide across the top of the highest part, where the weir had been, and slanted out and down to double that at the base. As the ground rose to it the dam widened, as though the king had ordered the builders to use in each hundred-foot run always the same number of three-foot cubes of red granite; so it spread out and became a paved promenade beside the lake. There the king had planted shade trees and set pavilions, small temples, and other buildings whose use Rodney could not guess. The irrigation channels had in those days taken off from the foot of the weir; the traces of them curved round the contours of the lower slope. He thought they must have been an afterthought, and the farmers' prosperity an accident of the king's arcadia.

The town of Naital had been upstream, to his right. The women would have walked down from it to the new lake and washed clothes. The cattle would have grazed at the edge of the hanging jungle, the fields below would have been rich, and all day a noise of people. The lake would have been nearly three-quarters of a mile wide and two miles long, and in the evenings veiled by gauzy drifts of wood smoke. When the king came with his court, they'd make another tapestry; the men of the village would stop work to watch the king flying his hawks at water fowl and heron, and would be happy in their privilege of seeing such a gorgeous sight.

That king had lived secure; his grandson had spent his energy in a struggle for survival against the Tiger State, Lalkot. Naital died; the weir broke, the gates vanished. The assault of a hundred and fifty monsoons had shattered hundreds of granite cubes and strewed the valley for miles downstream with the wreckage. As the town decayed, men had chipped other blocks into small pieces and used them to mend their houses and byres. Now the houses and byres were fallen down, and square-cut stones littered their levelled standings. Striped mosquitoes and huge gnats whined in a waste of tall brown reeds where the lake had been. From July to November it would be a marsh; at this season it was a dry and sour-smelling barren, with pools of black water hidden among the reeds and the little stream winding invisible through the middle. Egrets and the little herons, the paddy birds, haunted it, and a pair of sarus cranes lived at the lower end. Vivid kingfishers flashed down the secret aisles by day; and at night tigers stepped through the jungle to drink below the dam.

At half-past seven he and Piroo had crawled down the hill to reconnoitre. From a hiding place they saw that nine or ten soldiers appeared to be living in one of the pavilions on the dam, among a welter of dirty sacks, piled rifles, bedding rolls, and cooking pots. One of their number, apparently a sentry, sat under a tree and played on a bamboo flute. Rodney decided that the Rani's stores must be in the other buildings, noticing that the roof of one had recently been patched with wood and cloth. He wormed back up to the ridge here, Piroo behind him, and made his plan.

The cart had been standing among the trees in a shallow dip. Caroline was resting in it; outside, Mrs. Hatch was trying to keep Robin quiet. He walked over and, speaking harshly, ordered two of the men to take the cart to the top end of the valley and wait near the stream until he came.

Caroline smiled with weak cheerfulness and said, "Please don't worry, Rodney. I'll see he gets to Gondwara, whatever happens."

He stared at her, turned on his heel, and strode back to the ridge crest. He'd have a few more hours at least to remember her face.

The attack itself, to be executed by untrained villagers, had to be simple, and it did not take fifteen minutes to think out the plan. Piroo would stalk and kill the sentry; the rest, headed by Rodney, would then make a direct rush from close quarters and overpower the other soldiers. To get into position Piroo would work round well below the dam, cross the stream, and come in through the dried marsh from the opposite direction. He would take out the sentry an hour after noon, when all the soldiers were likely to be asleep. The reeds, the ruined steps of the dam, and the trees and buildings should give him ample cover; he was to be as silent as possible.

By that time Rodney's party were to be at the foot of the hill and as close to the promenade as they could get. When they saw Piroo attack the sentry, or when an alarm was raised, they would rush forward in a body and bear down the guard by weight of numbers. If it went well they would have three or four hours to destroy the stores and cannon before the Rani's forces came up the dusty road. He would have preferred to attack at night, but there was no time, for the army would be here by dusk and after that attack would be hopeless.

That was the plan, and so far there had been no hitch. It was past noon, Piroo had long been gone, and the valley drowsed in the heat. Rodney glanced at the sun once more and whispered to the old twin, "Are we all ready now?"

"Yes."

"Spread out then, and follow me, the way we practised back there. Stop when I stop—and for heaven's sake no one make a noise."

"*Bahut achcha.*"

As they moved off, a pair of long-tailed green parrots shrieked away among the trees; then the hillside dozed again, humming in the lazy heat of noon. The party advanced slowly, first on the right, then on the left, in the middle, the right again, two or three at a time. After twenty minutes they reached the foot of the slope, crossed the road, and were on a level with the top of the dam. The scattered buildings stood up in silhouette against the forest curtain across the marsh. The sentry sat under his tree, with his side face to them. Quickly Rodney edged the raiders over an uncomfortably bare stretch. Two minutes more and they were crouched forty yards from the dam in the thick evergreen hollows of some korinda bushes, the old irrigation channels winding close below them.

The valley stirred with the aimless noises of midday. Monkeys crashed distantly in the trees across the marsh. Behind and to the right of his party, where the town had stood, some bigger animal was moving across the hill; a peacock blared *hauk hauk,* a little brown and white cheetal stag trotted out of the willow cover, shook his horns, and ran across the flat place above. It might be a bear frightening them, or perhaps a tiger—but the stag had not been very alarmed. Pig—the peacock had made a mistake; the boar came out and sniffed the breeze; his sounder followed him— three sows and a score of piglets. They began rooting about among the stones under an arm of thin acacias sticking out of the jungle. The high sun moved infinitesimally across the sky. The opposite slope was thick with sal; through the hot weather, as the other trees wilted and faded, the sal had stood like dark green cathedrals among them. Now, in the harshest weeks of the year, they had begun their miracle and were putting out new leaves—freshest brightest green.

He could not see down into the marsh because of the dam,

but the paddy birds kept hopping up and flying round above the reeds. Piroo was on his way. The villagers' faces were tight, and their eyes moved from side to side. He muttered to them to be quiet and smiled at them.

The new sentry's yellow coat was unbuttoned, and his rifle leaned against the tree beside him. He sang quietly to himself, breaking the melody to puff at a cigarette. The smell of it crept across the slope to the watchers, tainting the hot clean jungle air.

Though he was looking full at the place, Rodney could not believe for a second that he saw a head coming over the far edge of the promenade. With no sense of urgency he noted the flat expression on Piroo's face, noted that he never stopped moving, noted that he searched with his eyes and came steadily snaking on and over and up. On to the promenade, over the flat stones, up to the sentry's tree. Rodney started in a nervous spasm of release.

"Get ready!"

He watched a play, the same that he had seen from the cart at Monkeys' Well. That had been a shadow drama, distorting the depth of death and cruelty into two flat dimensions, and therefore more horrible than this. Yet the sentry was a young man, humming a pleasant tune.

Piroo reached the tree, crouched, drew the black square from his waist and without a pause came on round the near side of the trunk. Without a pause the black silk whipped and the humming stopped. Piroo had his right foot jammed into the soldier's back, and strained away with the silk like a bar in his hands.

Rodney waited until the sentry's face was black. He sprang up. "Charge!"

The villagers ran towards the dam with a ragged scream, and waved their hoes and spades and axes in the air. Rodney bounded forward. This was it; he'd got them. He scrambled up the stone blocks, and at the top saw the soldiers beginning to tumble out of their houses and look around them with sleepy eyes and mouths foolishly open.

The Silver Guru rose like a splotched ghost from the shadow of a building and stretched out his arms. Rodney heard the villagers cry out and felt them check their pace. The Silver Guru said softly, "Stop!"

Rodney yelled, "*Come on!*" swung up the rifle, fired—and missed. He was alone, for every one of the villagers had stopped. He ran on, the bayonet point levelled. But three soldiers were out now, and their rifles pointed at his body.

The Silver Guru said again, "Stop!"

He stopped and lowered the point. It was all over. In the moment when the men of Chalisgon faltered it was over. It was that sort of plan; success rested on a particular second, and the second had gone. He could not reach the Guru before the three soldiers shot him down. More were out now, scared and fingering the trigger. The Silver Guru's reputation protected the dump better than any number of soldiers. Rodney wondered how long he had been here, and why he had come.

He stood sullenly, holding the empty rifle in front of him. The Guru told him to drop it, and he let it clatter to the stones. What would they do to the villagers? For their sake he would have to fight and make a diversion so that some at least could escape. From the corner of his eye he gauged the distance to the nearest soldier. The men of Chalisgon huddled foolishly on the edge of the promenade.

The Guru raised one silver arm, palm towards them, and said gently, "You are true men, and will be rewarded. Neither you nor your village will be harmed. You have my word, and you know who I am. I am the Silver Guru of Bhowani. Go quietly to your homes now. Be as true to your Rani, who is an Indian like you, as you have been to this Englishman."

Rodney eyed him coldly. He was a traitor, and would die for it, but he knew men. Perhaps he even meant what he said. If all the leaders of the mutiny were like him, the people might turn against the British. But, if even a few had been like him, India would never have needed the British, and the Honourable East India Company would still be the

trading company it started out to be. It didn't matter now.
All questions of right and wrong had been drowned in
blood; the words would mean nothing until there was no
more blood to spill.

The villagers shuffled away. The old twin turned as he
went and cast Rodney a despairing look, a mixture of shame,
anger, and resignation. A soldier found the dead sentry's
corpse and exclaimed angrily over it. Another ran out and
lifted his rifle to shoot at the villagers trailing dejectedly
down the path towards Chalisgon. Rodney realized that the
Silver Guru and the soldiers thought that his party had
killed their comrade. Piroo had got away.

The Silver Guru cried sharply, "Don't shoot. They are
brave men." He added, turning to the havildar, "You would
do well to place another sentry, and order one man to watch
the sahib here. Come with me please, Captain. Let us sit
down in the shade and wait till the Rani's army comes."

He led the way across the promenade and, bending his
knees, squatted straight-spined near the edge. His back was
to the marsh, and he faced the two temples where the cannon
were. Rodney, glancing over his shoulder, saw that the guns
had been assembled; there were four twelve-pounders in
each of the temples, surrounded by kegs and boxes. He
swore silently, but the soldier was inches behind him, and
the others were watching suspiciously, and he could do
nothing. He sat down very close to the Guru, who motioned
him off with a twinkle in his grey eyes.

"Not so close, please. You are a determined young man.
But don't try to escape now; no one will hurt you. When the
Rani comes, you can show us where your son and others are
hiding, and we will send you all back to Kishanpur and keep
you safe in the fort. You've been through enough. Stay in
Kishanpur until India has settled down. Then we'll escort
you to a seaport and you can take ship for England—unless
by then you have decided to stay with us."

He seemed more human, and at peace with himself. He
looked at Rodney or at the trees, not beyond them into

unimaginable distances as he used to. The thinker had stopped thinking, the seeker had found. The spirit which had wrestled to know right from wrong was only a man, doing the best he could, for the decisions had been made and the whirlwind had caught him up.

Rodney believed now that Prithvi Chand had spoken the truth—that the Rani was innocent of the massacre of the refugees in Kishanpur. But who could control the Dewan? Even now he might be plotting to overthrow the Rani. And if he succeeded—then what? Caroline and Robin and Mrs. Hatch would be safer trying the passage to Gondwara. Piroo would be on his way to them, and could guide them. They'd be safe there, for of course the mutiny would be stamped out. Of course, of course. Sir Hector wouldn't believe Caroline if she told him his Bengal regiments were concealing treachery. There'd be another massacre, and no one could hope to escape three times.

The Silver Guru said, speaking always in Hindustani, "The Company is going to lose India—at Gondwara—and it is right that it should. You're an Anglo-Indian, and your life and work are built on this Company; but you're English too, and the English have ideals of freedom, for themselves. How would you like to be ruled at home by an Indian Company of merchant-adventurers?"

"The Company is *not* going to lose India," Rodney said coldly. "And—and if it did, do you think Indians are fit to rule themselves, or protect themselves, yet? There'd be a year of anarchy, civil wars between rajahs mad for power. I know now why the Rani wanted me to command her army. And who would suffer in all that but the ordinary people of India? And afterwards—Russia!"

"Perhaps. But when a country has learned how to throw off one lot of foreigners, it can do it again. Let us not talk about it any more. Why don't you tell me where your child is hidden? You don't trust the Dewan? He can be controlled now. You know the Rani had one of his eyes put out the next day?"

Rodney said quietly, "The Dewan is an honourable gentle-man compared with you. We don't produce many traitors in England"—he stared at the suddenly softened face before him—"and you must be about the worst in our history. You're English. How *can* you think we're going to lose this war, or rebellion, or mutiny, or whatever you want to call it? How *can* you? I do, just, understand how your experiences could have deranged you and made you plot against your country. But I don't understand how you think we're going to lose, whatever the odds. Only foreigners think like that. And if you imagine you'll be forgotten when the time comes to clean up, you're mistaken. We'll hang you on your tree in Bhowani, and generations of English children will learn your name as the meanest rat England ever produced."

A veil fell over the Guru's eyes and he looked past Rodney at the glaring yellow slope of hill. He said, "You hid there, in those korindas? That was a good idea. Leopards use them often—the leopards of England this time, eh? I was looking the other way, north, or I might have seen you."

The Guru continued in English, and the soldier standing over Rodney shifted his feet in surprise at hearing the strange language. "You are a remarkable race. You can understand an Englishman being a traitor, if he's a little mad. But if he thinks England can possibly lose a war, then he's too mad to be English. Well, you're right, and I'm not mad. In *my* country the children will learn my name, and remember me as a man who fought their battle in a far place—for them."

"What is your name?" Rodney asked grimly. "I'd like to know—though we can always find out from the old rolls of your regiment."

"My name is Donegal Sean Shaughnessy."

The grey eyes were on him, and warm now with affection. They were not North Sea eyes but Irish Channel eyes. An evil cloud lifted from Rodney's mind. Whenever he'd thought of the Guru, the man's treason had soiled him and every Englishman with its filth. But the Guru had lied in the temple

about the smuggling, and lied when he said he was English.
Rodney gasped with the relief; in the time of cholera he saw
Mrs. Hatch, in the time of defeat he saw the Guru. This was
not a traitor, only an enemy—an Irish boy driven by famine
to take a shilling and a red coat, to suffer lashes and turn
to silver in the embrace of India. On burning roads without
end, and for nineteen years under the tree, the rain had
ripened his love of liberty and made it a fruit ready to put
out seeds.

The leper of Bhowani looked him in the eye. "You were
a child, Captain Savage. Now you have become great, and
will be greater. I said once to the Rani that this mutiny
which we planned would sow only ruin and merciless hatred.
It was at our first meeting, after we had heard from the east
what was afoot. I said that though we claimed to work for
great ideals—patriotism, religion, liberty—yet in fact meaner
things drove us. In her, jealousy—that the English ruled and
made peace where her kind had made only wars. In the
Dewan, revenge and licence to kill, and lust to take women
who were bound so that they could not turn away from his
face. In me, hatred—hatred of England, which is not the
same as love of Ireland. The merchant was the only honest
one. He wanted money, and said so—but you don't know
about the merchant?"

"I didn't—then."

"I see. I felt cold. I said our hands were not clean. We
weren't big enough. No one is." He sighed. "It was your fault
too. You English are proud, distant. You want power for
your country in the world. It is only in passing, by mistake,
that you work for India—all that good work, turned sour.
There was a moment then, in that meeting, when the Rani
cried out, 'India will be free and great and good—and one!'
The others turned away from her. Yet *you* would have agreed.
It was sad. It is sad. Ruin and merciless hatred, I said; for
the most part it will be true. But now I know that in some
places, in some people, the love has been born which I tried
to find in all the gods, and failed. I was cold then; I am warm

now. There *is* love, all kinds of love: you, Miss Langford, the sepoys at the gaol—oh, I've heard—the men and women of Chalisgon, the Rani. Poor girl, she'd never thought of that."

His silver hands rested at his sides. The branches of a wild fig laced over him and broke up the light on his skin. Behind him the reeds were still.

"You were right in another matter. We will lose. But I could not follow any other path than this. Do you know what tragedy is? The inevitable—nothing else. I've lived trying to love, but for many years I've known that I would die trying to hate. Given a certain birth, and descending stars, a man must follow his path though he sees Satan waiting with open arms at the end of it. Examine your own mind when the blood is washed away and the dead are buried. You have reached and passed your pains. For Christ, who loved us, remember and understand, afterward."

Rodney felt tears pricking his eyes. He whispered, "I will remember. Forgive me for thinking what I did of you. But I have a path to follow too. Women and children were murdered in Bhowani, through you. *You* did it, not the sepoys. And you did something far worse. You poisoned a wonderful trust, and it died. I know now that it wasn't the best, but it was something. It'll take a long time to grow again. In some ways it will never be the same. What I have to forgive you, I forgive. But I believe in the rule of law and I will do everything I can to bring you to trial."

The Silver Guru's face crinkled in a smile of extraordinary sadness, and he said, "And on the gallows I will say this. Only the hangman will hear, but I'll be speaking to every Indian and every Englishman, every soldier, priest, merchant, farmer, governor—and especially to you, who have the strength to be greater than rank or race or caste. I'll say: 'I therefore, the prisoner of the Lord, beseech you that ye walk worthy of the vocation wherewith ye are called, with all lowliness and meekness, with longsuffering, forbearing one another in love; preserving the unity of the spirit in the bond of . . .' "

The black silk banded his throat, Piroo's face hovered over his shoulder, and they were both gone. Out of sight the bodies bumped and crashed down the high stone blocks.

Rodney began to move. Every instinct sent him forward to break the strangler's lock and save the Guru from those flat eyes. But as his muscles sprang to action he saw a vision of Caroline, starving in the jungles, so that instead he shot over in a backward somersault. His boots hit the soldier behind him in the stomach, and the man fell down, his eyes starting out in superstitious horror. Rodney banged the man's head hard against the stone and snatched up his rifle. The others had seen and were coming fast. He dropped to one knee and fired. The havildar in the lead coughed and stumbled, the rest dived for cover. Bullets whistled past; Rodney jumped over the edge of the dam and hurled in great bounds down the steps.

The Guru lay face downward in three inches of stinking water. Blood running from his nose, Piroo crouched over him. When he saw Rodney he loosened the silk and chopped down with the side of his right hand. The short blow struck under the Guru's ear, and his neck cracked. Piroo tugged at the long hair, jerking the head back at an impossible angle. Then he laughed curtly and ran ahead of Rodney into the reeds.

In a second they were out of sight. Bullets smacked after them and whined in ricochets off the patches of hard earth. Paddy birds flew up and circled piping overhead. Sedge warblers twittered angrily. The sarus cranes flapped their heavy wings and lumbered into flight. After a minute the shooting stopped, and as Rodney and Piroo pushed aside the tall reed stalks and splashed through the scattered pools they heard the soldiers clattering down the side of the dam, then a groaning wail.

"He's dead. He's *dead*!"

# 24

H E STRETCHED impatiently and for the hundredth time worked out the date. Monday, June the twenty-second, and the monsoon visibly imminent. Today they should reach Gondwara. Today they must reach it, if they were to be in time. One of the bullocks had died the day after they left Naital, and progress along the jungle trails had been slow, painful, and dangerous.

Each day the enemy cavalry rode out ahead of the main body of the army; twice he'd seen the grey-and-silver horsemen of the 60th trotting down a valley floor parallel to the ridge paths which Piroo always used. Behind the cavalry the army must be moving fast, but they had no news of it. They had not dared to get down on to the Pike yet. It would be safe to do so now, for surely the general would have his vedettes as close as this across the river.

June the twenty-second, a stifling day, a low lead sky with slow-moving clouds, hot and dark, permeated by the hidden sun. Caroline slept, swaying to the jerk and jolt of the cart; Mrs. Hatch told Robin a fairy story in a low voice; Piroo walked in the dust beside the lone bullock. Rodney called out to him, "Piroo, turn down now. We'll risk it."

Piroo clucked, the bullock swung, and the cart turned right. They dropped off the baking red rock plateau and wound down through thick woods towards the valley of the Nerbudda River. At the lip of the escarpment the trail ran in the lee of a ruined wall, where once a fortress had stood guarding the pass. Lower down they met two bullock carts grinding up the hill, loaded with immense piles of straw. Piroo whined a greeting and a few words in a nasal dialect. Rodney heard one of the strangers answer, "They're close, friend; that's why we're going home. But they haven't reached the river yet. Be careful; the whites have gone mad too."

In the heat haze a white temple towered up against the yellow forest slope to the left of the trail. They were tolling a bell inside, its slow boom of sound shaking the air, and he saw priests scurrying about the platform. The bullock leaned back and stepped delicately, sliding forward so that the red dust, four inches deep, squirted up between its toes. Caroline awoke with a start; Mrs. Hatch left her story unfinished. They sat and wetted their cracked lips with their tongues and looked at each other, while Robin talked to himself and scrambled over their feet. Rodney gripped the rifle, flexing his fingers on the stock and trigger-guard.

At the foot of the hill the wheels grated and bumped; afterwards the cart rattled steadily on the ragged metalling of the Deccan Pike where it ran straight and level for half a mile by deserted fields. Peering through the crack in the front canvas, he saw another red fort, also in ruins, on the right of the road, and beyond it wide water stretching to a high bank, a mud wall, and a jumble of houses. The squeak of the axle slowed its rhythm; the rattling slowed to a bump and bump; Piroo muttered, *"Gora log—lalkurti."*

A rough English voice cried, " ''Alt—*roko*! Where are you furching *jata*, eh? Wo'er you go' in there, you black barn-shoot? Let's 'ave a *dekko—jildi* now."

A hand tore at the back canvas, and two brick-red faces poked through. The fronts of their shakos were spread with the blazon of a flaming grenade, and over it the royal crown of England, flanked by a pair of numerals—men of the Queen's Fusiliers. The first jerked up his rifle when he saw Rodney's tattered trousers and dark face. Then they slowly lowered their weapons, for the people in the cart were crying, and Robin's face was crumpled in abject terror, and outside Piroo bowed and whined, the black corner of silk inconspicuous in his loincloth. The soldiers called out over their shoulders. Boots slammed against the loose stones of the roadway, and half a dozen heads and shoulders blocked the view. Their voices droned in foul-mouthed tenderness, the sweat dripped from their foreheads and hands, and Rodney could not stop weeping and hugging Robin and clenching and unclenching his hand on Caroline's.

Piroo weighted the floor with heavy stones, a fusilier sat on the tailboard, and the cart rumbled down into the river. On the other side they climbed a steep bank and passed into Gondwara.

The streets were full of soldiers and deserted of townsmen, and stank of death. A furlong in from the river a narrow crooked alley ran off to the left between tall houses. Except for a swinging sign, its paint flaked and dim, there was nothing to show that this was the Street of the Rawans, famous all over India for its wealth and the skill of its craftsmen in precious metals. Below the sign a corpse lay bloated and shiny black, motionless under a curtain of buzzing flies. There were others, on the Pike and in the side alleys; they were Indian men and women, and white maggots clustered round the wounds which had killed them; the women's sexual parts were torn and bared to the flies. Beside the cart the escorting fusilier said curtly to Piroo, "Take a *dekko* at them, you. Same *ke mwafik* for you if you done these poor ladies and gents any 'arm." Rodney's eyes glazed over with the hurt of pity. What had he thought on the hill above Chalisgon? *Once in a thousand years,* and the chance for the true glory already nine-tenths gone.

Soldiers of both races were putting the finishing touches to breastworks at the corners of the houses. From their badges he saw that the 82nd Bengal Native Infantry had been allotted the left of the street and the Fusiliers the right. The first line of defence would certainly be on the river, but these preparations showed where the general intended to site his reserves.

Robin buried his face in Caroline's lap when he saw the sepoys, and Rodney's mouth dried up, and sweat made the palms of his hands slippery. Caroline, stroking Robin's head, tried to smile across at him, but he could not take his eyes off the sepoys and watched them as a rabbit watches a snake. He read every tone in their voices, every fleeting expression on their faces. They were soldiers preparing for battle with the unhurried skill and neutral eyes of the professional. They worked easily, and their officers did not give many orders— but all was ready and they did not need orders. He had seen it all before; he knew it.

The night of May the tenth—Shyamsingh's face! Rodney knew nothing. He could have sworn these men had no thought of treason, but he was certain they had. What could he say to the little general with the stony eyes? How could he make him believe?

Piroo stumbled from sheer weariness. The fusilier kicked him angrily and shouted, "Git up, you black sod!" Piroo picked himself out of the dust and walked on expressionlessly. Rodney's head ached. "Ruin and merciless hatred . . ." The Indian sepoys worked at their tasks without looking at the Indian bodies in the streets.

A horseman galloped up from behind and edged past the cart. He wore a dark blue coat, dark blue trousers with broad double stripes of gold, and a black schapska with a gold bag tied to its side; he carried a lance. Rodney recognized it as the uniform of a regiment of Bombay Lancers. A sepoy of the 82nd called from a rooftop, "What's the news, brother?"

"Contacted the enemy two miles up the Pike—a patrol of the Sixtieth!"

The lancer flung the words back over his shoulder as he hurried on, raising dust and swarms of flies. Rodney forgot the corpses and the horror in the streets. The call of bugles, the disciplined tramp of foot soldiers, the rumble of moving guns, all joined together and formed a familiar pattern in his head. His eyes sharpened to full alert awareness, and he began to think. Caroline, watching his face, sighed and relaxed, but he did not see her or hear her.

If the enemy cavalry were two miles up the Pike, their main body of infantry and guns would reach the river well before nightfall. The Lancer vedettes, the Fusilier outpost, and any more of the general's forces on the far bank would have orders to fall back slowly. New moon, pitch dark. The enemy might try to cross by night, but they would be wasting their artillery strength if they did; it was unlikely. The battle would be here, and tomorrow—a hundred years and seven hundred miles from the field of Plassey.

The soldier led into the courtyard of a large building with many ornate porticoes, and the cart stopped. Haggard white women ran out in stained clothes and surrounded it. Rodney climbed down and rested against the wheel, for his knees had turned to water. The fusilier supported him, stroking him as a mother strokes a terrified child, and whispering, "There, sir, there. You rest; don't you worry. We'll tear them swine in 'alf tomorrer; don't you worry."

Rodney shook his head and watched the crowding women help Mrs. Hatch and Caroline and Robin out of the cart. So the general had not been able to get the women and children away from Gondwara; in fact he'd had to abandon cantonments and bring them in here to the city when he moved the troops forward to defend the river line. He saw that Caroline and Mrs. Hatch walked with flat purpose, while these others trembled and moved jerkily, and spoke with a hidden quiver of panic in their voices. They expected the worst, but could not even yet believe it, and the strains of anxiety made deeper marks on their faces than all the trials of experience had left on Caroline.

Rodney turned impatiently to the fusilier. "Take me to the general, please, at once."

"I'm here, Captain Savage."

Sir Hector touched his elbow, and he drew himself upright and saluted. The pasty face crinkled in a smile. "I am glad to see you. Come with me."

The little man turned and strode across the courtyard, raising one hand continually to his plumed cocked hat as he went, his huge sword clanking on the stones. Rodney followed into a big room, cool-seeming and dark, and the

general pushed up a chair for him—they must have brought
this furniture in from cantonments. A hand seized his own
and a voice said, "Hullo, Savage—it is Savage, isn't it?
Thank God you're safe"—and he looked up. He recognized
the speaker as George Harris of the 82nd B.N.I., aide-de-
camp to the general, and a man he knew slightly. He nodded
and muttered, "Yes, I got away." There was another staff
officer in the room; Rodney did not know him but saw by
his badges that he was of the 26th Foot, Queen's service.
They were all three looking at him strangely, and he realized
he had the Kishanpur soldier's rifle in his hand, the bayonet
fixed. He put it between his feet and glanced over his
shoulder; an Indian clerk was writing slowly at a desk in the
corner; three maps hung on the wall to his left; dusty foot-
marks covered the marble floor; the afternoon light filtered
through tall Moorish grilles on to the general's impassive
face. Rodney opened his mouth to speak.

Harris was watching him, Harris of the 82nd Bengal Native
Infantry. And he, Rodney, was going to say that the 82nd
were planning mutiny. Harris would not believe it of his
82nd, any more than he himself had of his 13th. Harris
would persuade the general that Rodney was unstrung, mad.

He cleared his throat. "I'd like to speak to you alone, sir.
It's very important."

Sir Hector balanced on his toes, puffed out his chest, and
nodded slightly. "Very well. Leave us, if you please, gentlemen. Before you go—Mr. Harris, pray tell me, have the
latest orders been acknowledged by all commanding officers?
Excellent. And is Captain Cable coming here at four o'clock
p.m.? Excellent. I think all else is in train, and you know
where to find me. Thank you."

He stood beyond the table, his arms clasped behind his
back. Rodney gathered his wandering wits and in short
sentences told all that he knew and suspected. As the long,
muddled, dimly lit story unfolded, the general rocked incessantly on his toes and seemed to grow taller.

It sounded fantastic now, and unbelievable—like the

morning of May the tenth. When he had finished the general stroked his chin and looked at him for a minute without speaking, tugging at his beard. Rodney saw that the little man had stepped on to a thick book concealed behind the table.

At length the general said, "That is a remarkable story, Captain. I could wish I had known Colonel Bulstrode better. I might have taken other action on his report. He was a gross man, not informed by godliness. I did what I could—wrote in confidence to my superior. Nothing happened that I know of. Have you any more solid proof than the word of Captain Prithvi Chand that my Bengal regiments are going to mutiny?"

"No, sir, nothing. But there never will be any proof. At Bhowani it burst on us like a thunderbolt—worse."

Sir Hector put one hand inside the front of his dark blue frock coat, lowered his head, and stared out into the courtyard with unfocused eyes. A muted clatter came in through the grilles, and the building hummed with distant movement.

The general began to speak in a polite conversational tone. "I will tell you what my position here is, Captain. Do not think, please, that I am asking your advice. I have two regiments of Bengal Native Infantry—the Eighty-second, commanded by Lieutenant Colonel Handforth, and the Ninety-seventh, under Lieutenant Colonel Moray. I have the personal word of both those officers, given me with all the force at their command, that neither regiment is in a mutinous state. They assure me that their sepoys are inexpressibly shocked by what is taking place elsewhere in Bengal. I have not yet mastered the Hindustani language myself, unfortunately, or I would know the truth at once. I have noted that the men's demeanour and actions corroborate their commanding officers' opinions. They have caught various deserters and handed them over for punishment, and they fought gallantly in a small skirmish to relieve Marka a week ago."

Rodney bowed his head. He had known it would come to this; this was how he would have reacted himself. Handforth and Moray and the others would not be British Officers of the Bengal Army if they could distrust their regiments. That sightless, lovely faith was better than his memories. He had no right to poison it; let it slide over the fall in a clear stream.

The general was saying, "Colonel Handforth has told me that to disarm the regiments now—supposing it were possible —would break their spirit, and that many of the men would certainly be so grieved that they would, after a time, join the enemy. It is also obvious that they might resist being disarmed, conscious of their own loyalty. Furthermore, Captain, perhaps you are not aware that my total force of British comprises one regiment of infantry—the Fusiliers—and eight six-pounder guns of Cable's European Troop, Bengal Horse Artillery. My cavalry is Native—one troop of Bombay Lancers, whose commander was killed at Marka. It is now therefore under the command of a Native Officer, a Rissaldar Rikirao Purohit."

Rodney sat up with a jerk, his weariness forgotten. A cold hand moved up the back of his neck, and he stammered, "I —I thought you had an infantry regiment of Bengal Europeans, sir, and a regiment of Dragoons, and a company or more of twelve-pounders."

"I did." The general never raised his voice, and there was no special intonation in his quiet words. "I had the Fourteenth Bengal Europeans. I was ordered to send them and the twelve-pounders to Jubbulpore as soon as the news of the mutiny reached headquarters. The Dragoons had already set out for China shortly before. This troop of Bombay Lancers which I have arrived a few days ago to replace them —one hundred Hindus instead of two thousand Christians. Pray allow me to continue. I know the enemy have two well-armed and disciplined regiments of infantry from Bhowani—your Thirteenth and the Eighty-eighth—and one of cavalry, the Sixtieth. My information is that they also have the equivalent of three regiments of Kishanpur infantry, who will have no great fighting value. Until just now I had counted on their being without any artillery, except a few of the Rani's six-pounders."

"I'm sorry, sir. I tried; I couldn't get at them——"

Sir Hector inclined his head with a wintry smile. "Your courage and devotion have been beyond praise. There are the facts. The British women and children of the old garrison are here, nearly two hundred of them. The regiments that were ordered away left their families when they went, and I have not felt that my position here justified me in sparing men to escort them down country. You say the Bengal sepoys are about to mutiny, but I know I am about to be attacked. If I somehow disarm and disband the Bengal regiments and the troop of Bombay Lancers, I will fight at a disadvantage of one to six. We faced them one to sixteen at Plassey, and beat them, but the sepoys of 1857 are not the same men as the ragged half-hearted rabble who followed Suraj-ud-Dowlah in 1757. I will consider now what is best to do, and pray for God's guidance. Without some more definite proof, I consider it unlikely that He will decide to disarm the sepoys. In an hour from now they must move to their battle positions."

Rodney stared at his knees. Sweat trickled down his back, and his hands were numb and clammy. His head throbbed and he could think of nothing to say. In an hour the sepoys would be committed to action stations and out of the general's hand; after that they could never be disarmed. The Almighty would decide. There was one more thing that must be said. Painfully, hesitatingly, he muttered, "Very good, sir. There are dead Indians in the streets—raped, murdered. The B.N.I can see them. If the men who did it have not been punished we will have no moral right to expect anything else ourselves, should the regiments—should we —if——"

He couldn't finish the sentence. Sir Hector said, "I am aware of it. It is a vile, base thing—but I have not been able to find the perpetrators, and I receive no co-operation from the officers or noncommissioned officers of the Fusiliers and the Artillery in the matter. I try to guide my actions by our Saviour's words, Captain, but I confess that for the first time in my life I am torn by doubt. These are Englishmen, and they have heard what happened in Bhowani. Their passions are too inflamed now; it is impossible to guide them to a true Christian forgiveness. As an officer in general command of troops, in whose hands rest so many innocent lives, I cannot prevent myself thinking how much more effectively the English soldiers will fight if their fury is allowed to run riot, and encouraged. I am still not sure. I must uphold discipline; I must win a battle, depending on these men; I must not torture the Bengal regiments in their hour of agony."

Rodney looked up as the little general paused. Nothing showed in Sir Hector's face. This was a harder man than Dellamain, though formed, like him, of many men. What conflicts raged at night behind that high forehead, between the reassuring thunders of a personal Almighty, the limpid syllables of the Sermon on the Mount, the icy concepts of a new Napoleon?

Sir Hector stepped down from his book, came round the table, and touched Rodney on the shoulder. "There is another thought which will affect my decision, Captain, about the Bengal regiments. I have told no one else. I dare not. A general is a lonely man. We will win this war, sooner or later. By winning we will condemn ourselves and all India to generations of hatred, unless somewhere, somehow, a new affection is born on the battlefields to replace the old. The new will never be quite the same—remember Bhowani, look about in the streets here—but it will be strangled at birth, finally and for ever, unless the Native regiments here remain loyal tomorrow—loyal to themselves, Captain. Without new, powerful evidence against them, I must give them the opportunity."

There was nothing to say now. Rodney knew he was

facing a great man, and in the general's place, on the facts before him, would have prayed for the courage and long-seeing wisdom to think as he was thinking. Sentence of death, after so many trials, came in unexpected, beautiful words. "I must give them the opportunity." Now he had to face the last minutes, prepare himself, and at the last die fighting as a professional fighting man should—hot, but not bitter.

Rodney dragged himself upright, saluted, and walked to the door. There he turned, came back, and picked up the rifle and bayonet. The general looked at him quickly as he went out.

There was a sepoy walking down the passage with a paper in his hand, his heels clicking on the stone flags. Rodney glanced dully at the big 82 on the man's shako. There was something about the face; it was strained and sick. He walked on; he had seen that expression before. The light from the door behind him bathed the sepoy's face. He groped in the dregs of his memory and walked slowly.

Naik Parasiya, at the children's party, the Saturday afternoon in Bhowani—that was the look of animal hurt.

Rodney could not move his feet, and he put his hand against the wall for support. A voice was speaking close to his ear. He did not listen but fought harder to concentrate on a memory. Naik Parasiya's expression—but he had seen the face itself before. "Go away! There is no sahib here." His eyes focused, and he saw it was Sir Hector who had followed him and was talking to him, urging him to lie down and rest. "Dismiss, you drunken owls. *Hut!*" He shouted the words aloud, and the general stared. The sepoy had turned into a room off the passage; he had a broad back and long arms.

Rodney grabbed the little general by the elbows, squeezing hard, and shook him. "Did you see that sepoy who's just passed? He was in the temple at Kishanpur the night of the Holi, with the other ringleaders, getting instructions, making plans. I can see it now, smell it. Oh, God, sir, I *know* they're going to mutiny!"

Sir Hector stepped away. He rocked once on toe and heel and looked pensively down the passage and up at the ceiling. He said quietly, "Very well. The Almighty's hand is here. I will require your services as an extra aide on my staff. In one hour's time in the city square, if you please—you know it? It is at the end of the Street of the Rawans. Mr. Harris will find you a horse. I have certain things to do, if you will excuse me."

Struggling for breath, Rodney went along to the room where the women were. Everywhere people moved about in the building, preparing for battle. Caroline met him at the door and he pulled her out into the passage. Over her shoulder he saw women tearing sheets into bandages. He heard Mrs. Hatch make a raucous joke and cackle with laughter; the other women looked up at her with slack mouths. Robin was there, asleep. Dusty sunlight poured through the windows, and thunder rumbled in the hills to the south.

He closed the door gently and took Caroline's left hand and held it to his cheek. He said, "After the battle, dear."

"After the battle?" She shook her head slowly. "No, now. We've travelled a long way together. We've lived in misunderstandings, little ones and big ones. We've been no better than poor Mr. Dellamain, thinking he was a fox when he was only a rabbit to be killed. Or Colonel Bulstrode, who knew so much he couldn't believe the truth. It's not going to happen to me again. I know your wife was killed before your eyes a few weeks ago, and you think you can't say anything, but—there's going to be a battle. I love you. I've loved you since I first saw you. I must say it now because—I'm still me. Because of the things that have happened to us. I've never had much use for womanly modesty, but I did have pride once. Because—there's going to be a battle."

"I thought you were so hard and selfish, once," he said; "then that you were somehow unreal—interested in things and ideals, not people."

"I was jealous, and furious that I couldn't keep myself away from you. I don't want to know anything about the Rani, but I hate her. Major de Forrest couldn't understand me; I don't blame him."

"Then I thought you were a saint."

"I was terrified of it. I could see you kneeling in your mind. Oh, I was so deliriously happy after I got out of that wardrobe. Wasn't that ridiculous?" She laughed softly. "Because you looked at me as a woman. There was something holding you back before then, something terrible, but —I wanted it."

"I thought—imagined, dreamed—vile things about you, Caroline."

She ran one hand through his hair. "I'm a woman. Do you know I tremble for you in the night, and no man's ever touched me? In the last six months I've found out everything about love—except that. I didn't believe love existed between men and women, only domination and submission; and now I've explored every corner of it—except that. I'm not ashamed. Touch me before you go."

He put his hands on her back and kissed each breast in turn. Her nipples stood up under the stained cotton of her sari, and he brushed the places with his lips. She started and gasped and pressed his head closer. After a minute she bent and whispered in his ear, "Is this it, the mystery?"

He rode back up the Pike towards the river until he came to the Street of the Rawans, and turned right into it. Squads of soldiers filled the narrow shaft, all moving the same way, now swinging rapidly along, now shuffling to a halt as blocks developed ahead. Dust rose, accoutrements clinked. It was again the early hours of May the tenth. If a fire glared over the houses he would go berserk and start fighting his way back to Caroline and Robin. The soldiers did not look round to see who pressed them, and from the saddle he heard them muttering in their languages.

"Wot's all this, Tom?" "Nap the Noughth's going to give us one of 'is sermons I expec'. 'E'd better not ask us to be kind an' 'oly this time." "Wot are we loaded for, anyway? Bloody dangerous if yer asks me." "Keep yer trap shut."

"Where are we going, brother?" "To the market square, I think. The general-sahib will doubtless exhort us before the battle. It is customary." "It is customary. The general-sahib speaks like a lion. I do not understand what he says."

He listened carefully to the intonation of the sepoys' voices. The words were innocent, but he knew what to listen for, and it was there—a subdued tension, an anxiety, a waiting. They didn't know what the signal would be, but they were ready and they could not hide it.

The street ran from the west into a cobbled square and continued out again on the other side. Another even narrower alley led into the square from the south—the right as he looked. On his left the row of houses was unbroken, and behind them he knew the river must be close. The general, astride his monstrous charger, faced into the square near where this Street of the Rawans entered it. He was talking to two men. One was a black-avised lieutenant colonel of Fusiliers, on foot; that would be R. C. L. Dempsey. The other was a horseman and had a tiger skin under his saddle and wore the brass helmet and black horsehair crest of the Bengal Horse Artillery—Captain Cable. The twilight showed Dempsey's face hard and Cable's mouth firm-set. Rodney heard the general say, "Just the one. This is no time for prolonged investigations. To your posts, please, gentlemen."

The two saluted and went away, and Rodney reported himself for duty. Another rider trotted up and without a word took station a horse's length behind him. He saw it was a rissaldar in the dark blue and gold of the Bombay Lancers—a slight, grizzled, old man with high cheekbones, grey whiskers, and a tight mouth.

The infantry tramped by into the square and fell in on their markers. The housetops began to lose their hard outlines, and stars brightened in the first dusk. The half-light washed the housefronts; their boarded windows looked out unseeing over the men. There was no sound but the tramp and click of soldiers, and the noise of the general's horse blowing breath through its nostrils. Rodney could distinguish the dull scarlet coats of the mass in the square above the white of their trousers; in front, thirty-five feet from the general, was the first rank of Fusiliers; behind it, more Fusiliers; behind them, rank upon rank of Native Infantry; but they were all infantry, and he saw no sign of the rissaldar's Lancers, or of the British gunners of Cable's troop. There were noticeably fewer ranks in the Fusiliers than in either of the sepoy regiments behind, and he decided that the Fusiliers must be providing all the outpost detachments watching the river and the approaches to the ford. Bayonets were not fixed; he looked at a dim red sea, white-based, black-capped.

The front rank of the Fusiliers stood motionless in front of him, set back that little distance. They were stunted children of England's new slums, with bad teeth and sharp suspicious faces. They were muttering to each other, passing some message down the ranks. He looked beyond them at the sepoys—and he was on the Pike at Bhowani in front of Dellamain's burning courthouse. He caught his breath and swayed in the saddle. Their eyes moved from side to side; they fidgeted in tiny movements; every man searched for a sign or a signal. They held rifles in their hands, their pouches were full of ammunition, and the British soldiers had their backs to them. With a wordless moan he urged his horse forward.

Sir Hector Pierce stood up in his stirrups. "Parade— *'shun!*"

Rodney stopped; three thousand men cracked to attention. While the echo still shook the houses, wheels rumbled and hoofs beat in the Street of the Rawans behind. The general edged his horse out of the way and motioned curtly to Rodney to follow suit. One behind the other eight guns crashed out of the narrow opening, turned right and left, and bounced across the cobbles to fill the space in front of the Fusiliers.

Rodney watched the faces of the sepoys behind. In desperation they awaited a signal, but no signal came. They could not see through the tight ranks of Fusiliers, but saw the mounted gunners and heard the rumble of the caissons on the cobbles. Behind them and to their left squads of Fusiliers appeared, blocking the other exits from the square, and stood at ease. To their right the row of houses offered no escape. Before, there had been no gleam of metal—only the scarlet and black and white. Now points of steel glinted in the street openings, and the murky light shone on gun barrels, wheel treads, brass helmets.

Cable sidled his horse alongside the general's, and a sudden flare lit up the barred tiger skin under his saddle. In the sepoy regiments the shakos stirred and nodded. Rodney caught a glimpse of Colonel Handforth's incredulous face.

The artillerymen flung their weight on wheel and trail. The trails crashed to the cobbles. Charges in, ramrods stabbed; grapeshot in, the ramrods stabbed. The gun nearest to his right had not been loaded with shot. The ramrods flew through the air, the waiting gunners caught them. They stood round their guns in stiff attitudes. At each gun one man stood by the breech, and held the burning portfire in his hand.

Cable muttered, "Ready, sir."

The general threw back his head and shouted, "General salute. *Present—ARMS!*"

In the two sepoy regiments the rifles jerked up to the Present. The British Officers swept their swords up to their mouths, kissed the guard, and swung the point down and out in the salute. The regiments stood rigid and helpless.

For on the order the Fusiliers did not come to the Present. Each man turned on his heel to face the Native Infantry behind, and jerked straight up into the aim. At regular intervals men moved forward and sideways, opening alleys through the ranks. At the end of the alleys the guns stood; the sepoys stared down the muzzles of loaded rifles, down corridors of men into the black mouths of the cannon; the portfires burned bright in the gloom, the smoke wisps rose from them.

The foremost ranks of sepoys wavered. In the thicker dark Rodney could not see the expression on their faces. The general called out in English, "Colonels Handforth and Moray, kindly order your men to lay down their arms— bayonets too. Tell them that if there is any hesitation both regiments will be blown to pieces. Otherwise they will not be hurt. Be so good as to remove your British Officers to a flank."

In front of the 82nd, Colonel Handforth raised his head to stare at the general over the intervening Fusiliers. The cold voice cut in. "Obey my order, please—at once."

Handforth repeated the general's words in choking Hindustani. Behind him, Moray stammered to the 97th. The black shakos rippled down. The men laid their rifles on the ground and straightened up. The British Officers did not move. Rodney had heard Handforth's order to them to stay in their places and, after a pause, Moray repeating it.

Handforth kissed the hilt of his sword and snapped it suddenly across his knee. He unbuckled his swordbelt and dropped it on the ground before him; fumbling at the two medals on his coat, he tore them loose and threw them down beside the broken sword. All the other British Officers in the two regiments were following his example.

Some sepoys stood stiffly at attention; some wept and threw down their medals and tugged at their buttons like their officers. They did not know what they had been going to do; many would have no idea even now. But whatever it was, it was gone, and in its room was disgrace. The Fusiliers stared along the rifle barrels at them; the portfires flared over the touch-holes of the cannon. They were sepoys of the Bengal Army, and they and their officers stood disgraced in the presence of British private soldiers. The cannon loaded with powder but no shot pointed at Colonel Handforth's stomach.

Rodney lowered himself stiffly to the ground. The torture, and the miles of dusty road were behind him. He had done his work and fulfilled his duty. He must go to the sepoys, the farmers, the friends, and help them stare down these white guttersnipes. He began to walk forward, a tic working in his left cheek.

The rissaldar leaned down from the saddle and caught his shoulder. "It's not over yet, sahib-bahadur."

The old man's lips were white-rimmed, and his eyes shone with a dark compassion. Rodney stumbled to a halt and waited, the rissaldar's thin hand biting into his shoulder. The horse nuzzled his back, and he caught at its snaffle.

The general rapped an order. The Fusiliers, holding their rifles in the aim, shuffled backward pace by pace, flowing back like the tide, slipping back between the rank of guns. At last they were pressed back against the walls of the houses, a sweep of dark scarlet on the housefronts, all their rifles pointing always inward. The row of guns stood nakedly exposed on the cobbles, so many lashes in the face, so many spears in the proud heart. The Bengal Native Infantry sighed together, and Rodney moaned; it was the sigh of the Bhowani night, the groaning crowd-wail.

A file of Fusiliers marched out of the Street of the Rawans and passed forward between the guns. In their ranks marched the sepoy of the passage, the man of Kishanpur. Behind him the pioneer sergeant of the Fusiliers, wearing the traditional apron, carried an axe and a hammer. The file halted.

The general said, "Colonel Handforth, translate after me to your men, please, phrase by phrase: Sepoy Girdhari Lall Pande, Eighty-second Bengal Native Infantry, having been found guilty of treason . . ."

"*Sipahi Girdhari Lall Pande, be-arsi Bengal ka paltan, sir-had ki qasur gunegar hone ki sabab se . . .*"

". . . is sentenced to death, by being blown to death from a gun . . ."

". . . *top phutne se maut ka saza hukm hogya . . .*"

". . . the ancient and customary punishment of his crime . . ."

*. . . jo issi qasur ka am saza hai . . .*"

". . . the sentence will be carried out forthwith."

". . . *yeh saza ek dum karna ka hai.*"

The pioneer sergeant ripped the buttons off Girdhari Lall's chest. With a bayonet he slashed the back of the coat and tore it off savagely, rocking the man's wide frame. Then he took his hammer and began to shackle on leg-irons, but Girdhari Lall burst free and marched out alone in front of the unshotted gun. There he arched back until the muzzle touched the centre of his spine.

The general called out, "British Officers, please move to a flank."

Colonel Handforth flinched but did not move. No one moved, and the rissaldar's grip tightened on Rodney's shoulder.

Girdhari Lall shouted in a strong voice, "Remember Mangal Pande! Now and for ever! Rise! It is not too late. Rise!"

The general raised his hand, paused, and let it drop. The gunner dropped the fire to the touch-hole.

The air split and clapped together, and the boards on the windows rattled. Girdhari Lall's head flew up and spun like a black football against the orange glare in the sky. The vacuum of the blast sucked back pieces of flesh and spattered the gunners with blood and bowels. The body flew apart like a bursting water jar, and a shower of entrails and pieces of bone and flesh splashed the faces of the British Officers and Indian sepoys. Colonel Handforth, his face a red mask, clapped his hands to his ears and rolled on the ground.

A fusilier fainted and fell clattering beside his rifle on to the cobbles. Rodney would have gone but for the hand so hard on his shoulder that it hurt. The artillerymen looked out, grim and still, through eyes rimmed with blood. The houses were a wall of darkness and only the portfires twinkled in the square. The stars were going out, one by one, behind a low cloudbank. Thunder grumbled closer to the south, marching over the Mahadeo Hills down into the valley of the Nerbudda.

He stood a long time in darkness of mind. He had a new memory to set beside the others—the corpses in so many rooms and streets and gardens—and live with. The memory would not be of Girdhari Lall, but of the faces of the English gunners. It was right for them to execute a mutineer; but they had liked doing it. The tales had been told, and they had listened. They would behave like animals, and kill every Indian who crossed their path, and burn the land from end to end, and do it joyfully. "Ruin and merciless hatred . . ."

From a long way off he heard the general's small voice. "Eighty-second and Ninety-seventh Regiments of Bengal Native Infantry, march back to your lines in cantonments, in that order. British Officers, I look to you to stay with your men and keep them in the lines, in good discipline, until I can issue further orders." He paused a long moment, and spoke gently. "Gentlemen, it was for them." And, suddenly harsh, "*March off!*"

There was a silent wait. Then, one by one, muttered half-hearted commands; the tramp and crash of professional fighting infantry on the march, but lacking something—no arms in their hands, no steel at their hips; swinging into step, rhythmic, but the rhythm dead and cold.

When Rodney looked up the square was almost empty. A few fusiliers were gathering up the rows of abandoned arms and throwing them into two bullock carts. Nearby a groom held a torch, the red glare of it shining on the general's face. The general did not know how to weep; and he was in the care of his Almighty, so perhaps he did not feel the pains of other men. But his face was soft as he turned to the rissaldar and said in English, speaking slowly, "Rissaldar-sahib, under God, India is in your hands tomorrow. May He guide you."

The man in the worn blue and gold uniform looked at the general. He did not understand English, but he understood what had been said to him. The realization burst on Rodney, then, that the Bombay Lancers had not been disarmed. The rissaldar's grim old face showed nothing. He saluted, swung his horse, and trotted out of the square. Rodney stared at the general, his heart suddenly pounding and over-full. After everything, after the massacres and the murders and the execution and the hate, the general would throw on the troopers of the Lancers this staggering cross. He was not asking them to be loyal to the British, or to the enemies of the British, but to hold faith with themselves who were simple men and had sworn an oath and under it had taken the Company's arms. This was not the General's Almighty, or the shade of Napoleon, but love which spoke.

It was dark. Sir Hector fumbled in his pocket and brought out a small book. The groom held up the torch so that its light fell on the pages. In the empty square Sir Hector began to read aloud the Christian service for the burial of the dead. A grave and reverent sincerity lifted his voice, and he almost sang. The party of Fusiliers went on with their noisy work, not knowing or caring what the little man was doing now. Rodney, numbed by many shocks and wonders, listened to the words and, between the words, to the rifles and bayonets crashing, ringing into the carts.

At the end Sir Hector closed the book and said in an altered tone, "Come, Captain, let us go to our place. The enemy will attack two hours after dawn."

# 25

THE TENSION flowed out of him in the night of waiting—a thunderous night, electric but rainless. The merciless urgency of the past weeks had reached its climax at dusk, in the roar of the execution gun. The future lay in the lap of the battle which would be won or lost, here and now, without hurry. The rains must break soon, but they could not affect the outcome now. They would drop the final curtain of a tragedy, to announce its ending and fix its result unchangeably in the mould of history.

When the morning came he saw that the river ran only seven hundred yards wide, and he saw the twinkle of bayonets, spear-points, sabres, and guns on the far bank. The dawn pressed down like lead on a world waiting for rain, so that the smoke of the enemy's cooking fires did not drift away but made a hazy line above the scrub jungle at the edge of the fields. The level bases of the clouds scraped the roofs of the city behind him, and dimmed the lustre of the Rani's standard hanging from the tower of the ruined fort across the river. The water tumbled over the rock reefs in the ford and ran smooth and oily between. Buildings cast no shadows because the sun, after its rising, hung invisible behind the clouds and spread its heat and light through all the surcharged air.

He stared across the river, straining his eyes into the sourceless glare of the day. Directly opposite, dots and blobs and squares of colour moved in rhythmic patterns among the faded green of the foliage, and he saw that the enemy infantry were forming columns. The white of their trousers flickered to and fro in the scrub, and their bayonets were already fixed. Failing a last-moment flank march along the river bank, which would be dangerous because of the watching British guns, their attack must surely come straight across the river in the shallowest part of the ford, along the line of the Deccan Pike. Here, in front of Rodney, the Fusiliers stood ready to receive it. They were in the British soldier's favourite formation, a threadlike scarlet line, behind the low mud wall which marked the river's flood level. In the centre of the line a gap in the scarlet was densely filled by the blue coats and brass guns of Cable's troop. There the soldiers had broken down the mud wall so that the muzzles of the guns could be depressed to sweep the slope of cracked red earth leading up from the water's edge.

The ford was wide, and all this was at the downstream, western end; horsemen could cross anywhere from here for a quarter of a mile upstream, to the right. Beyond the right of the Fusiliers' line the walls of the city stood back a few yards from the top of the sloping bank, and that long strip of flat ground was empty of men; sticks and stones, dead dogs and little heaps of garbage littered it—but no soldiers. Four hundred yards up, the walls of the city bent away from the river, and there, at the point which marked the eastern, upstream limit of fordable water, fifteen or twenty mango trees stood in a lonely huddled grove above the bank. The troop of Bombay Lancers waited under its dark green leaves, but Rodney could not see them. He turned away, frightened of his thoughts, but he could not stop them. Sir Hector had posted the Lancers there to guard the flank— and they were not gods or heroes but Mahrattas, Indians, Hindus, men of flesh and blood, and heart and spirit and brain.

Across the river the sabres of the enemy cavalry (the 60th, the enemy!—he laughed shortly and bit his lip) the sabres twinkled, an acre of spilled diamonds behind the centre of their infantry. The Dewan might send *them* cantering to cross the ford up there in face of the Lancers. They'd move too fast for the guns to hurt them much until they got into the water, and then it might be too late. What if the Lancers couldn't hold them—wouldn't? Why should they, with the

brown girls ripped and flyblown and bloated in the streets
and murder in men's eyes? What if a torrent of sabres—
and lances—poured down that noisome strip of river bank
and struck the Fusiliers in flank?

Trrrr*mp*, trrrr*mp*. He lifted his head in quick astonishment. After the double roll of drums, the bands struck up in
the lilting swell of "Lilliburlero"; he remembered when the
bandmaster was having so much trouble teaching the tune
to the 88th's band. Trrrr*mp*, trrrr*mp*, and the shrill fifes. The
Dewan must have gone mad; or was this the signal for
mutiny, gone tragically astray? On the far bank the bushes
waved and shook and of a sudden were bright with colour.
In nine columns, three dark green of the 13th, three primrose
of Kishanpur, three scarlet of the 88th, the enemy moved
down to the river's edge, their bayonets flickering like steel
carpets in the livid light. On the right and left the white
trousers of the sepoys swung in regular rhythm; in the centre
the Kishanpur soldiers' bare legs were almost invisible
against the earth, and their yellow coats came on like floating
flowers. At the head of the 88th the Colours hung limp on
the staffs—the Union of Great Britain at the right, the Regimental of the Honourable East India Company at the left.
These were the Colours which used to hang in the mess,
cased and crossed like huge rockets, under a portrait of
Queen Victoria. The Kishanpur infantry surrounded two
primrose standards, and by them rode a single man on horseback. Rodney recognized the Dewan and no longer heard
the strains of the massed bands. He threw away the cheroot
and felt the tip of his bayonet with his finger. The columns
marched on and into the water. The 60th Light Cavalry were
not with them. He slowly ground the stub of the cheroot
under his heel and tried to dry the palms of his hands on his
torn trousers.

Behind him Sir Hector, benignly disinterested, peered
down on the scene from a flat housetop, rocking his five
feet and one inch back and forth on heels and toes, his hands
clasped under the tails of his frock coat. The Fusiliers had

unbuttoned their coats and put handkerchiefs under their shakos in a futile attempt to protect their necks from the all-pervading sun. The sweat soaked dark through the scarlet tunics; the cheap black dye of their cuffs ran, and stained their foreheads as they wiped them with their sleeves. Under the mixed colours their faces were strained and white, and ugly with expectancy. Piroo squatted comfortably by Rodney's heels, his fingers in his ears. Cable's guns, lined up wheel to wheel, poked silently over the shattered wall; by them the portfires flared out like a row of street lamps. Upstream all was quiet; in the deep water downstream fish were rising and a moving crocodile dragged light ripples under the bank. Beneath the music of the bands he heard the swish and splash of wading men. The general nodded.

The scene shivered, split in horizontal bars, and came wavering together again. A single concussion rocked his head. The eight six-pounders of Cable's troop had fired all together. The shock chased trembling shudders across the water, and before they died the guns fired again and sent new little waves to run shivering after them.

The foremost ranks of wading infantry dissolved. Men plunged hither and thither, turning back, losing their balance, falling over. The Colours faltered and swayed wildly. On the far bank the music trailed away in a discordant cacophony of sound. Cable's gunners fired with quick savage precision; in the distinct regular pauses between the explosions Rodney heard the wail and shout of the stricken army. A black patch covered one of the Dewan's eyes.

The artillery's regular fire, the parade-ground stillness of the Fusiliers, the stretch of quiet river, all gave the battle a detached and panoramic quality. This was a painting—this carnage in the water, those dragging shapes and lumps which were men and shakos and knapsacks and severed legs, those light dots running to and fro on the far bank.

He saw a puff of smoke jet out from the scrub on the right of the Pike, opposite the ruined fort. The shell shrieked by and exploded against a temple behind Cable's guns. Dust settled in a grey pall as the thud of the piece crept lagging after. One by one more guns opened fire, and he counted anxiously: fourteen or fifteen altogether, including twelve-pounders. The gunners over there were amateurs and they had not had much time to practise with their new weapons—still, it was a heavy weight of metal. Fountains of dirty water sprang up from the river, balls whizzed far overhead; but already they were beginning to steady their aim.

Under the British fire the Kishanpur infantry broke ranks. Rodney watched grimly; they had never met anything like this, or been given the training and discipline to face it. For a minute or two the sepoy regiments looked to be in equally bad shape; then the Native Officers got control and the regiments continued to advance. For one moment—a moment of mixed exultation and horror—he thought the Dewan would allow them to press home the hopeless attack. Then through the smoke and the turmoil of broken water he saw men wading across the front of the columns, shouting and gesticulating. At once the sepoys turned about, each in his place, and the regiments ploughed back as steadily as they had advanced, while the guns bit off piece after piece from the rear of the columns and strewed the wreckage in the river. The Kishanpur infantry became a distraught mob, their yellow coats everywhere—upstream, downstream, scrabbling through the green and scarlet ranks, running in clusters along the far bank. One, in his crazed panic, splashed furiously towards the British and reached the shelving slope in safety; at a word a single Fusilier stepped out of rank, leaned on the wall, and shot him in the head.

The enemy shells burst over the line of British guns in a steady crescendo. A pair of artillerymen sank down by their piece; another dropped in the dust and crawled round in circles on his hands and knees. The dust cloud rose thicker, drifting sluggishly to the east across the front. Over there the bands began to play defiantly louder, but uneven now. The river was quiet again, and nothing to mark the slaughter; all drifted down on the stream, except a corpse bent over a snag, jerking and swaying as the current tugged at its shoulders.

The opposing artilleries settled down to a duel. Rodney breathed out in a long slow sigh, lit a fresh cheroot to stay the shaking of his hands, and looked about him. The stakes were on the board, all the love gone for nothing, and the dispute left for decision to the blind cannon. The infantry must stand and listen while St. Barbara of the Artillery spoke. *Ultima ratio regis*—the king's last argument. He glanced upstream. Today the last word probably lay in the heart of a man, an old nearly toothless horseman from the Deccan plateau.

The enemy bombardment was concentrating on Cable's troop. A direct hit blew George Harris, at Sir Hector's side, into a red mush; splinters droned endlessly over the wall, and men fell silent in the dirt; the wall crumbled; the Fusiliers shifted uneasily as stray shells struck their line, and when their officers were not looking they would peer secretly round at the prim little general. Across the river the steel-tipped hedge of colour had re-formed, and flurries in it marked where British shells ploughed through.

Rodney felt his mind slipping away from him as the heat and noise and dust racketed him to the edge of insanity. To bring it back, he tried to keep the ash long on his cheroot; like that he wouldn't wince or duck involuntarily as the shells swished past. Surely to God no one could stand this much longer—not very much longer?

Still the guns cracked at his eardrums. The Fusiliers relaxed their shoulders, mopped their brows, and watched the gunners die, each man thanking God that choking hand was not at his throat. The clouds settled lower overhead. Rodney ground his teeth: stick it out—for a century they'd been drumming it into the sepoys there over the river. His mind leaped back eleven years. He saw the field of Chillianwallah, where he and they had stood for murderous hours through the unseen battle of the cannon. He remembered his terror, and Jemadar Narain's stern compassion, supporting him without weight of words. They'd stuck it out together then. He groaned. Not very much longer—it couldn't be.

After an hour the British rate of fire had slowed perceptibly. Blue-coated gunners sprawled beside their guns and died of heat-stroke where they lay. Cable's lieutenant knelt on the ground, his brass helmet bright beside him and spurts of blood dyeing the crest. An artillery sergeant caromed, babbling, along the sides of the houses like a drunken ape, to collapse frothing at Rodney's feet. A gunner threw down his ramrod and ran down the bank and plunged into the river. The dripping, sweaty dead were dragged out of the way and piled round the caissons in a welter of splintered wood, twisted iron, and spilled powder. Direct hits overturned three of the eight guns so that their muzzles pointed at the sky or rammed at an angle into the dust.

Over the pandemonium bugles blared across the water. Shells howled in at Cable's troop, breaking the distant band music into tiny dislocated snatches. The Fusiliers straightened their backs and stood alert, a little eased now and not frightened.

For the second time the bushes on the far bank parted, the masses of colour wheeled and swung down through them, down the bank and into the water. The formation was the same; the Kishanpur infantry lost their line and dressing before they reached the water; still there was no sign of the cavalry. Looking now, as the heads of the columns approached in the river, Rodney saw the expressions on the faces of the sepoys, and felt sick. As they reached the centre point of the stream Cable screamed, "*Action front! Canister!*" The muzzles swung, paused, and poured out long streams of orange fire. After the duel only three of them remained in action, and those undermanned. They fired irregularly, each crew as fast as it could. Cable had taken station as layer on the centre gun and shouted continuous commands in a cracked voice.

At the third round the Kishanpur infantry broke and scattered. Rodney saw the Dewan using the flat of his sword, then the edge, on the men struggling back past his horse. The golden youth who had been the Ensign of the Body-guard cannoned into the tight scarlet ranks of the 88th and scrabbled insanely to get through them, away from the canister scythes. A havildar of the 88th lifted his rifle and shot him down.

The sepoy regiments came on, separated by a wide gap where the Kishanpur infantry had been. Any minute now they would be within effective rifle range. Watching them, his mind saw again the hundred troopers of the Bombay Lancers who waited silent in the mango grove. He saw the old rissaldar's pinched face, the blue and gold uniforms, the lances pointing upwards. Resting his hands on the wall, he stared dim-eyed at the oncoming sepoys, wading through water waist and neck high while Cable's guns poured canister into them and hurled the men like broken branches into the stream. The six columns, scarlet and rifle-green, loomed nearer. The Fusiliers waited. Piroo stood up, taking a firm grip of his pickaxe.

The columns reached the shallows. On top of the bank a hundred yards away the gunners depressed the muzzles and fired with the desperation of lunatics. The Fusiliers jerked up their rifles. The roar of artillery could not quite blow away the shouted commands of their officers.

"Fire! Load! Rod! Home! Return! Cap! Fire a volley at one hundred yards, ready! Present! FIRE! Load! Rod! Home! Return! Cap! Volley one hundred, ready! Present! FIRE! . . . FIRE! . . . FIRE!"

Rodney heard his own voice gabbling. "FIRE! Oh, God, get out your skirmishers, man. . . . FIRE! . . . Vishnu's hit. The Fusiliers haven't been touched yet by the guns. You crazy swine, FIRE! Retire; give the Fusiliers half an hour of shrapnel FIRE! and try again *with* the cavalry. Narain, what are you doing here? FIRE! Spread out—bayonets and charge! FIRE! Oh, Christ, oh, God. . . ." He shut his eyes.

At last, under a swelling roar from the enemy artillery, the remnants turned and marched back for a second time through the oily river. It took ten minutes; during that time the enemy guns, suddenly accurate, all but smashed the British line. The storm of shell cut the Fusiliers to ribbons; one of Cable's remaining guns was shattered and Cable himself killed. Sir Hector watched the retreating columns through a telescope and as soon as the heads began to climb the far bank, turned and shouted a command down to Colonel Dempsey. The Fusiliers broke line and streamed back across the narrow strip of land and down the alleys into the town. The general stayed on his housetop, and at thirty-yard intervals along the wall single Fusilier sentries remained to watch the river. For a moment the enemy guns did not seem to notice the movement, then they all turned on to the general.

Sir Hector peered down on Rodney and called gaily, "Hot work, Captain. Let us hope they use up their ammunition on me. I doubt if they will have much left by now."

As though the sense of the remark had carried across to the enemy, their guns one by one hiccoughed into silence. A haze of black smoke and pink dust surrounded the general, and a small fire had started in a house behind his. He said, "Come on up here, my boy."

Swaying on his feet, Rodney climbed the single narrow flight of stairs. At the top he found that Sir Hector had been standing all the while on a pile of loose bricks, and still was. The little man looked round. "Do you think they will come again?"

"Yes," he answered dully. Of course they'd come again.

The general said, "Faith, faith. You have a great regiment, sir."

"They'd be in here now, with any sort of decent leadership. It's murder," Rodney broke out tensely.

Sir Hector raised the telescope to his eye and looked upstream, saying softly, "I know, Captain, I know. All quiet up there—no sign of their cavalry. Ours have a vedette at the edge of the grove—two men. Their chance will come. Victory or defeat will be decided there—two

Native Officers and ninety-eight rank and file of the Bombay Lancers."

He put the telescope under his arm, thrust his head a little forward, and stuck one hand into the front of his frock coat. He continued, "In a few minutes, Captain Savage. Perhaps I have done wrong. But indeed"—his voice was metallic—"if we can trust no one in this whole country, after a hundred years of dominion, we deserve the annihilation our all-wise Father will certainly mete out."

And Robin? And Caroline? Must your Father who is all-wise roast my darlings alive over slow fires because we are not wise?

"Here they come! Stand to! Stand to!" It was his own voice.

The enemy columns marched out of the scrub for the third time and quickly down into the water. They were still columns, but in a more open formation. There were only six of them, composed of the two sepoy regiments, and no band was playing. He saw the 13th bass drummer, six foot four inches tall, carrying a rifle in the front of the regiment's centre column. The general waved his arm, messengers ran, bugles called. The press of Fusiliers tumbled out of the sheltering city through the few narrow alleys. Simultaneously the enemy guns opened fire and a torrent of shells burst over the openings. The Fusiliers quailed before it, and their dead and wounded began to pile up. The texture of the air thickened every second, so that it could hardly be breathed. The sepoys struggled on, murky figures in a shrieking grey-black panorama, splashed with orange fire. Their battalions had lost two-thirds of their men; the Fusiliers were losing heavily now, as they ran in confusion to their places under the shells. The two six-pounders cracked once, then four enemy shells, coming together, obliterated the crews. Men ran from the wagon lines to take their places. In a dark twilight the artillery flashes rippled and sparkled across the water.

"FIRE! ... Load! Rod! ... FIRE! FIRE! FIRE!"

The six columns, scarlet and rifle-green, loomed nearer and nearer. The Union Colour fell, and a sepoy snatched it up. Men turned their heads quickly in the desperation of their firing, looked upstream, and muttered to themselves. The sepoy skirmishers splashed out, fanning forward in half-moons; the ragged volleys of the Fusiliers had no effect now; there were too many targets, too many green and scarlet pieces darting forward. The sepoy centre began to form line. The crackling stopped. Dempsey screamed, *"Fix your—* BAYONETS!" The thin steel skewers clicked home.

Sir Hector ran down the steps, drew a sword nearly as large as himself, scrambled nimbly on to the wall and stood there, insecurely balanced, staring up the river. The mango grove was dark and quiet, the water smooth. Watching him, Rodney saw him open his mouth, hesitate, and shut it again. Here was the terror of decision. Only a bayonet charge could save the Fusiliers' position now—and once it was launched nothing could hold enemy cavalry if the Lancers didn't.

A shell blast blew the cocked hat off the general's head. He brandished the sword and said politely, "We will take the bayonet to them now, if you please, Fusiliers."

Rodney vaulted the wall and ran down over the fissured earth, levelled bayonets riding the slope to right and left and a dry harsh cheer echoing in his ears. The sepoys fired one scattered volley and came on too. Sir Hector galloped five yards in front of the Fusiliers, his bald head wet with sweat, his knees up and toes turned outwards; but no one could catch him up. Rodney heard distant music as he ran, and felt the charging Fusiliers sigh. Quickly he glanced to the right.

Shimmering above the reach of water, a silver and grey squadron of the 60th Bengal Light Cavalry debouched in extended order from the scrub and cantered down into the river. Their many trumpets gave out a wild sweet calling. Oh, Caroline! Caroline!

Then he could not look again but knew as he fought that troop after troop of the 60th followed the first. This was insanity, to hack at Sepoy Rupchand, to shout "Hurrah!" as his bayonet slid through the green cloth of Naik Mahdev's tunic, just below the third black button. No single thing, not even such a dawn as May the tenth, could wipe out eleven years. Madness, madness in nightmare! They all recognized him, so conspicuous in their dark green among the scarlet Fusiliers. He laughed crazily to see that in the moment of recognition some shifted their aim away, others turned deliberately to shoot at him. Those would be the leaders; there was Naik Parasiya, he wore a major's coat, badly fitting —Weasel Anderson's.

And to the right, the vivid snatched cameos: the water boiled at the chests of struggling horses; shells burst among them, broke the strong lines; one horseman turned back, another stumbled and fell and rolled helplessly down river. The light was iron-grey over all, and the heat increasing, and the mango grove silent.

Ten yards away he saw the Dewan's brocaded coat. The lust to kill froze him, and he headed straight for the man, striking out silently with big swings of his rifle. No one heard the guns; the rifles were silent; the fight was a fury of grunting and gabbled swearing. He knocked Parasiya down, trampled him under water, and snatched his sword. A wedge of Fusiliers clubbed and bayoneted forward beside him. The Dewan showed his teeth, waved his jewelled sabre, and spurred his horse on. The Colours surged forward.

The maddened horse plunged over Rodney and he swung his weight back, his curved sword whirling silver against the black sky. They were like dogs snarling at each other. The Dewan's single eye shone luminous and angry. The neck there, if he could reach it, the soft neck just above the collar . . .

Agony struck his right elbow and flashed in white fire through his body. The sword spun away in a glittering arc and he fell coughing, retching, and bubbling beneath the water.

Hands forced under his armpits and dragged him back. He

heard, ten miles away, an insistent bugle repeating over and over again the regimental call of the Fusiliers, followed by the Retire. He was on his feet, stumbling in giddy nausea between two bearded private soldiers. To right and left the sepoys re-formed their ranks and followed up, cheering in wild exaltation.

They would find Caroline and Robin back there, holding hands, waiting. He groaned, threw off the soldiers' arms, and turned to face the enemy.

No one was moving. The hand of God pressed down in the cloud and held them still. Awestruck and dumb, the men who had been fighting stood together and looked up the broad reach of the Nerbudda to the east. They held their breaths and waited, poised like stiff puppets. The infantry waited in the river; on either side the gunners did not fire their guns.

Upstream there the leading troop of the 60th Bengal Light Cavalry came to the edge of the river. The horses shook themselves, neighed, and trotted out in the shallows. The riders shouted to the Lancers in the grove; the greetings echoed back from the walls of the city.

"Comrades! Brothers! Remember Mangal Pande! Join us! For your gods, join us!"

Rodney bowed his head. Not again, not again—not again Bhowani, and Kishanpur, and the execution, and the phantasmal arms of love, distorted, disfigured, which came to strangle him in the nights.

A single trumpet shrieked *Charge!* He raised his head. A blue wave galloped furiously out of the mango grove and down the slope. The golden strands of cap line and shoulder knot flew back and sparkled in the morning darkness. The horses stretched their necks, their hoofs struck the hard red earth in thunder. At the crest of the wave the upright lance points swept slowly down, the pennons whipped in circling arcs of red and white, bending down; the riders leaned into the long horizontal shafts, the trumpet screamed and screamed. The lances ripped through the grey and silver and scattered it and sent it rolling down the stream in a broken jumble of wreckage. The charge went home, and the shock of it thudded along the banks.

Somewhere, a long way off, a gun fired. The soldier puppets moved sharply and sighed together. The men in the river moved. The sigh became a shout, swelled to a choking roar, and Rodney turned again to his front.

A single raindrop splashed on his bare head, and another. Huge slow warm drops fell thicker and faster, and danced on the river and on the baked earth of the bank. He turned his head and saw the general, back on the wall, wave his sword. The two black cannon mouths gaped at him. Vivid orange flames streaked from the muzzles, and an avalanche of canister roared inches over his head into the sepoys. All the Fusiliers, officers and sergeants and rank and file, danced under the solid rods of rain, singing and shouting like berserkers. He crept on his knees up the bank towards them. Piroo ran down to drag him in.

And always, upstream, the ceaseless battering charges of the Lancers, the single trumpet's commands: *Charge! Break! Retire! Re-form! Charge!* At first a hundred, then eighty, sixty, forty men. *Charge! Break! Retire! Re-form! Charge!*

The two six-pounders swept the slope at point-blank range, laying green and scarlet windrows at the water's edge. A few sepoys ran forward and charged alone into the blast; a few crept back into the river; the Fusiliers fired in an utter disorder of fury. The Dewan's primrose coat turned and vanished into the wall of falling rain. The 13th and 88th regiments of Bengal Native Infantry re-formed their ranks, struggled up the bank, were blown away by cannon and rifles, and came again, and again. The Union Colour of the 88th fell broken into the stream and floated away. The white Regimental Colour, woven of silk, bright with the Company's crest and the regiment's scrolled battle honours, came on, and the sepoys came on under it. The ravenous guns devoured them all and scattered them in fragments of sodden hair and flesh and cloth over the foreshore.

Behind their wall the remnants of the Fusiliers joined in the slaughter with steaming rifles. At Rodney's side a squat private soldier fired and fired, muttering all the while under his breath, "Filthy furching black bastards. You wite! You wite!"

Rodney laid his head on the wall and burst into tears. The warm tears splashed down with the raindrops while a heavy pain clenched inside his stomach.

The general said something. The cursing fusilier put a hand under his shoulder and walked him, unresisting, back to the house where the women were. The soldier's voice murmured like a soft river.

"There, there, sir. You was wonderful. Mind tha' puddle, sir. You must of killed a 'undred of them furching niggers yourself, sir, begging your par'n, sir. I's all right, sir, i's all right, don't you worry. We'll kill every nigger in the coun'ry, we know wo' they done to you. Don't you worry, sir. . . ."

Piroo helped him at his other side.

Caroline waited upright and still in the door of the ground-floor room which they had made into a dressing-station. Shuffling across the courtyard, he saw she had been listening to the guns, and carried a pistol in a sash at her waist. Lips parted, she peered into the rain and, as he came closer, ran out, took his left hand, and stood a second touching him. Inside the building the darkness hid her and he could not stop crying. She led him to a pallet, whispered to him to lie down, and began to cut away his sleeve.

Sobbing, he stared up into the blackness and muttered, "It's finished. We've won. We've won, and I wish I were dead."

She knelt beside him and put her arm under his head; he turned and pressed his eyes against the swell of her breast. She ran her fingers slowly through his hair. Outside the rain drummed and hissed, drowning all other sounds.

It drowned at last his throbbing hurt and drowned physical pain, until he felt nothing but the touch of her fingertips and a slow tide of love rising to fill him as the sea floods a scoured channel.

The surgeon came and bent over him. Caroline knelt at the head of the pallet, keeping her hand on his temple. Dimly he heard the surgeon say, "It's not broken, Captain, but it is very extensively bruised. You must stay here; we'll make up a bed for you inside."

Caroline's cool fingers rippled the love in him, and he dared not look away from her eyes. He said, "Not yet. Later."

"While you are in my hospital you are under my orders, sir."

The voice was from a long way off, and his own answering it. "I can't help that. I'm sorry."

A pause, a shuffle, feet moving away in the straw. His eyes saw a little depth in the dusk; three hand lanterns cast a feeble glow into the barren room and gleamed back yellow from instruments and bandages and sweating faces ranged on the straw round the walls.

"You should stay here." Her voice was doubtful and wondering.

He put his hand over hers. "No, I shouldn't. You mean— you want me to stay, don't you? Let us always be accurate."

He smiled up, mocking her old didacticism. Surely now there would be a tomorrow, and a time to savour each other. She hung her head lower and nodded, and he thought she blushed. She pulled her hand away; his happiness caressed him so that he laughed, stretched his legs, and said, still in caricature of the abruptness which had been her manner to the world, "Dress my wound. And be quick."

Amelia Hatch's anxious red face loomed over them, and he burst out giggling. She must have found a pot of henna in the night to re-dye her hair. In the tattered sari she looked indescribably raffish, like some kindly long-retired Bombay harlot. When she saw him laughing she leaned over, wagging her forefinger. "Ai'm ashamed of you, Captain Sevvidge, reely Ai am! And you, miss! A-'olding 'ands in 'ospital!"

Caroline worked quickly at the bandage, smiling to herself. Mrs. Hatch rattled stridently on, then suddenly bent and smacked a kiss on Rodney's cheek. "There, ducks, don't attend to me."

He sniffed meaningly, and she drew herself up. "Not one drop, Capting—at least, h'only one!"

She turned away and swooped on the wounded soldiers. Their drawn faces lightened under the familiar flood of her cockney scolding. Caroline patted the knot of the sling. "There, that's all right—if you insist on going out."

"Thank you, Caroline. How's Robin?"

"He's upstairs with a badly wounded artilleryman. We doubt whether the man will live, but he wants Robin to stay with him. Would you like to see him?"

"Yes—no, I must go. I'll be back soon, I expect. Piroo!"

"Sahib!"

"Come on."

She followed him to the courtyard. He walked quickly on into the rain, without daring to look back, for what would show in his face.

Soldiers staggered by them through the deep puddles, carrying wounded men in litters improvised of bamboos and blankets. A couple of riderless troop-horses galloped side by side down the narrow lane, joyfully kicking up their heels and forcing everyone back against the houses. Behind the temple the horses of the gun teams waited patiently in tethered rows, their heads drooping. It was twenty degrees cooler, and the rain brought a rich smell out of the earth, not wholly pleasant but full and real.

Down a side turning he saw a group of English gunners bending over something green and dirty white. They were kicking it, and he saw it was a sepoy of the 13th. The man knelt in the mud. His coat was a rag, and his bowels hung out of his stomach, trailing on the earth. One gunner held his neck and tried to make him lick the ground; another jerked him back by his hair and rammed axle grease down his throat. His eyeballs were rolled up out of sight, and he did not know what they were doing to him or who they were. Rodney ran forward, trying to shout, but no words would come through the tight contraction in his throat. As he came near, one of the gunners stood aside and said roughly, " 'Ere, that's enough. This barnshoot might 'ave a brother in them Lancers."

The sepoy was dead. Rodney turned away, the gunners staring at him, their faces exultant, angry, and ashamed in the rain. With Piroo holding his good arm he went forward to his place.

They had cleared away the worst of the debris from the firing line. The rank of Fusiliers stood to their posts, soaked to the skin, and laughed as the water streamed off their shakos and ran down their noses into their mouths. The steady rain poured down on the foreshore, and on the corpses and wreckage there, and bounced on the river's yellow surface. Two hundred yards out it became an impenetrable curtain, veiling the rest of the stream and the far bank.

Sir Hector stood a little apart, as always, balancing up and down on the tips of his toes, his beard pearled and his bald head ashimmer with raindrops. A trooper of the Lancers, holding a horse's head, was talking to him. The trooper rocked on his feet, as if mesmerized into imitating the general's habit. Rodney came up to hear the trooper saying, *"Huzoor sahib, gaonwala-ne khabbar liya kih . . ."*

When he had finished Rodney turned to the general. "He says, sir, that a villager has reported a small party of Indians —five or six—hiding in the charcoal burners' huts at Harna, two miles up river on this bank. The villager didn't know who they were, but thought they came over from the other side last night, in a boat."

Sir Hector eyed the lancer, examining with care his torn tunic and the broken lance in his hand. He said, "They're tired—exhausted—but it must be done. Captain, kindly take out a patrol of Lancers, about a dozen men, and see what there is. Your horse is behind the house still. Pray give my compliments to Rissaldar Rikirao on your way, and ask if he can spare me five minutes."

Twenty minutes later, with the weary file of troopers splashing behind him, Piroo loping at his stirrup, and the rain falling in sheets from the silent trees, Rodney came to Harna.

Wisps of smoke rose from two or three carefully stacked banks of wet wood, each the size of a small room. The smoke mingled with the rain and drifted in eddies across an open space full of tree stumps, where the charcoal burners had cut back from the river. In the centre stood a group of their huts, sketchy frameworks of split wood on which they had latched overlapping layers of brown leaves to form walls and roofs. The squad rode among the huts and stopped, facing all directions, in a tangle of pushing horses.

Striving one-handed to bring his horse round, while two others backed into it and all the troopers swore, Rodney saw the Rani of Kishanpur. She stood looking at him, bareheaded and alone, fifty yards away in the jungle beyond the edge of the clearing. Before he had thought what he was doing, he jerked his head in a sideways motion. She hesitated, then stepped behind a tree and out of sight.

Automatically he told the troopers to dismount and search the huts, and watched blank-faced while they did it. He could capture her easily now, and see her executed. Surely she deserved it? But when he opened his mouth it was to call out to the N.C.O., "Anything there, Daffadar?"

"Nothing, sahib. Someone's been here recently though. I found this."

He took the ruby ring from the man's hand and absently pushed it on to the little finger of his left hand. So they'd found poor Prithvi, found the ring in the bushes and given it back to her, and she'd lost it again. Piroo had marked the unease of his manner and was looking at him intently; Piroo knew him through and through by this time. Suddenly he recalled the exact timbre of Caroline's voice on the hill above Chalisgon. "Rodney, Rodney, you are so strong. But nothing's worth the loss of your humanity. Be stronger still."

He said, "Very well, Daffadar. Go back at once and report that. I will follow slowly; my wound hurts."

He flushed in saying it, for half of the dozen troopers were wounded at least as badly. The daffadar peered at him anxiously. "Are you sure you're all right, sahib? We can easily come along with you. There's no hurry now."

"No, no, you may be needed. Piroo here will look after me."

He walked his horse slowly after them until the little trotting column disappeared into the jungle, their backswept lances knocking showers of water from the lower branches. When the creak and jingle died he slid to the ground, gave Piroo the reins, and walked painfully back under the thunderous monotone of the rain towards the place where he had seen her.

She had moved forward to the edge of the trees, and he saw her there. An aching sadness checked his step; he had thought she was stronger than he, as strong as Caroline. He was wrong; a little pistol glinted in her hand and there was somebody with her, hidden in the bushes. He sighed and stood still, waiting for the bullet. Caroline would know.

The Twenty-seventh Rajah of Kishanpur, three years old, scrambled out of his hiding place and caught at Sumitra's dress. Proud careful hands had made him a miniature replica of a great prince—embroidered slippers, tight white trousers, long primrose coat, black sail-like hat with egret plume and diamond ornaments, tiny jewelled sabre. But the rain had spoiled it all, so it was only a bedraggled, frightened child who stood beside his mother and stared at Rodney with solemn eyes.

The Rani said in a hard voice, "Do not be alarmed, Captain Savage. The pistol is for us, if you try to make us prisoners."

The familiar blackness moved in her eyes; her soaking dress clung to the shape of her, moulding under her breasts and between her thighs; a fallen leaf stuck to her shining black hair, and mud splashes streaked the sari's hem.

He said slowly, "You saw the troopers go."

"Oh, the great English sahib must have all the glory! He will not share it with any Indian—not even lickspittle swine of lancers—and then there will be a reward. Can I buy you off with a ruby ring?"

He flushed but did not answer, looking down at the child beside her. After half a minute he summoned a smile and said, "Highness, you are hungry? You are? Well, I have chupattis and coarse sugar on that horse. The little man will give you some."

The boy licked his lips and stared from Piroo to his mother. The fire died from her eyes and tears started out; she said at last, looking still at Rodney, "Yes, go on."

The boy ran off, stumbling over his toy sabre. Slowly the Rani bowed her head, put her joined hands to her forehead, and stooped to touch Rodney's knee and foot. Her voice trembled. "My lord, you are hurt."

He raised her up and said gently, "A little, Sumitra. But tell me what has happened. Why are you two here alone like this?"

The silent storm of her weeping had washed all passion out of her face. She spoke like a woman who reads from a long and dull document.

"We come over in a little boat last night—we two, the new captain of my Guard and the lieutenant, the head priest, my tire-woman, and another servant. Today is the hundredth anniversary of Plassey. There was a prophecy that English rule would last a hundred years and be broken on the field of battle. It is the first day of the new moon, which is auspicious. It is Vishnu's Jattra. It is the first day of the rains. How could there be failure? We came across to give special honour to the regiments in Gondwara, for rising in rebellion and destroying the British soldiers in the night—they were going to bring elephants out here. He, the little one, would have been the first to enter the town, escorted by them. At noon he would have been enthroned King of Kishanpur, King of Gondwara, Viceroy of the Nerbudda, Prince of the Sindhya Hills, Lord of the Waters of the Kishan and the Ken and the Betwa—all our old lands."

The rain spread kohl and mascara in streaks across her face. The mud squelched in over her thin slippers as she shifted her feet.

"When the others saw what happened in the battle just now they took the boat and rowed away without telling me. They knew I would not turn back. Treason, double treason —the regiments fought against us. We knew we could not force the ford. It was to be given up to us."

"The two Bengal infantry regiments did not fight on either side, Sumitra. They were disarmed last night, and Girdhari Lall blown from a cannon's mouth."

She shivered. "You again, and the pale girl. Only you could have known enough. The Lancers——?"

"Were true to their salt."

"True to their treachery!"

"True to themselves! It doesn't matter now. Sumitra, give yourself up. Your army has been smashed——"

"I can raise another!"

"Only to make more widows. Lalkot will desert you now; the other princes will never come in. The Sikhs won't, even if they ever intended to. Everything depended on this—they must have told you that at the tiger hunt—and you've lost. Your own people don't want you. They're helping us all they can. How do you think I and two women and a child ever reached Gondwara, through a hundred miles of your territory, helpless, starving, sick, penniless, beaten? There's been too much blood. I don't know now what's right for India—I thought I did once. I don't know who should decide —there are too many different voices. The poor people speak from ignorance and poverty; you speak from jealousy; we —I don't know. I only know that you and your bloody intrigues which can start a thing like this must go. You have

destroyed your army; you've massacred my regiment. I'll
make you come and look at them——"

"Stop, stop!"

"That's not the worst. Men, brown men and white men,
are turning into wild beasts. The Silver Guru saw it all. India
will never recover from the hatred. The longer it goes on,
the worse it gets. Perhaps there's a beginning of something
new and better—God knows. Give yourself up. Caroline and
I can prove you were not responsible for the massacre in the
fort. You'll never rule Kishanpur again, but the boy might
—if you help us now when we need help; we won't for long."

Under the urgency in his words she grew quiet, and he
saw she had not changed. Still sunshine and shadow, storm
and calm, love and hate, possessed her in rapid succession,
each equally fierce, each obvious in every look and word.
She said, "Will you take my son?"

Rodney stared, disbelieving his ears.

"Yes, my son, the Rajah, that prince there, eating gur
from the hand of a casteless thug! King of Kishanpur, King
of Gondwara, Viceroy of the Nerbudda, Prince of the Sindhya Hills, Lord of the Waters of the Kishan and the Ken
and the Betwa!"

She trembled violently. Rodney answered slowly, "I'll take
him, if you wish. I'll raise him with my own son. You and I
will never understand each other, but perhaps they will. It's
going to be important."

"Promise! Because there is no other hope for him. Oh,
I know you're right about the rebellion! You will win, we
will be destroyed. Our cause was lost here at dusk, through
you—and this morning, through a few Lancers."

"They were too great for causes," he interrupted quietly.
"They could only do what they had to, so that they could
live with themselves."

She flung out her hand. "But the rebellion will go on, until
I and those who will follow me are wiped out. My fate is
there. My lord, *I* cannot turn back now, *I* cannot survive, as
many will, a silk and diamond doll. For me it is written,

decided! I know my road, I can see my end. And no one will ever take me, to tie me to your cold cannon, while your English soldiers devour my body with their blue eyes—ugh —like the sky seen through a skull—like yours."

She stopped and finished in a breathless rush. "I hate you so much, and I love you."

A deep breath lifted her breasts. She opened her arms, stumbling forward, and pressed her wet body against him. "My lord, you know? You have suffered this? I am proud, and you love the pale girl. Kill me."

His arm in the sling hurt savagely where her breast throbbed against it. He gasped at the pain and jerked away. She sprang back, eyes glittering and lips spitting, and raised the pistol to shoot him. Then she realized; her face softened, and she opened her mouth to speak.

Before she could say anything, Rodney cried, "Here, Piroo. Quick!"

He pressed the horse's reins into her hand, and helped Piroo to heft her, unprotesting, into the saddle. He turned his face up into the rain and shouted, "Go on, there's a little ford thirty miles up river. Go on! Good-bye—and I promise."

She looked down from him to her son, while the big gelding reared and snorted under her. Then she gathered the reins and galloped for the river. Rodney cried out and ran a few paces after her. She forced the horse over a high bank and plunged into fast deep water. The curtains of mist and rain parted a moment, and he saw her dark head in the river; then it was gone and he saw nothing but the torn water and heard nothing but the hiss of the rain. He turned on his heel and walked away.

A yard ahead of him the little brown boy in the brilliant clothes rode on Piroo's shoulder, drumming on the old man's head with his fists, and shouting, "Hola! Get up, elephant! I am the king. Why did my mummy jump in the water?"

Piroo's whining voice answered,

"Your Majesty, Your Excellency . . ."

They could cashier him if they found out, or shoot him perhaps. He'd have to make up a story for the general, and Sir Hector Pierce was a wise and inward-seeing man. The horse might finish up in the shallows of the ford for all to see—and so might Sumitra Lakshmi, Rawan, Rani-Regent of Kishanpur, musk and sandalwood woman, flame of courage.

But he had reached the uttermost end of his strength and must lie down a space and let the storms of the Great Bengal Mutiny roar where they would over the land. He had fought himself, and found himself. He had fought his enemies, who were his friends, and won—and lost. He had fought Caroline, and lost—and won. She must be there to accept his surrender, so that he could lie down at her feet and sleep. He whistled tunelessly and walked faster into the surge of the rain.

# Glossary

With the exception of a few well-known names, such as "Peter the Hermit," "China," "Gladstone," etc., all places and persons mentioned in the story but not covered by notes in this glossary are imaginary.

The meanings given for Hindustani words apply only to this story; other meanings and shades of meaning are not given. Long phrases already translated in the text are not explained.

Inevitably, the expert will consider many of these brief notes inadequate, if not actually misleading; nevertheless, in connection with this story, they may be helpful.

*achcha* (utcha), good.

*Addiscombe*, village near Croydon; site of the H.E.I.C.'s military cadet college.

*admi* (ahdmi), man.

*Afghanistan*, various references in the book are to the First British–Afghan War, 1839–42.

*Agra* (Ahgra), city, 27.10 N., 78.00 E.

*a-gya* (ah-geea), has come.

*Al Kadhimain* (Al Kadhimain), mosque near Baghdad.

*Almora* (Al-mora), village, 29.37 N., 79.41 E.

*Anglo-India(n)*, the British community in India; at this time people of mixed British and Indian blood were referred to as "Eurasians."

*ankus* (unkas), pointed elephant goad, with a hook on one side.

*anna* (anna), coin; sixteenth part of a rupee.

*Auckland*, George Eden, Earl of Auckland; Governor General of India 1835–42.

*ayah* (eye-ya), children's nurse.

*baba* (baba), baby.

*babu* (bahboo), clerk, educated man (literally, father).

*bahadur* (b'hahda), brave; used as suffix when addressing military men, e.g., sahib-bahadur.

*bahin* (bine), sister.

*bahut* (bote), much, very.

*baje* (budgey), o'clock.

*bannia* (bun-ya), merchant.

*Bareilly* (B'relly), town, 28.30 N., 79.30 E.

*barnshoot*, corruption of *bahin ka chute*

*Barrackpore*, town and military station fifteen miles north of Calcutta.

*Bengal Proper*, roughly, the modern province of Bengal (in 1857 "Bengal" would usually have meant the much larger Presidency of that name).

*Berhampur* (Berram-pore), town and military station, 24.07 N., 88.10 E.

*Betwa* (Bate-wa), south-bank, tributary of the Jumna; junction at 25.54 N., 80.13 E., forty miles south-south-west of Cawnpore, q.v.

*bhi* (b'hee), also, too.

*Bhowani* (B'wahny), imaginary town. To get a geographical bearing on the story it should be imagined to be about where Jhansi really is—25.27 N., 78.33 E.

*Bhurtpore* (Bhurtpore), town and fortress, 27.13 N., 77.30 E.

*Black Water*, ocean, sea (direct translation of Hindustani *Kala Pani*).

*B.L.C.*, Bengal Light Cavalry (Native).

*B.N.I.*, Bengal Native Infantry.

*Brahmin* (Brahmin), member of the highest Hindu caste.

*buddha* (boodda), old.

*burqa* (boorka), shapeless one-piece garment, usually of white cotton, covering the whole person; worn in public by most Mohammedan and some high-caste Hindu women.

*Canning*, Charles John, Earl Canning, Governor General of India 1856–62.

*Carnatic* (Car-nattic), name formerly used for a part of the southeast coast of the Indian peninsula.

*Cawnpore*, city on the Ganges, 26.28 N., 80.30 E.

*Chandernagore* (Chundra-n'gore), small territory belonging to

France; on the Hooghly twenty miles north of Calcutta.

*Chillianwallah* (Chillyun-wolla), town in the Punjab, 32.45 N., 73.35 E. Site of a hard-fought battle, January 1849, between British and Sikhs.

*chhe* (chay), six.

*cheetah* (cheeta), hunting leopard.

*cheetal* (cheetle), common spotted deer of India, *Cervus axis*.

*chokra* (choke-ra), youth, boy.

chor do (chor doe), let go!

*chupatti* (ch'patty), flat disk of unleavened wheat bread.

*chute* (choot), vulva.

*civil, the*, non-military officials of the government (Anglo-Indian jargon). Stemming down from the Governor General there were governors (of presidencies); lieutenant governors (of provinces); commissioners (of divisions); collectors, or deputy commissioners (of districts). A resident was the Governor General's ambassador to a princely state, and thus not part of the administration of British India. In the story, Mr. Dellamain's job was that of a collector, but he is ranked as commissioner because he was also resident to Kishanpur under the peculiar circumstances of that (imaginary) state.

*collector*, see *civil*.

*Colvin*, John Russell, Lieutenant Governor of the N.W. Provinces of Bengal, 1853–57.

*commissioner*, see *civil*.

*cornet*, see *ranks*.

*Cuddalore* (Cudda-lore), town and seaport, 11.44 N., 79.45 E.; site of many battles between the French and English.

*daffadar* (duffa-dah), see *ranks*.

*Dalhousie*, James Andrew Broun Ramsay, 10th Earl and 1st Marquess of Dalhousie, Governor General of India 1848–56.

*Deccan* (Dekk'n), unofficial name for the part of peninsular India south of the Nerbudda River.

*dekhana* (d'khahna), to show (tr.).

*dewan* (D'wahn), chief minister of an Indian ruler.

*Dinapore* (Dinah-pore), town and military station near Patna, q.v.

*down country*, closer to a Presidency capital (Anglo-Indian jargon).

*dum* (dum), breath.

*Dum-Dum*, town, military station and arsenal four and a half miles northeast of Calcutta.

*ek* (eck), one.

*ek dum* (eck dum), at once (literally, one breath).

*ensign*, see *ranks*.

*follower*, one of the noncombatants, usually of low caste, who accompany armies in India to carry out menial tasks.

*gaddi* (guddy), throne (literally, heavy cushion).

*gaonwala* (gown-wolla), villager.

*ghat* (gaht), step, platform.

*ghi* (ghee), clarified butter.

*ghusl* (ghoosl), bath.

*Goa*, town and territory belonging to Portugal, 15.28 N., 73.50 E.

*gold-mohur* (mo-hoor), tree, *Poinciana regia*.

*Gond* (Goand), member of aboriginal race inhabiting jungles of central India.

*gora* (gora), pale-faced.

*gurdwara* (goord-wahra), Sikh place of worship.

*guru* (goorroo), teacher.

*Gwalior* (Gwollyor), princely state; also, its capital city, 26.13 N., 78.10 E.

*hai* (hay), is.

*havildar* (huvvle-dah), see *ranks*.

*hazri* (hahzri), breakfast.

*Hearsey*, Major-General commanding Presidency Division of Bengal in 1857.

*H.E.I.C.*, the Honourable East India Company.

*Hindi* (Hindy). Aryan dialect of northeast India; now the lingua franca of the Republic of India.

*hogya* (hoe-geea), finished, done.

*Holi* (Holy), Hindu religious festival, in early spring.

*howdah* (howdah), framework for carrying passengers on elephant back.

*hut!*, exclamation.

*huzoor* (h'zoor), honorific term of address (literally, presence).

*Hyderabad* (Hydra-bad), city and state of the Deccan, between Bombay and Madras; not to be confused with the town of Hyderabad, Sind.

*Jaipur* (Jye-poor), princely state of Rajputana, intersected by 27 N., 76 E.

*jai ram!* (jye rahm!), a form of greeting.

*jata* (jahta), going.

*Jattra* (Juttra), a pilgrimage.

*jemadar* (jemma-dah), see *ranks*.

*-ji* (-jee), polite suffix added to, e.g., *babu*, *guru*.

*jildi* (jildy), quickly (British soldiers' corruption of Hindustani *jaldi*).

*Jodhpur* (Joad-poor), princely state of Rajputana, intersected by 26 N., 72 E.; also the Rajput type of trousers.

*John Company*, nickname of the H.E.I.C.

*Johnny Sepoy*, generic term for sepoys.

*Jubbulpore* (Jubble-poor), city, 23.10 N., 80.03 E.

*ka* (ka), postposition, meaning "of" (cf. " 's" in English).

*Kalpi* (Kulpy), town, 26.07 N., 79.45 E.

*ke mwafik* (k'mwahfik), postposition, meaning "like," "similar to."

*Ken* (Ken), south-bank tributary of the Jumna River—junction fifty miles south-southeast of Cawnpore, q.v., at 25.48 N., 80.32 E.

*khabbar* (khubber), news, information.

*kih* (k'), that (conj.).

*koi hai* (kwa hi), a call for service (literally, is anyone there?); used instead of "boy!" etc.

*Konkan* (Konkahn), a region on the western coast of the Indian peninsula.

*Kotdwara* (Coat-dwahra), town, 29.48 N., 78.33 E.

*lagao* (l'gow), put on!

*Lake*, Gerard, Viscount Lake, Commander-in-Chief in India 1800–1805.

*lalkurti* (lahl-koorty), redcoats; hence British soldiers as opposed to Indian sepoys, though many of the latter also wore red coats.

*Laswari* (L'swahry), village seventy-eight miles south-south-west of Delhi. Here, November 1, 1803, the British under Lord Lake defeated the Mahrattas.

*liya* (leeah), brought.

*log* (loag), people.

*mahout* (ma-hoot), elephant driver.

*Mahratta* (ma-hratta), member of Hindu race inhabiting the western and central parts of the Indian peninsula; at times they overran India.

*maila* (mile-ah), dirty.

*Mangal Pande* (Mungle Pundy), sepoy, 34th B.N.I.; attacked the adjutant of his regiment March 29, 1857; tried April 6, executed April 8.

*Meerut* (Mare-oot), town and military station, 29.00 N., 77.43 E. (twenty miles northeast of Delhi).

*Monghyr* (Mung-geer), town and military station on the Ganges, 25.22 N., 86.29 E.

*mullah* (moolla), Mohammedan priest.

*murari sanp* (m'rahry sahnp), milk snake.

*mynah* (mine-ah), bird of starling family.

*Nagpur* (Nahg-pore), city, 21.10 N., 79.10 E.

*nahin* (na'ee *or* nay), no, not.

*naik* (nike), see *ranks*.

*namaste* (n'musty), gesture of obeisance made by putting hands to forehead, palms inward.

*nautch* (nawtch), dance.

*Nawab* (N'wahb), princely ruler (always a Mohammedan).

*-ne* (-nay), meaningless appositive used after the subject of a sen-

tence when the verb is in the past tense.

neem (neem), tree, *Azadirachta indica*.

*Nerbudda* (Nerbudda), river, flowing westward into the Gulf of Cambay about lat. 21.35 N.

*nini* (ninny), sleep (baby-talk for Hindustani *nind*).

*Nizam* (Nye-zam), ruler of the princely State of Hyderabad in the Deccan.

*Oudh* (Ood), kingdom; capital Lucknow, 26.52 N., 80.55 E.; annexed by the British, February 7, 1856.

*panchh* (pahnch), five.

*Pande* (Pundy), name of Brahmin sub-caste.

*pandit* (pundit), teacher, wise man (also used as title).

*pani* (pahny), water.

*Pashupatti* (Pushoo-puttee), one of the eight principal manifestations of Shiva; represented under the material form of fire.

*Patna* (Putna), town, 25.35 N., 85.12 E.

*peepul* (peeple), large fig tree, *Ficus religiosa* (the Bodhi under which Lord Buddha sat was a peepul).

*pice* (pice), coin; one-fourth of an anna.

*pie* (pie), coin; one-twelfth of an anna.

*pher* (fair), again, once more.

*Plassey*, village on the Hooghly eighty-five miles north of Calcutta. Here, June 23, 1757, the British under Clive defeated Suraj-ud-Dowlah.

*Pramathas* (Pr'mahtas), demons, servants of Shiva.

*punkah* (punkah), fan.

*Queen's*, the epithet denoted that the official, officer, soldier, regiment, etc., was based in the United Kingdom; it would be contrasted with, e.g., "local," or "colonial," or (in India) "Company's."

*Rajputs* (Rahjpoots), Hindus, divided into numerous clans, who regard themselves as descended from the ancient Kshatriya or Warrior caste; also the rank below Brahmins in the Hindu religious hierarchy.

*ram ram* (rahm rahm), a form of greeting.

*rani* (rahny), wife of princely ruler; also, a woman ruling in her own right.

*ranks*. British officers' ranks were the same as to-day, except that the lowest rank, corresponding to modern second lieutenant, was ensign in infantry and cornet in cavalry. Below the British Officers there were three grades of Native Officers, the titles of which again varied in infantry and cavalry: infantry—subadar-major, subadar, jemadar; cavalry—rissaldar-major, rissaldar, jemadar. The three-striped non-com was havildar (inf.) or daffa-dar (cav.); the two-striper was naik (inf.) or lance-daffadar (cav.). The private soldier was sipahi (sepoy) in infantry, sowar in cavalry.

*regiments*. The 19th, 24th, and 34th B.N.I. were real and did the things they are said in the story to have done. All other regiments mentioned are imaginary.

*resident*, see *civil*.

*rissaldar*, see *ranks*.

*Rohilkand* (Roe-ill-kund), the district round Bareilly, *q.v.*

*roko* (roe-koe), stop!

*sab* (sub), all, every.

*sadhu* (sahdoo), religious mendicant.

*sal* (sahl), large tree, *Shorea robusta.*

*sambhur* (sahmba), the Indian elk, *Rusa aristotelis.*

*sanp* (sahnp), snake.

*sarhe* (sahray), half-past; and a half.

*sari* (sahry), female outer garment.

*schapska*, lancer's headdress, shaped rather like a scholar's mortarboard.

*secondary jungle*, jungle which has once been cleared: marked by denseness of undergrowth.

*Shaiva* (Shye-va), one of a sect of Hindus who regard Shiva as principal member of the divine triad, and identify him with creation and reproduction as well as with destruction.

*shikari* (sh'kahry), professional hunter, hence sportsman.

*Shiva* (Sheeva), third god of the Hindu triad, later regarded as the Destroyer.

*Shiva Purana* (Sheeva P'rahna), a tale of Hindu mythology.

*Sholingur* (Sho-ling-gur), town, 13.08 N., 79.26 E.

*Simla*, hill town 31.07 N., 77.05 E.; was the hot-weather capital of British India.

*Sind*, a large area of western India astride the Indus River.

*Sinigaglia*, town in Italy seventeen miles north-west of Ancona; here in 1501–1502 Cesare Borgia murdered Vitelozzo Vitelli, Oliver-

otto da Fermo, the Signor Pagolo, and the Duke di Gravina Orsini.

*sirdar* (sir-dar), title of honour, particularly of and to Native Officers.

*state* (in this book), a territory ruled by an Indian prince—rajah, maharajah, Nawab, Nizam, etc. —and thus not part of British India. All the states mentioned are imaginary, except Hyderabad, though there are in fact villages named Kiloi, Purkhas, etc., in various parts of India.

*subadar(-major)* (sooba-dah), see *ranks.*

*subordinate*, an Anglo-Indian or Eurasian below commissioned rank or its civil equivalent (Anglo-Indian jargon).

*sunta* (soonta), hearing (pres. part. of verb).

*suraj* (soor'j), sun.

*Suraj-ud-Dowlah* (S'rahja Dowla), Nawab of Bengal; responsible for the Black Hole of Calcutta, 1756; defeated by Clive at Plassey, 1757.

*suttee* (suttee), custom of Hindu widow immolating herself on her husband's funeral pyre; a woman so acting. (Suttee was abolished by Lord William Bentinck, Governor General of India, in December 1829.)

*sweeper*, domestic servant, always of untouchable caste; employed to clean out toilets and incidentally to sweep floors.

*thug(-gee)* (thug, thuggee), member of religious association that lived by highway murder and robbery; the association and its acts. (Thuggee was in reality destroyed by several men under

the leadership of William Slee-
man.)

*topi* (topey), hat.

*up country*, farther away from a
Presidency capital, cf. down
country (Anglo-Indian jargon).

*Varuna* (Va-roona), the supreme
god among those of the Hindu
Veda; the deity of the waters.

*Vauban*, Sébastien le Prestre de,
1633–1707; French military engineer and marshal.

*Vishnu* (Vishnoo), the second
member of the Hindu triad; the
Preserver.

*Yama* (Yahma), the Hindu god of
death and penance.

*zenana* (z'nahna), women's apart-
ments, also called *harem*.